Violent Women and Sensation Fiction

Also by Andrew Mangham

WILKIE COLLINS: Interdisciplinary Essays (*editor*)

Violent Women and Sensation Fiction
Crime, Medicine and Victorian Popular Culture

Andrew Mangham
Lecturer, School of English and American Literature, University of Reading

palgrave
macmillan

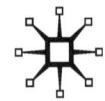

© Andrew Mangham 2007

All rights reserved. No reproduction, copy or transmission of this publication may be made without written permission.

No paragraph of this publication may be reproduced, copied or transmitted save with written permission or in accordance with the provisions of the Copyright, Designs and Patents Act 1988, or under the terms of any licence permitting limited copying issued by the Copyright Licensing Agency, 90 Tottenham Court Road, London W1T 4LP.

Any person who does any unauthorised act in relation to this publication may be liable to criminal prosecution and civil claims for damages.

The author has asserted his right to be identified as the author of this work in accordance with the Copyright, Designs and Patents Act 1988.

First published 2007 by
PALGRAVE MACMILLAN
Houndmills, Basingstoke, Hampshire RG21 6XS and
175 Fifth Avenue, New York, N.Y. 10010
Companies and representatives throughout the world

PALGRAVE MACMILLAN is the global academic imprint of the Palgrave Macmillan division of St. Martin's Press, LLC and of Palgrave Macmillan Ltd. Macmillan® is a registered trademark in the United States, United Kingdom and other countries. Palgrave is a registered trademark in the European Union and other countries.

ISBN-13: 978–0–230–54521–2   hardback
ISBN-10: 0–230–54521–1   hardback

This book is printed on paper suitable for recycling and made from fully managed and sustained forest sources. Logging, pulping and manufacturing processes are expected to conform to the environmental regulations of the country of origin.

A catalogue record for this book is available from the British Library.

A catalog record for this book is available from the Library of Congress.

10 9 8 7 6 5 4 3 2
16 15 14 13 12 11 10 09 08

Printed and bound in Great Britain by
CPI Antony Rowe, Chippenham and Eastbourne

For Emily, Rosie, Olivia, and Joseph

Contents

List of Illustrations — ix

Acknowledgements — x

Introduction — 1

1 Explosive Materials: Legal, Medical, and Journalistic Profiles of the Violent Woman — 7

    The body in the kitchen — 7
    Young women and adolescents: 'The mad fury of that lovely being' — 9
    Motherhood I: Maternal maniacs — 23
    Motherhood II: Morbid influences — 29
    Female old age: Sick fancies — 39

2 'The Terrible Chemistry of Nature': The Road Murder and Popular Fiction — 49

    'The fussy activity about the nightdress of a school girl' — 49
    Popular fictional representations — 63
    'A tragedy of blood and tears': *Aurora Floyd* — 64
    'Smooth as polished crystal': *St. Martin's Eve* — 71
    'Detective fever': *The Moonstone* — 79

3 'Frail Erections': Exploiting Violent Women in the Work of Mary Elizabeth Braddon — 87

    Poking the embers: The hysterical violence of young women — 87
    Unmotherly glances and sickly sentimentality: Dangerous maternities — 103
    Uncultivated waste: Post-menopausal women — 116

4 'Nest-Building Apes': Female Follies and Bourgeois Culture in the Novels of Mrs Henry Wood — 126

    A man of two wives/a man of two lives: Divided masculinity and domestic ideology in *East Lynne* (1862) — 129
    'Looking back': The mother's influence in *Danesbury House* (1860) and *Mrs Halliburton's Troubles* (1862) — 137
    'The matrimonial lottery': Choosing a good wife in *Lady Adelaide's Oath* (1867) — 143

'Evil heritages': Superstition and morbid heredity in
The Shadow of Ashlydyat (1864)   149
A moth in the upturned tumbler: The control and display
of passion in *Verner's Pride* (1863)   158

5 Hidden Shadows: Dangerous Women and Obscure Diseases in the Novels of Wilkie Collins   169

'What could I do?': *The Woman in White* (1860)   172
'In a glass darkly': *No Name* (1862)   182
'The shadow of a woman': *Armadale* (1866)   196

Conclusion   209

Notes   212

Bibliography   233

Index   242

List of Illustrations

4.1 Unknown artist, 'Nest-Building Apes', *Once a Week*, 19 July 1862, p. 112   128

Acknowledgements

This book is based on a Ph.D. thesis I submitted at the University of Sheffield in 2005. I was fortunate to have Sally Shuttleworth as supervisor. It was her work which first interested me in the links between science and popular fiction, and I am indebted to her for her kind, inspiring, and diligent help with this project and many others besides. I also want to thank Janice M. Allan. Her complex and insightful ideas on sensation fiction convinced me to study the subject back in the 1990s. Since then she has become an invaluable friend and mentor.

This book has benefited a great deal from the insightful comments of Jenny Bourne Taylor, Neil Roberts, Angela Wright, Joseph Bristow, and the anonymous reader at Palgrave Macmillan. I would also like to thank the following people for answering inquiries and/or recommending sources: Michael Flowers, Gabrielle Malcolm, Kate Mattacks, Jennifer Carnell, Amanda Mordavsky Caleb, Janice Norwood, Karin Lesnik-Oberstein, and the late Chris Willis. I would also like to thank the patient and helpful staff at the following libraries: The British Library (including the Document Supply Centre in Boston Spa), Sheffield City Library, The Harry Ransom Centre in Texas, and the Special Collections and the Universities of Sheffield and Leeds. This project was funded, in part, by the University of Sheffield and the Arts and Humanities Research Council. For this I am very grateful.

I would like to thank the wonderful people who have made my work so much easier by providing an intellectually inspiring network of friends. These include Sarah 'PB' Bell, Anne-Marie Evans, Anne-Marie Beller, Greta Depledge, Ana Maria Garcia Dominguez, Holly Furneaux, Tatiana Kontou, and Stefani Brusberg-Kiermeier. I would also like to acknowledge Gerry Taylor's very kind assistance with printing the manuscript.

Finally, I want to thank my family for being so understanding and patient. It is to my parents that I owe the greatest debt of all. Their untiring and unquestioning support has allowed all of my studies to be feasible and enjoyable. They remain the most inspiring people in my life. I am dedicating this book to the four little individuals who often found it difficult to understand the unsociable habits of my work. Because I wasn't always available to play, this book is for Emily, Rosie, Olivia, and Joseph.

Introduction

In 1838, J. E. D. Esquirol, the chief physician at the Charenton asylum, identified pyromania (an insane compulsion to commit arson) as a distinct form of insanity. Although he argued that the condition could be developed by both men and women, he claimed, in *Mental Maladies: A Treatise on Insanity* (1838), that 'young women are [...] more subject to *pyromania* than young men'.[1] The reason for this, he alleged, is that men are not subject to the range of constitutional weaknesses that frequently affect women. More specifically, he argued that biological processes like menstruation, pregnancy, childbirth, and the menopause weakened women's psychological defences against violent compulsions. This, according to Esquirol, is why more women committed arson than men. He supported his contention with 'the case of a woman, who set fire to a house near her own, through jealousy of another woman'.[2]

Seven years later, his ideas seemed to find validation in the British criminal case of Jane Crosby. As reported in *The Times*, Jane severely disliked her youngest daughter. Unlike her older sister, Sarah Ann Crosby had had a closer relationship to her father and was, *The Times* noted,

> in the habit of telling him on Saturday nights what her mother had done during the week; and on that account the mother, from time to time, manifested a most inveterate and inhuman dislike and hatred to her younger child.[3]

Her mother decided

> to put an end to the child's existence. In order to carry this barbarous and unnatural resolve into effect, on Thursday evening, the 28th ult., she made up a large fire in the kitchen of her own house, with the determination of sacrificing her child in the flames prepared by her own hands. For reasons known to this wretched woman herself, she stripped off the child's clothes and hid them in a hole behind the inner door and in the ash-midden, and

having done so took the child by its legs and arms and literally roasted it to death. [...] The wretched woman then took the child off the fire, and held her on her knee by the fireside till life was nearly extinct, the little innocent faintly asking her other sister for a drink of water.[4]

This incident was witnessed only by Crosby's eldest daughter. As the court found evidence given by the latter to be unsatisfactory because of her age, Jane was acquitted.

Twenty-one years later, Mrs Henry Wood, one of the most popular novelists of the period, wrote *St. Martin's Eve* (1866). The novel features Charlotte St John, a woman so incensed with hatred for her stepson that she allows him to burn to death. As her lady's maid recounts:

"She did not purposely set him on fire: she did not. I have gathered a great deal from words she has let drop in her paroxysms, and I know it was not done purposely. '[... He] set fire to his pinafore [...]', she said one night when she was moaning [...]."

"But she bolted the door on him."

"Ah, yes, she did that; bolted it upon him, knowing he was on fire; there's no doubt of it. I have gathered that much. I think at the moment she was mad, unconscious of what she did. She is not naturally cruel, only in these uncontrollable attacks".[5]

Unlike Jane Crosby, Charlotte's actions are not allowed to go unpunished. Continuing a tradition that ran through the sensation novels of the 1860s, Charlotte is sent to a lunatic asylum where she lives out the remainder of her days.

When placed side by side, such harrowing tales suggest that ideas and images worked, with fascinating fluidity, across generic and disciplinary boundaries during the nineteenth century. The above examples demonstrate, specifically, how notions of women as insanely violent moved across legal, medical, and fictional texts. All of these subjects have been written about, at length, in the last twenty years or so. A number of volumes have concentrated on the Victorian notion of madness, especially female madness, and its treatment;[6] historians have uncovered the often-gruesome details of many notorious murder cases,[7] and sensation fiction now has an established place in the canon due to a large number of works outlining the importance of popular fiction.[8] When it comes to linking these fields, however, or, more accurately, studying how they were *already* linked, no single work has made the important connections.[9] As the above examples of pyromania imply, cultural intersections existed between a number of nineteenth-century discourses on the subject of female violence and this book aims to highlight where and how they operated. Yet this is not a study that aims solely to uncover previously unnoticed connections. Rather, it is my argument that, by exploring the links between a number of Victorian disciplines, one learns a great deal about each one of those fields and the larger culture into which it was embedded. Such interdisciplinary research has become increasingly voluminous in recent years. Since the 1980s and 1990s, when writers like Gillian Beer and Helen Small published innovative studies of literature and science,[10] a canon of works has emerged with the intention to link two, but rarely more than two, avenues of nineteenth-century thought. My book suggests that much is still to be learned by adding the dimension of legal history to the more customary combination of science and literature. I concentrate on the insanely violent woman as a key point of focus and trace her provocative progress through a varied selection of nineteenth-century sources.[11]

The aim of my first two chapters is to ask important questions about the connections between criminal trials of real women and emerging medical theories of psychosomatic female pathology. This is the context through which I analyse, in the subsequent three chapters, the novels of Mary Elizabeth Braddon, Ellen (Mrs Henry) Wood, and Wilkie Collins. When it comes to studying the links between fiction writers and scientific material, academics tend to concentrate on writers considered more 'serious' or 'canonical'. Hence, Charlotte Brontë, George Eliot, and Thomas Hardy are well represented in interdisciplinary research.[12] Although such work has helped to form new ways of thinking about most types of literature, it has left the vital connections between non-fictional material and *popular* fiction largely unexplored; when one considers how these works had the greatest audiences, such omissions are difficult to account for. Braddon, Wood, and Collins have been chosen as the focus for this research because they were the best-selling writers of their period. At a time when Dickens was relatively inactive, their best-selling stories provide an important testament to what was of popular interest at the time.

Although works like *The Woman in White* (1860), *Lady Audley's Secret* (1862), and *East Lynne* (1862) have had no shortage of scholarly interest, such texts are rarely placed in a historical context.[13] I use a large amount of space, in this book, outlining the real events and theories that inspired the sensation novel. Such work is important because of the reciprocal exchange of inspiration that existed between the novels and non-fictional writings. On the one hand, historical sources have a good deal to tell us about the plots, styles, and characterisations of the sensation genre. This book aims to show that fiction, especially popular fiction, provides historians, as well as literary critics, with some important and enlightening documents. Yet such documents are crucial, in this context, only if they are not studied in isolation. I suggest that, in the very act of moving one idea from non-fictional documents to the fictional page, sensation novelists have a lot to teach us about their own history and culture. In short, history tells us lot about fiction, and fiction also tells us much about history, but it is with the links, exchanges, and slippages between the two that this book is primarily concerned.

All three of the authors I deal with in this book had interesting and evocative links with the medical and legal fields. Braddon, for example, had experiences of psychopathology throughout the 1860s. Mary Maxwell, the first wife of her husband John Maxwell had gone insane shortly after childbirth: 'She went mad', writes Robert Lee Wolff, 'sometime after the birth of the seventh [child], and entered an asylum near Dublin at a date which cannot have been very long before 1860'.[14] In 1868 Braddon experienced a mental breakdown caused by exhaustion and the deaths of her mother and sister. She described her condition as follows:

> My brain is much over excited & I scarce know what I write. [...] For more than six months [...] life [has been] a blank, or something worse than a blank, an interval in which imagination [runs] riot, & I [am] surrounded by shadows.[15]

Braddon was pregnant at the time and she and Maxwell feared that her malady would develop into insanity: 'Please do not allude to anything I have said about my long illness', Braddon implored Edward Bulwer-Lytton, 'as that is a point on which my husband is sensitive'.[16] Sensitive or not, Braddon and Maxwell consulted physicians and medical literature to ascertain the exact nature of her mental problems.

Mrs Henry Wood's intimate friends included important scientists. Among these she counted Sir William Lawrence, physician to Queen Victoria, as a close acquaintance. Lawrence had gained notoriety earlier in the century by propounding the notion that the human mind was contained entirely in the dense nerve fibres of the brain. Such a materialist view was violently opposed by John Abernethy, who argued, more traditionally, that man's intellect was a principle that transcended biology and connected humans, spiritually, with God.[17] Additionally, and, according to Mrs Henry Wood's only biographer (her son Charles), her husband owned a large and comprehensive medical library which Mrs Wood consulted.[18]

Wilkie Collins owned scientific and medical textbooks as part of his library, some of which were gifts from their authors. Through Dickens, he would have known nineteenth-century psychiatrist John Conolly, in addition to John Forster, secretary to the Lunacy Commission, and Lord Shaftesbury, chairman of the same.[19]

Collins's training as a barrister cemented a long-standing interest in legal matters. As I outline in chapter two, he is also known to have followed and discussed some of the period's infamous murder trials. He even admitted that such crimes inspired his best-known plots:

> I was in Paris wandering about the streets with Charles Dickens [...] amusing ourselves by looking into the shops. We came to an old bookstall – half

shop and half store and I found some dilapidated volumes of records of French crimes, a sort of French *Newgate Calendar*. I said to Dickens "Here is a prize." So it turned out to be. In them I found some of my best plots. *The Woman in White* was one.[20]

Braddon had a similar indebtedness to real crimes: 'I think', she wrote to Bulwer, 'I shall once more make my dip in the lucky bag of the Newgate Calendar'.[21] Mrs Henry Wood, according to her son, showed an avid interest in real murder cases:

> She took the keenest interest in all great trials. She followed out the threads and points of an intricate case with the greatest clearness and insight. In all important trials where mystery or complications were involved, or doubt and indecision as to right and wrong, guilty or not guilty, she quickly made up her mind at an early stage, saw the strong and the weak points, and was scarcely ever wrong in the opinion she formed. She often said that had she been a man, she would have made a first-rate lawyer, with a passionate love for her work.[22]

Such evidence suggests that the sensation novelists drew on scandals that were raging through the Victorian age, but this was by no means a passive appropriation. Sensation novelists constantly changed details, added subplots, and neutralised some of the more shocking elements of real events and theories where women were accused of extreme violence. Such alterations are fascinating and revealing insights into Victorian mores and concerns as well as the nature of the era's print media.

Many significant intersections between legal, medical, and literary materials were the result of the context in which popular novels were printed: the Victorian family magazine.[23] Periodicals were a powerful forum in which ideas and voices from a range of disciplines came together and interacted.[24] Sensation novels were mostly serialised in magazines like *Temple Bar* and Dickens's *All the Year Round*, through to more up-market publications like the *Cornhill Magazine* and *Macmillan's*. These weekly and monthly publications all featured, in varying degrees, articles written by scientists, lawyers, and journalists exploring new ideas and current events. Famous trials were frequently outlined and, in order to create continuity between features, writers of fiction often drew on such non-fictional material to construct stories that had resonances for contemporary readers. What is more, non-fiction writers of both criminal reports and medical texts employed literary devices to explain and explore ideas. Melodramatic tableaux that one might associate with popular fiction became a useful way to market 'factual' crime reports and, for medical writers especially, make complex ideas more accessible to general readers. In this book I take account of the non-fictional articles sensation fiction has printed alongside in order to understand how Victorian readers would have construed specific passages, themes, and characterisations, plus what such exchanges reveal about some of the period's most pressing issues.

Considering how popular novels like *The Woman in White*, *East Lynne*, and *Lady Audley's Secret* have proved to be with academics, it is difficult to explain why books written by the same hands, around the same time, have remained an untapped resource. This book aims to uncover some of those forgotten narratives, all the while considering what they tell us about the more canonical texts. This, combined with an interdisciplinary methodology, aims to highlight the complex nature of the sensation novel, and suggest that, if we are to gauge an accurate understanding of the genre, one needs to take account the richness of its original context.

1
Explosive Materials: Legal, Medical, and Journalistic Profiles of the Violent Woman

The body in the kitchen

On 25 October 1849, *The Times* suggested that the upcoming trial of Maria and Frederick Manning would be one of the most important of the century:

> It has undoubtedly happened in all times and ages that certain examples have taken a stronger hold than others of the public mind, have created more lively horror and more continuous interest, and have been preserved in the traditions of successive generations as illustrating the stage of social progress at which they occurred. That such will be the case with the Bermondsey murder, whatever may be the issue of the pending case, we cannot doubt.[1]

Earlier that year, the Mannings had invited Patrick O'Connor – a wealthy soldier with whom Maria had been having an affair – to dinner. Meeting a friend *en route*, O'Connor proudly showed his dinner invitation, which read 'we shall be glad to see you, Maria'.[2] This was the last time O'Connor was seen alive. After failing to turn up to work, he was reported missing and, as he had last been seen heading towards the Mannings', the police commenced their search at the couple's home. By the time the local constabulary arrived, husband and wife had already fled. During a search of the house, one officer noticed how the mortar holding a kitchen flagstone in place was wet. Removing the floor, he discovered the battered corpse of Patrick O'Connor. Identifiable only by his false teeth, he had received a gunshot to the head and eighteen wounds from a blunt instrument. After a highly publicised search, Maria and Frederick were captured at different locations.

At their trial, focus was laid almost exclusively on Maria, who became the inspiration for Dickens's Hortense in *Bleak House* (1853).[3] She was described by the papers as a 'comely woman' with 'dark hair and eyes' and a 'slight foreign accent'.[4] She was Swiss by birth and had served as lady's maid to the Duchess of Sutherland. Frederick, according to *The Times*, was the 'weaker vessel' of the two. It was his wife who had purportedly masterminded the killing of O'Connor. She was, the newspaper added, 'Lady Macbeth on the Bermondsey Stage', 'Jezebel to the life', 'the ready arguer, the greedy aggrandizer, the forger, the intriguer, the resolute, the painted and attired'.[5]

Both defendants were found guilty of O'Connor's murder and executed before a crowd of thirty thousand people.[6] Before his death, Frederick gave a full confession. He admitted that he had helped bury the victim's body, but claimed that the murder had been solely committed by his wife. She persuaded her victim, he said, to walk into the cellar and wash his hands before dinner. Following him down the stairs she wrapped one arm around his neck and shot him in the head with the other. Frederick allegedly fainted and, when he eventually came to, Maria had inflicted eighteen additional wounds with a crowbar.

What appears most interesting about the Manning case is how it emerges, in the period's journalism, as a story in which the 'ordinary' domestic functions of Maria are indistinguishable from the brutal act of murder. Journals and newspapers laid enormous emphasis on Mrs Manning's dinner invitation and the fact that O'Connor had been buried beneath the kitchen floor. According to Frederick's dubious confession, Maria had dug her victim's shallow grave three weeks before the murder. The victim had even walked past the hole several times and inquired as to its purpose. On hearing of O'Connor's disappearance, shortly before she and her husband absconded, Maria is alleged to have uttered 'Poor Mr. O'Connor'. The prosecutor saw this as evidence of her 'hypocrisy' and 'consummate wickedness'.[7] 'Why Poor Mr. O'Connor?' he asked her openly in court, 'you knew his body was mouldering in your kitchen'.[8] The *Standard* claimed that Maria had even cooked a Sunday goose over O'Connor's rotting remains.[9] The act of cooking a goose, however, was actually Maria's own euphemism for killing O'Connor. During preparations for the crime she is alleged to have said 'now I shall get things ready to cook his goose'.[10] Maria had no intentions of cooking O'Connor a real goose, as *The Times* emphatically reported that *'nothing had been prepared in the way of food'* the night he was murdered.[11]

According to Isabella Beeton's book on household management, cooking and the maintenance of a good kitchen is one of woman's first and foremost concerns:

> It is in serving up food that is at once appetizing and wholesome that the skill of the modern housewife is severely tasked; and she has scarcely a more important duty to fulfil. It is, in fact, her particular vocation, in virtue of which she may be said to hold the health of the family, and of the friends of the family, in her hands from day to day.[12]

When it came to reporting the Bermondsey case, newspapers stressed how woman's 'particular vocation' had become indistinguishable from a burst of extreme aggression. In this murder, cooking – or, more specifically, 'cooking a goose' – had terrible connotations. The kitchen, according to Beeton, is 'the great laboratory of every household [... where] much of the "weal or woe", as far as regards bodily health, depends upon the nature of the preparations concocted within its walls'.[13] The work concocted within the walls of the Manning kitchen was certainly tending more towards 'woe' than 'weal'. For Beeton and many of her contemporaries, the kitchen was the hallowed centre of every home yet, in the Mannings' kitchen, a nasty secret mouldered beneath its flagstones.

What this suggests is that far from being limited to the 'angel in the house' imagery, popular nineteenth-century conceptions of femininity, influenced as much by cases like this as by advice manuals like Beeton's, perceived there to be a ghastly, destructive energy lurking beneath female spaces and feminine graces. The Bermondsey murder did not combine murder and the home in a way that was horrifying and unexpected (as one might presume), but confirmed growing suspicions that every home and every woman could harbour the potential for extreme violence.

Young women and adolescents: 'The mad fury of that lovely being'

In 1863, Mary Fortune, a little-known crime writer using the pseudonym 'Waif Wander', composed a short story entitled 'The White Maniac: A Doctor's Tale'. Curious, risqué, and, at times, absurd, the story was eventually published posthumously in 1912. It is narrated by Charles Elverton, a young London physician specialising in the treatment of mental disorders. Elverton is called to attend a beautiful, twenty-year-old, foreign princess. Living in the London suburbs, the aptly named Blanche D'Alberville is entombed in a house completely devoid of colour:

> From the extreme top of the chimneys to the basement, roof, windows, everything was pure white; not a shade lurked even inside a window; the windows themselves were painted white, and the curtains were of a white muslin that fell over every one of them. Every yard of the broad space that one might reasonably have expected to see decorated with flowers and grass shrubberies was covered with a glaring and sparkling white gravel, the effect of which, even in the hot brilliant sun of a London afternoon, was to dazzle, and blind, and aggravate.[14]

Visitors to the weird mansion are requested to wear white suits before they enter. Blanche's uncle, the Duke de Rohan, explains that his niece is kept in this surreal, colourless environment because the colour red initiates a maniacal fury in her:

> 'My wretched niece is mad'.
> 'Mad!'
> 'Alas! yes, frightfully – horribly mad!' and he shuddered as if a cold wind had penetrated his bones. [...] 'The sight of one colour has such an effect on the miserable girl that we have found out, by bitter experience, the only way to avoid a repetition of the most fearful tragedies, is to keep every hue or shade away from her vision; for, although it is only one colour that affects her, any of the others seems to suggest that *one* to her mind and produce uncontrollable agitation. In consequence of this she is virtually imprisoned within the grounds of the house I have provided for her, and every object that meets her eye is white, even the ground, and the very roof of the mansion.[15]

The scenario may seem incredible, but it was not without its parallels in Victorian medical treatises. The anonymous writer of 'Woman in Her Psychological Relations' (1851), an article in *The Journal of Psychological Medicine and Mental Pathology*, for example, noted that the red uniforms of soldiers were likely to ignite 'improper' feelings in young females:

> The soldier is *par excellence* the most attractive to the sex; his warlike profession, his manly moustache, the scarlet and gold, the nodding plume, the burnished helm of his uniform, his glittering arms, and the tout-ensemble of his accoutrements, often, where there is a special susceptibility to the sexual influence of form and colour, awake strange mysterious emotions in the young female just bursting into womanhood.[16]

Mary Fortune's plot is a bizarre extension of Victorian medical theories of *normative* female behaviour. Elverton discovers no obvious signs of 'strange mysterious emotions' in the Princess: 'I was looking in the eyes of the beautiful being before me for a single trace of the madness I had been told of, but I could not find it'.[17] Being an 'enthusiastic youth',[18] Elverton inevitably falls in love with the young woman and fully believes her suggestion that it is her uncle, not she, who is the true maniac. It is, she claims, 'his mania to believe *me* mad'.[19] Believing Blanche to be 'the most perfect of women',[20] Elverton asks her to marry him. Horrified, the Duke writes to Blanche's father, asking him to explain his daughter's insanity to her new fiancé. D'Alberville responds with the following 'fearful paper':

> Sir, – You wish to wed my daughter, the Princess D'Alberville. Words would vainly express the pain with which I expose our disgrace – our horrible

secret – to a stranger, but it is to save you from a fate worse than death. Blanche D'Alberville is an anthropophagus, already has one of her own family fallen victim to her thirst for human blood.[21]

The misogynistic 'Woman in Her Psychological Relations' testifies to the cannibalistic longings experienced by women like Blanche:

> Dr. Laycock quotes Dr. Elliotson as mentioning in his lectures that a 'patient has longed for raw flesh' (the carnivorous appetite) 'and even for live flesh, so that some have eaten live kittens and rats'. Languis, a German writer, tells a story of a woman who lived near Cologne, who had such a cannibalish longing for the flesh of her husband, that she killed him, ate as much of him as she could while still fresh, and pickled the remainder. Another longed for a bite out of a baker's arm![22]

Rather than believing that Blanche is one such 'anthropophagus! a cannibal!' Elverton becomes convinced that she is the victim of 'some detestable plot [...] for what vile purpose, or what end in view [he is] ignorant'.[23] He determines to expose the plot by presenting Blanche with a bouquet of 'flaring scarlet verbena'.[24] Bursting into the white house, in his white suit, Elverton presents his 'bride' with the nosegay, resulting in the following scene:

> Her eyes [...] flashed into madness at the sight of the flowers as I turned. Her face grew scarlet, her hands clenched, and her regards *devoured* the scarlet bouquet, as I madly held it towards her. [...] How well I remember that picture to-day. The white room – the torn brilliant flowers – and the mad fury of that lovely being. [...] Then there was a rush, and white teeth were at my throat, tearing flesh, and sinews and veins; and a horrible sound was in my ears, as if some wild animal was tearing at my body![25]

In order to separate her from Elverton's throat, Blanche has to be killed. While he is recovering from the attack, the surgeon is told of the first time Blanche had become aggressive:

> The first intimation her wretched relatives had of the horrible thing was upon the morning of her eighteenth year. They went to her room to congratulate her, and found her lying upon the dead body of her younger sister, who occupied the same chamber; she had literally torn her throat with her teeth, and was sucking the hot blood as she was discovered.[26]

Closing the story, Elverton admits being haunted by his bride: 'I have never since met with a case of anthropophagy, but I fancy I still feel Blanche's teeth at my throat'.[27]

It is possible to trace in the story's extraordinary details the influence of a number of mainstream Victorian texts. The image of a woman buried in whiteness, for example, is clearly indebted to *The Woman in White* (1860) and *Great Expectations* (1860–1), while the notion of one sibling attacking and drinking the blood of another replicates Bertha Rochester's assault on her brother in *Jane Eyre* (1847). Recounting his sister's attack, Bertha's victim cries, 'she sucked the blood: she said she'd drain my heart'.[28] Fortune's short story not only echoed narratives contained in literary and medical books, but also seems to have repainted, in melodramatic colours, stories from the period's journalism. For example, in 1860, the *Annual Register* ran the story of a 'Double Murder by an Insane Sister'. In Manchester, Joseph Scholes became alarmed one morning when none of his family joined him at breakfast. Searching the house and discovering no one, he eventually broke down the door to his sister's bedroom, finding the following:

> The sister was sitting in a chair, the father and son were lying on the floor together, quite dead. They had been strangled by the insane woman, neither, owing to physical infirmity, having been able to offer much resistance, though there were marks of blows about the room, as though by a stick. [...] From a statement of the poor maniac, it is supposed that the old man and his son went to the woman's room to coerce her into quiet; and that on their striking her, she had turned upon them with a maniac's strength and fury, and strangled both with her hands.[29]

Although Miss Scholes's alleged insanity seems to have been initiated by a blow from a family member, while Blanche's is triggered by her eighteenth birthday, their histories share the image of a young woman destroying her family with a sudden and unpredictable burst of insane violence. Miss Scholes was immediately committed as insane without a murder trial.

As Roger Smith shows, in *Trial by Medicine* (1981), 'it was in the nineteenth century that lawyers, medical men and the public increasingly expected medicine to be represented in the criminal law'.[30] The Victorians established the practice of having expert medical witnesses in criminal and civil trials. As Smith demonstrates, this was not a smooth development as doctors, lawyers, and journalists repeatedly argued over what constituted diminished responsibility. From a legal point of view, the question was settled by the trial of *R. v. McNaughten* (1843). Following Daniel McNaughten's acquittal on the grounds of insanity, the Lord Chancellor created a precedent named the 'McNaughten Rules'. These rules stipulated that a criminal prosecution was sustainable only if the defendant's mental state did not interfere with their sense of right and wrong. Psychologists complained that this was too simplistic. They argued that in many mental conditions the patient knows the difference between right and wrong but cannot resist the urge to commit crime. This was especially seen to be the case with women.

Women, as already noted, were believed to be driven by their bodily processes – processes, moreover, that were considered to be inherently pathological. Hence, according to some medical witnesses, many violent women had tried to fight the urge to commit crime but, because of the pressures of their psychosomatic organisations, had lost the battle. Despite the fact that they knew they were doing wrong, such women, the medics argued, could not resist the criminal impulse.

The expert medical witness thus became a vocal presence in the Victorian courtroom, and, had Miss Scholes been indicted for murdering her relatives, a psychologist would probably have been called to testify to her mental state (assuming, of course, that she had the financial means to secure his services). The authorities were satisfied, however, that Miss Scholes's insanity made her unfit to attend trial and so no alienists had the chance to comment on her condition.

It does not require an extensive combing of contemporaneous medical texts, however, before one discovers clinical pronouncements on insanely violent young women. Adolescence, in particular, was considered to be a precarious and explosive time for women. In 'Woman in Her Psychological Relations', for example, the type of woman whose mind is most likely to be disordered by the sight of a virile young soldier is identified as 'the young female just bursting into womanhood'. In a series of lectures delivered at the Bristol Medical School in 1855, psychologist James Davey claimed of puberty that

> at this period of life, a general revolution of the whole system takes place. [...] At the age of puberty, a new order of functions elicits desires and wants which have been until then unfelt. All nature seems to bear a different aspect: imagination on Icarian wings, takes a bold flight to unknown regions; the limits of the universe become unbounded.[31]

Such ideas were not exclusive to specialised medical literature, as in 1864, *Macmillan's Magazine* featured an article by Dinah Mulock Craik entitled 'In Her Teens'. It suggested that, for females,

> the years between twelve and twenty are, to most, a season anything but pleasant; a crisis in which the whole heart and brain are full of tumult, when all life looks strange and bewildering – delirious with exquisite unrealities, – and agonized with griefs equally chimerical and unnatural.[32]

Thirteen years later, gynaecologist Lawson Tait (whose work was the first to discuss – in any great detail – pathologies of the fallopian tubes) articulated similar ideas, but applied them more exclusively to the development of insanity:

> A dormant tendency to mental disease becomes roused into action; and acute mania forms one of the risks through which many young women

have to pass at the period of puberty. [...] I have several times seen girls so afflicted indulge in gestures and language which puzzled us to guess how the patients became acquainted with them, the girls were so young and had been so well brought up.[33]

According to Tait, primal, irrational behaviour (which had remained dormant in a family's hereditary biology for generations) could become manifest in the 'gestures and language' of the insane, pubescent female. This is apparently corroborated by Blanche's attack on Elverton, which reads like a form of atavism:

A horrible sound was in my ears, as if some wild animal was tearing at my body! I dreamt that I was in a jungle of Africa, and that a tiger, with a tawny coat, was devouring my still living flesh.[34]

As Tait suggests, primal, dormant behaviour has here found vent in the passions of an adolescent female. Indeed, 'The White Maniac' has many elements that appear to have been appropriated from concurrent ideas on the dangers of female puberty. Elverton admits an interest in Blanche's case, for example, because 'the subject was just now engaging the attention of the medical world in a remarkable degree'.[35] Like Tait's, Craik's, and Davey's image of the volatile adolescent, Blanche's first insane outbreak occurs on her eighteenth birthday – the day that the Victorians would have recognised as heralding her move into womanhood.

In his influential treatise on *Mental Maladies* (1838), Esquirol outlined the case history of one of his patients. The story has a lot in common with Blanche D'Alberville's:

She has always, however, had a proud and intractable disposition; an aversion to labour; a relish from early life, for blood, and for meat, which she sometimes eats raw. Long since, she felt herself irresistibly inclined to homicide, in order to shed blood. She has been seen to cut into pieces, with an expression of joy, birds, or other animals which fell into her hands. Marriage did not modify this horrible instinct. [...] She repeats that a crime must be committed; and that she must slay her mother, and all who approach her. The human race must die, and the earth inundated with blood.[36]

What is noteworthy about these medical examples is how they perceive the *ordinary* phases of female adolescence to be the predisposing causes of *extraordinary* behaviours. Esquirol's blood-lusting patient, like Blanche D'Alberville, has not gone insane because of some irrecoverable shock or accident, but developed a predilection for the taboo of cannibalism through the 'bewildering tumult' of her biological organisation.

Such narratives naturally fostered a climate of fear and observation around the adolescent female. 'Does it not behove us', asked Craik, 'to look a little more closely after our "girls"?'[37] Medico-legal expert Alfred Swaine Taylor had a stark reminder to 'look a little more closely' when visiting Esquirol at the Charenton:

> On one occasion, in accompanying Esquirol round the Asylum of Charenton, the author was suddenly seized from behind by a tight grasp round his neck, by which he was rendered powerless, and felt almost strangled (garrotted). Esquirol and other physicians, who had gone forward, on hearing the wild shriek of his assailant, turned back, and rescued him from a somewhat perilous position. One of the female patients, who a few minutes before had presented nothing but a calm appearance and quiet manner, had silently crept behind him, being the last of the party, and had suddenly thrown both her arms around his neck, apparently with a view of throttling him.[38]

Like Elverton, Taylor takes 'a calm appearance and quiet manner' for granted and, turning his back on Esquirol's patient, has to have her removed from his neck (as Elverton does with Blanche). Taylor's experience, although it occurred within the walls of an asylum, served as a graphic reminder that the 'sweet and innocent' appearances of 'girls' could not be trusted. Like Blanche and the Charenton inmate, any young woman, it was implied, could develop an unexpected violent mania.

In the same volume featuring his assault in the Charenton, Taylor outlined the criminal case of Sarah Minchin. In 1853, seventeen-year-old Minchin was tried for wounding thirteen-year-old Frederick Smith. At the time, Minchin was a servant of the Smith household. On 17 June, *The Times* reported how

> about 7 o' clock on the morning of the 22nd May shrieks were heard from the bedroom occupied by the prosecutor, and upon a young man named Cushion, who slept in another room close by, going in, he found the prisoner in the act of endeavouring to cut the throat of the lad with a carving knife.[39]

Because Minchin had no apparent motive for the crime, her defence lawyer claimed that she was under 'the influence of a frightful dream or in a state of somnambulism'.[40] No medical witnesses were called to testify to the claim, however, as the defendant could not afford their services. In his *Principles and Practice of Medical Jurisprudence* (1865), Alfred Taylor rejected the idea of somnambulism, adding 'there was nothing to show that the prisoner was not aware of what she was doing'.[41] Nonetheless, Sarah could not account for her actions; on being asked 'what could have induced her to make an attack of so murderous a nature [...], she made no reply'.[42] She was found guilty of Grievous Bodily Harm but given a lenient sentence.

The Minchin story seemed to follow a pattern set by Victorian literature and medicine: a family member opens a bedroom door to discover a murder scene presided over by an adolescent female. Yet, possibly the most significant factor in the case of Sarah Minchin (and perhaps the reason why the crime received so much media attention) is the fact that the violence seemed to have challenged (albeit momentarily) the class and gender power dynamics of the Smiths' bourgeois household. On 3 June, *The Times* featured the testimony of the victim, Frederick Smith:

> While fast asleep in bed, I was awoken by feeling a violent pain in my neck. I saw the prisoner close to me, and on putting up my hand to protect myself, she drew a knife through my hand, which was much cut. I felt the knife a little bit into my throat. She then struck at my neck again with the knife and tried to saw it. I cried out 'Murder' as well as I was able, but the prisoner did all she could to prevent my giving an alarm, by kneeling upon me and putting her hands over my mouth.[43]

As most victims in the cases against Victorian murderesses were killed, Frederick's testimony, given from the victim's point of view, is a rare thing. According to *The Times*, it 'excite[d] the commiseration of all';[44] looking at it closely, it reads like the evidence of a rape victim. Notice, for example, how Frederick is forced into position and silenced by Sarah while she penetrates his body with a carving knife. Although neither the victim nor the perpetrator could offer an explanation for the assault, there is the possibility that Sarah and Frederick, both in their teens, had a sexual relationship that neither were willing to admit to – a cross-class relationship between servant and master, upstairs and downstairs. Sarah's attempt on Frederick's life certainly reads like a sexual encounter between the classes, as well as an inversion of traditional gender roles. As such, Minchin's visit to Frederick's bedroom that night, as reported by *The Times*, seems to have offered some resistance to the hierarchical ordering of the Smiths' middle-class home.

Similar challenges to traditional family structures are also evident in 'The White Maniac'. As the Duke explains to Elverton, 'the honour of a noble house is deeply concerned' in his niece's story, and the scandal generated by Blanche's murdering of her sister compromises the value of the D'Alberville name.[45] It is, the Duke admits, 'the unspoken curse that rests on our wretched name' and, according to Blanche's father, 'our disgrace – our horrible secret'.[46] The taint that Blanche's first act of violence injects into the D'Alberville family is also represented, ironically, by the whiteness that envelops her suburban home. Like Satis House in *Great Expectations*, the building is like an 'enchanted castle'[47] where former splendour is overwritten by current grotesqueness:

> My companion led the way up a broad staircase covered with white cloth, and balustraded with carved rails, the effect of which was totally destroyed by their covering of white paint. [...] Without having beheld such a scene, one can hardly conceive the strange cold look the utter absence of colour gave it.[48]

In a reversal of the traditional 'stained whiteness' metaphor, Blanche's transgression is signalled by a lack of colour that bleaches out the magnificence of the home and the respectability of the D'Alberville name. The domestic, family environment, which ought to be a comforting stronghold, is transformed by her aggression into a lifeless, haunting atmosphere.

Like Sarah Minchin's alleged attack on Frederick Smith, Blanche's violence is also not without its sexual connotations. The D'Albervilles enter their daughters' bedroom to discover the just-matured Blanche on her sister's body, drinking her 'hot blood'. As in the Minchin case, where the female is discovered violating the male, Blanche's first transgression offers a similar violation of the gender status quo and carries proto-lesbian connotations. A similar breach of roles occurs in Blanche's second and final attack on Elverton. Like Taylor's underestimation of the woman in the Charenton, Elverton's presentation of Blanche with a scarlet bouquet results in him being completely unmanned. This is reflected immediately before the attack when the doctor catches sight of himself in a mirror:

> The mirror reflected, in unbroken stillness, the cold whiteness of the large apartment, but it also reflected my face and form, wearing an expression that half awoke me to a consciousness of physical indisposition. There was a wild look in my pallid countenance, and a reckless air in my figure which the very garments seemed to have imbibed, and which was awry; the collar of my shirt was unbuttoned, and I had even neglected to put on my neck-tie; but it was upon the blood-red bouquet that my momentary gaze became riveted.
>
> It was such a contrast; the cold, pure white of all the surroundings, and that circled patch of blood-colour that I held in my hand was so suggestive![49]

Of course, the exposed neck, white costume, and 'red patch' could be suggestive of Elverton's vulnerability to the upcoming violence, yet they could also symbolise how Elverton and his 'bride' have exchanged roles. Dressed from head to foot in white garments, and carrying a scarlet bouquet, Elverton's mirror image seems bridal and the subsequent attack could be read as a violent reversal of the marriage consummation. Unlike post-marital coitus, however, the bodily contact between Blanche and Elverton is more preoccupied with extinguishing life than creating it.

'The White Maniac' was thus a story that seemed to draw on existing ideas about the incendiary nature of female adolescence. What the narrative reveals, when combined with coexisting medical and journalist material, is that stories of pubescent women's violence were often stories featuring momentary assaults on the sanctity of the home and the family. As with concurrent medical debates, such narratives seemed to underpin the view that young women, and the homes they were central to, needed careful and sustained surveillance if established hierarchies were to be maintained.

The association of the female adolescent body with violence fostered more widespread fears regarding the destructive potential of female sexuality and reproduction. In particular, the period's constructions of hysteria show distinct associations between sexual desire and aggression. Victorian definitions of the hysterical condition were riddled with inconsistency and contradiction. Medical writers would often categorise the condition by defining what it was *not* rather than what it was. In 1864, for example, Frederick Skey, one of the era's main specialists in the area, admitted with reference to one of his patients: 'I had no doubt whatever that it would prove to be a case of hysteria. It appeared obvious that it must be so, simply because it was most improbable that it could be any other disease'.[50] Thought to have reached 'little epidemic' status by mid-century,[51] hysteria became what Janet Oppenheim has usefully termed a 'catch-all classification'.[52] Its 'clinical criteria', explains Jane Wood, 'could be modified in order to diagnose all the behaviours which did not fit the prescribed model of Victorian womanhood'.[53] Yet, as the origins of the word 'hysteria' suggest ('derived from *hustera*, the Greek for uterus'[54]), one characteristic that remained constant throughout the disorder's long history was its link with the female sexual body. Julius Althaus observed how, prior to the mid-nineteenth century,

> pressure of the uterus upon the various organs of the body was considered to be the mainspring of all the sufferings of hysterical patients. Where there was a feeling of suffocation, it must be due to the uterus compressing the throat and the bronchial tubes; coma and lethargy in hysterical women proceeded from the womb squeezing the blood-vessels travelling towards the brain; palpitations arose from the uterus worrying the heart; and if there were a feeling of pain and constriction in the epigastrium, it must again be the womb engaged in a relentless attack on the liver.[55]

By the mid-Victorian period, this notion of the 'wandering uterus' was, as this passage illustrates, being discredited. A correspondent to the *Lancet* observed in 1853, for example, that it was 'a mistake to designate by a uterine name a disease which is not of uterine origin'.[56] Indeed, as shown by

Mark Micale's extensive work on the subject, the period's leading specialists aimed to show how men were also prone to the disorder, albeit much more rarely.[57]

Notwithstanding these developments, the Victorians still held to the idea that menstruation was crucial to the development and diagnosis of hysteria. Although Althaus dismissed earlier clinical emphases on the mobile uterus, he nevertheless claimed (in the very same text) that 'hysterical attacks occur almost always after sudden suppression of the menstrual flow', adding that 'in all cases of hysteria, we must take care that the ordinary functions of life, especially menstruation and alimentation, should be in proper order'.[58] Robert Brudenell Carter, author of a monograph on the condition, wrote of 'faulty menstruation' that 'it will be found that, although affections of this kind often arise consecutively to hysteria, still women suffering from them are more liable than others, *cæteris paribus*, to be the subjects of the disorder'.[59]

Indeed, the idea of women suffering from mental alienation because of a defective menstrual flow was not unfamiliar to the era's medical professionals. The flow and ebb of menstruation was seen to determine both the reproductive and mental states of women. James Prichard wrote in his *Treatise on Insanity* (1837), for instance:

> Sudden suppressions of the catamenia are frequently followed by disease of the nervous system of various kinds. Females [...] undergoing powerful excitements, experience a suppression of the catamenia, followed in some instances immediately by fits of epilepsy or hysteria, the attacks of which are so sudden as to illustrate the connexion of cause and effect.[60]

The uses of words like 'immediately' and 'sudden' in this passage are not insignificant. According to Prichard, stoppage of the catamenial discharge creates a build-up of energy that eventually results in the eruption of pressurised, volcanic mental conditions of which hysteria is one.

In the criminal courtroom, such ideas formed the foundations of a number of insanity defences. In 1863, for example, Sarah Mitchell was arraigned for the murder of her baby. Having been abandoned by her lover, Mitchell stabbed the child in the chest twice before attempting to cut her own throat. At the trial, three medical witnesses claimed that the defendant was not responsible for her actions because she was hysterical. The surgeon William Cathrow declared that

> he always found her excessively nervous. Her husband, she said, did not behave kindly to her, and she was always extremely jealous. Occasionally she was subject to hysteria. [...] In his (witness's) opinion no woman could have done what she did unless in a state of insanity. She showed, also, a great deal of cunning in throwing them off their guard, which was another mark of insanity.[61]

Sarah was under treatment for hysteria at the time of the murder. Cathrow had considered 'whether there was any necessity for putting her under restraint', prior to the killing of her infant, 'but she threw them off their guard with her excessive cunning'.[62] The surgeon's evidence seems to corroborate Carter's opinion that the hysteric displays an 'extraordinary development of cunning by means of which [she] often carr[ies] out most complicated systems of deception and succeeds in baffling the watchfulness, even of very close observers'.[63] Mitchell's sister Elizabeth also testified that 'there was something strange and peculiar in her manner'[64] and, in a letter to Elizabeth, Mitchell's lover explained his reasons for abandoning Sarah. According to him, 'her violence has been such that I have become hopeless of our ever getting on comfortably together'.[65] Elizabeth explains that 'after that event she became still more excited' – an excitement, medical experts claimed, that culminated in the killing of the child.[66] It took the jury 'about a minute' to return a verdict of '*Not Guilty*, upon the grounds of insanity'.[67] The case of alleged accumulative and unreasonable violence corroborated, and was endorsed by, scores of similar such narratives in the period's medical literature. Through vehicles like the *Annual Register* and *The Times*, such material was now reaching the general public in graphic and lurid detail.

In the 1845 trial of Martha Brixey, the notion of menstrual dysfunction instigating a sudden act of violence also formed the crux of the defendant's insanity plea. Like Sarah Minchin, who was arraigned for the grievous bodily harm of Frederick Smith, Brixey (an eighteen-year-old servant) cut the throat of one of the children in her care. Unlike Minchin, however, Brixey was successful in killing her victim. John Ffinch, the baby's father, explains how, on that morning, a police magistrate happened to pay him a social call:

> I was sitting in the dining-room, at about quarter to ten o' clock, with my wife and Mr. Traill, the police-magistrate, when the prisoner entered the room in a very excited state, and addressing me said, 'Oh, Sir what have I done? What have I done?' I rose, as, indeed, we all did. The prisoner said, 'Oh, Sir, I am a murderer. I have murdered the dear baby. I have cut the dear baby's throat'. I instantly ran from the room and proceeded to the nursery, I found my child in his cot with his head very nearly cut off. There was an ordinary tableknife lying across the child covered with blood; and I saw that my child was dead.[68]

At the trial, it emerged that Martha had been experiencing menstrual irregularities and her defence lawyer was eager to exploit the fact to secure an acquittal. He called on the Ffinch family physician, John Mould Burton, to give evidence as follows:

> I am a surgeon, and attend the family of Mr. Ffinch. By desire of Mrs. Ffinch, I have since the 31st of March sent the prisoner some medicines to remove

some constitutional irregularities to which young women are especially subject.[69]

Drawing on his professional experiences he adds:

> I have frequently had occasion to attend young women who have been subject to temporary suspensions of the action of nature and I believe any suspension of that action is calculated very much to derange the general constitution. [...] The patient is subjected to fits of irritability and great excitement and passion. These symptoms will present themselves very suddenly.[70]

Burton had even recommended earlier that Martha be dismissed because her medical condition rendered her unfit to manage children. *The Times* reported how one day, prior to the murder, Martha – being dissatisfied with her uniform – 'ripped the body from the skirt, and thrust it with the poker into the fire'.[71] Burton believed that 'that act was likely to have arisen from the difficulties or disease under which she was labouring' and 'unfitted her to be among young children'.[72] When Brixey cut Robert Ffinch's throat almost to the point of decapitation, she seems to have validated the surgeon's warnings.

In *Principles and Practice*, Alfred Taylor utilised the Brixey case as evidence of how 'amenorrhoea (suppressed menstruation) may be a cause of insanity among girls', adding:

> By the sympathy of the uterine functions with the brain there may be some intellectual disturbance, indicated by waywardness of temper, strange and immoral conduct, morbid appetite, and great irritability with excitement from slight causes. A crime may be suddenly perpetrated by such persons without apparent motive.[73]

Taylor concludes, therefore, that Brixey was rightly acquitted on the grounds of insanity.[74]

The employment of medical evidence in the courtroom thus seemed to vocalise a set of associations that already existed in medical texts. In nineteenth-century clinical discussions of the female body (particularly the pathologies of hysteria and amenorrhoea), we observe very close connections between women's reproductive abilities and their potential for violence. James Davey, for example, combined hysteria with mania to coin the hybrid term 'hysteromania', while Esquirol evocatively referred to hysteria as 'uterine fury'.[75] According to Davey, 'no class of patients manifest a more continuous and perverse moral sense than [the hysterical] one'[76] and it seemed that homicidal tendencies and sexual promiscuity went side by side.

Such an association is particularly clear in the 1857 indictment of Madeline Smith. Accused of murdering her secret lover Emile L'Angelier,

Madeline seemed, as Mary Hartman has observed, to be on trial for her sexual fallenness rather than the murder.[77] Her case excited an extraordinary amount of public interest. At each hearing, the courtroom was filled to capacity and crowds gathered outside to hear the latest developments. In a report occupying an unprecedented sixty-one double-columned pages of the *Annual Register*, it is recorded that 'from the first announcement of the arrest of the accused, this *cause célèbre* excited the deepest interest in Scotland – an interest which was raised to the highest point of excitement during the trial'.[78] When Madeline was eventually set free through the Scotch verdict of 'not proven', the crowd seemed delighted: 'Instantly on the announcement of these last words, a vehement burst of cheering came from the audience, especially from the galleries, which was again and again renewed with increasing loudness'.[79] The public reaction suggests that the defence lawyer's claims had been better received than the prosecutor's. The former had set out to portray Madeline as a 'poor girl' led astray by the 'ingenuity and skill' of a 'vile', 'corrupting', and 'nefarious' adventurer.[80] George Young, the defence, even claimed that the L'Angelier death was suicide:

> The character of this man – his origin, his previous history, the nature of his conversation, the numerous occasions upon which he spoke of suicide – naturally suggest that as one mode by which he may have departed this life.[81]

The prosecution alleged that in order to free herself from an engagement to L'Angelier Madeline laced her lover's cocoa with arsenic. Indeed, Madeline's guilt appeared at first sight to be a foregone conclusion. She had had the motive and the opportunity for poisoning L'Angelier; plus, it was proven that Madeline had bought large quantities of arsenic shortly before her fiancé's death.[82] Yet, the bulk of the prosecuting evidence relied on compromising letters to L'Angelier, written by Madeline, in which she admitted having sexual relations with him. The affair, the Lord Advocate (prosecution) claimed, 'assumed a criminal aspect [...] not once or twice, but I have evidence to show clearly that repeated acts of improper connection took place'.[83] He then read aloud a number of letters, written by Madeline, featuring comments such as 'beloved, if we did wrong last night, it was in the excitement of our love', 'you might rest assured, after what has passed, that I cannot be the wife of any other, dear Emile', and 'our intimacy has not been criminal as I am your wife before God'.[84] These letters, the prosecutor maintained, 'speak [a] language not to be mistaken'[85] and

> show as extraordinary a frame of mind, and as unhallowed a passion, as perhaps ever appeared in a court of justice. [...] She uses the most disgusting and revolting language, exhibiting a state of mind most lamentable to think of.[86]

Significantly, he then suggests that the jury's verdict ought to be determined by the evidence found in those letters:

> If you think it such a just and satisfactory inference [that Madeline and L'Angelier were together the night he died and] that you can rest your verdict upon it, it is quite competent for you to draw such an inference from such letters as these.[87]

Thus, for the prosecuting advocate, the proof of Madeline's guilt in the murder of L'Angelier is synonymous with the evidence of her sexual liberties. In his case against the defendant, there is no distinction between coitus and killing. The fact that the prosecution's case was unsuccessful, moreover, does not necessarily indicate that the jury rejected these connections. It appears, instead, that they chose to believe the defence's claim that Madeline was the passive, innocent dupe of an adventurer. Madeline's lawyer presented an image of the accused as neither sexual nor murderous – as if reaffirming the idea that it was impossible for a woman to be one without being the other. Hence, in *this* trial we see, melodramatically played out, existing assumptions that there were firm links between female sexual desire and the development of destructive behaviour.

This highlights how, for the Victorians, normative female behaviours (or, perhaps more accurately, feelings and developments considered essential to female development) regularly placed women on the verge of violent insanity. Medical, legal, and journalistic texts exchanged ideas and images relating to the explosive nature of female adolescence and found that it was a volatile and dangerous time for all women. Yet, what also emerges from discussing medical, legal, and journalistic materials alongside each other is a glimpse of how the Victorians were able to maintain a firm vigilance over the 'nation's girls' by imagining them as explosive materials. As Helen Taylor poignantly observed in 1866, 'many people do fancy that, in dealing with women, we are dealing with very explosive materials'.[88] When it came to applying similar ideas to the nation's mothers, issues of reproduction and caste control also became the focus of an intense scrutiny.

Motherhood I: Maternal maniacs

In 1860, the obstetrician Charles Routh published what the *British Medical Journal* praised as 'the most elaborate treatise on the feeding of infants that has ever emanated from the British press'.[89] Immensely popular and influential, *Infant Feeding and its Influence on Life* (1860) aimed to lower infant mortality figures by providing a thorough and practical guide on the care of babies. The book opens with a very idealistic portrait of family life:

> The mother has suffered in her travail, and the husband has grieved over his wife's sufferings. But even in her weakness it is an unalloyed pleasure

to gaze on the little babe that sleeps by her side. First, helpless to a degree, it commends itself to her protection; and gradually, as the stream of life acquires power, new feelings of love expand her maternal heart.[90]

This sentimental babe-in-arms image yields to one of disharmony and misery, however, when bad maternal management results in sickness:

> How different the picture when illness creeps in! How sad the looks are now of those who loved it: the little babe itself, how changed in aspect! It is sorrowful to behold its now haggard, now excited, restless look, and to hear its pitiful moan. The wellspring of pleasure has become an occasion of grief and despondency, and who knows how soon, like the blighted floweret, it may droop beyond recovery?[91]

Routh's melodramatic opening moves, with a massive jolt, from a familiar, romantic notion of maternity to a more painful image of motherhood that (considering the period's infant morality rates) would also have been familiar to his Victorian readers.[92] His message seems to be that one should not become confident in the health of the home when all within that hallowed circle *appears* to be well. Like female adolescents, who could bring death and destruction into every family home, mothers, it was argued, could be a similar source of devastation. Although, in Routh's text, such consequences are caused by maternal mismanagement or neglect, the opening page echoes the era's larger notions of motherhood as simultaneously life-giving and destructive. In the criminal cases of women accused of killing their children, moreover, nineteenth-century professionals found a dramatic crystallisation of what was already a widespread belief: that the biological phases of motherhood engendered the possibility of violence in all women.

Like Routh's *Infant Feeding*, some of the period's other medical texts perceived no stage of maternity to be exempt from the prospect of violence. Adolescence, as noted above, was seen to be a preparation for the reproductive state. Pregnancy, the next stage in the maternal process, was assumed to be imbued with similar risks. Esquirol wrote about 'mania', for example, that 'attacks burst forth spontaneously. [...] With some women the attack bursts forth at every pregnancy'.[93] According to some psychologists, the period of gestation placed a strain on women's bodies and minds that could eventually result in a sudden and destructive psychological disorder. Observe, for instance, how Esquirol repeats the term 'burst forth'; it highlights how, for this alienist, the madness caused by pregnancy was not an introspective, melancholic disorder but a violent and explosive condition.[94]

This theory found expression in the Central Criminal Court in 1863 during the arraignment of Mary Ann Payne. In June of that year, Mr Sedgewick, a London surgeon, was called to attend upon the injuries of twenty-one-year-old Payne, who had jumped from a second-story window. When he examined the room from which she had leapt, he discovered the body of her son Charlie. His throat had been cut with 'a common table knife'.[95] At the trial, it emerged that Payne was 'four months in the familyway [sic]' when she committed the crime.[96] When giving evidence, Sedgewick argued that it was not uncommon for pregnant women to experience 'a morbid state of mind' and 'derangement of the mental faculties', adding,

> sometimes when in a morbid state women in the familyway [sic] would commit acts of cruelty on those nearest and dearest to them. It was said the prisoner when pregnant had always exhibited a peculiar horror of knives and razors, and that when apprehended her first exclamation was, 'where is Charlie?'[97]

Payne was acquitted on the grounds of insanity. Two years later, the Old Bailey tried the similar and shocking case of Esther Lack. Considered 'a kind, respectable woman' by her neighbours,[98] Lack killed three of her children by cutting their throats with a razor. On being arrested, she gave an account of the killings as follows:

> I know what I am doing. I woke a little before 3 o' clock, and went downstairs and brought razors from the kitchen. I came up and killed Christopher first; I then leant over the baby and killed Eliza. I then killed Esther, and after I did so I kissed the baby.[99]

Lack's statement, which became crucial to her defence, reads like a gruesome inversion of Routh's opening to *Infant Feeding*. Whereas Routh presents the image of motherly compassion turning sour when influenced by bad maternal care, Lack's statement sees the act of motherly tenderness as the culmination of an act of extreme brutality. In the above extract, for example, it would be easy to misread 'kissed' as 'killed' and *vice versa*. It illustrates how, in the nineteenth century, a fine line was considered to exist (in some cases) between mothering and murdering.

As in Mary Ann Payne's case, Esther Lack's defence proposed that her actions were the result of the strains of motherhood. Yet, unlike Payne, it was alleged that suckling, rather than pregnancy, had driven Lack to kill her offspring:

> Mr. Sleigh then addressed the jury on behalf of the prisoner. He said he thought he should satisfy them beyond all reasonable doubt that the wretched woman now standing at the bar charged with the commission of an offence which was so utterly revolting to our common nature was wholly irresponsible for her act.[100]

Sleigh subpoenaed Mary Gardner, a widowed friend of Lack's, who had visited her on a number of occasions. She testified that 'at the time of the occurrence she was nursing her daughter. [... Gardner] persuaded the prisoner to cease suckling her child, owing to the weakness of which she complained in her head'.[101] The jury declined to hear the testimony of further witnesses, intimating that they were 'fully satisfied' with the evidence of Lack's insanity, and acquitted her on that basis.[102]

The story of Esther Lack echoes many similar cases outlined in treatises on insanity. In *Mental Maladies*, for example, Esquirol cites the case of a thirty-two-year-old patient who similarly exhausted her psychological and somatic faculties through breast-feeding:

> At the eighth month of lactation, she becomes sad, impatient and irritable towards her husband. She was heard to complain that she had children. She is impetuous in her treatment of her nursing child. Several times, she was observed to press it, as if with a view to stifle it. In one instance, during the absence of her husband, she threw it out of the window.[103]

Again, we observe a fine divide between acts associated with motherhood and violence; a maternal embrace can suddenly become suffocating, smothering (s/mothering).[104] As with pregnancy, breast-feeding was considered to be a drain on women's biological and moral strength; like menstruation, lactation was understood to be a regimen that both determined and testified to the state of women's health. Esquirol warned that 'we must be ever watchful of these metastases and suppressions'.[105] When the flow was stemmed, the accumulation of lochial discharge led to a pressurised, volcanic mental condition: 'the lochia are suppressed, and the milk is not secreted. Mania bursts forth on the same day. [...] The lochia are suppressed and an irruption of mania takes place'.[106] It was an old belief (discounted by many nineteenth-century medics) that unspent breast milk travelled into the cranium, causing insanity and death.[107] Esquirol's suggestive use of words like 'burst' and 'irrupt' underscores the prevailing notion that mothers could harbour explosive capabilities. Routh's sugary image of maternity as the 'wellspring of unalloyed pleasure' is something, it seems, he and his contemporaries were wary of taking for granted.

The phase of maternity that was considered to put the most strain on women's psychosomatic systems, however, was childbirth itself. As shown recently by Hilary Marland, the Victorian era developed a highly nuanced idea of puerperal insanity.[108] Classified as one of the 'most appalling diseases incident to human nature' by Robert Ferguson (Physician Extraordinary to the Queen) in 1859, puerperal insanity, or puerperal mania, was considered extensively by Robert Gooch in 1839.[109] His *On Some of the Most Important Diseases Peculiar to Women* was, according Ferguson, a landmark text in the treatment of medical conditions thought exclusive to women. In it, Gooch wrote of puerperal mania:

> During that long process, or rather succession of processes, in which the sexual organs of the human female are employed in the forming, lodging,

expelling, and lastly feeding of the offspring, there is no time at which the mind may not become disordered; but there are two periods at which this is chiefly liable to occur, the one soon after delivery, when the body is sustaining the effects of labour, the other several months afterwards, when the body is sustaining the effects of nursing. [...] The sexual system in women is a set of organs which are in action only during half the natural life of the individual, and even during this half they are in action only at intervals. During these intervals of action they diffuse an unusual excitement throughout the nervous system. [...] There is, therefore, something in the state of the constitution induced by lying-in or nursing capable of producing the disease.[110]

Although Gooch's definition is rather vague ('something in the state of the constitution'), it nevertheless concludes that childbirth was one of the most precarious events in the psychosomatic lives of women. Other texts from the period carried his suggestions even further by linking the state of 'lying in' with murder. The *British Medical Journal* claimed in 1865, for example, that

in that particular form of mania, again, called puerperal – the mania of women, which sometimes follows upon childbed – the mother becomes melancholy, and is at times seized with an 'uncontrollable impulse' to destroy herself, ay! Even to destroy her own offspring – the doting mother murdering her own beloved child – and she is horrified with herself all the time, because of the dreadful crime to which she feels impelled. Does such a woman (becoming a murderess) deserve our deepest sympathy; or ought she to be handed into the hangman's hands?[111]

The passage's combination of sentimentality and horror, 'the *doting* mother *murdering* her own beloved child', is, as we have seen in Routh, a standard technique in texts dealing with the issue of motherhood. Medical writers were eager to show how childbirth could, and often did, lead women – against their will – into murdering their 'unoffending' babies. In a treatise predating Gooch's by three years, James Cowles Prichard cites the case of 'a country woman, twenty-four years of age', who had been 'ten days confined with her first child, when suddenly, having her eyes fixed upon it, [...] was seized with the desire of strangling it. The idea made her shudder' and she was compelled to separate herself from her infant, not trusting her ability to resist throttling it.[112] Another woman, Prichard observes, would not use a knife when eating if her newborn baby was nearby.[113]

In 1857 these ideas were ventriloquised at the Central Criminal Court in the trial of Martha Bacon. After the birth of her second child it was claimed that Bacon developed violent puerperal insanity. It is recorded in the *Annual Register* how, 'after the birth of her last child, Mrs Bacon was very strange in her manner. She was under delusions, and had threatened to destroy the lives of her dearest relatives'.[114] Before she committed any violence, Bacon was sent to St Luke's Asylum where she remained for five months. On being discharged, her husband Thomas 'seems to have been very uneasy about her'.[115] Leaving for work one day, he arranged for a neighbour, Harriet Munro, to check on his wife and children. When Munro arrived at the Bacon's house it appeared to be empty. She returned the following day, with a friend, and met Martha Bacon in the street. She

> suddenly burst out with, 'Some one had got into the house by the back window, and a man had killed the two children and had cut their throat, and she was going to pay her rent and tell her landlord what had happened'.[116]

The article's use of the term 'burst out' parallels the favoured 'burst forth' of medical writers. Harriet Munro and her friend searched Martha's home and

> upon going into the back room on the ground-floor they saw the little boy, sitting on a chair, his head resting on a table, and with his throat cut. [...] Subsequently a police constable was fetched, and then the body of the little girl was found lying upstairs on the floor. Her throat, too, was cut, and she was quite dead.[117]

Because Martha had been previously confined as a puerperal maniac, the jury seemed to find little difficulty in acquitting her on the grounds of insanity. Her trial was a matter of celebrity and, on reading of its particulars in the newspapers, some of Martha's former neighbours began to see a previous family scandal in an entirely new light. It emerged, after her acquittal, that Martha's former home 'had been burnt down under somewhat suspicious circumstances'.[118] Thomas Bacon's mother had also died very suddenly. Her body was exhumed and examined by Alfred Taylor. He discovered traces of arsenic in most parts of Mrs Bacon's anatomy. Oddly, and perhaps because Martha was 'confined in safe custody during Her Majesty's pleasure' by then,[119] Thomas Bacon was arrested and tried for his mother's murder. He was found guilty and hanged. The *Annual Register* rightly questioned the verdict, adding: 'It must not be forgotten that there was present in the household another person, who has since been found guilty – as far as an insane person can be guilty – of the murder of her two children'.[120] According to the journal, the birth of Martha's last child had driven her to killing her mother-in-law, burning down her husband's house (Bertha Rochester-style), and slaughtering her two children. This willingness (on the part of the journal) to connect Martha's alleged puerperal insanity with the two previous crimes reveals an eager (automatic even) association between women in the puerperal state and any acts of destruction (real or anticipated) committed in connection with their homes and families. According to the Victorians, mothers were as capable of extinguishing life as they were of creating it, and it was the process of mothering *itself* that frequently led to murder.

Motherhood II: Morbid influences

According to Routh's guide on *Infant Feeding*, babies should always be fed, when appropriate, by their mothers. Again invoking a sentimental tableau, he writes:

> It is always delightful to perform a duty, how much more a maternal obligation! Is there a more delightful occupation for a mother than to watch the little babe hanging upon her breast, so helpless, and yet so fondling, nestling so closely to her, and feeding so contentedly upon her milk? Is there any means by which love can be more riveted between two beings in such intimate and close relation?[121]

However, he continues, there are conditions under which a woman ought to 'forget her suckling child';[122] particularly when she carries a disease or runs the risk of developing a medical problem.[123] In such cases, Routh maintains, it is necessary to employ a wet nurse. 'It is usual in our profession', he admits, 'to select fallen women'.[124] Such women, he says, are employed for philanthropic reasons:

> Surround such a person by a virtuous family, let benevolence be shown to her, let her recover a respect for herself, and in the kindly attentions received, and those she tenders to the child she now suckles, and under the happy influence of religion, you may stop her downward course – you may arrest the tendency to a repetition of the offence – you may preserve a useful member to society, and thus save her from ruin.[125]

Notwithstanding the above, Routh then suggests that employing fallen women as wet nurses was a grave mistake. Allowing such women into the inner sanctum jeopardised 'the purity of the domestic home' with 'the spectacle of vice rewarded'.[126] Such women, he proposes, have the ability to corrupt and mislead wives, servants, and husbands with their promiscuity. Their influence on children was more baneful still. Fallen women, he conceded, often concealed venereal diseases and addictions to opium or gin in order to be considered for employment. When it came to suckling, therefore, their breast milk was 'the vehicle of poison'.[127] He also hinted at the possibility that mental and moral 'peculiarities' are transferable through breast-feeding: 'A curious point here presents itself for inquiry, – Are mental peculiarities of a good or bad kind transmitted through the milk of a wet nurse, as well as bodily infirmities?'[128] As the issue is 'extremely difficult or doubtful of proof', he considers it 'wise not to discuss it here'.[129] Yet he does discuss it, albeit less directly, four pages on, answering the 'curious inquiry' in the affirmative:

> [Cancer] is known to be hereditary; and therefore it is necessary to be doubly cautious in making a selection where any blood relative of the

nurse has laboured under the malady. What is true of cancer I would equally apply to *insanity*. This is also a hereditary disease, the taint of which, even if not actually transmitted as insanity, often develops itself in after life, in analogous, although milder, affections. Extraordinary peculiarities, eccentricities, strong dispositions to crime or sexual indulgences, more frequently a deficiency in intellectual power, are apt to follow – evils greatly to be deplored, and therefore, if practicable, to be avoided.[130]

As before, Routh avoids making any direct connection between breast-feeding and the transference of mental aberration,[131] yet he does intimate in the above citation that children suckled by insane women have a greater chance of developing madness in later life.

Such issues were brought into the foreground by the notorious trial of Mary Ann Brough. Forbes Winslow, one of Victorian England's most prominent psychologists, was also one of the period's most frequent medical witnesses in criminal cases. In addition to editing the *Journal of Psychological Medicine* from 1848 to 1860, he wrote, among other works in psychology, *The Plea of Insanity in Criminal Cases* (1843) and *On Obscure Diseases of the Brain and Disorders of the Mind* (1860). In 1854, he gave evidence in Mary Brough's trial, claiming that at the time she committed her crimes she was acting under the influence of insanity. Brough, infamously, cut the throats of six of her children, killing them all, and attempted suicide by cutting her own.[132] Before she bled to death from her own injuries, Brough was rescued by a stranger who had noticed blood through her bedroom window. She promptly received medical attention for her wounds and almost as promptly received legal attention for the murders. In her trial, Winslow was called to give evidence in support of her use of the insanity defence. Her plea was successful and she was sent to Bedlam where she died eight years later.[133]

At the time of giving evidence, Winslow gave a full and gruesome account of the murders, in the *Journal of Psychological Medicine*, outlining his reasons for diagnosing them as 'symptomatic of insanity'.[134] Shortly before she murdered her children, Brough had separated from her husband following his discovery of her in the act of fornication. According to some contemporary commentators on the case, this marital rift signified how the murders aimed to prevent the husband gaining full custody of the children. In his *Unsoundness of Mind in Relation to Criminal Acts* (1854), for example, John Charles Bucknill, another key expert in medico-legal issues, gave his opinion that this 'horrible domestic massacre' was the result of an 'atrocious', 'vindictive', and 'poison[ous]' motive.[135] In response, Winslow undertook a lengthy and contradictory defence of his diagnosis in his journal. His article claimed that – because the crime went so far against the natural, sentimental instincts of motherhood – it *had* to be the result of insanity. Writing in his characteristic purple prose, he asked whether it is possible

> for one moment to suppose that this unhappy woman, who was admitted to have exhibited to her children, up to a short period antecedent to their death, the most kind and tender affection; nursing them with apparent motherly fondness [...], could *in full possession of her senses*, have coolly murdered them, solely because she had been detected in an act of infidelity! [...] The idea is preposterous. [...] We cannot, for a single instant, believe that any mother, however lost to all sense of shame, and deeply steeped in vice, could, in violation of one of the most powerful instincts wisely implanted in the human heart, proceed deliberately, in defiance, and in total disregard of appeals that would have roused even the affection, and wrung the heart of a Hottentot or New Zealand savage, destroy six of her unoffending and innocent children![136]

This passage seems out of place in a scientific context. Medical experts like Winslow were attempting to argue that maternal instincts and the organic phases of motherhood were not as remote from brutal violence as one would assume. Pregnancy, suckling, and childbirth were all, it seems, associated with insane violence at mid-century. Indeed, Winslow's article features the court testimony of Mr Izod, a surgeon who had treated Mary prior to the murders. He claimed, at the trial, that the defendant had had mental anomalies since the birth of her youngest child. 'In September, 1852', he testified,

> she was delivered of a child, and eight days afterwards she was attacked with paralysis, and completely lost the use of her left side. She also lost her speech, and her face was distorted. She gradually recovered, but never entirely regained her power, and [I] observed symptoms of a disordered brain. In consequence of this, [I] constantly advised her to avoid excitement of every description, and [I] felt satisfied that any sudden excitement would be dangerous to her.[137]

Winslow 'agreed with Mr. Izod that the condition of the prisoner's brain rendered her peculiarly liable to suffer from excitement; and he had no doubt that her brain had been in a disordered state ever since the attack of paralysis'.[138] Although modern readers are likely to recognise the fit as (what we today call) a stroke, her symptoms exemplified the medical belief that childbirth was not infrequently followed by paroxysms of madness and violence. By characterising Brough's violence as grossly different to the 'norm', therefore, Winslow's argument was not supported by the medical climate it ostensibly emerged from. He is too eager, it seems, to represent his evidence in the trial of Mary Brough as the only reasonable conclusion available to him. He emphatically writes, for example, that *'the act itself bears insanity stamped on its very face!'*[139] His vehement attempt to defend his definition of Mary Brough as a maniac (as opposed to a calculating killer) was clearly an attempt to legitimise his previous findings. Brough's case became one of national celebrity for reasons intimated in the *Annual Register*'s unreserved reporting of the case. Besides the obviously shocking details of the crime, Brough's act fuelled gossip because the defendant had been a wet nurse to the Prince of Wales. She had been dismissed from service at Buckingham Palace 'for some disobedience of orders'.[140] The journal added that, following Brough's acquittal,

> a strange notion appeared to pervade the minds of the vulgar that the crimes of this wretched woman would be some stain upon the future of the Prince of Wales, whom she had nursed, and *that she never could be found guilty of murder*, because it would attach some imputation on the Prince for ever.[141]

If, therefore, mental impulses *were* transferable through breast milk, the Prince of Wales would have suckled on milk instilled with a maniacal or homicidal taint. Brough's trial vocalised the medical ideas on how 'mothers' were capable of inflicting more insidious forms of harm than direct violence. Through her biological links to the nation's children, the unsuitable wet nurse could, it was urged, have a dire effect on future generations.

The morbid influence of unhealthy mothers was an idea that midnineteenth-century medical texts often returned to. Besides breast milk, the umbilical cord was also understood to allow for the passage of sickly forces. In 1865, for example, Dr Meadows claimed in the *British Medical Journal* that 'mind [...] acts upon matter' and that there was a 'direct connection between the nervous system of the mother and that of the foetus through the umbilical cord'.[142] The period's obstetrical textbooks were flooded with case histories of women whose excessive emotions or licentious behaviour lead to the birth of an unhealthy child. The idea is ancient in origin but it is interesting how it survived at a time when one would assume it to have been outdated. As late as 1875, for example, in a medical tract entitled *Maternal Impressions*, surgeon Robert Lee used Francois Mariceau's 1716 warning against excessive emotion during pregnancy:

> Above all, [ensure] that [the mother] may be not affrighted, nor that any melancholy news be suddenly told her. [...] Wherefore, if there be any news to tell a high-belly'd woman, let it rather be such as may moderately rejoice her (for excessive joy may likewise prejudice her in this condition); and, if there be absolutely necessity to acquaint her with bad news, let the gentlest means be contrived to do it all at once.[143]

Lee gives the following list of things that may frighten a woman into giving birth to an unhealthy child: 'thunder-storm, the sight of a child run over in the streets, a violent attack of hæmoptysis [coughing up blood] to her husband, and escape from being blown from a railway bridge', and so on.[144] In 1867 J. Waring-Curran reported to the Obstetrical Society the case of 'Mrs. E'. During pregnancy, she had told him, 'I was passing through a hayfield, when a young man, picking up a frog, threatened to throw it at me. I begged him not; but he did so, striking me in the face'.[145] So severe was the shock that Mrs E eventually gave birth to 'a monster':

> Having gone full time, she was delivered, after a tedious labour, of a monster, bearing, as far as the head, neck, and shoulder went, a striking resemblance to a frog. It breathed a couple of times, and then happily died.[146]

It is interesting how Waring-Curran refers to the unfortunate offspring as 'it'. What Mrs E gives birth to is neither male nor female, human nor inhuman. It is, essentially, a hybrid creature that belies all such categories. Like a frog, which, as an amphibian, is able to live in and out of water, Mrs E's androgynous offspring is a creature that staggers between types. This story is matched in absurdity by one told in the same context by J. Hyde Houghton, surgeon to the Dudley Dispensary. He claimed that one of his patients, 'Mrs. C', had had an affair with a grocer and conceived. When the child was delivered, it was a 'healthy girl' but, Houghton writes,

> on the body and limbs of that poor child I counted forty nævi [skin blemishes], varying in size from a small pea to a walnut, and looking as though the skin was dotted with prunes and grocers' raisins and currants! It is not in my power to describe the consternation of the mother when she saw the child (and was told that nothing could be done for the *immediate* removal of those 'horrid spots'); the amazement of the attendants, and I may add, of the doctor; and the 'confirmation strong as Holy Writ' which the event gave to the previous scandal. The poor child died when about three months old, and after it the scandal gradually died too.[147]

The way in which Houghton decides to associate the baby's nævi with the scandal of her mother's illicit liaison is revealing. In his outline of the facts, it seems as though the infant bears the hallmarks of her mother's fallenness. The scarlet letter has been figuratively passed to the next generation through biological osmosis. What is also significant is that Mrs C's affair is with her working-class grocer. As with Routh's stories of families being 'poisoned' by the breast milk of prostitutes, Mrs C's experience is one of cross-class contamination. The baby's nævi are the physical reminders of the abominations that may be produced by mixing genes from two widely different classes.

Fortunately for all involved, the daughter of Mrs C, like the frog-like offspring of Mrs E, does not live to propagate its inherent biological substrata.

In addition to their purported function of advancing medical knowledge, the roles of such stories, in a hegemonic bourgeois culture, were manifold. The cases of Mrs E and Mrs C, for example, warned of the dire consequences women faced when they did not adhere to acceptable notions of female behaviour. Mrs E failed to maintain a lady-like reserve, while Mrs C satisfied her desire for an extramarital, carnal relationship with a man below her station.

A different set of theories, yet ones that continue in many ways these traditional forms of mindset, are those relating to the issue of heredity. Following the landmark publication of Darwin's *Origin of Species* (1859), ideas on breeding and biological conditioning became a constant source of speculation across all forms of media in the Victorian period. What is more, 'Darwinian Theory' lent its support to a diverse range of social ideas. In 1869, for example, Darwin's cousin Francis Galton published a book on *Hereditary Genius*. Openly indebted to Darwin's work, the treatise aimed to show 'that a man's natural abilities are derived by inheritance'.[148] Although no mention of the nineteenth-century class system is made directly, Galton warned that hybrid forms are not always a favourable combination:

> Let us consider the nature of hybrids. Suppose a town to be formed under the influence of two others that differ, the one a watering-place and the other a fishing-town; what will be the result? We find that particular combination to be unusually favourable, because the different elements do not interfere with, but rather support one another. [...] Let us take another instance of an hybrid; one that leads to a different result. Suppose an enterprising manufacturer from a town at no great distance from an incipient watering-place, discovers advantages in its minerals, water, power, or means of access, and prepares to set up his mill in the place. We may predict what will follow, with much certainty. Either the place will be forsaken as a watering-place, or the manufacturer will be in some way or other got rid of. The two elements are discordant.[149]

Galton's choice of metaphor ensures that it is impossible to read this passage outside of its historical context. The image of a manufacturer setting up his mill in a place rich in natural resources is not incidental in an era making landmark developments in industry and international colonisation. Indeed, the watering-place and manufacturing town setting had firm class associations for the Victorians. The latter, for example, was assumed to be peopled by working-class 'hands' and mill owners who had worked their way to a fortune as Dickens's Bounderby does. Watering-places, by contrast, were the haunts of languishing invalids; men and women who could afford the luxury of trying what natural spring waters might do for their rheumatic ailments.

Seaside towns were likewise considered to be the favoured destinations for individuals experiencing respiratory difficulties. The seaside town therefore makes a healthy combination with watering-places. The elements of manufacturing towns, however, would become engaged in a 'struggle for survival' with those belonging to the watering-place. As different forms of society are incompatible, Galton suggests, so are the individuals from those dissimilar groups. From his book, therefore, one might read support for the idea of retaining traditional social formations and a warning against cross-class reproduction.

Indeed, writings on heredity often have a didactic subtext, urging for the control of social and individual behaviour. According to Henry Maudsley, one of the period's most influential authorities on psychology and biological determinism,

> observation reveals more and more clearly every day how much the capacity and character, bodily and mental, of the individual is dependent upon his ancestral antecedents. It is impossible to deny that a man may suffer irredeemable ill through the misfortune of a bad descent.[150]

Insanity and 'peculiarities of mind', therefore, could be explained as the inescapable destinies of many children. Fathers, it was argued, were as capable as mothers of transmitting morbid cerebral influences, hence there was no need for the mediating influence of the umbilicus or breast milk. Yet it was widely understood that mothers were more likely to bequeath insanity. In 1867, for example, W. Jung wrote in the *Journal of Mental Science* that 'the hereditary influence of the father is slightly less than that of the mother' and 'women have a greater tendency to be affected with hereditary insanity than men'.[151] Esquirol expressed the idea in less-measured terms: 'Insanity is rather transmissible by mothers, than fathers'.[152]

Writing about the implications ideas on heredity had for the understanding of criminal behaviour, the surgeon Frederick James Brown inquired, in the *British Medical Journal*:

> Are the children of lunatics equally responsible with the children of sane persons? I trow not. There ought to be a compromise, in the way of punishment, between that appointed for sane persons and that for lunatics. Human responsibility is a variable quantity: it is never two days equal, from the cradle to the grave. Such being the case, allowance should be made for mental infirmity as an inheritance either actually or by predisposition. The mind, equally with the body, is inherited.[153]

It is significant that this article appeared in 1866 as it works with ideas that Cesare Lombroso developed, ten years later, in *Criminal Man* (1876). Lombroso believed that the criminal was an unhealthy freight – a diseased organism in the otherwise progressive development of humanity. For all his work on degeneration, as Daniel Pick argues in *Faces of Degeneration* (1989), Lombroso was optimistic about science's ability to arrest the atavistic decline of humanity.[154] With scores of photographs dedicated to providing an accurate face of criminality, *Criminal Man* aimed to provide a chart of physical signs through which the criminal type could be identified and eliminated from the procreative bloodstream. Frederick Brown's article in the *Journal of Mental Science* seems to have prefigured the idea that the criminal was a born criminal. His or her delinquent destiny, he claims, is inescapable and it is therefore necessary that he or she is given lenient treatment by the criminal courts. In other words, the criminal was seen to belong to a subgroup – a different species almost – and it was therefore only humane to show tolerance for a crime that the perpetrator was incapable of resisting.

The journal in which Brown's article appeared was edited by Maudsley from 1862 to 1878. Although Maudsley agreed with Brown that 'the mind, equally with the body, is inherited', his theories drew on the work of Bénédict Augustin Morel to suggest that, rather than being just the trait of a subgroup, criminal and insane tendencies could lurk, unforeseen, in certain generations. The child of a lunatic, he writes, 'has a native constitution of nervous element which, whatever name we give it, is unstable or defective, rendering him unequal to bear the severe stress of adverse events'.[155] Such ideas drew on Morel's theory of *dégénérescence*. Pick notes that 'madness, for Morel and many of his colleagues could not necessarily be seen or heard, but it lurked in the body, incubated by the parents and visited upon the children'.[156] As we will see, the theory of heredity supported insanity pleas in the nation's courtrooms, yet it also drew on, and revised, the 'smouldering fires' concept of female insanity. Through the work of Morel and Maudsley, nineteenth-century psychiatry once again characterised women's madness as a 'something' loitering in the blood; 'something' that needed to be watched for and governed.

In 1872 the death sentence of poisoner Christiana Edmunds was lessened after the Home Secretary consulted evidence that she had a hereditary predisposition towards insanity. Alfred Taylor wrote:

> In some trials there has been a tendency to rely upon hereditary predisposition as almost the sole proof of insanity in the criminal. In the case of *Christiana Edmunds*, convicted of the crime of poisoning on an extensive scale, no evidence of intellectual insanity or of homicidal impulse could be found. There was a motive, an endeavour to fix the crime upon others, great skill in its perpetration, concealment with a full knowledge of the consequences of the act and an endeavour to avoid this punishment by a false plea of pregnancy. In short, the conduct of the woman throughout was that of a sane criminal. The jury found her guilty; but in

consequence of proof being furnished that many members of her family had suffered under insanity in some form, it was supposed that there might be some latent degree of insanity in her case, not discoverable by the ordinary methods of examination. This led to the commutation of her sentence.[157]

He concludes that 'there was nothing to indicate unsoundness of mind either in a medical or a legal sense in this woman'.[158] In the trial itself, Edmunds's mother testified that a number of the defendant's immediate relatives had been insane:

In 1843, my husband became insane, and was sent to a private lunatic asylum. [...] He was very strange in his manner a long time before he was sent there. He raved about having millions of money and attempted to knock down his medical man with a ruler. [...] I had a son named Arthur Burns Edmunds. He was subject to epileptic fits from a child. In February, 1860, we could not manage him. He was very violent at times, and was at length taken to Earlswood Asylum, where he remained until 1866, and died there. I had a daughter, a sister of the prisoner. She is now dead. She suffered from hysteria, and attempted, when in a fit, to throw herself from a window. She was about 36 when she died. She was always excited and suffered from hysteria. My father, Mr Burns, was a Major in the Army. He died at the age of 43. He was paralysed before he died, and died in a fit. He had to be fastened in a chair, and was quite childish before he died. I had a brother who had a daughter. She suffered from weakness of intellect. She was quite imbecile.[159]

According to the *Annual Register*, the prisoner's family was thus 'saturated with hereditary insanity'.[160] Because Edmunds was 'so very like her father', her mother had 'always had a dread of her in relation to that time of life' (her early forties) because that was the age her father went insane.[161] In order to support the mother's claim that Edmunds's family had a hereditary predisposition towards madness, the defence enlisted medical experts (including Maudsley) from all over the country to testify. The prosecution claimed, however, that insanity in the family was not evidence, in itself, that Christiana committed her crimes under the duress of mental impairment:

Referring to the suggestion of hereditary taint, [the prosecution, Mr Serjeant Ballantine] said that was a favourite specific with doctors of a certain class. [...] He did not deny that 'the hereditary taint' was a matter that might be fairly raised in matters of lunacy, but it is not itself a ground, in the absence of anything like distinct evidence of insanity, for believing that a person was insane.[162]

With so much possible social danger inherent to the state of breeding, it was considered imperative that healthy, well-balanced matches were made. As indicated by Galton, a bad sexual match is paid for by the new generation. Hidden behind such stories is a didactic, reactionary message: in order for the social scaffolding of mid-Victorian society to be preserved, middle-class behaviour and cross-class sexual activity needed to be checked. Like adolescents, the nation's mothers were watched for signs of insanity. Yet, because of the latter's more obvious links with breeding, myths of maternal violence helped to maintain a keen scrutiny over issues of national development.

Female old age: Sick fancies

> Pity the sorrows of a Poor Old Maid,
> Who long a Proud Coquette disdain inspir'd,
> Who long a beauteous face and form display'd,
> And flush'd with flattery herself admir'd.
>
> Amidst the throng in Theatres and Parks,
> I used to shine in newest fashions dress'd,
> Receive the homage of the Dashing Sparks,
> And fired with envy every female breast.
>
> As time advanced mankind forsook my train,
> I then with Birds and Beasts some comfort found,
> But now, oppress'd with sorrow I complain,
> For, Oh, my Parrot's dead – my Monkey's drown'd![167]

As is indicated by this popular street ballad, the old maid was often perceived as a figure of ridicule during the mid-nineteenth century. Reaping loneliness and sorrow for her previous coquettishness, and with her absurd whims and fancies, the ageing female seemed to offer an amusing respite from the period's more inclement discussions of women's rights. Yet, by looking at the interactions between medical, legal, journalistic, and literary representations of female senescence, it is possible to glean how the ageing woman was a figure of high symbolic importance for the Victorians. She was, in fact, a complicated, multidimensional character who seemed to confirm the era's conservative ideas on women, while simultaneously offering new ways of thinking about gender.

Unlike young women and mothers, who were seen to be under the watchful control of parents and husbands, old maids appeared to have a significant degree of independence. In 1861, Anne Thackeray Ritchie asked in the *Cornhill*:

> May not spinsters, as well as bachelors, give their opinions on every subject, no matter how ignorant they may be; travel about anywhere, in any

costume, however convenient; climb up craters, publish their experiences, tame horses, wear pork-pie hats, write articles in the *Saturday Review*?[168]

It is better, postulates Ritchie, to be an old maid than an unhappy wife:

> And if Miss A. considers herself less fortunate than Mrs. B., who has an adoring husband always at home, and 10,000*l*. a year, she certainly does not envy poor Mrs. C., who has to fly to Sir Cresswell Cresswell to get rid of a 'life companion', who beats her with his umbrella, spends her money and knocks her down, instead of 'lifting her up'.[169]

The image of the self-sufficient, single, and ageing woman finds its way into some of our best-known Victorian novels. Although not quite fulfilling the attractive image offered by Ritchie, Mrs Henry Wood's Cornelia Carlyle (*East Lynne* [1862]) and Dickens's Betsy Trotwood both have a single status and management over their own affairs. Such also seems to be the case with Dickens's more disturbing creations of Miss Havisham and Mrs Clennam – women whose traits of 'old maid' independence are central to the grotesqueness of their characterisations.

The old maid seems to have stood, first and foremost, as a sign of the period's surplus of women. In a short story for the *Cornhill*, R. Ashe King created a fictional dialogue between two characters discussing the apparent preponderance of old maids. One speaker remarks:

> If we were Spartans we could expose on some Mount Taygetus the surplusage of our female infants; if we were Hindoos we could get rid of all widows by suttee; but as we are Christians we must not interfere with the course of nature, however strange and vexatious it may be.[170]

The British toleration of old women, even as comic figures, seems indulgent when compared to barbaric Eastern predilections for sacrificing women of advanced age. Yet, as King's story also reveals, the old maid was a figure connected with the alarming overplus of Victorian women. Anne Ritchie writes, for example, that

> statistics are very much the fashion now-a-days, and we cannot take up a newspaper or a pamphlet without seeing in round numbers that so many people will do so and so in the course of the year. [...] So many will be old maids in the course of time. This last number is such an alarming one, that I am afraid to write it down.[171]

Three years later King wrote in the same magazine that

> if I took up a paper, the extraordinary number of female births was sure to be the first thing to strike my eye. When I got into my 'bus to get to

my office, I had to work my way to a seat gingerly, as if treading amongst eggs, I was so begirt with bonnets, bandboxes, and babies. [...] There were a few black specks of manhood, like the sparsely-sprinkled currants of a meagre school-cake. [...] Billow after billow of crinoline and then a black speck struggling to the surface; then another succession of foamy billows, and another unfortunate could be seen deep in the trough of the sea.[172]

The imagery that King chooses for his story is revealing. Men are portrayed as drowning in a sea of crinoline and the excess of women is described as a 'strange and vexatious' part of nature. The passage also gives the impression of a fantasy being overfulfilled. The school-cake metaphor, for instance, appears to underscore the notion that male Victorians have too much of a good thing. The superfluity of women is portrayed as a characteristically modern phenomenon. Both King and Ritchie portray a world where readers of newspapers are shocked by statistics and census returns. The issue spills over into omnibuses on the daily commute to the office. Although the notion of having too much choice (as opposed to a scarcity of it) might seem like an edifying one at first glance, for an age that valued self-control and self-restraint, the old maid became a haunting signifier of surfeit and excess on a national scale; on an individual level, however, they were seen, conversely, as creatures of deprivation.

In his 1860 textbook on the *Obscure Diseases of the Brain*, Winslow included the description of a hallucination as narrated by one of his peers' patients. It reads:

I am in the habit [...] of dining at five, and exactly as the hour arrives I am subjected to the following painful visitation. The door of the room [...] flies wide open; an old hag [...] enters with a frowning and incensed countenance [and] comes straight upon me with every demonstration of spite and indignation [...]; she [...] then strikes me with a severe blow with her staff. I fall from my chair in a swoon. [...] To the recurrence of this apparition I am daily subjected. [...] 'Then', said the doctor, 'with your permission I will dine with you today *tête-à-tête,* and we will see if your malignant old woman will venture to join our company'.[173]

At the usual time of the old woman's appearance, the doctor tries to distract his patient with what he calls 'conversation [...] of the most varied and brilliant character', but 'a moment had scarcely elapsed when the owner of the house exclaimed, in an alarmed voice, "The hag comes again!" and dropped back in his chair in a swoon, in the way he had himself described'.[174] For all its strangeness, the description of the hallucination is not out of key with the period's fears surrounding the old maid figure. Why, for example, is the apparition female? Why is she violent? Medical literature from the period features many inglorious representations of the aging female. In 'Woman In Her Psychological Relations', for example, the

> 'Old Maid' is the pest and scourge of the circle in which she moves; and in extreme cases – verging upon, if not actually the subject of – worse insanity, she is little less than a she-fiend. Her whole life is devoted to an ingenious system of mischief-making, she delights in tormenting – corporeally and mentally – all that she dare to practice upon. She is intrusive, insolent, regardless of the ordinary rules of politeness; ever feeling insults where none were intended; ungrateful, treacherous, and revengeful – not sparing even her oldest and truest friends. Add to these mental characteristics, a quaint untidy dress, a shrivelled skin, a lean figure, a bearded lip, shattered teeth, harsh grating voice, and manly stride, and the *typical* 'Old Maid' is complete.[175]

Such descriptions suggest that the old maid figure was a highly threatening one for the male population. In the opening to *Uneven Developments*, Mary Poovey uses W. R. Greg's famous 'Why Are Women Redundant' (1862) to powerful effect and explains why the old maid was perceived as so fearsome. Poovey observes how women who had not been integrated into the domestic sphere through marriage became disturbing images of women's rejection of the home life and the natural instincts it was seen to complement.[176] According to Greg,

> there is an enormous and increasing number of single women in the nation, a number quite disproportionate and quite abnormal ... There are hundreds of thousands of women – not to speak more largely still – scattered through all ranks, but proportionately most numerous in the middle and upper classes, – who have to earn their own living, instead of spending and husbanding the earnings of men; who, not having the natural duties and labours of wives and mothers, have to carve out artificial and painfully sought occupations for themselves.[177]

The 'problem' of surplus women thus became an issue, according to Poovey, through which Greg and his contemporaries aimed to 'naturalize [...] monogamous marriage, a sexual division of labour, and a specific economic relation between the sexes, in which men earn and women "spend" and "husband" the earnings of men'.[178] Hence, by presenting a hideous picture of what women *would* be without marriage and children, writers like Greg, Winslow, and the anonymous author of 'Woman In Her Psychological Relations' argued in favour of preserving and reinforcing traditional gender roles.

It is vital we recognise, however, that ideas on the hideousness of old age were not exclusively applied to spinsters. In Victorian eyes, the old maid's married or widowed sisters were also considered to be prey to the dreadful effects of ageing. Married or unmarried, virginal or otherwise, all women were deemed prone to developing a dangerous form of insanity due to the biological 'change' they experienced at middle age. Clinical considerations of old age in women tended to focus on ideas of transition. As soon as they hit forty years of age, women were seen to be at risk from the great 'change of life'. The menopause, often called the 'climacteric' and 'critical' stage, was viewed as a period when women were prone to profound alterations in character. Among these, Dr Francis Skae includes 'depression, [...] sleeplessness, restlessness, [...] inattention to ordinary domestic affairs [relevant in relation to Greg's arguments ...] various delusions', paranoia, suicide, and even homicide.[179] Edward Tilt's *The Change of Life* (1857), purportedly the only medical treatise on menopause produced at this time, added that 'the c[hange] of life so completely modifies the constitution of woman'.[180]

Moreover, when it came to aging women, ideas of 'change' were never far removed from those of deterioration. In 1844, for example, a correspondent to *Blackwood's Edinburgh Magazine* tellingly referred to old women as society's 'uncultivated waste'.[181] At the autumn stages of women's lives, Eliza Lynn Linton added:

> The brightness fades, the roses fall from the wall, the sweetest muscatelles are but sourish Hambro's, the stars are dim, and the songs all out of tune, and the happy home grows dull and dead, for its merry ghosts have all departed.[182]

Typically heavy handed in its use of organic imagery, the passage reveals how, in Victorian opinion, the female role, once it had become surplus to reproductive requirements, changed from what was once alive, bright, fertile, and sweet into something dead, dull, barren, and sour. It is an image that Dickens drew upon, prior to Linton's article, for the first description of Miss Havisham:

> I saw that everything that was within my view, which ought to be white, had been white long ago, and had lost its lustre, and was faded and yellow. I saw that the bride within the bridal dress had withered like the dress [...] and had no brightness left but the brightness of her sunken eyes. I saw that the dress had been put upon the rounded figure of a woman, and that the figure upon which it now hung loose, had shrunk to skin and bone.[183]

Characters like Miss Havisham certainly testified to the inevitability of change, but in passages like these, the change is not a progression but deterioration. As a site of negotiation between images of development and decay, the aging female figure seemed to represent, in microcosm, the era's larger fears of degeneration. Critics like William Greenslade and Jane Wood have viewed the concept of degeneration as a post-Darwinian preoccupation of the 1880s onwards.[184] Yet, as descriptions of older and surplus women reveal, concerns about the nature of aging and what it reveals about modern life were finding their way into medical, journalistic, and literary texts much earlier.

Writing in the *Journal of Mental Science* in 1865, Skae noted:

> Various psychological authors [...] have [...] observed the frequency of insanity in women at that period, and have referred to the 'change of life' as the exciting cause of a large proportion of those cases of insanity which are met with between forty and fifty years of age.[185]

Skae and his colleagues defined a specific type of mania called 'climacteric insanity'. They claimed that because of the 'exciting' influence of the 'physiological changes then taking place'[186] in the female body (especially the 'overplus of blood' caused by ceased menstruation),[187] women were prone to a host of uncharacteristic psychological symptoms. One of Esquirol's patients, 'fifty-two years of age', had been, he writes, 'constantly walking about, seeking to do mischief' ever since the cessation of her menses.[188] Miss Havisham's desire to 'wreak revenge on all the male sex'[189] could also be read as symptomatic of the troublesome tendencies supposedly developed by women over a certain age. In *The Change of Life*, Tilt wrote:

> There is often unusual peevishness and ill-temper, sometimes assuming the importance of moral insanity. Some make their once peaceable homes intolerable by their ungovernable temper; others bear hatred, for a time, to the long-cherished objects of their affection. [...] Some of my patients at this period were constantly troubled with the temptation to kill their grandchildren, and they feared to dine with them because of the knives.[190]

Here Tilt echoes Prichard's story of the mother who would not use a knife when dining if her baby was nearby. The similarity between Tilt's climacteric old woman and Prichard's puerperal mother serves as an illustration of how all women (regardless of their age and social and biological statuses) were believed to have the smouldering fires of insanity within them. According to Tilt, 'time dulls the eye, robs the cheek of its bloom, delves furrows in the forehead, but cannot quell the [...] fire burning in the heart of women'.[191]

In 1872, these ideas were used to defend Christiana Edmunds, the notorious 'Brighton Poisoner'. Though discussed briefly by Judith Knelman,[192] Edmunds's remarkable story seems to have been largely overlooked by modern historians. In 1871 Christiana allegedly had an affair with her married physician, Charles Beard. *The Times* noted how 'there seemed to have ripened into a state of things which did not ordinarily exist between a medical adviser and his patient, and there could be no doubt the patient herself entertained very strong feelings indicating considerable affection towards him'.[193] So considerable was Edmunds's affection that she purportedly gave Mrs Beard a box of sweetmeats laced with strychnine. On finding the sweets to have a bitter taste, Mrs Beard accused Edmunds of trying to poison her and Dr Beard suspended his visits. In an attempt to vindicate herself, Edmunds complained to the confectioner, claiming that he had sold her contaminated goods. She also sent some of them to be forensically examined by a surgeon. Over the next few weeks, Edmunds seemed to do everything she could to make the confectioner (John Maynard) look like the true poisoner. She asked children she met in the street to buy cakes from his shop, adulterated them with poison and returned them. She also randomly gave poisoned sweets to children – often waiting outside school gates to do so. As a result, a significant number of the Brighton population experienced symptoms of poisoning. On 12 June 1871, Sidney Barker, a boy of four-years-old, died of strychnine intoxication after eating chocolates purchased from Maynard's shop. Edmunds attended the child's inquest and declared that Maynard had also poisoned her and Mrs Beard. She also wrote three anonymous letters to Sydney's father, signed 'An Old Inhabitant and a Seeker for Justice', 'G. C. B.', and 'A London Tradesman now in Brighton', urging him to prosecute the confectioner. An expert graphologist later claimed, at her trial, that they were all in Edmunds's hand.

It appears that Edmunds obtained poison by sending forged letters to a chemist, Isaac Garrett, claiming to be a rival pharmacist, Messrs Glaisyer and Kemp. One of them read 'Messrs Glaisyer and Kemp will be much obliged if Mr Garrett could supply them with a little strychnia. They are in immediate want of half an ounce'.[194] When Sydney Barker died, Edmunds sent another forged letter to Garrett, claiming to be from the local coroner, requesting the loan of his poison book. She wrote 'you will tie up your book and send it at once by the bearer; it shall be returned to you as soon as you need it'.[195] When the book was returned, however, the pages referring to Edmunds's purchase of poison had been torn out. In court, the graphologist identified the handwriting of these letters to be Edmunds's as well. Her extraordinary criminal career (which reads like the plot of a popular novel) was eventually brought to an end when she wrote, in her own name, to the detective investigating the poisonings (Inspector Gibbs). Besides urging Gibbs to arrest Maynard, Christiana displayed knowledge of the poisonings which only the perpetrator could have. Gibbs 'took her into custody on the 17th of August at her residence on the charge of attempting to poison Mrs Beard. She replied, "I poison Mrs Beard! Who can say so? I've been nearly poisoned myself!"'[196] It was for the murder of Sydney Barker, however, that she was eventually indicted a year later.

The evidence, as Crown prosecutor, Mr Serjeant Ballantine, claimed, suggested that Edmunds was a 'woman exhibiting powers of great contrivance and considerable cunning'.[197] Yet, at her densely populated trial, medical witnesses (including Maudsley) claimed that her crimes were the result of a 'great change' she had experienced some months before (and probably the reason she was attended by Charles Beard). Although the menopause, 'a delicate subject to speak of' was never mentioned directly in her trial, the meaning of 'great change' is unmistakable.[198] It had led, doctors William Wood, Charles Robertson, and Maudsley agreed, to her becoming morally insane: Wood 'gave it as his opinion that the prisoner was of unsound mind', Robertson 'regarded her as bordering between crime and insanity', and Maudsley

> found a deficiency of moral feeling. She did not appear to me to realize her position. In reference to her moral sense I consider her mind to be impaired.
>
> Cross examined by Mr. Serjeant Ballantine – What do you mean by the term 'impaired moral sense'?
>
> Witness – I mean a want of moral feeling with regard to events or acts regarding which a perfectly sane person might be expected to exhibit feeling. I should say that anybody who deliberately committed crime was deficient of moral feeling.
>
> Do you consider that insanity? – Certainly.[199]

Maudsley's, Wood's, and Robertson's evidence concurred with the contemporaneous medical idea that post-menopausal women were 'constantly walking about seeking to do mischief' Miss Havisham-style.

What emerges from the reports of Edmunds's trial and its report in newspapers and journals is an image of the defendant as a witch-like poisoner of Brighton's children:

> The prisoner was charged with the wilful murder of Sidney Barker, a boy of tender years who was unknown to the prisoner, and against whom therefore she could have no malice. [The defence lawyer, Serjeant Parry] did not pretend that on certain occasions she did not give poisoned chocolate creams to several children.[200]

When passing the death sentence on Edmunds, the judge observed that she had 'turned [her] attention to the poisoning of these innocents'.[201] Yet it was not *just* by giving adulterated sweets that Edmunds seemed to contaminate the children of Brighton. She was alleged to have used them as a way of orchestrating her crimes – selecting boys from the street to buy her poison, return adulterated sweetmeats to Maynard's confectionary, and gain possession of Garrett's poison book. To contemporary followers of the trial, Edmunds's criminal career must have seemed as though life was imitating art as the infectious old maid had been a staple fictional representation for years. Like Edmunds, Miss Havisham uses a child, Estella, to inflict her revenge on the male population. Her bitterness over a disappointment in love, like Edmunds's, is something that infects (and is eventually played out by) 'these innocents'.

In the interim between the publication of *Great Expectations* and the Edmunds trial, the *Cornhill* featured William Cyples's short story 'Granny Leatham's Revenge' (1866). Following her family's loss of a fortune and the rejection of her grandson by a neighbour's daughter, Granny Leatham determines to be avenged on her neighbours, the Astburys. She is described as follows:

> A century ago Granny would not unlikely have been the witch of the parish, and run a risk of the horse-pond, if not of something still worse. Her temper, which had always been high, seemed only to have grown bitterer with age; and the recent misfortunes which had overtaken the family had made her disposition still sourer.[202]

Although, like *Great Expectations*, the story aims to locate the source of Granny Leatham's bitterness in some disappointing circumstance, it nevertheless leaves the connections between age and sourness unchallenged. As Granny grows older, she grows more spiteful. Like Miss Havisham, who metonymically replaces Estella's heart with ice, Granny Leatham is also suspected as having a spoiling effect on her granddaughter Matty. As one of the family's servants tells Granny, 'I dunner like to be near yo'; an' yo'n spoil Matty yet'. The narrator adds:

> This young creature was granny's constant companion; the two – the one so old and the other so young – being on the most level and equal terms, though, luckily, the child showed nothing of the temper of the dame.[203]

The 'dame's' influence on Matty grows deeper, however, when Granny, like Christiana Edmunds and Miss Havisham, uses the child to orchestrate her revenge. Late one night Granny Leatham and Matty steal an infected cow from a near-by farm and introduce it to the Astbury herd: 'the plague had been wilfully introduced into another parish! [...] the half-crippled old woman at [the plagued cow's] heels, relentlessly urg[ed] it on whenever it attempted to stop. [...] She flourished both crutch and stick, and, striking the panting cow cruelly, hissed it forward'.[204] It is noteworthy how Cyples chooses to set his short story among cattle breeders. It allows him to locate the old female figure among issues of breeding and caste control. Notice, for example, how the infected cow and Granny Leatham share infirmities: the half-crippled woman shadows the staggering animal and her coarse hissing echoes the cow's frail panting. Like the sick animal, the old woman is figured as an unhealthy element (in this short story and, more broadly, Victorian culture) – alien to the procreating group, yet operating within it, the old woman sours and infects those she comes into contact with. Granny Leatham's revenge introduces a plague risk into the entire parish; Miss Havisham's bitterness is something that influences the full plot and *dramatis personae* of *Great Expectations*; and Christiana Edmunds's alleged attempt to kill Mrs Beard resulted in a significant part of the Brighton population being poisoned. The predictable conclusion to 'Granny Leatham's Revenge' is that the Astbury herd does not pick up the desired infection, but Granny carries it back to her own cattle.

The destructive actions of Granny Leatham, Christiana Edmunds, and Miss Havisham highlight the relentlessness with which the myth of woman as 'explosive material' worked its way through a wide range of nineteenth-century ideas. Even the old and infirm, it seems, were not exempt from the onset of destructive potential and this reflects how the myth itself worked ubiquitously across a number of discourses and disciplines. The notion that women were frequently on the brink of violent insanity was applicable to all stages of women's lives and helped change the shape of the period's fiction, journalism, medicine, and criminal law. That the myth facilitated a more robust control over the female population is true but only partly so. The idea of explosive female violence actually became a powerful form of expression. For some it indicated that, more than ever, Victorian women needed to know their place; yet, as the next chapter will aim to demonstrate, it also became a basis through which some traditional forms of power could be scrutinised and questioned.

2
'The Terrible Chemistry of Nature': The Road Murder and Popular Fiction

'The fussy activity about the nightdress of a school girl'

On 3 July 1860, *The Times* reported how 'a shocking murder was perpetrated at Road, a village about four miles from Frome':

> About 7 o'clock, it was found that one of [Samuel Savile Kent's] sons, a fine lad of just four years of age, was missing from his cot in the nurse's room, in which he usually slept, and after an hour's search his body was found stuffed down the seat of a privy on the premises, the throat being cut so as almost to sever the head from the body, and a large stab being apparent near the heart, evidently inflicted after death, as no blood had flowed from it. The body was wrapped in a blanket belonging to its bed, and he appears to have been killed while still asleep.[1]

Discussing the murder's wider possible significance, the newspaper's first reaction was to invoke the popular notion of the home as 'sacred' and to cast the murder as a shocking encroachment of its values:

> It is certain that the value of human life, the security of families, and the sacredness of English households demand that this matter shall never be allowed to rest till the last shadow in its dark mystery shall be chased away by the light of unquestionable truth.[2]

Although he does not focus specifically on the Road Murder, A. D. Hutter has suggested that crime was often figured, in the mid-Victorian period, as a foreign energy – infecting the lifeblood of the family from outside its established parameters.[3] It is a contention clearly supported by *The Times*'s characterisation of the Road Murder as a ghastly slur on the otherwise untainted profile of British domesticity. Yet, as Anthea Trodd and Elizabeth Rose Gruner have rightly observed, the Road controversy also generated an impression that crime was no alien introduction to the family, but a factor generated from within the home itself. The death of Francis Kent, Gruner writes, 'suggested that the Victorian family [... was] itself the source of many of its complexities and dangers'.[4] Paradoxically, this is also supported by *The Times*'s reporting of the murder: 'We cannot divest ourselves of the belief', the newspaper admitted, 'that the child suffered death at the hands of some one belonging to the house'. It concludes: 'It is evident that the guilty person must have been in the house over night, for all the fastenings were exactly as they had been left the previous night, when Mr Kent himself saw they were secure'.[5] Taken in conjunction with *The Times*'s earlier claim that the murder went forcibly against the nature of the family, the above citation provides modern scholars with a cautionary example of how events like the Road Murder do not communicate a unified and consistent message. In the same newspaper, for instance, the murder of Francis Kent is represented as both a monstrous breach of the home's traditional parameters and an element generated from within the Kent family itself. Rather than presenting nineteenth-century observers with an example of how crime invaded the home or grew from within its sanctified walls, the Road Murder was a paradigm of both. The crime, in fact, became a stage on which competing ideas as to the natures of women, the home, and society at large were enacted and discussed.

The Road Murder was, additionally, a site of conflict between cultural subgroups. It fuelled contests between the home and the police, women and medics, doctors and lawyers, and professionals holding violently opposed views. From such disagreements, it is possible to construct a case study of how mid-century uses of images relating to insane female violence formed part of a complex attempt to moderate and maintain the bourgeois home. By revealing ways in which certain factors of the Road Murder were appropriated and transformed in popular fiction, it is also possible to glean how, in the hands of novelists, the Road controversy provided a powerful idea with which the totalitarian nature of the homely ideal could be explored and challenged. Writing on Wilkie Collins's use of the murder, Gruner claims that 'if we read *The Moonstone* [(1868)] in the context of the famous murder case on which it was in part based, we find a scathing commentary on the Victorian family in Collins's selective recapitulation of the details of the case'.[6] As the novels of writers like Collins reveal, however, popular, literary uses of notorious crimes were neither subversive nor reactionary but had the potential to be both. Mary Braddon, Mrs Henry Wood, and Wilkie Collins, in particular, appropriated the Road Murder's details and, in so doing, appear to have replicated its ability for both supporting and critiquing the period's conservative ideas on gender. I will return to this issue later.

In congruence with many of the period's other murder cases, the Road Murder seemed to suggest that homicide and the 'ordinary' duties of women were not unrelated factors. In some reports of the crime, for example, journalists emphasised details that seemed to combine images of murder with domesticity. One article observed,

> that the child had been taken up, wrapped in the blanket which was between the quilt and the sheet, and that the [way the] clothes were afterwards arranged, seemed to indicate that a woman's hand had been concerned in the work.[7]

Elizabeth Gough, Francis's nurse (who was herself arrested and later released), suggested that the crime 'must have been done by a female hand, it was done so neatly'.[8] Although it reads like an odd claim, Gough's statement is actually not, as we saw in the previous chapter, out of key with contemporary beliefs in killing and destruction as possible extensions of women's ideological roles. The hyperbolic image of the murderer tenderly arranging Francis's cot with one hand and slashing his throat with the other recalls Maria Manning's ominous goose cooking of 1849. The Victorians appear to have been inundated with stories where home management had lapsed into unpredictable acts of aggression. Such associations appear, writ large, in the period's most canonical fictions. In *A Tale of Two Cities* (1859), for example, Madame Defarge's knitting, ordinarily a harmless, domestic pursuit, forms a deadly register of people to be guillotined. Mrs Joe's sewing in *Great Expectations* (1860–1) takes on a similar sinister function when her thimble is used to 'play the tambourine' upon Pip's head.[9] Her apron, stuck full of pins and needles (that often find their way into the food she prepares for Joe and Pip) converts what ought to be comforting symbols of domestic propriety into menacing images of danger. As with these Dickensian grotesques, the Road Murder (as it appears in contemporaneous journalism) combined impressions of domestic routine with the potential for homicidal brutality. It fostered a notion of the home as a deceptive place of conflict between latent dangers and misleading appearances. In his outline of the Road Murder, the Kents' family physician, Joseph Stapleton, wrote that the crime had fuelled the following image of domestic life:

> Upon the sunny slopes of the Sicilian shore the most luscious grapes are seen to grow and ripen where the vines take root in a volcanic soil. Beneath the fair outside the terrible chemistry of nature is at work, and the explosion of Mount Etna sweeps in a moment both the vineyard and the fruit away. So, in many an English household, the amenities of social life are found to clothe with grace a rugged and shallow crust. The stranger lingers out there a short holiday. He is deaf to the ominous rumblings around him. The tempest is stifled in his presence. But it gathers strength in those deep recesses where the crater is instinct with fire; and, as he retires, it bursts out, in its fury, to hurl parents, children, servants, into one common, inevitable, and promiscuous destruction. The figure

is unequal – oh! How unequal – to the reality; and this reality has come to pass in England![10]

As with concurrent negotiations of female psychology, Stapleton finds explosive and volcanic metaphors a useful apparatus in considering the implications the Road Murder had for the ubiquitous domestic idyll. Notice how images of fecundity (the growing and ripening grapes) overlay notions of the 'terrible chemistry of nature'. Such ideas were crucial to nineteenth-century understandings of womanhood.

As I discussed in the previous chapter, such links often fostered an idea that women and the home needed to be watched. It is hardly surprising, therefore, that commentators on the Road Murder began to question whether any such vigilance had been employed in the Kent household prior to the killing of Francis. According to one letter in *The Times*, signed 'S. P.', the Kent affair was the result of three possible causes: 'In conjecturing the circumstances which could have led to the murder of a child of such tender age, the probable causes reduce themselves to three, – hatred, lunacy or somnambulism, and fear'. The correspondent rejects hatred as unlikely and claims that fear is the most probable reason.[11] SP's consideration of lunacy and somnambulism, although he or she aims to discount them, is nevertheless revealing:

> Lunacy or somnambulism would hardly manifest itself with such startling results, unless symptoms had previously appeared which it would be the business of the police to discover, and which would go far to identify the author of the crime.[12]

According to SP, murder committed by a family member, under the influence of mental impairment, would have been foreshadowed in the eccentric behaviour of that individual before the crime itself. His opinion concurs with that of various psychological writers, including William A. Hammond, who wrote in his *Insanity in its Relations to Crime* (1873) that

> it is no more possible for a person to be insane without other evidences of disease than mental derangement, than for pneumonia to exist with no other symptoms than disturbed respiration. [...] All the previous and subsequent circumstances, as well as those attendant upon the act, should be thoroughly investigated, and due weight should be given to those physical symptoms, the existence of which will always be revealed by careful examination.[13]

The search for the perpetrator of the Road Murder henceforth became a search for signs of psychopathology in the histories of the Kent family members. As we shall see, such evidence was not unforthcoming.

Some nineteenth-century psychologists and observers of the Road Murder investigations claimed that signs of insanity were not always as clear as SP and Hammond supposed. In direct contrast to the former's letter, another communication to *The Times* editor, dated two months later, asked: 'Every attempt to establish a motive for a murder in this mysterious case having hitherto failed, will it admit of any other explanation? Does not the deed itself bear the impress of insanity?' The writer (signing himself 'Medicus') then outlines the facts of the case, laying specific emphasis on the fact there were no warning signs before the deed. He concludes with the following:

> Which of the inmates, seized with one of these paroxysms of insanity the culminating point of which too frequently is homicide, could have gone over all the phases of this tragedy without disturbing any other of the inmates?
>
> It is unnecessary to horrify your readers with a recital of any of the numerous instances on record of homicidal monomania. The Road mystery embraces the combined caution, craft, inconsistency, bodily power, and mental abstraction and desperation of such crimes.[14]

Thus, unlike SP's suggestion that anyone suffering from insanity would have manifested a number of preceding warning signs, this writer suggests that, because the peace of the Kent household had remained undisturbed during (and before) the night of the murder, insanity must have been an integral factor. His use of the term 'homicidal monomania', which had entered into popular linguistic currency by 1860, exploits the notion of murderous insanity as having an elusive and misleading symptomatology. Esquirol, the man responsible for coining the term, inquired,

> does not the fury of the homicidal monomaniac burst forth instantaneously, so that no antecedent circumstance may have forewarned the victim? [...] Certain motives, more or less plausible to their minds, determine them, and they select for their victims the objects of their strongest attachment. They commit the homicide with composure, at least in appearance. After having consummated their purpose, they are not disturbed, nor uneasy.[15]

Esquirol defined monomania as a form of insanity where the sufferer is violently motivated towards one object or subject only. Thus, he would consider Blanche D'Alberville's obsession with the colour red (discussed in chapter one) as a textbook case. Regarding everything else, the monomaniac, Simon During notes, appears rational and mentally sound:

> Monomaniacs could 'think, reason, and act like other men'. Thus, to appear normal no longer meant to be sane, at least in the disease's acute form.

Unlike delirium or mania it could be revealed in a single bizarre act disrupting a superficially ordinary life. [...] No causal nexus, no narrative could explain acts emerging from monomania. [...] The condition is, in an often used term, 'motiveless', *essentially* unfathomable.[16]

Hence, homicidal monomania was defined as an elusive and misleading form of mental impairment that gave no timely warnings. Murder was not only seen, therefore, as an alien energy, invading the home from outside its boundaries, but could also be viewed as an element that lurked, undiscovered and practically undiscoverable, within those familiar parameters. Affectionate family ties, moreover, offer no resistance to the urges of homicidal monomaniacs who select their dearest relations as victims. Thus, in claiming that the Road Murder was the result of homicidal monomania, a conclusion that he draws from the apparent ordinariness of the Kents, Medicus engages with a wider belief that middle-class, domestic normalcy could contain the secret potential for destruction. In the letters of SP and Medicus, moreover, we catch a glimpse of a mid-century change in attitudes regarding the relationship between women, the home, and violence. Contradicting ideas that crimes like Francis's murder were the result of an extraordinary, foreseeable mental paroxysm, Medicus (drawing on the ideas of Esquirol) suggested, as did Stapleton, that the ordinary, day-to-day affairs of family life were not incompatible with the incubation of murderous desires.

This is not to argue, however, that Esquirol and his followers perceived observation of the potentially insane to be useless. Like SP, Esquirol believed that a homicidal monomaniac's history, prior to a murderous act, would reveal signs of mental impairment. Yet, because monomania was such a deceptive and elusive clinical condition, observation needed to be rigorous and sustained:

> No skill of the physician, no degree of experience however great, no penetration or reach of thought, will suffice at a glance to decide this momentous question.
> Careful observation of the bodily health, and particularly those organic functions that are beyond the control of the will; and watchfulness by day and by night, to as great an extent as possible, of the mental operations and acts of the patient [...] will eventually and rightfully decide the case.[17]

Of course, knowing when to apply such a keen observation is a difficult business when dealing with a form of insanity as equivocal as monomania. Esquirol conceded that insanity would often go undetected until reaching its critical and often fatal climax. He was concerned with looking for symptoms, but unlike William Hammond and SP, the focus of *his* investigations were not moments of absurdity or eccentricity, but the *ordinary* 'organic functions' of his patients. His writings give a sense that normality is not to be trusted.

Following an inconclusive inquest into the Road Murder, the Home Secretary commissioned Sergeant Whicher, a Scotland Yard detective who had rose to fame by apprehending Maria Manning in 1849, to investigate the case. Within days of his dispatch, *The Times* announced Whicher's 'apprehension of Miss Constance Kent', Francis's sixteen-year-old stepsister. In the preliminary Magistrates' inquiry into her arrest, Whicher testified:

> I am an inspector of detectives. I have been engaged since Sunday last in investigating the circumstances connected with the murder of Francis Savile Kent. [...] I have made an examination of the premises, and believe that the murder was committed by some inmate of the house. [...] I sent for Constance Kent on Monday last to her bed room, having previously examined her drawers and found a list of her linen [...] in which were enumerated, among other things, three night dresses as belonging to her. [...] I said, 'Here are three night dresses; where are they?' She said, 'I have two; the other was lost at the wash the week after the murder'. [...] This afternoon I again proceeded to the house and sent for [Constance] into the dining-room. I said, 'I am a police officer, and I hold a warrant for your apprehension, charging you with the murder of your brother Francis Savile Kent'.[18]

As we shall see, the unintended innuendo in 'examined her drawers' is not an unfitting one. Based on the evidence of a missing nightgown, and that evidence alone, Whicher confined Constance to the county gaol. However, Magistrates agreed with an overwhelming public opinion that there was not enough evidence against her and ordered her release. Yet, because the police search became centred on the nightgown of an adolescent girl, a garment that was afterwards revealed to be heavily stained with blood, the arrest of Constance, and the publication of its details in national newspapers, offer twenty-first-century scholars a rare snapshot of the cultural and ideological values that the Victorians invested in the process of menstruation. Elaine and English Showalter have observed how, in the nineteenth century, there is an 'almost total disappearance, outside of scientific literature, of any explicit allusion to this large area of human experience'.[19] In journalistic reports of the Road investigations we are presented with an exception. Although Constance was arrested on the evidence that a nightdress was missing from her wardrobe inventory, Whicher was unaware that a nightgown, saturated in blood, *had* been found on the day following Francis's murder. In one of the later inquiries into the murder investigation, local police constable Urch gave evidence on how it was discovered:

> I went into the kitchen and scullery, and on searching about in the scullery and opening the door of the boiler-furnace, I saw something wrapped up there. I pulled it out, and found what appeared to me to be a shift wrapped up in a piece of brown paper. [...] On opening the bundle in the stable I found it to contain a shift in a very dirty state; it was very bloody. [...] Mr. Foley [another local policeman] stated that when the shift was handed to him he shuddered to think the man that found it was so foolish as to expose it. By his (Foley's) directions it was afterwards shown to Mr. Stapleton, surgeon. [...] He was perfectly satisfied that the shift had nothing to do with the murder.[20]

It is extraordinary how the discovery of a bloodstained garment was considered insignificant evidence the day after a sanguinary murder had been committed on the same premises. Yet, Elaine Showalter notes, in *The Female Malady* (1987), that in the middle-class Victorian home, 'to manage the hygiene of menstruation in a household where it could not be acknowledged or revealed created a sense of anxiety and shame'.[21] Hence, the custom of shamefully hiding bloodstained garments was, it seems, a standardised practice. The discovery of the bloody nightshift in the Kent house was never reported to Sergeant Whicher. Instead, the garment was discreetly placed back into the boiler and was subsequently lost.

This incredible blunder eventually came to light during the investigations of Thomas Saunders. In an unprecedented move, the Home Secretary commissioned Saunders, a retired barrister, to conduct an examination into the crime and its investigation by local policemen. After hearing how Stapleton had dismissed the evidence of the nightgown as insignificant, Saunders asked Urch whether the surgeon had 'look[ed] at it with a microscope?'

> Witness. – No, I should think he did not!
> Mr. Saunders. – Then, if I have read in French works on jurisprudence that a Minister of Justice had ordered such a garment to be examined by a microscope, I think it will not appear so absurd as it seems to be thought that such an examination was not made.

In an attempt to create or eliminate a link between the murder and the bloodstained garment, Saunders then asked, 'I am told that, after a laborious search, that [a] piece of paper was found [at the scene of the crime]. Did the blood on that paper bear any resemblance to the blood which was found on the shift?' The witness replied, defensively, 'No, it did not'.[22]

Three days after this report was circulated in *The Times*, a letter, echoing the offended tone of Urch, appeared in the same newspaper from

Joseph Stapleton. Responding to Saunders's claim that the nightgown ought to have been examined through a microscope, he wrote:

> In the case at Road I was five miles from home, and without a microscope at hand; but I had no hesitation in advising the authorities that the night-dress shown to me (as to its condition, and the appearance respecting which I was consulted) furnished no clue to this crime. The grounds and value of my opinion seem to have been explained to the satisfaction of the magistrates, and I hoped that the night-dress was withdrawn forever from public observation.
>
> However, Mr. Saunders has dragged it from its obscurity again, and, as it seems to me, in wanton and useless violation of public decency and private feeling. In a capital felony, and upon a question of science, he opposes the gossip of a country village and the fading and fragmentary recollections of his own reading to the testimony of competent and responsible witnesses.[23]

Two days later, *The Times* featured a response from Saunders. The barrister 'denied that he had indulged in any forensic medical criticisms at Mr. Stapleton's expense', and sardonically added:

> For [my] own part, [I] thought that a microscopic inspection of that article would have been highly satisfactory, and that opinion was concurred in by professional gentlemen in London who wrote M.D. after their names, while Mr. Stapleton subscribed himself merely 'M.R.C.S., Lond'. [...] Who were satisfied with Mr. Stapleton's explanation, and with his hopes that this nightdress had been withdrawn for ever from public observation? [...] [I leave] it for the public to say whether [I have] dragged this matter from its obscurity in wanton and useless violation of public decency and public feeling; but [I say] this openly, that in case of murder, which [is] a capital felony, no observations which might be levelled at [me] should prevent [me] from doing what [I] believed to be a public duty in a private character.[24]

What is particularly interesting, in this exchange between medic and lawyer, is how the nightdress, brought in and out of the kitchen boiler, metaphorically represents the way menstruation (as a subject) is similarly exposed to, then hidden from, public view. Aiming to retain medicine's apparently exclusive hold on matters relating to the female body, Stapleton criticises Saunders's 'wanton', public discussion of a supposedly private matter. He also defends his professional ability to differentiate between menses and blood shed from an open wound. Saunders, by apparent contrast, argues that in the investigation of murder, the boundaries between private and public are no longer viable. Yet, although Stapleton and Saunders appear to be in heated opposition to each other, their argument forms part of the same process through which images of control worked their way into discussions of the menstruating body. I argued in the previous chapter that, at mid-century, the female sexual body was often linked with murder in the characterisation of uterine processes as requiring indefatigable control and surveillance. In the exchange between Stapleton and Saunders we observe how these links between murder and menstruation allowed professional minds to anticipate the control and regulation of women and the home.

Following the pattern set by the case of Madeline Smith, which became an inquiry into the defendant's sexual encounters with her lover, the Road investigation developed into an inquisition on the menstrual habits of Constance Kent and her sisters. Unaware of the nightshift that had been found and replaced in the kitchen furnace, Whicher launched a wide-scale hunt for the nightgown missing from Constance's wardrobe. On 26 July 1860, *The Times* reported how

> every possible exertion is being made by the police to collect further evidence, and to find, if possible, the missing nightdress belonging to Miss Constance Kent [...] and, with the view of inducing the inhabitants of the village to assist in the search, a placard has been issued, offering a reward of 5*l*. to any person finding the nightdress and delivering it to the police.[25]

SP, the correspondent I quoted earlier, suggestively called this search the '"fussy activity" about the nightdress of a schoolgirl'.[26] For him (or her), the missing nightshift was insignificant evidence and the search a waste of police resources. Yet the search is interesting because it reveals how, in the narrative that emerges from journalistic representations of the Road Murder, there is little or no distinction between menstruating and murdering for male investigators. For Whicher, in particular, the search for the Road murderer focussed on the missing, bloodstained nightdress of Constance Kent. Some notable Victorians similarly believed there was a link between the catamenial flow and the development of insane female violence. Henry Maudsley, for example, writing on pubescence, makes use of some very interesting and revealing terms: 'A sudden suppression of the menses has produced a direct *explosion* of insanity; or occurring some time before an *outbreak*, it may be an important *link* in its causation'.[27] Like his professional peers, Maudsley uses words like 'suppression', 'explosion', and 'outbreak' to form an idea of women's mental aberration as volcanic and energetic. Yet Maudsley's description of menstruation as 'an important *link*' to those subterranean fires seems to have had a particular significance for the Victorians. In Gillian Beer's interdisciplinary study of the notion of the 'missing link' in nineteenth-century discourses, she identifies the 'missing link' as

> a hypothetical type between two life forms, particularly between mankind and other primates. [...] It also bore for the Victorians a freight

of conflicting political meanings that called on spatial terms: particularly those of distance and closeness between kinds, classes, and peoples. It raised questions of boundaries: what's in, what's out: the object and the abject.[28]

The 'missing link' was thus a connection between two apparently opposing entities; one of which was often 'acceptable' and 'proper' while the other existed beneath social acceptability. Despite its potential threat to social barriers and power distribution, the search for the 'missing link' was, Beer writes, a compulsive one for the Victorians; they were, it seems, obsessed with searching for something they did not want to uncover.

This set of ideas, I argue, is echoed by mid-century perceptions of menstruation and the Road Murder investigations. As 'an important *link* in [insanity's] causation', menstruation is figured by Maudsley and his colleagues as the 'missing link' between women's ostensible proprieties and the inner, destructive fires smouldering within her. This is perhaps most obvious in the often-repeated notion that women vented their subterranean fires through the menstrual flow. The obstetrician Charles Locock argued, for example, that the 'menses were the outlets of "peccant humours"'.[29] Applied to the Road Murder, however, this suggests that the search for Constance's bloodstained nightdress (the 'fussy activity about the nightdress of schoolgirl') was also a search for the 'missing link' between the unruffled, domestic respectability of the Kent family and the inward, fiery inclination towards violence assumed to be a possibility in all households. In the murder case itself, the link was actually a missing one as the nightdress was misplaced. Like the evolutionists' search for the ancient ape-man hybrid that would link contemporary society with brutes, the Road police were similarly engrossed in forging links between the 'sacredness of English households' and an act of violence that for 'hideous wickedness [was] without parallel in [their] criminal records'.[30]

After many investigations, and investigations into those investigations, the Road Murder seemed to go unsolved. The case never left the pages of British newspapers between 1860–5, but in April of the latter year it was sensationally reawakened:

> The proverb 'murder will out' has often been discredited in our time by the lasting mystery which has enveloped great crimes, but an event has now occurred which will recall it to every mind. The 'Road Murder', that dark deed which filled the country with amazement and painful curiosity five years ago, and the incidents of which were studied as a dreadfully fascinating problem in every household, seems now likely to receive a full explanation. Yesterday, Miss CONSTANCE EMILY KENT, one of the unfortunate family, a young lady of only 21 years of age, surrendered at Bow-street and made a voluntary confession of the crime.[31]

Now that Constance had confessed, the press began to consider her guilt in earnest. In the July of the same year, she was arraigned for the murder of Francis and was found guilty. Despite receiving the death sentence, she was reprieved by the Home Secretary and served twenty years of penal servitude. No medical men were commissioned to speak at her trial, yet many speculated as to the true state of Constance's mentality. *The Times* observed, for example, that

> Constance Kent has achieved a celebrity which eclipses the pacification of half the world, and will certainly last as long as the English language is spoken. She is not only the heroine of a foul murder, but an example in the science of mind. As a psychological type she will long survive the vulgar crowds of poets, philosophers, and historians.[32]

A few days before the trial, the *Lancet* attributed the crime's motive to Constance's age. The twenty-one-year-old woman who now stood in the dock and the sixteen-year-old-girl who murdered her brother were not, the journal claimed, the same woman. In 1860

> girlhood was struggling into maturity amidst the contending influences of physical sympathies and hereditary predispositions; now womanhood, in all its ripeness has for the time triumphed. [...] Then a bewildering sense of that *new existence* and the vague subordination of mind to matter which marks the mystery of female maturity held reason as the mere reflection of an organism incapable of determining its relations. [She is] the same witness in name but nothing else. Five years have elapsed; the girl is now a woman.[33]

This 'new existence' is obviously meant to delineate the growth of Constance as a sexual woman. Notice how the line 'subordination of mind to matter which marks the mystery of female maturity' alliterates words beginning with 'm', as if stammering over, and ultimately failing to use, the word 'menstruation'. The article suggests, like Lawson Tait and other medical writers on the subject of female development, that at sixteen years old, Constance was susceptible to her 'hereditary predispositions' to madness. Back in 1860, *The Times* had uncovered evidence of mental inaptitude in three of Constance's maternal relatives. The first Mrs Kent, mother to Constance but not Francis, was described as 'having for several years previous to her death been afflicted in her mind and incapable of attending to the discharge of her household duties'. *The Times* continued:

> It has also been ascertained that the grandmother of Constance Kent was decidedly of unsound mind, and [...] her mother was for many years considered to be of weak intellect. An uncle of the accused has been twice

confined in a lunatic asylum, so that should the evidence produced be sufficient a warrant to the committal of the prisoner, there is no doubt that the question of hereditary insanity will be raised as having prompted the perpetration of such a fearful crime. [...] Two medical men acquainted with her [one being Stapleton] have given it as their opinion that in a paroxysm of mental aberration she might have committed the offence with which she stands charged.[34]

The *Lancet* fused this evidence of morbid inheritance with considerations of Constance's age to reiterate that puberty was a time when such unhealthy taints manifested themselves:

The daughter of a lunatic, at the time when the functions of the female organism were becoming developed, committed an act, which, if a crime, is entirely deficient in every attribute by which crime is usually recognised. [...] Strange and horrible cravings will frequently arise which entrap their victims to the perpetration of [...] crime – motiveless crime – motiveless except so far as to gratify some vague, undefined, consuming, craving desire, or to fulfil the suggestion of an equally inexplicable but not less terrible impulse.[35]

Forbes Winslow claimed that 'out of forty-two young persons in whom [...] mental disease commenced between fourteen and sixteen years of age, eighteen inherited the affection from their parents; and in by far the greater number of cases the disease manifested itself contemporaneously with the age of puberty and menstruation'.[36] In *The Great Crime of 1860*, Joseph Stapleton, who had treated both Constance and her mother, commented that

we shall find, in the heritable character of the passionate temperament, some explanation for the revolting and atrocious crimes which during the last few months have startled and destroyed the security of our domestic relations. The tiger's cub is at first an amusing and gentle playfellow to handle and to pet; but it will, on quick occasion, show that it inherits, with a tiger's face and fangs, a tiger's instincts too.[37]

He conceded that the first Mrs Kent had 'exhibited symptoms of insanity' and a knife was once found hidden under her bed.[38]

As with Christiana Edmunds, Constance Kent seemed to have a multitude of insane relatives who could be invoked as evidence of her insanely murdering her stepbrother. She thus appeared to confirm the growing belief that insanity could be biologically transmitted, especially through the female line of descent. Her story provided the Victorians with another example of how female biology, the roles of mothers, and issues of descent needed to be the objects of a keen vigilance. The hereditary taint, unwatched and uncared for in the female descendants of the first Mrs Kent, had purportedly culminated in the brutal killing of a 'fine', 'healthy lad', whose destiny it was to continue the Kent caste.

Despite observations to the contrary, the murder of Francis was not the first time that the alleged actions of his stepsister had disturbed the composure of the Kent household. In the very first report of Francis's murder *The Times* reported the 'singular fact' that, three years earlier, 'the two younger children of Mr. Kent's first wife – Constance and William – considering themselves to be ill-treated, started off, both dressed in male attire, and were not found for two days'.[39] The flight was considered no insignificant incident and *The Times* later added:

> Some three years since one of the daughters of Mr. Kent by his first wife absconded from her home with her brother William, she having before leaving cut off her hair and dressed herself as a boy. It was into this water-closet [the one in which Francis's body was discovered] that she threw her own clothes after assuming male attire.[40]

In this report, focus is taken away from William and laid exclusively on Constance. The writer may have had the story of Maggie Tulliver, who cut off her hair and later ran away in *The Mill on the Floss* (1860), in mind when drawing up his report. Commentators certainly read Constance's cutting of her hair and adoption of male clothing as evidence of her ability to kill her stepbrother. She was 'a flighty young girl', *The Times* alleged, 'who had already given signs of an erratic disposition, and who might be guilty of many eccentricities'.[41] Constance's father admitted that such behaviour was evidence of how she lacked 'feminine delicacy' and added that '"she had wished to be independent", a quality which was laudable in a boy, but hardly considered a virtue in one of the female sex'.[42] When Constance came to trial in 1865, her legal representation sought the opinion of John Bucknill on whether or not it was feasible to use the insanity plea on her behalf. Bucknill focussed on what Constance's flight from home 'indicated' and 'foreboded':

> The peculiarities evinced by Constance Kent between the ages of 12 and 17 may be attributed to the then transitional period of her life. Moreover, the fact of her cutting off her hair, dressing herself in her brother's clothes, and leaving her home with the intention of going abroad, which occurred when she was only 13 years of age, indicated a peculiarity of disposition and great determination of character which foreboded that, for good or evil, her future life would be remarkable. This peculiar disposition, which led her to such singular and violent resolves of action, seemed also to colour and intensify the thoughts and feelings.[43]

As in the case of Sarah Minchin, *The Times* and Bucknill laid a particularly heavy emphasis on Constance's alleged contravention of gender roles and used this to link her with the murder of Francis. Like Minchin's attack on Frederick Smith, Constance's alleged murder of her brother can be read as a sexual role reversal. It was proposed that Constance had made a nocturnal visit to a male family member's bedroom and penetrated him more than once with her father's razor. Like Blanche's attack on her sister in 'The White Maniac', this version of the story seems to have incestuous connotations and, when considering Francis's age, paedophiliac ones too. All these suggestions combine to create an overriding sense that the Road Murder was a very weird affair. It presented pictures of sexuality and family life that were far from the healthy, procreative ideal favoured by the Victorians. Yet, as we have seen, newspaper reports, doctors' letters, and a mass of other sources were eager to point out that such weirdness was generated from within the ordinary biological developments of the Kent women and, therefore, such 'developments' needed to be analysed and discussed at length.

Popular fictional representations

Wilkie Collins, Mary Elizabeth Braddon, and Mrs Henry Wood, the most popular novelists of the 1860s, were notorious for using actual crimes as the foundations for their plots. If 'a crime of extraordinary horror figures among our *causes célèbres*', Henry Mansel famously wrote in 1863, 'the sensationist is immediately at hand to weave the incident into a thrilling tale, with names and circumstances slightly disguised'. There is, he continues, 'something unspeakably disgusting in this ravenous appetite for carrion, this vulture-like instinct which smells out the newest mass of social corruption, and hurries to devour the loathsome dainty before the scent has evaporated'.[44] Although Mansel's article has been much used by modern scholars, it is still a worthy representative of the castigation novelists earned for allowing crimes like the Road Murder to feed into their fictional storylines. 'Murder, conspiracy, robbery, fraud, are the strong colours upon the national palette',[45] wrote Margaret Oliphant the same year, and, it seems, the popular novelists were eager to exploit the widespread predilection.

Literary critics and biographers have repeatedly cited the Road Murder as a fascination of Collins's. It is evident that he and Dickens discussed it in the letters they sent to each other. In a letter from Dickens to Collins, for instance, dated the October following the crime, Dickens gives his opinion that Mr Kent was the true murderer:

> Mr. Kent intriguing with the nursemaid, poor little child awakes in crib and sits up contemplating blissful proceedings. Nursemaid strangles him then and there. Mr. Kent gashes body to mystify discoverers and disposes of the same.[46]

In addition to mentioning the Road Murder almost directly in *Aurora Floyd* (1863), Braddon admitted having 'pored and puzzled' over journalistic material when researching her book of verse *Garibaldi and Other Poems* (1861): 'With a business-like punctuality of a salaried clerk', she wrote to Charles Kent, 'I went every morning to my file of the *Times*'.[47] It is around this time that the journalism I have been discussing appeared. Unfortunately, there appears to be no direct reference to the Road Murder by Mrs Henry Wood. Yet, as outlined previously, in the introduction, her son Charles wrote that 'she took the keenest interest in all great trials'.[48] The murder of Francis Kent and the trial of his sister, which had an extraordinary journalistic life of more than five years, is very likely to have been one of the 'great trials' that Mrs Wood ardently followed.

In focussing on their appropriation of the Road Murder, it is possible to show how Collins, Braddon, and Wood adopted and created a literary style that was highly responsive to contemporary social developments, especially those relating to crime and psychology. The Road Murder, in particular, appears to have inspired three of the era's best sellers: *Aurora Floyd* (1863), *St. Martin's Eve* (1866), and *The Moonstone* (1868). While we cannot ignore the commercial benefits of using a graphic story like the Kents', I will argue that the fictional uses of the crime also allowed Collins, Braddon, and Wood to explore the alleged links between female biology and the development of insane violence.

'A tragedy of blood and tears': *Aurora Floyd*

Aurora Floyd was serialised in *Temple Bar* from 1862 to 1863 and therefore appears within the boundaries of the Road Murder's two major developments: the death of Francis and Constance's confession. The plot involves a murder committed within the confines of a bourgeois home. It has a central young woman suspected of murder, and a Scotland Yard detective whose job it is to investigate her. Additionally, the omniscient narrator draws a clear parallel between the plot and the Road Murder. Commenting on the effect *Aurora Floyd*'s crime has on the home, Braddon writes:

> It was a weary and a bitter time. I wonder, as I write of it, when I think of a quiet Somersetshire household in which a dreadful deed was done. The secret of which has never yet been brought to light, and perhaps never will be revealed until the Day of Judgement, what must have been suffered by each member of that family? What slow agonies, what ever-increasing tortures, while that cruel mystery was the 'sensation' topic of conversation in a thousand happy home-circles, in a thousand tavern-parlours and pleasant club-rooms. [...] God help that household. [...] God help all patient creatures labouring under the burden of an unjust suspicion, and support them unto the end.[49]

It is clear from this passage that *Aurora Floyd* was written before Constance's confession.[50] For Anthea Trodd, this reference to the Road Murder, and the novel's appropriation of the case in general, reveals a clear tension between the home, the crime, and police investigation. For her, the murder investigations into the deaths of Francis Savile Kent and James Conyers are both figured as an invasion of the sacred domestic space and a ghastly breach of the boundaries between public and private.[51] While *Aurora Floyd* is a text that reproduces and seems to confirm these fears, it also aims to explore them in relation to the male gaze. Braddon's second-most popular book is a work that draws connections between female violence and biology yet raises important questions about the veracity of those links by orchestrating them through the eyes of men.

Aurora Floyd is a novel that opens as sensationally as it means to continue. The opening scene, set in Felden Woods, is steeped in a red gleam:

> Faint streaks of crimson glimmer here and there amidst the rich darkness of the Kentish woods. Autumn's red finger has been lightly laid upon the foliage – sparingly, as the artist puts the brighter tints into his picture: but the grandeur of an August sunset blazes upon the peaceful landscape, and lights all into glory. [...] Every object in the fair English prospect is steeped in a luminous haze. [...] Upon the broad *façade* of a mighty red-brick mansion [...] the sinking sun lingers long, making gorgeous illumination. The long rows of narrow windows are all a-flame with the red light, and an honest homeward tramping villager pauses once or twice in the roadway to glance across the smooth width of dewy lawn and tranquil lake, half fearful that there must be something more than natural in the glitter of those windows, and that maybe Maister Floyd's house is a-fire.[52]

This opening introduces images that Braddon uses, throughout her novel, to portray its passionate heroine. The 'crimson glimmer' that 'lights all into glory', for example, prefigures Aurora's fiery nature, whose name is indicative of her bright and brilliant exteriority. Yet, notice also how the 'natural' opening scene is filtered through the gaze of two male observers (the painter and the villager). Here the text seems to be foreshadowing how, despite the novel's use of fiery imagery to represent Aurora, her brilliant exteriority will be constantly viewed, watched, and judged by male characters. Similarly, the sexual connotations behind 'autumn's red finger lightly laid upon the foliage', prefigure how Braddon's novel will represent these threatening, fiery images as not unrelated to the sexual desires of the male onlooker.

In its aesthetic exploration of femininity, *Aurora Floyd* utilises the two main characters, Aurora and Lucy Floyd. Aurora, bright, exotic, and Cleopatra-like, is contrasted with the vapid, controlled, and pious nature of her cousin. Whereas Aurora is introduced as

> a divinity! Imperiously beautiful in white and scarlet, painfully dazzling to look upon, intoxicatingly brilliant to behold [...] the beauty of this woman was like the strength of [an] alcoholic preparation; barbarous,

intoxicating, dangerous, and maddening. [... She is an] imperious creature, [a] Cleopatra in crinoline.

(p. 33)

Lucy is

exactly the sort of woman to make a good wife. She had been educated to that end by a careful mother. Purity and goodness had watched over her and hemmed her in from her cradle. [...] She was ladylike and accomplished.

(p. 48)

Talbot Bulstrode, the man from whose perspective both these views are made, looks upon Lucy 'as calmly as if she had been a statue', perceiving a

delicacy of outline, perfection of feature, purity of tint, all were there; but while one face dazzled you by its shining splendour, the other impressed you only with a feeble sense of its charms, slow to come and quick to pass away. There are so many Lucys but so few Auroras.

(p. 48)

For Bulstrode, the division between Lucy and Aurora is clear. Lucy is the personification of perfection, a 'fair-haired ideal' (p. 47). Aurora, however, is 'like Charlotte Corday with the knife in her hand', a 'black-eyed Siren' (p. 47) that he believes might lead him and his aristocratic name to destruction.

Aurora Floyd is a book that seems to support the idea that women were divided into angels and demons. It is a dichotomy that has overshadowed studies of Victorian representations of women for years. In one essay on the novel, for example, Jeni Curtis utilises this binary, arguing that it is the novel's main aim to discredit it.[53] It seems, she argues, that Aurora is the novel's most dissident portrait of femininity while Lucy's characterisation remains well within acceptable, reactionary classifications. Yet, because Aurora is continually described as 'Eastern' and 'exotic', Aurora, 'apparently rebellious, is, in fact, the conformist, complying to [...] masculine constructions of womanhood, the temptress',[54] and Lucy is the novel's most 'non-conformist' female portrait. Using Cixous's ideas on the unspeakable feminine, she argues that the silence of Lucy is indicative of an inner female strength that cannot be expressed using the language (and within the social environment) created by men. What I propose, however, is that this argument reproduces a nineteenth-century construct that was far from subversive. The writer of 'Woman in her Psychological Relations', for example, warned the article's readers not to take for granted that 'the most beautiful and perfect physically' are necessarily 'the most excellent and perfect mentally'.[55] Lucy Floyd is probably more accurately read as a fictionalisation of the era's ubiquitous belief that all women, however calm they may appear, harboured passionate and destructive hidden fires. Lucy is often described as a site of contradiction between inner passion and outer control: 'How hard it is upon such women as these that they feel so much and yet display so little feeling!' admits the narrator:

> These gentle creatures love, and make no sign. They sit, like Patience on a monument, smiling at grief; and no one reads the mournful meaning of that sad smile. Concealment, like the worm i' the bud, feeds on their damask cheeks. [...] Their inner life may be a tragedy, all blood and tears, while their outer existence is some dull domestic drama of every-day life. The only outward sign Lucy Floyd gave of the condition of her heart was that one tremulous, half-whispered affirmative; and yet what a tempest of emotion was going forward within!
>
> (p. 160)

Lucy is like the Kent family in their pre-murder days. Like them, she has an unruffled exteriority and a 'tragedy [of] blood and tears' concealed from outside observers. Indeed, the reference to blood and tears relates back to the medical idea that the non-secretion of such bodily fluids could cause a pressurised build-up of energy in women. The fact that Lucy *is* able to control her passions converts her into Bulstrode's idea of perfection. Rather than offering a paradigm of an unspoken female resistance, therefore, the characterisation of Lucy Floyd draws on the mid-nineteenth-century belief that true feminine propriety resided in skills of control and concealment.

With Aurora, the novel offers an exact inversion of her cousin. Aurora's fires are not smouldering on the inside, like Lucy's, but are blazing on the outside:

> The dark-eyed, impetuous creatures, who speak out fearlessly, and tell you that they love or hate you – flinging their arms round your neck or throwing the carving-knife at you, as the case may be – get full value for all their emotion.
>
> (p. 160)

As earlier, when she was described as Charlotte Corday with knife in hand, Aurora's passions are represented as murderous; the image of such 'impetuous creatures' 'flinging their arms around your neck' one moment and 'throwing a carving-knife at you the next' is a clear echo of the women I discussed in chapter one, mothers especially, whose embrace could become deadly without warning. Indeed, Aurora Floyd is a character heavily invested with images of danger and destruction. Her dark eyes are often described as 'flashing forked lightnings of womanly fury' (p. 28), and she is portrayed as 'strange, [...] wicked and unwomanly' (p. 47), a 'terrible woman, with her unfeminine tastes and mysterious propensities' (p. 49). It is not surprising, therefore, that long before anyone is murdered in the novel, Aurora becomes

68 *Violent Women and Sensation Fiction*

the object of strict scrutiny from those around her. Her lady's-maid Mrs Powell 'hate[s] her' (p. 133) and watches patiently for a time when she can cause her trouble. Steeve Hargraves, a former stable man, similarly anticipates the 'chance of doing [her] any mischief' (p. 140). Talbot Bulstrode constantly directs his 'straight penetrating gaze' (p. 38) in her direction.

This surveillance of the heroine is apparently justified by one of the novel's key scenes. After witnessing Hargraves (the 'Softy') mercilessly kick her lame old dog, Aurora, with riding-whip in hand, launches a violent attack upon her servant:

> Aurora sprang upon him like a beautiful tigress, and catching the collar of his fustian jacket in her slight hands, rooted him to the spot on which he stood. The grasp of those slender hands, convulsed by passion, was not to be easily shaken off; and Steeve Hargraves, taken completely off his guard, stared aghast at his assailant. Taller than the stable-man by a foot and a half, she towered above him, her cheeks white with rage, her eyes flashing fury, her hat fallen off, and her black hair tumbling around her shoulders, sublime in her passion. [...] She disengaged her right hand from his collar and rained a shower of blows upon his clumsy shoulders with her slender whip; a mere toy, with emeralds set in its golden head, but stinging like a rod of flexile steel in that little hand.
>
> 'How dared you!' she repeated again and again, her cheeks changing from white to scarlet in the effort to hold the man with one hand. Her tangled hair had fallen to her waist by this time, and the whip was broken in half-a-dozen places.
>
> (p. 138)

John Mellish, Aurora's husband, 'turn[s] white with horror at beholding the beautiful fury', and, seeing 'the convulsive heaving of Aurora's breast [... and] the violent emotion', believes it will surely 'terminate in hysteria, as all womanly fury must, sooner or later' (p. 139). The extraordinary episode is packed with oxymoronic images: 'beautiful tigress', 'sublime in her passion', 'beautiful fury', 'womanly fury', and a 'mere toy' of a riding-whip that is able to give a hefty beating. As with Constance Kent's apparent rejection of her gender role through cutting her hair and dressing as a boy, this passage involves the potential destabilisation of traditional gender attributes. Aurora towers over her male adversary and overpowers him, employing a strong grasp with slender woman's hands. When Mellish witnesses her violence he attempts to reaffirm more traditional power relations, telling Aurora, 'you should not have done this; you should have told me' (p. 139). He then horsewhips the Softy with the prefacing statement: 'It wasn't Mrs Mellish's business to horsewhip you, but it was her duty to let me do it for her; so take that, you coward' (p. 140). The whipping he administers with his large manly whip hardly measures up to the one Aurora delivers with her emerald-set toy. Like many of the era's non-fictional writers, furthermore, Mellish links the violence of his wife with the possibilities of hysteria. It is significant that he makes this connection (mentally) at a time when his mind is panicked by the spectacle of his wife's improper violence. It suggests that not only are the links between women's bodies and violence the products of a male imagination, but also that those connections are forged from minds beset with fear, panic, and a desire to retain traditional power delegations. Indeed, this is made especially clear when the Softy himself links Aurora's violence with her body. He admits how he dreams of her thus:

> I've seen her in my dreams sometimes, with her beautiful thro-at [sic] laid open, and streaming oceans of blood; but, for all that, she's always had the broken whip in her hand, and she's always laughed at me. I've had many a dream about her; but I've never seen her dead or quiet; and I've never seen her without the whip.
>
> (p. 191)

This image of Aurora, envisioned through the male, erotic-oneiric imagination, is, I argue, a poignant reconfiguration of mid-century conceptions of female violence. As in the attack that Mellish expected to become hysterical, Aurora holds the phallic riding-whip while humiliating and emasculating the Softy by laughing.[56] These assaults on the masculinity of the Softy are combined with images that underscore Aurora's presumed somatic debility as a woman. The portrait of her throat 'laid open, and streaming oceans of blood', for example, not only invokes the aggressive death of Francis Kent, but also seems to be a particularly menstrual image. Aurora's emasculating violence is linked, for both the Softy and John Mellish, to her biological position as a woman. *Aurora Floyd* is thus a novel that draws on the associations, forged throughout the nineteenth century, between women's bodies and violence. Yet, the way in which the text represents these links as the products of the disturbed male imagination seems to suggest that the connections have more to do with an unbalanced, masculine viewpoint than any forms of reality.

The beating of the Softy is not, however, the only violent act charged against Aurora; she is later suspected of murdering James Conyers. She married Conyers while at finishing school. Some years later, believing him to be dead from an erroneous newspaper report, she marries Mellish and moves into his wealthy Doncaster estate. Conyers gains employment as Mellish's estate manager and attempts to blackmail his unintentionally bigamous wife. When Conyers is shot dead one evening, Aurora – who has exhibited violent propensities and was with the victim on the night of the murder – becomes the main suspect. Readers who have witnessed Conyers's bribing scenes and know that (like Madeline Smith) Aurora has a motive are encouraged to believe, as they are with Lady Dedlock in *Bleak House* (1853), that she is the murderer. To draw all of these things together, Braddon introduces the character of Captain Prodder, Aurora's maternal uncle, who, like the reading public, learns these facts individually and forms the opinion that his niece is a murderess. He witnesses, for example, Aurora giving Conyers a large amount of cash:

> She stamped her foot upon the turf, and tore the lace in her hands, throwing the fragments away from her. [...]
> 'You'd like to stab me, or shoot me, or strangle me, as I stand here, wouldn't you now?' asked [Conyers] mockingly.
> 'Yes', cried Aurora, 'I would!' She flung her head back with a gesture of disdain as she spoke.
>
> (p. 283)

Prodder then hears about her beating the Softy:

> He was not particularly elated by the image of his sister's child laying a horsewhip upon the shoulders of her half-witted servant. This trifling incident did not exactly harmonize with his idea of the beautiful heiress, playing upon all manner of instruments, and speaking half-a-dozen languages.
>
> (p. 185)

Then, on the very next page, Prodder hears the gunshot that kills Conyers:

> The broad-shouldered, strong-limbed sailor leaned against the turnstile, trembling in every limb.
> What was that which his niece said a quarter of an hour before, when the man had asked her whether she would like to shoot him?
>
> (p. 186)

Appearing in such close succession, these passages draw together the factors that incriminate Aurora: her sexual indiscretions with Conyers, her secrets, and her passionate nature. The way Aurora tears the lace of her dress and flings it from her echoes how Martha Brixey had torn her nursemaid's uniform and thrown it into the fire. The medical witness at her trial, John Mould Burton, concluded that the action was evidence of her dangerous nature, rendering her unfit for the care of children. Prodder appears to think in a similar way by linking Aurora's behaviour, in the interview with her first husband, with the shooting. Aurora's beating of the Softy is also echoed: the gun used to murder Conyers is described 'as pretty as a lady's toy, and small enough to be carried in a lady's pocket' (p. 260). The description invokes the image of Aurora's emerald-set riding-whip, which was also described as a 'mere toy'.

Unlike in her previous novel, *Lady Audley's Secret* (1862), however, Braddon reveals how her heroine's murder of her first husband exists only in the suspicions of her readers and male characters. The detective in *Aurora Floyd* is not employed to *expose* female responsibility, as Whicher seemed to do in the

Road Murder, but absolves Aurora of the guilt that overhangs her. Written at a time when Constance Kent was suspected as the murderer of her stepbrother, and before her confession, Braddon exploits preconceived expectations of female guilt and dismantles them by portraying the Softy as the true murderer. In so doing, *Aurora Floyd* is a novel that encourages its readers to reassess the foundations upon which the image of insane female violence is built. While the novel apparently accepts that, in the masculine imagination, femininity and violence are firmly associated, her guiltless heroine is a characterisation that questions the reliability of those associations.

'Smooth as polished crystal': *St. Martin's Eve*

St. Martin's Eve appeared in volume form one year after Constance's confession and trial. We can surmise from this that the novel was being written as the details of those events were unfolding in the newspapers. Despite Mrs Henry Wood's prudish reputation, the plot of her 1866 novel is one of the most shocking of all popular fiction produced during the mid-nineteenth century. It commences with the birth of Benja St John, a complicated delivery resulting in the death of his mother. In a sentimental deathbed scene, typical of Wood, Benja's mother urges her husband to choose a second wife carefully:

> Choose one that will be a *mother* to my child. Be not allured by beauty, be not tempted by wealth, be not ensnared by specious deceit; but take one who will be to him the loving mother that I would have been. Some one whom you know well and can trust. Not a stranger, not a –[57]

She is interrupted by her husband's avowal that he will never remarry. Within a year, however, George St John begins looking for another wife and, allured by the beauty of Charlotte Norris, he appears to disregard the warnings of his first wife by marrying a virtual stranger. He dies shortly after of an inherited, constitutional weakness, leaving his son Benja and his new son Georgie to the care of Charlotte. Impassioned by jealousy of Benja, who outranks her own child as heir to the estate, and provoked by hereditary insanity, Charlotte is violent towards her stepson. After a family row, she witnesses Benja set himself on fire from a toy church made of paper and candles. Seeing an opportunity to rid herself of the heir and secure the estate for her own child, she leaves the child to burn by locking him in the nursery. Although suspicion falls on Charlotte from other characters, the death is generally understood to be an accident. Notwithstanding, Charlotte is haunted by visions of Benja with the lighted toy and frequently imagines the noise of his screams. Her own child Georgie later dies from the shock of having seen Benja's body, and after attempting to secure herself another wealthy husband and kill two other female characters, Charlotte is eventually committed to a lunatic asylum.

There are a number of factors to suggest that *St. Martin's Eve* is a fictionalisation of the Road Murder. Most obviously, both stories pivot around the death of a young boy in a bourgeois household. There is also the shared imputation that Benja and Francis were killed because of the jealous animosities generated by a second marriage and the creation of a stepfamily. As we shall see, also, the Road Murder and *St. Martin's Eve* share the suggestion that a hereditary predisposition to insanity might offer some explanation for the central crime. Like the actual murder of Francis Kent, the nursery door in *St. Martin's Eve* becomes a significant source of evidence. In a dialogue with Mrs Dallimore, a policeman's wife, Elizabeth Gough revealed how the nursery door in Road Hill House must have been opened by an experienced hand on the night of the murder: 'the door creaks', Mrs Dallimore inquired, 'how could it have been opened by a stranger without making a noise?' To which Elizabeth replied, 'a person accustomed to opening it could do it without making a noise'.[58] In *St. Martin's Eve*, Honour Tritton, Benja's nurse, discovers that the door to the nursery in which Benja's body is found has been locked from the outside: 'When I left him upstairs', she says, 'I left both doors open; that is, unfastened. [...] When I got back again, both were fastened; the one on the inside, the other on the out. *I want to know who did it*' (pp. 155–6, italics in original). The doors reveal something terrible in both stories: in the Road Murder it was evidence that Francis's murderer had to be one of the family members; in *St. Martin's Eve*, it proved that someone had locked the door on the burning child.

Interestingly, the novel originates from a short story Wood wrote for William Harrison Ainsworth's *New Monthly Magazine* in 1853. That story, also entitled 'St. Martin's Eve', differs from the novel in such a way that implies Wood was influenced by the Road Murder when writing the 1866 version. In the story, the evidence of the nursery door is not an important factor in discovering Charlotte's culpability. Moreover, Charlotte does not become the locus of an intense investigation as she does in the novel. In the 1853 version, additionally, Charlotte does not leave Benja to die, but actually *holds* him into the fire that kills him:

> She commenced the onslaught with a furious blow on his ear. The startled child dropped the church, and its paper walls took fire.
> A short struggle ensued. Instinct caused Benja to endeavour to spring away from the flames, but Mrs. Carlton held him with a firm, revengeful hand, beating him about the head and ears, and the blaze caught his pinafore. [...] Oh, wicked woman![59]

The earlier version is actually more shocking than the later one. The burning Benja gets on his knees and begs Charlotte to save him before she finally leaves him to 'burn slowly away to death'.[60] The *New Monthly* story seems to have more in common with the Jane Crosby case, which, as outlined in the introduction, involved a woman holding her child in the kitchen fire. By the time it was lengthened and revised in 1866, Mrs Wood's harrowing tale seems to have appropriated additional details from the Road Murder.

It is necessary that we bear in mind that, while suspicions of 'murder from within' (apparent in both the Road Murder and *St. Martin's Eve*) were horrible, they were not completely unexpected. I discussed above, for example, how the Road Murder was conceived to be a confirmation of the belief that 'smouldering fires' lurked beneath the social respectability of every household. In Mrs Henry Wood's novel, fire and burning imagery runs throughout the text to suggest that danger was always an integral part of the St John home. For example, long before we are introduced to Charlotte, the text opens with the image of Alnwick Hall as a tranquil place harbouring threatening, fiery interiors:

> The day had been wet and cold: and the sodden leaves that strewed the park of one of England's fair domains did not contribute to the cheerfulness of the scene. [...] A cheerful house, [...] which on this ungenial day gave out as wretched an *appearance* as did all else of *outward nature*.
> But if the weather was rendering the demesne desolate, it seemed not to affect the house itself. Lights, gleaming from many of its numerous windows, were passing from room to room, from passage to passage; and fires added their red glow to the general brightness. A spectator might have said that some unusual excitement or gaiety was going on there. Excitement in that house there indeed was, but of gaiety none; for grim Death was about to pay it a visit: not to call any waiting for him in wary old age, but to snatch away the young and lovely.
>
> (p. 1, italics added)

As with *Aurora Floyd*, *St. Martin's Eve* is a story that begins as it aims to proceed. The image of the 'young and lovely' being snatched away by death prefigures the death of Benja and was likely to have struck a significant note with contemporaries familiar with the Road Murder's details. The park in which Alnwick Hall stands is passionless and uneventful; yet the house itself is ablaze with 'lights gleaming' and a 'general brightness' that peeps out from its windows, suggestive of the chaotic scene unfolding within (namely the birth of Benja and the death of his mother). Like the explosive images used by medical writers to describe women, Mrs Wood portrays the St John estate as a site of conflict between a cold, controlled, uneventful exteriority and a fiery, dramatic interiority.

The ways in which the novel transforms the events of the Road Murder, moreover, allow a closer, stylistic engagement with this model of femininity. The original act of stabbing, for example (the means through which Francis Kent died), is converted by Wood's narrative into burning. Prior to his death, a model church at a fair transfixes Benja. Made from wood, paper, and candles,

> Benja's attention had become riveted by the pretty model of a church rising from the midst of green moss. It was white, and its coloured windows were ingeniously shown up by means of a light placed within it. [...] How little did Honour think that the sight was to exercise so terrible an influence on the unconscious child!
>
> (pp. 125–6)

Proper, decorous, and pious on the outside, yet with a flame burning dangerously on the inside, the church is also a model of womanhood, as understood by many Victorians. Honour builds Benja a similar model and, on being left alone with it, he sets himself on fire. *St. Martin's Eve* thus appears to be a text that not only draws on the details of the Road Murder, but also appropriated the idea, found within journalistic accounts of the crime, that a calm exterior often belied stronger, destructive energies.

This is most apparent in the characterisation of Charlotte St John herself. From the moment she is introduced to her future husband, her majestic beauty is frequently described as conflicting with 'a most peculiar expression that would now and again gleam from her eyes' (p. 13). It is after the birth of her son Georgie, however, that these tensions become hazardous. From the excessive love of her own child, Charlotte develops a strong hatred for Benja:

> The frail little infant of a few days had become to her the greatest treasure earth ever gave; her love for him was of that wild, impassioned, all-absorbing nature, known, it is hoped, but to few, for it never visits a well-regulated heart.
>
> And in proportion to her love for her own child, grew her jealousy of Benja – nay, not jealousy only but dislike. [...] The jealousy and the dislike had come – the hatred would only too surely follow.
>
> (pp. 39–40)

What is perhaps most interesting about this passage is the narrative suggestion that Charlotte's passions seldom visit 'a well-regulated heart'. It implies that not only does Wood appropriate prevailing notions of women as sites of conflict between inner fires and outer propriety, but that such passionate violence could be avoided with self-regulation and self-control. As the love for Georgie becomes more intense, so too does Charlotte's violent hatred of her stepson, which is often the result of an uncontrolled impulse: 'it is true that once or twice, upon some very slight provocation, [Charlotte] had fallen into a storm of passion that literally rendered Honour motionless with alarm, seizing the child somewhat after the manner of a tiger, and beating him furiously' (p. 40). Writing about deep-seated resentments in women, Joseph Stapleton commented:

> In a perpetual and compulsory solitude, woman nurses her revenge. It grows up into an absorbing and remorseless passion. Opportunity and time and talent are all centred in the scheme to seek and strike the victim of its wrath. Rarely indeed does a woman's revenge fail in its design or falter in its execution. Once conceived, it grows within her into form, and receives a terrible vitality and power, till, at length, her secret longings prompt and precipitate the moment where she sees and exults over the travail in her soul.[61]

Apparently confirming this, *St. Martin's Eve* outlines a scene of domestic violence in which Charlotte, believing she has witnessed her husband showing Benja more affection than Georgie, gives her stepson a furious beating:

> She had seen it all; the loving meeting with one child, the neglect of the other. Passion, anger, jealousy, waged war within her. [...] In that one moment she was a mad woman.
> What exactly occurred upon his entrance, George St. John could not afterwards remember. [...] A strange, wild look on his wife's face, telling, as it seemed to him, of madness; a wail of reproaches, such as had never been addressed to him from woman's lips; Benja struck to the ground with a violent blow, and his cheek bleeding from it, passed before his eyes as a troubled vision. [... Charlotte] had sunk on a sofa; pale, trembling, hysterical.
>
> (pp. 43–4)

Although, like Aurora Floyd's beating of the Softy, Charlotte's violence is termed 'hysterical', her condition seems to have more in common with the behaviour of puerperal maniacs. Puerperal mania, termed a 'fiery ordeal' by Winslow,[62] was (as noted in the previous chapter) often depicted by nineteenth-century medics through flaming and volcanic imagery. In their influential encyclopaedia on psychology, for example, John Bucknill and Daniel Tuke wrote about the condition:

> Every medical man has observed the extraordinary amount of obscenity, in thought and language, which breaks forth from the most modest and well-nurtured woman under the influence of puerperal mania. [...] Religious and moral principles alone give strength to the female mind; and that, when these are weakened or removed by disease, the subterranean fires become active, and the crater gives forth smoke and flame.[63]

Like the puerperal women portrayed in this passage, Charlotte's attack on Benja is 'impassioned', 'violent', and 'hysterical'. She is a 'mad woman' who levels a 'wail of reproaches such as had never been addressed [...] from woman's lips' at her husband, echoing how the Victorians were sometimes shocked by the language and actions of their female family members when afflicted with psychosomatic maladies. In Bucknill and Tuke's description, moreover, it is only when the lack of 'religious and moral principles' have left an opening that the 'smoke and flame' of insanity is allowed egress. Like the characterisation of Charlotte St John, these alienists appear to hold the opinion that puerperal women's emotions and morals required staunch vigilance and control because, when these become weakened, the womanly fires were given vent.

George St John is given a number of warnings that his wife is a danger to his heir. In addition to the attack on Benja cited above, for example, he is warned by Honour and Charlotte's physician Mr Pym (an emphatic five times in just three pages) that, if he dies, he must not leave Benja under his wife's care:

> If you fear that you will be taken from us, *don't* leave this child in the power of Mrs. St. John. [...] Leave him in the power of anybody else in the world, but don't leave him to Mrs. St. John. [...] To anyone else in the world, sir! [...] To any of your own family – to Mrs. Darling – to whom you will; but do not, do not leave him in the power of his step-mother! [...] Don't leave Benja under your wife's charge [...] Do not leave Benja under the charge of your wife.
>
> (pp. 64–7)

As with Burton's suspicion that Martha Brixey's small acts of passion rendered her unsuitable for the care of children, Charlotte St John's occasional, impassioned attacks on Benja are correctly understood as signs of her violent potential. Like Samuel Kent, however, who ignored what warning signs Constance's flight may have offered (and Ffinch's disregard of Burton's warning), St John only half listens to the forebodings of Honour and Pym. Aiming to resolve the situation with a compromise, he leaves his estate to Benja instead of Charlotte. In his amended will, she and Georgie are entitled to remain at Alnwick Hall as long as Charlotte acts as Benja's guardian. In managing his affairs thus, however, St John only exacerbates his wife's anger. Charlotte's hatred and jealousy against Benja are fuelled by her husband's posthumous favouritism. The text converts the metaphorical 'smouldering fires' into a literal conflagration, and Charlotte's heated passions get vented onto poor Benja.

In reproducing the idea that the puerperal condition invested women with the capacity to murder, Wood's text thus appears to offer support for the views offered by medical writers and journalistic reports of real crimes. Yet, as the novel considers the more complex issues surrounding heredity, particularly the expectations that those ideas were assumed to foster, it is possible to see a more ambivalent interpretation of the same. One such obvious disagreement is the novel's review of psychiatry's belief that 'girls are far more likely to inherit insanity from their mother than from the other parent'.[64] Charlotte, by contrast, inherits lunacy from her father. In the closing stages of the novel, Charlotte's mother, Mrs Darling, and her physician, Mr Pym, admit that Charlotte's father died in a fit of insanity. One thing is indisputable', says the former, 'that she inherited her father's jealousy of disposition':

> In her it was in excess so great as to be in itself a species of madness. She was not, that I ever heard, jealous of her husband; it displayed itself in her jealous love for her child. Until he was born, I don't think she had one of those paroxysms of violence that those about her called 'temper'. [...] These fits of passion, coupled with the fierce jealousy that was beyond all reason, all parallel in my experience, were very like madness.
> (p. 427)

Charlotte's violent paroxysms are explained as a dangerous mixture of congenital insanity and a weakness in will augmented by the puerperal state. Again, this echoes certain elements of the Road Murder as the *Lancet* had suggested of Constance Kent that the 'transitional period of life, influenced by an hereditary predisposition to insanity offered the most probable as well as humane explanation of the horrible transaction'.[65] Charlotte St John, as a new mother, is also at a 'transitional period' in her life. Yet, unlike Constance (and more like Christiana Edmunds), Charlotte inherits her father's insanity, thus questioning the idea that insanity is mostly transferred through *female* lines of descent.

Yet, perhaps the text's strongest dissent from the idea that female biology predisposed all women to the onset of aggressive mania comes from the suggestion that violence such as Charlotte's is actually the result of self-fulfilling male expectations. With reference to Charlotte, Frederick St John asks Pym, 'do you not think she must be insane?' Pym admits that it is something he has 'always' been on the watch for:

> 'I cannot say that. But I may tell you that I have always feared it for her'.
> 'Her father died mad, you wrote word to the dean'.
> 'He died raving mad. [...] His madness, as I gathered at the time, was hereditary; but he had been (unlike his daughter) perfectly well all his life, betraying no symptoms of it'.
> (p. 424)

Once again, the question of insanity pivots on the search for 'betraying symptoms'. Pym's acknowledgement that there *have* been such symptoms in Charlotte carries the suggestion that his fears have led to his watching for signs of her morbid inheritance. It is not only Charlotte's alleged destiny to develop insanity, therefore, but she is equally fated to carry other people's expectations of her instability and the scrutiny that naturally follows.

It is this vigilance that leads, directly, to some of Charlotte's most aggressive behaviour. Her violent moments in the novel (namely when she locks the nursery door on Benja and attacks Georgina Beauclerc and Honour Tritton) all occur shortly after her mental condition has been in doubt and measures have been put in place to control her alleged madness. Despite her apparent puerperal insanity, for example, Charlotte would not have reached her heightened levels of fury, had it not been for her husband's legacy, which forces her to be Benja's guardian. The will was executed in response to Pym and Honour's five ominous warnings against Charlotte's temper. Ironically, the controls actually *fuel* the acts they were created to prevent; the narrative sequence reveals a connection between the anticipation of insane violence, attempts to control it, and its manifestation. Similarly, Charlotte's attempted attack on Georgina Beauclerc and her savage, Bertha Rochester-like assault on Honour Tritton provide the climax to a scene in which Frederick St John has closely watched her for signs of madness. It is suggested to Frederick, by Charlotte's half-sister Rose, that the former may have inherited insanity from her father. Like Pym and Charlotte's mother before him, Frederick thus becomes compulsively obsessed with watching Charlotte for signs of lunacy: 'the doubt had been already implanted in him by Rose Darling; but for that, he might never have so much as glanced at the possibility' (p. 390). He thereafter becomes 'secretly busy as ever was a London detective, watching [Charlotte]. He had been watching her closely [...] and he persuaded himself that he did detect signs of incipient madness' (pp. 386–7). Frederick's surveillance of Charlotte, which becomes 'all impulse and excitement' (p. 423), is like the 'fussy activity' surrounding the bloodstained nightdress of Constance Kent. Like the Road Murder investigation, Frederick is driven to expose the links between Charlotte's calm and collected exteriority and the internal chaos that he believes to be raging within her.

Her appearance, however, is unforthcoming in these clues, and this leads to Frederick questioning the validity and limits of his own gaze:

> At one moment he recalled all the queer and horrible tales he had heard of people killing or injuring others in their madness, previously unsuspected; the next, he asked himself whether he were awake or dreaming that he should call up ideas so unlikely and fantastical. [... Charlotte] sat down to the piano, and sang some low, sweet music, charming their ears, winning their hearts. Had all the doctors connected with Bethlehem Hospital come forward then to declare her mad, people would have laughed at them for their pains; and Mr. St. John amidst the rest.
>
> (p. 391)

The Dean of Westerbury joins the others in watching Charlotte. *His* gaze, however, gets redirected:

> Calm, impassive, perfectly self-possessed, she stood [...] looking singularly attractive, one of the beautiful crystal chessmen held between her slender fingers. Not a woman in the world could look much less insane than did Charlotte [...]; and the dean turned his eyes on Frederick, in momentary wonder at that gentleman's hallucination.
>
> (p. 411)

Charlotte's external blankness is so effective that it reflects the gaze of Frederick and redirects the dean's. The result is that both men begin to question *Frederick's* sanity. As with the Duke in 'The White Maniac', they believe it is Frederick's mania to believe Charlotte mad. She becomes like the crystal chess piece she holds between her slender fingers; 'her beautiful features [...] smooth as polished crystal' (p. 15) reflect and refract the interpretive, subjective gaze of her observers. The text consequently inquires, as do many sensation novels, how far the process of detecting madness is itself an unhealthy fixation.

Hence, although *St. Martin's Eve* tells a story that exploits and reproduces many of the period's medico-legal associations between female violent insanity and women's biology, the text also explores how these links may be generated by the expectant male gaze. How far, the novel appears to ask, do medical and legal specialists create the problems they are employed to uncover? And how far might this in itself be symptomatic of mental pathology?

'Detective fever': *The Moonstone*

Of the three novels that I deal with in this chapter, *The Moonstone* is the one that engages most obviously with the details of the Road Murder. The novel was serialised, weekly, in *All the Year Round* from January to August 1868, three years after the sentencing of Constance. As with the Road Murder story, which is told through a series of fragmented and often contradictory journalistic articles, *The Moonstone* is narrated through a string of testimonies concerned with a crime committed within the confines of a bourgeois home. In both the Road Murder and *The Moonstone*, there are indications that one of the house's inmates is responsible; local policemen perform inadequate investigations, and a Scotland Yard detective arrives on the scene to become preoccupied with discovering a stained nightdress. While the similarities are unmistakable, it is the *differences* between the two stories that are the most revealing, particularly the way Collins's appropriation of the Road Murder appears to be a bloodless fictionalisation. In her biography of Wilkie Collins, Catherine Peters claims that the most obvious difference between the Road Murder and Collins's fictionalisation is that the central crime is changed from murder to theft. This, she suggests, was a means through which Collins rendered his narrative less shocking than the original crime. Despite being credited with creating the sensation genre, Collins, according to Peters, 'disliked the personal violence of murder'.[66] This argument, however, is hardly supported by the text, as the Moonstone, the stolen diamond, has a particularly bloody heritage. Its original seizing in the siege of Seringapatam, for example, opens the novel with a particularly sanguinary event:

> I [...] saw the bodies of two Indians [...] lying across the entrance, dead. [...] A third Indian, mortally wounded, was sinking at the feet of a man whose back was towards me. The man turned at the instant when I came in, and I saw John Herncastle, with a torch in one hand, and a dagger dripping with blood in the other. A stone, set like a pommel, in the end of the dagger's handle, flashed in the torchlight, as he turned on me, like a gleam of fire.[67]

From the beginning of the novel, therefore, the Moonstone has firm associations with bloodshed. It is, after all, set into the handle of a dagger used to kill its three guardians. We might also argue that the jewel has a particularly murderous influence on the text's cast of characters as a trail of deaths marks its procession through the narrative. The way in which the diamond first appears, for example, among the corpses of the Indians, is echoed by how it ultimately leaves the bodies of Lady Verinder, Rosanna Spearman, and Godfrey Ablewhite in its wake. Rather than avoiding the 'personal violence of murder', therefore, the Moonstone (the ominous centre of the novel) appears to epitomise death and destruction.

Additional links with blood are also apparent in the symbolic associations that can be drawn between the diamond and menstruation. Its name, *Moon* stone for example, elicits the idea of monthly periodicity.[68] In her historical study of gynaecology in England from 1800–1929, furthermore, Ornella Moscucci notes how medical writers were indebted to mythological associations between women's bodies and lunar cycles:

> Woman's seemingly mysterious capacity to bring forth and nurture life evoked ancient beliefs about the moon and the sea, which bio-medical writers translated into the language of science. In the mythology of a number of cultures the lunar deity was represented as female and was related to the fertilisation of the earth, the harvesting and planting of crops and the cycle of the seasons.[69]

Additionally, as with the beginnings of the menstrual age, the gem testifies to Rachel Verinder's procession into womanhood as it is given to her on her eighteenth birthday. Like the enigmatic bloodstain on the nightdress in the

Road Murder case, which confused the distinctions between menses and blood shed during murder, the Moonstone is a similar hybrid of these images as it has links with both murder and menstruation.

In her analysis of *The Moonstone* in relation to nineteenth-century psychological ideas, Jenny Bourne Taylor has argued that the diamond is 'a source of unconscious energy which, when lost, produces hysteria'.[70] The jewel produces hysteria, however, long before it is lost. Gabriel Betteredge explains, for example, how it is presented to Rachel in a scene of scattered senses and screaming women:

> The light that streamed from it was like the light of the harvest moon. When you looked down into the stone, you looked into a yellow deep that drew your eyes into it so that they saw nothing else. It seemed unfathomable; this jewel that you could hold between your finger and thumb, seemed unfathomable as the heavens themselves. [...] It shone awfully out of the depths of its own brightness, with a moony gleam, in the dark. No wonder Miss Rachel was fascinated: no wonder her cousins screamed. The diamond laid such a hold on *me* that I burst out with as large an 'O' as the [cousins] themselves.
>
> (p. 74, italics in original)

Like Charlotte St John, whose 'beautiful features, [...] smooth as polished crystal' hid the demonic, destructive depths of her character, the Moonstone is also characterised as a fascinating object of beauty harbouring awful, unfathomable depths. In addition, the jewel has 'a defect, in the shape of a flaw, in the very heart of the stone' (p. 50), a description that recalls contemporaneous definitions of women as polished on the outside, yet fundamentally flawed and defective on the inside. The gem's central fault means that, as a commercial commodity, the diamond is worth more cut into a number of smaller jewels:

> The flawed Diamond, cut up, would actually fetch more than the Diamond as it now is; for this plain reason – that from four to six perfect brilliants might be cut from it, which would be, collectively, worth more money than the large – but imperfect – single stone.
>
> (p. 51)

Such descriptions of the diamond as defective, multifaceted and, potentially, fragmented associate the stone with Victorian ideas of female nature. The diamond has a close symbolic relationship with its owner, Rachel, a character who becomes increasingly hysterical as the novel progresses. Betteredge describes her, for example, as 'possessing a host of graces and attractions' yet, like the diamond, she 'had one defect', which he identifies as her having 'ideas of her own' (p. 65). Not only does Rachel have a central defect like the gem, but she also shares its associations with fragmentation and multiplicity. Speaking to Godfrey Ablewhite later, she cries:

> Go away! I must be out of my mind to talk as I am talking now. No! you mustn't leave me – you mustn't carry away a wrong impression. I must say, what is to be said in my own defence. Mind this! *He* doesn't know – he never will know, what I have told *you*. I will never see him – I don't care what happens – I will never, never, never see him again! Don't ask me his name! Don't ask me any more! Let's change the subject. Are you doctor enough, Godfrey, to tell me why I feel as if I was stifling for want of breath? Is there a form of hysterics that bursts into words instead of tears?
> (p. 242, italics in original)

Rachel's speech is broken up by small sentences, exclamations, rhetorical questions, parentheses, and emphases. Like the narrative sequence of the novel, and the faceted Moonstone itself, which narrowly escapes being split into a number of smaller gems, Rachel's self-diagnosed 'hysterics', which here take the form of words instead of tears, synchronise with concurrent notions of hysteria. Such contradictory, fitful displays of emotion, argued Frederick Skey (in the same year that *The Moonstone* was published) 'are the predominant signs of hysteria', particularly 'fits of crying, sobbing, [and] laughing. [...] The frequency of hysteria', he continued, 'is no less remarkable than the multiformity of the shapes that it puts on'.[71] Thus, with its central flaw and multifarious polished surface, the Moonstone becomes a fitting symbol of nineteenth-century ideas on the somatic nature of women. In addition, the gem has clear links with bloodshed and death and, by constructing the jewel as an amalgamation of violence and female biology, the novel appears to confirm prevailing ideas on the close relationship between those two factors.

Yet, despite appearing to reproduce these ideas, Collins's narrative explores how far they form the foundations for the unhealthy fixations of professional and unprofessional detectives. Like Constance Kent's bloodstained nightdress, the Moonstone becomes the object of a frenzied investigative search. The preliminary suspicions of Sergeant Cuff, a London detective modelled on Sergeant Whicher, tend towards Rosanna Spearman, a former thief rehabilitated by Lady Verinder into a housemaid. 'It was plain that Sergeant Cuff's suspicions of Rosanna had been raised' (p. 125), admits Betteredge, by the fact that she had a criminal history:

> The upshot of it was, that Rosanna Spearman had been a thief. [...] There was certainly no beauty about her to make the others envious; she was the plainest woman in the house, with the additional misfortune of having one shoulder bigger than the other.
> (pp. 34–5)

Thus, Rosanna is considered a suspicious woman, not only because of her criminal history, but because of her physical deformities as well. Notice how the investigative, male gaze moves seamlessly (in the above passage) from issues of criminality to biology. With her criminal propensities and physical deformities, Rosanna personifies the delinquent proclivities and somatic incapacities that were central to mid-Victorian definitions of femininity.

In addition, the connections between the investigation of the theft and the (pathologised) female body are most obviously negotiated in Collins's depiction of the Shivering Sands, a setting firmly associated with Rosanna. Both are introduced, for example, in the same episode: 'Having now told the story of Rosanna', Betteredge moves on 'to the story of the sands':

> The sand-hills here run down to the sea, and end in two spits of rock jutting out opposite each other, till you lose sight of them in the water. One is called the North Spit, and one the South. Between the two, shifting backwards and forwards at certain seasons of the year, lies the most horrible quicksand on the shores of Yorkshire. At the turn of the tide, something goes on in the *unknown deeps below*, which sets the whole face of the quicksand *shivering and trembling* in a manner most remarkable to see, and which has given to it, among the people in our parts, the name of The Shivering Sand.
>
> (p. 36, italics added)

The description seems to employ images of the female body and psychopathological symptoms. The sands are located, for example, between two rocks 'jutting out opposite to each other' – mimicking images of the female genitalia between the two pelvic protrusions.[72] References to the 'unknown deeps below' recall the images of the Moonstone as having 'unfathomable depths' and the notion of women as divided between outer calmness and a dangerous, unknown interiority. Like the hysterical woman, the sands shiver and tremble as though manifesting corporeal reactions to a mental stimulus. Indeed, the following citation from a description of the Sands employs many of the images used by contemporaneous medical writers to describe hysteria:

> The horrid sand began to *shiver*. The broad brown face of it *heaved* slowly, and then *dimpled* and *quivered* all over. 'Do you know what it looks like to me?' says Rosanna, catching me by the shoulder again. 'It looks as if it had hundreds of suffocating people under it – all struggling to get to the *surface*, and all sinking lower and lower in the *dreadful deeps*! Throw a stone in, Mr Betteredge! Throw a stone in, and let's see the sand suck it down!' (pp. 38–9, italics added; Collins's italics replaced with underlining)

As with the hysterical fit, the sands shiver, heave, dimple, and quiver as though suffering from the loss of mental control. Like Charlotte St John and the Moonstone, also, the Sands appear to have ghastly, chaotic depths and the flow and ebb of the tide echoes Victorian associations of the female body with the sea.[73] It is hardly surprising, therefore, that Rosanna (a personification of criminality and somatic incapacity) feels a strong connection with the landscape: 'Something draws me to it', she admits, 'I try to keep away, from it, and I can't. [...] I think that my grave is waiting for me here' (p. 38). Circumstances later compel her to commit suicide by jumping into the quicksand.

It is Rosanna's attachment to the Sands that leads Franklin Blake, not knowing himself to be the thief, to search for the Moonstone there. He understands from her suicide note that she has hidden something there and, bearing in mind how similar the portrait of the Shivering Sands is to the image of female genitalia, his investigation becomes a highly sexualised process:

> The bared wet *surface* of the quicksand itself, glittering with a golden brightness, hid the horror of its *false brown face* under a passing smile. [...] I saw the preliminary *heaving* of the Sand, and then the awful *shiver* that crept over its surface – as if some spirit of terror lived and moved and shuddered in the *fathomless deeps beneath*. [...] The sight of it so near me, still disturbed at intervals by its *hideous shivering fits*, shook my nerves for the moment. A horrible fancy that the dead woman might appear on the scene of her suicide, to assist my search – an unutterable dread of seeing her rise through the *heaving surface* of the same, and point to the place – forced itself into my mind, and turned me cold in the warm sunlight. I own I closed my eyes at the moment when the point of the stick first entered the quicksand.
>
> (pp. 312–3, italics added)

Again, the description of the landscape is permeated with psychosomatic symptoms and the suggestion of hidden depths. The search for clues to a woman's crime, or a crime that Blake *believes* to be a woman's, becomes a sexual act of penetrating the surface to get to hidden realities. Like the detective and journalistic searches for the 'missing link' between Constance Kent's outer propriety and her alleged inner violence through the 'fussy activity about the nightdress of a schoolgirl', Blake's inspection of the Shivering Sands seems to be a compulsive, figurative search of the female sexual body for hideous conclusions. Franklin avoids looking into the sand as his stick begins to penetrate it, reading like an anticipation of Freud's 'vagina dentata' idea – where the male is neurotically afraid of the gratification of his own desires. This could be because, like the investigators of the Road Murder, Blake is searching for evidence he is half-afraid to discover – evidence that crime and violence resides within the 'fathomless deeps' of nineteenth-century respectability. Whether or not those links exist, the narrative suggests that the process of searching for them is an unhealthy fixation.

If additional support were needed to highlight similarities between the Road Murder and the plot of *The Moonstone*, it is certainly provided by the fact that, in Collins's novel, the search for the Moonstone becomes the search for a stained nightdress. When Sergeant Cuff begins investigating the crime scene, he notices a smear in a painted door in Rachel's room. The local policeman believes the smear to be inconsequential but Cuff corrects him:

> 'I made a private inquiry last week, Mr Superintendent', he said. 'At one end of the inquiry there was a murder, and at the other end there was a spot of ink on a tablecloth that nobody could account for. [...] Before we go a step further in this business we must see the [garment] that made the smear, and we must know for certain when the paint was wet.
>
> (p. 109)

Cuff's suspicions are correct; Franklin, the true thief, creates the smear, which leaves a stain on his nightgown. Peters believes that the change from a bloodstain to paint is evidence of Collins's attempt to neutralise the Road Murder of its bloody details.[74] Yet I propose that, in changing the stain from blood to paint, the novel better engages with issues of sexuality and creativity. The stain on the nightgown in Collins's narrative is caused by the more masculine creative endeavour of painting as opposed to menstruation. Thus, when Franklin finally recovers the box Rosanna has hidden in the Shivering Sands, he discovers that his search has, in fact, been self-referential – a search for his *own* responsibility:

> Putting the case *between my knees*, and exerting my utmost strength, I contrived to draw off the cover. [... Inside] it was a nightgown. [...I] instantly discovered the smear of the paint from the door of Rachel's boudoir!
>
> My eyes remained riveted on the stain, and my mind took me back at a leap from the present to the past. [...] I had discovered the smear on the nightgown. To whom did the nightgown belong? [...] The nightgown itself would reveal the truth; for, in all probability, the nightgown was marked with its owner's name.
>
> I took it up from the sand, and looked for the mark.
> I found the mark, and read –
> MY OWN NAME.
>
> There were the familiar letters which told me that the nightgown was mine. [...] I had penetrated the secret which the quicksand had kept from every other living creature. And, on the unanswerable evidence of the paint-stain, I had discovered Myself as the Thief.
>
> (pp. 313–4, italics added)

Franklin's search of the Shivering Sands is heavily imbued with sexual imagery: he places the box between his legs and refers to himself as having 'penetrated the secret' of what occurred that night in Rachel's boudoir. There are also indications that Franklin's search is not the work of a healthy mind. Notice how the fragmented, broken sentences of this scene echo Rachel's hysterical fit. The soiled nightdress reveals no evidence of female culpability but links him directly to the crime; the contents of the case are objects of his *own* creation, his own painting. Franklin's compulsive, convulsive search for the missing link between outer propriety and alleged hidden depths of femininity has been a search for a link of his own forging. Like Frederick St John's investigation of Charlotte and masculine interpretations of Aurora Floyd's character, the detective searches of Blake have revealed more about the detective than they have about the detected. It is significant how Franklin himself begins to evince symptoms of hysteria. It is a display that exposes *him* as the most pathological party, not Rosanna or Rachel. The object linking Blake to the crime, a smeared painting, is highly symbolic: it suggests that the male, investigative process that links women and crime is, in fact, a distorted and malformed creative process (as indicated by Franklin's disfigured painting). Like Braddon and Wood, Collins utilises images from the Road Murder, which forms the basis for his complex, narrative exploration of the Victorian, masculine obsession with discovering and defining female insane violence. Blake's own culpability not only suggests that connections between female sexuality and crime are the fictive objects of a male fabrication, but that that 'fabrication' is a symbol of masculine psychopathology.

3
'Frail Erections': Exploiting Violent Women in the Work of Mary Elizabeth Braddon

> I am racking my own brain – or trying to rack it – in search of a rag of plot whereon to hang three volumes of words. The worst part of the business is that the books with murders in them – Lady A. & H. Dunbar – the whole interest concentering [*sic*] in the murder – sell better than any others, & the critics say Thou shalt do no murder. However, I think this time I shall once more make my dip in the lucky bag of the Newgate Calendar.[1]

So wrote Braddon to her 'literary mentor' Edward Bulwer-Lytton in 1872. By then Braddon had established herself as one of Britain's best-selling novelists and, as this citation shows, she owed much of her success to her willingness to dip into the *Newgate Calendar* for inspiration. Yet, such letters also reveal Braddon's long-standing unease regarding the aesthetic value of plots centred on murder. 'I want to serve two masters', she admitted to Bulwer in 1863, 'I want to be artistic & to please *you*. I want to be sensational, & to please Mudie's subscribers'.[2] Although such sentiments may have been an attempt to please an author she greatly admired, they nevertheless reveal Braddon's belief in a divide between 'high' and 'popular' art. This is a tension visible in much of her work from the 1860s and which seemed to shape the young author's handling of insane female violence. Although Braddon frequently drew on her era's ideas on the links between the female body and violent insanity (an appropriation that ensured the commercial success of her novels), her texts also contain an ambivalent exploration of how such ideas could be exploited for individual gain.

Poking the embers: The hysterical violence of young women

In *Lady Audley's Secret*, Braddon's best-known novel, Robert Audley, the plot's amateur detective, appears to experience the same 'detective fever' felt by Frederick St John and Franklin Blake. He wonders:

> Why was it that I saw some strange mystery in my friend's disappearance? Was it a monition or a monomania? What if I am wrong after all?

What if this chain of evidence which I have constructed link by link is woven out of my own folly?[3]

As Jenny Bourne Taylor and others have noted, the investigations of Robert Audley, like Blake and St John, reveal more about the detective than they do about the detected. '*Lady Audley's Secret*', Taylor writes, 'is as much about the instability and tenuousness of the masculine detective consciousness as about the threatening femininity it investigates and controls'.[4] While such conclusions on the relationship between Robert and Lady Audley are very revealing, however, the association between the eponymous central character and the only character she *does* manage to kill (Luke Marks) has remained largely unexplored. The reason for this, no doubt, is that Robert has a much more pivotal role in the narrative than Luke does. His role as the text's investigator and problematic protagonist gives the reader a sustained insight into his thoughts and feelings, as is demonstrated by the above passage. Yet, despite his infrequent appearances, Luke also has an important, exclusive role in the narrative. Unlike Lady Audley's attempted murder of George Talboys, for example, the killing of Luke is not elided from the text and narrated retrospectively. Instead, Lady Audley's destructiveness is outlined in brilliant and graphic detail. Robert Audley may be the intended victim, but Luke's death secures him as the victim of Lady Audley's most destructive act of violence.

Having had her history discovered by Robert Audley, who threatens her with exposure, Lady Audley attempts to kill Robert by setting fire to the inn (owned by Luke Marks, her maid's husband) in which he is sleeping. Immediately prior to the arson, Lady Audley is portrayed as follows:

> The red blood flashed up into my lady's face with as sudden and transient a blaze as the flickering flame of a fire, and died as suddenly away, leaving her more pale than winter snow. [...] With every pulse slackening, with every drop of blood congealing in her veins, [...] the terrible process [...] was [...] transform[ing] her from a woman into a statue. [...] An unnatural crimson spot burned in the centre of each rounded cheek, and an unnatural lustre gleamed in her great blue eyes. She spoke with an unnatural clearness and an unnatural rapidity. She had altogether the appearance and manner of a person who has yielded to the dominant influence of some overpowering excitement.
>
> (pp. 306–9)

As with many investigations into Victorian murder cases like those outlined in chapter one, this passage focuses on the circulation of blood in the female perpetrator's body. Observe, for example, how the blood flows and ebbs from my lady's face; how the crimson spots burn in her cheeks, and every drop of blood congeals in her veins. What characterises the sanguinary state of Lady Audley is its excesses. Like Martha Brixey, whose menstrual blockage had allegedly led to her cutting the throat of the baby under her care, this passage suggests that an overplus of blood in Lady Audley's body is linked to the murderous act she is about to commit. The novel also links the bodily state of Lady Audley to her violence through its use of the ubiquitous 'smouldering fires' metaphor. The rush of blood to her face, for example, is compared to the 'flickering flame of a fire' and, similarly, the crimson spots in Lady Audley's face 'burn' in her cheeks. There is, Braddon adds, a 'flame in her eyes' and her blonde hair resembles a 'yellow flame' streaming above her (p. 316). Like Charlotte St John's inner fires, which become a literal conflagration that consumes the object of her hatred, these fiery passions of Lady Audley eventually result in the destruction of the inn and its owner.

As with mid-Victorian discussions of hysteria and reports of cases like Madeline Smith's, Lady Audley's most violent act appears to support the prevailing notion that there was a fine line between female brutality and women's carnality. The arson scene, for example, leaves Lady Audley in a state of undress: 'the wind had torn her heavy cloak away from her shoulders, and had left her slender figure exposed to the blast' (p. 320). In this description of her, Lady Audley could be mistaken as walking away from a sexual encounter, rather than one in which she has inflicted murderous violence. She is also described as an 'angry mermaid' (p. 316), a mythical figure that Nina Auerbach has shown to combine images of destruction and sexuality for the Victorians.[5] Indeed, in this last confrontation between Luke and his killer, the narrative is awash with sexual connotations. For example, Phoebe, Lady Audley's maid and Luke's wife, warns her mistress that Luke may become vulgar, 'you – you won't be offended, my lady, if he should say something rude'. Lady Audley replies, 'what should I care for his rudeness? Let him say what he likes' (p. 314). It is his actions, however, rather than his words, that are the most 'rude':

> Luke sat with his clumsy legs stretched out upon the hearth; with a glass of gin-and-water in one hand and the poker in the other. He had just thrust the poker into a great heap of black coals, and was shattering them to make a blaze, when his wife appeared upon the threshold of the room.
> (p. 314)

When he discovers Lady Audley to be on the threshold too, 'the poker dropped from the landlord's hand, and fell clattering amongst the cinders on the hearth' (p. 315). Like the riding-whip in *Aurora Floyd* and Franklin Blake's walking stick, the poker seems to become, in this sequence, a phallic metaphor. The flaring of the fire at the moment Lady Audley enters the threshold, for example, as well as Luke's dropping of the poker, prefigure how Luke's masculine threat will be annihilated by Lady Audley's use of fire. Yet, the image of the hot coals, flaring up on being poked could also represent, metonymically, the nineteenth-century idea that sexual gratification was, for women, a very precarious business. In the anonymously penned *My Secret Life*, assumed to be written in the 1880s, for instance, the author describes his first sexual encounter as being followed by a hysterical paralysis in the servant girl he has taken advantage of:

> I became conscious that she was pushing me off her, and rose up, she with me, to a half-sitting posture; she began to laugh, then to cry, and fell back in hysterics, as I had seen her before.
>
> I had seen my mother attend to her in those fits, but little did I then know that sexual excitement causes them in women and that probably in her I had been the cause.[6]

Although the servant girl's hysterical fit does not result in violence, this passage reveals how sex was thought to lead women into psychopathological conditions that could (as shown in chapter one) *culminate* in violence. Like this writer's carnal contact with the servant girl and Franklin's penetration of the Shivering Sands, Luke's poking of the embers is like another anticipation of the 'vagina dentata' metaphor. Both images suggest that the male penetrator desires what he fears and fears what he desires. Incidentally, Wilkie Collins used a very similar image six years earlier. In a humorous short story for *Bentley's Miscellany* entitled 'A Passage in the Life of Perugino Potts' (1856), the eponymous Potts, a painter, is advanced upon by one of his live female models. The painter describes how she 'coolly desired me to pull the foot-warming pipkin from under her robes, [...] to poke the embers, and then to put it back again; speaking just as composedly as if she were only asking me to help her on with her shawl!'[7] In apparent agreement, the 'poking the embers' metaphor in *Lady Audley's Secret* is connotative of sexual activity that, it was assumed at the time, could cause the inherent fires of womanhood to flare up with destructive consequences.

Yet *Lady Audley's Secret* is also a text that unsettles these assumptions by linking them to the commercial exploits of male characters and by portraying the central 'villainess' as an objectified pawn in those schemes. Clearly, the reader's sympathies are never with Luke Marks and we almost applaud his death. This is largely because, like James Conyers, Luke has played the role of blackmailer. Discovering that Lady Audley has a child by a previous marriage, he extorts from her the money with which he buys the inn. The scene where he discovers the evidence of the lady's bigamy also reads like a sexual connection. Luke is given a tour of Lady Audley's chambers:

> He went on cutting and chopping at a rude handle he was fashioning to the stake. [...] 'It's a mortal dull place, Phoebe', he said. [...] 'I've heard tell of a murder that was done here in old times'.
>
> 'There are murders enough in these times, as to that, Luke', answered the girl. [...Luke] uttered a cry of wonder when he saw the ornaments glittering

on white satin cushions. He wanted to handle the delicate jewels; to pull them about and find out their mercantile value. [...] 'What's this?' he asked presently, pointing to a brass knob in the framework of the box.

He pushed it as he spoke, and a secret drawer, lined with velvet, flew out of the casket. [...] There was not much in it; neither gold nor gems; only a baby's little worsted shoe rolled up in a piece of paper, and a tiny lock of pale and silky yellow hair, evidently taken from a baby's head. Phoebe's grey eyes dilated as she examined the little packet. [...] I'd rather have this than the diamond bracelet you would have liked to take', she answered; 'you shall have the public-house, Luke'.

(pp. 30–4)

The sexual nuances of the scene are driven mainly by its characterisation of Luke as a penetrating force and Lady Audley's possessions as various parts of the female sexual body. Luke, for example, sharpens a stick meant for a stake, which prefigures his later 'poking the embers' scene. He desires to 'handle' Lady Audley's 'delicate jewels' and the casket containing the baby's tokens is suggestively similar to the female genitalia: it is 'lined with purple velvet' and has a 'brass knob in the framework of the box', connotative of a clitoris, which Luke pokes as he does the embers. The jewellery box produces tokens belonging to a baby and reflects, crudely, how the female sexual organs produce infants. The scene has much in common with Victorian gynaecological descriptions of the vaginal examination. In his highly influential *Practical Treatise on the Diseases of Women* (1868), for example, Theodore Gaillard Thomas wrote:

> The index finger of one hand, being introduced into the vagina, the other fingers being flexed into the palm and the thumb laid upon them, passes directly to the cervix uteri, assuring the investigator as it goes of the perviousness of the vaginal canal. Upon reaching the os, this part is carefully examined with reference to size, consistency of lips, and character of discharge, a patulous os, with soft, velvety sides covered by a glutinous secretions, admonishing him of the existence of inflammation of the os and cervical canal.[8]

The passage makes graphic reading, but has some very interesting similarities with Luke and Phoebe's exploration of Lady Audley's chambers. Notice, for example, how the gynaecologist is described as the 'investigator' of the female body. Like Lady Audley's jewellery box, the genitalia has 'velvety sides' and contents that should be examined and assessed carefully. In Thomas's book, the search for tumours is like Luke and Phoebe's examination of the 'delicate jewels' in Lady Audley's 'box'.

In addition, Luke and Phoebe's penetration of Lady Audley's chamber is endowed with images of murder and death: he and Phoebe discuss the murders, past and present, that have been committed at Audley Court and the baby's tokens, concealed in a casket and including a lock of hair, would have invoked, for the Victorians, popular images of infanticide and child mortality.

While all of these interconnecting images suggest close associations between female sexuality and death, however, the scene's imagery also indicates that these associations were not without economic potential for the male 'investigator'. Phoebe and Luke, for example, weigh the 'mercantile value' of Lady Audley's jewels, the priciest of all being the infant's tokens. It is this 'little packet' that buys Luke his public house. Thus, in many ways, Luke's progress echoes that of the Victorian self-made man. Beginning in a position of obscurity, he manages to climb a step on the social ladder.

The inn itself, however, the crux of his social rise, is hardly a magnificent testament to what male exploitation can achieve:

> The cruel blasts [of wind] danced wildly round that frail erection. They disported themselves with the shattered pigeon-house, the broken weathercock, the loose tiles, and unshapely chimneys; they rattled at the window-panes, and whistled in the crevices; they mocked the feeble building from foundation to roof, and battered and banged and tormented it in their fierce gambols, until it trembled and rocked with the force of their rough play.
>
> (p. 314)

This passage portrays the public house with the same biological idioms used to represent Luke's exploitations. Like the broken riding-whip in *Aurora Floyd* and the dropped poker, the inn is an image of warped manhood. It has a 'broken weather*cock*', 'unshapely chimneys', and an overall appearance of a 'frail erection'. The description also uses a number of hysterical images as the 'feeble' and 'shattered' body of architecture 'trembles' under contact with the wind. Like Luke's actions throughout the text, the penetrating wind ravishes the tottering edifice with its 'rough play' and whistles 'in the crevices'. The roles have been reversed. Luke, once the penetrator of Lady Audley's suggestive chambers, now has his own 'frail' spaces invaded.

While *Lady Audley's Secret* is apparently willing to allow the idea of female biology as linked to insane violence to remain unchallenged, then, the text also questions how far those links are inseparable from the commercial endeavours of men. Fortunes built upon such foundations, Braddon's most celebrated novel seems to imply, are doomed to be as pathological as the 'insane' women they exploit.

This notion appears to have been a preoccupying theme for Braddon in the years preceding the publication of her best seller. Her first step into the literary market was made, not with a sensation novel, but with a book of verse based upon the Neapolitan Revolution. *Garibaldi and Other Poems*

(1861) featured the poem 'Under the Sycamores'. Set in seventeenth-century Colonial America, the piece allowed Braddon to explore the links between female insanity and the fantasies of male, social ambition. Omnisciently narrated, the poem tells the story of Menamenee, a beautiful American-Indian princess, who falls immoderately in love with a Scottish colonialist named Roderick. Roderick, who has a wife who will join him once he has built a settlement, informs Menamenee that her wild and passionate love is destined to remain unrequited. The news drives Menamenee insane and she leaves her tribe to live alone in the wilderness:

> Her long loose hair, in damp and tangled locks,
> Veiled her wan face, and vexed her bloodshot eyes
> Which were more mournful for their tearlessness,
> And the redoubled lustre of their gaze;
> Fever and madness mingling in their light,
> Until their brightness made them well-nigh blind.
> Her dress hung loose, and torn by branching shrubs.[9]

One of Menamenee's tribesmen is unsuccessful in convincing her to return home:

> He saw she was mad. She would not go
> Back to her home with him. With a strange laugh,
> She said, 'My home is in the forest now,
> Wilder and statelier than my old abode,
> More fitting for a princess such as I'. [...]
> He sought in vain, and sad and slow returned
> To tell the tribe the story of her woes,
> Which had obscured her brain and driven her mad.
> (pp. 198–200)

This outline of Menamenee's insanity carries, as does *Lady Audley's Secret*, images of fire and blood rushing to the Princess's face and eyes. Driven mad by love, and tottering on the brink of a pool overgrown with sycamores, Menamenee embodies the trope of love-sickness explored by Helen Small.[10] Like the love-mad female, Menamenee becomes inseparable from the wild landscape, which becomes a metonymic extension of her madness: 'My home is in the forest now, / Wilder and statelier than my old abode, / More fitting for a princess such as I'. It is not insignificant, therefore, that Roderick's cultivation of the landscape is figured as a particularly sexual act:

> He came,
> [...] to erect a home, and in the wilds
> Of the dark forest to hew out a spot

> Where he might rear an altar to his God. [...]
> [Menamenee] saw him, leaning, with his axe in hand,
> Against the monster tree he had hewn down,
> Lost in grave thought; his dark-blue eyes were closed,
> As if he would shut out the world he loathed, –
> As if he would shut out the weary sun;
> And, turning his eyes inward on his heart,
> Die of the tortures locked within its depth.
> (p. 180, p. 200)

Roderick is tortured because he must reject Menamenee in favour of his wife. His hewing of the essentially feminine landscape bears many similarities to Franklin Blake's penetration of the Shivering Sands. Like Blake, who closes his eyes and averts his face at the point his cane enters the surface, Roderick's cleaving at the 'monster tree' is also achieved with closed eyes and an amalgamated feeling of pleasure and disgust. Roderick aims to 'erect a home' and livelihood using the American wilderness as his foundations. As such, his conduct echoes that of Luke Marks, who builds *his* 'frail erection' using the untamed passions of Lady Audley as its cornerstone. The American landscape, as we have seen, is linked to the passions of Menamenee. Although Roderick is only ever compassionate towards the Indian Princess, the text nevertheless suggests (on a purely metaphorical level) that his colony (like Luke's inn) is built by exploiting the wild energies of Menamenee via the landscape she inhabits.

As with Luke's manipulation of Lady Audley, however, Roderick's colony is doomed to failure because the seeds of its destruction are sown firmly into its foundations. Aptly, the Indian princess shoots the coloniser with his own gun. The shooting, like the arson scene in *Lady Audley's Secret*, teems with biological imagery:

> He saw that she was mad. 'Menamenee!'
> 'Oh, do not speak to me!' she cried; 'I bore
> To look on you, but cannot bear your voice.
> That music sends the blood into my brain,
> Until the burning surges make me reel,
> As if the seas were tossing in my head! –
> You see I'm not too mad to know I'm mad!'
> (p. 202)

This last line is clearly the product of an age that also created the concept of monomania. In the portrait of Menamenee's insanity, it is possible to be insane *to a degree* and in reference to one object only. For Menamenee, this object is Roderick. Again, the poem utilises images of blood rushing to the brain, turning Menamenee mad as the smouldering fires surge within.

Unlike Lady Audley's burning of Luke, however, it is not the vented fires of Menamenee's insanity that kill Roderick but his own weapon. Menamenee's handling of the firearm is pregnant with illicit connotation:

> One little restless hand [was] upon her gun,
> With the incessant motion that betrays
> The unhinged mind. [...]
> The little clicking sound betrayed the hand
> With which she cocked the gun. [...]
> Her hand upon the gun while she speaks,
> The left hand on the barrel, and the right
> Driving the ramrod down upon the charge. [...]
> She laughed aloud the maniac's laugh.
> (pp. 206–9)

Menamenee's maniacal laughter resurrects the image of her Creole sister Bertha Rochester who, in *her* arson scene, effectively emasculates her husband by destroying his house and blinding him.[11] Menamenee's fondling of Roderick's weapon suggests that, like Aurora's riding-whip and Luke's poker, the gun is a metaphor for the phallus. Notice how her 'driving the ramrod down upon the charge' positions her as the penetrator while Roderick's position, as the one being shot, is the penetrated. Like the broken riding-whip and dropped poker, the gun (in the princess's hands) symbolises Roderick's emasculation. This is not, however, Roderick's first encounter with madness: 'He had met / With madness ere to-day' and, echoing the mid-Victorian medical idea that madness could be controlled and treated with an intense authoritative gaze, Roderick's

> stern dark glance
> Caught hers, and fixed it, till her frenzied gaze
> Trembled and wandered from him restlessly;
> Her hand relaxed its grasp, until the gun
> She had just lifted, slid towards the ground.
> (pp. 206–7)

The melodramatic sequence becomes a contest between Menamenee and Roderick for masculine, penetrative power. Roderick employs the alienist's gaze to regain authority – resulting in the gun suggestively losing its erect status and sliding to the ground. Unfortunately for him, Roderick's Scottish wife finally arrives at this crucial moment and, averting his gaze 'to wonder at his love' (p. 211), he is shot dead by the hysterical Menamenee.

The retaliatory aspects of Menamenee's story seem to elicit an interpretation of her story as subversive. The Indian princess, unlike so many of her English, Ophelian counterparts, appears to reject her love-mad fate in order to deny Roderick the benefits of the civilisation he has built upon the wilderness of her despair. Like *Lady Audley's Secret*, however, the poem characterises Menamenee's violence as not unrelated to the build-up of incendiary, sanguinary energies from within the female body. This suggests that, rather than enacting her revenge, Menamenee has succumbed to the pathologies to which all women were considered prone. Yet, by setting 'Under the Sycamores' in the colonies of North America, Braddon appears to suggest that images of female, insane violence were inseparable from the schemes of self-advancement and progress held by the male population. As with Lady Audley's destruction of Luke's inn, Menamenee's murder of Roderick suggests that the structures built upon such a basis are as volatile as the mad women and wild landscapes they inhabit.

While writing *Garibaldi*, Braddon was also attempting to write her first novel *Three Times Dead* (1861). Renamed later by the author as *The Trail of the Serpent*, the book sold over a thousand copies during the first week of publication. As with 'Under the Sycamores' and *Lady Audley's Secret*, the novel explores the passionate violence of young women. It features a beautiful Spanish countess, Valerie de Cevennes, whose passions lead her to poison her husband in the early stages of the text. She is first introduced to the reader, and the villain who later capitalises on her hysterical nature, during an opera performance at which she is a spectator. Some of her admirers observe: 'she is in the box next to the king; don't you see her diamonds? They and her eyes are brilliant enough to set the curtains of the box on fire', adding, 'she is handsome; but there's just too much of the demon in those great almond-shaped black eyes and that small determined mouth. What a fortune she would be to some intriguing adventurer'.[12] Valerie has much in common with some of sensation fiction's most memorable female characters. Like Rachel Verinder, she has an affinity with her diamonds and, as with Charlotte St John, her appearance is 'smooth as polished crystal'. Like Aurora Floyd, her dazzling beauty is akin to a dangerous conflagration as well.

In *The Trail of the Serpent*, Valerie's observers notice how she would be 'a fortune' to 'an adventurer', as Lady Audley proves to be for Luke Marks. Jabez North determines to become such an 'adventurer' and closely scrutinises Valerie with his opera glasses. His gaze uncovers her strong sexual desire for the opera singer Monsieur de Lancy, a man whom she has secretly married:

> 'My glass is well worth the fifteen guineas I paid for it', [Jabez] whispers to himself. 'That girl can command her eyes; they have not one traitorous flash. But those thin lips cannot keep a secret from a man with a decent amount of brains'.
>
> (p. 122)

Jabez follows Valerie home and, obtaining an interview with her, convinces her that De Lancy is an adulterer. The meeting becomes an investigative contest between Jabez's vigilant observation of Valerie's passions and the countess's ability to conceal them. When he first enters her chamber, for example, 'he sees that the young and beautiful girl is prepared to give him battle. He is disappointed. He had counted upon her surprise and confusion, and he feels that he has lost a point in the game' (p. 132). Suggestively slicing open the leaves of a book with a knife, Valerie is gradually led into betraying more of her feelings as the interview progresses:

> She tries to resume her employment with the paper-knife, but this time she tears the leaves into pieces in her endeavour to cut them. Her anguish and her womanhood get the better of her pride and her power of endurance. She crumples the book in her clenched hands and throws it into the fire. Her visitor smiles. His blows are beginning to tell.
> (p. 134)

Valerie's behaviour here recalls that of Martha Brixey who had thrown a fragment of her uniform into the fire. Like *her* physician's opinions on what those actions implied, Braddon's text suggests that this is a case of Valerie's womanhood getting the better of her. Convinced that Jabez is telling the truth, Valerie displays a set of symptoms that appear to have been lifted directly from the era's medical textbooks:

> Valerie [...] sat facing him, with her eyes fixed in a strange and ghastly stare. Once she lifts her hand to her throat, as if to save herself from choking; and when the schemer has finished speaking she slides heavily from her chair, and falls on her knees upon the Persian hearth-rug, with her small hands convulsively clasped about her heart. But she is not insensible, and she never takes her eyes from his face. She is a woman who neither weeps nor faints – she suffers. [...] There is a rushing sound in her ears, as if all the blood were surging from her heart up to her brain.
> (p. 136, p. 143)

The passage lapses into present-tense narration in order to present its images with more urgency and energy. Like Menamenee, Lady Audley, and the countless cases used as examples in medical texts, Valerie has a rush of blood to her head and experiences the choking sensation (*globulus hystericus*) associated with hysteria. Like Lucy Floyd and Charlotte St John, the Countess's body becomes a site of conflict between inner passions and the individual's ability to contain them. The more emotion Valerie betrays, the more successful Jabez becomes in his manipulation of her. This clearly concurs with the portraits of Luke Marks and Roderick building their homes and livelihoods upon the dangerous passions of Lady Audley and Menamenee. Intending to marry Valerie himself, Jabez persuades her to poison her husband.

The poisoning is committed moments before her husband performs, aptly, in the opera *Lucretia Borgia*. Meeting him before the performance,

> she held [an] antique diamond-cut glass with a steady hand while Gaston poured the wine into it. The light from the wood fire flickered, and he spilt some of the Madeira over her dress. [...] 'Your uncle's wine is not very clear', [de Lancy] said; 'but I would drink the vilest vinegar from the worst tavern in Paris, if you poured it out for me, Valerie'.
>
> (pp. 158–9)

De Lancy then leaves Valerie to give his performance. In an extraordinary scene that, like the Provençale's murder in *Middlemarch* (1872), crosses the boundaries between theatricality and reality, Valerie's husband 'dies' onstage and off:

> To [Valerie's] clouded sight the opera-house was only a confusion of waving lights and burning eyes; and that, in the midst of a chaos of blood and fire, she saw the vision of her lover and her husband dying by the hand that had caressed him.
>
> (p. 162)

Witness how the phrase 'chaos of blood and fire' anticipates the 'tragedy of blood and tears' experienced by the undemonstrative Lucy Floyd. Valerie's smouldering fires are vented onto her husband. Combined with De Lancy's avowal that he would 'drink the vilest vinegar' so long as Valerie poured it out for him, the line 'dying by the hand that had caressed him' is an echo of the cases, discussed in the preceding two chapters, featuring women accused of murdering their nearest relations. One of Valerie's opera companions ironically observes that performances like *Lucretia Borgia* 'set a dangerous example':

> Lucretia Borgia, in black velvet, avenging an insult according to the rules of high art and to the music of Donizetti is very charming, no doubt; but we don't want our wives and daughters to learn how they may poison us without fear of detection.
>
> (p. 161)

The assertion, which echoes concerns voiced by many of the period's medical writers, is apparently validated by Valerie's murder of her husband. The performance supplies her not only with the inspiration to kill her husband, but also with the means to do it. The speaker of the lines above fears murder without detection. In giving evidence in the trial of Catherine Wilson in 1862, Alfred Taylor suggested, 'in my experience I have frequently discovered that cases of death which have been registered as having been occasioned by cholera were, in reality, deaths from poison. I have known this to be so in eight cases where the bodies have been exhumed'.[13] His comment sparked what *The Times* referred to as 'a panic fear of wholesale poisoning',[14] and, when Wilson was sentenced to death for murdering her best friend, the judge admitted that, had she not been found guilty, 'the public would no longer sit down to their daily meals with safety'.[15] With its representation of Valerie poisoning her husband beneath the veneer of wifely love and theatricality, *The Trail of the Serpent* seems determined to confirm such fears.

The implication that appearances cannot be trusted is well illustrated by Braddon's use of the wineglass metaphor. As with the brilliant opening scene of *A Tale of Two Cities* (1859) in which the spilling of a casket of wine over the Parisian pavement forebodes the spilled blood of the guillotined, Valerie's 'diamond-cut glass', full of poisoned Madeira, similarly uses wine as connotative of blood.[16] With its multitude of crystal facets and, filled to overflowing with a red, innocuous liquid (that suggestively spills onto Valerie's dress), the glass of polluted wine reverberates with many of the images already discussed. Like the Moonstone, for example, it has a beautiful, multifarious exterior and flawed interior. Like Charlotte St John, it has a surface of 'polished crystal' and a deadly energy lurking beneath. More broadly, like the period's constructions of women, the beautiful appearance conceals a hideous, destructive reality.

It needs to be remembered, however, that while these characteristics appear to corroborate some of the era's negative ideas of women, the portrait of Valerie, like those of Lady Audley and Menamenee, associates such notions with the social scheming of the central male character. Through his exploitation of Valerie's passions, Jabez North, who starts life in a workhouse, takes a massive pecuniary leap upwards, becoming the millionaire Count de Marolles. As the omniscient narrator observes, Valerie was 'a pitiful puppet in the hands of a master fiend!' (p. 305).

As in *Lady Audley's Secret* and 'Under the Sycamores', however, the 'frail erections' built upon the pathology of female violence in *The Trail of the Serpent* are portrayed as vulnerable to the very emotions they exploit. Valerie's retaliation is not criminal, but actually atones for her murderous past. Having been married to Jabez for eight years and leading a corpse-like, automaton existence, Valerie overhears the conversation of one of Jabez's accomplices at a Belgravian dinner party. It reveals that De Lancy was not an adulterer. Valerie immediately regains her old fiery flare and assists the police in tracking Jabez for his previous crimes. When she confronts her husband after her rekindling, Jabez wonders:

> What is it? – this change, this transformation, which has taken eight years off the age of this woman, and restored her as she was on that night when he first saw her at the Opera House in Paris. What is it? So great and marvellous an alteration, he might almost doubt if this indeed were she. And yet he can scarcely define the change. It seems a transformation, not of the face, but of the soul. A new soul looking out of the old beauty. A new soul? No, the old soul, which he thought dead. It is indeed a resurrection

of the dead. [...] Has she indeed gone mad, and is this new light in her eyes the fire of insanity?

(pp. 322–3)

The text again utilises the images of an insane subterranean fire. This time, however, Valerie's passions work in a moral direction. Her retaliation not only amends the wrongs done to *her* by Jabez, but also atones for the injuries inflicted on other characters. The countess's story, therefore, suggests that her violent energies are a case of mischannelled energy. When women's passions are guided in the right direction, the text appears to imply, they can achieve good as well as evil. Unusually, Valerie appears to escape the miserable fate in store for other fictional murderesses. She is neither charged with murder, killed off by the narrative, nor imprisoned in a lunatic asylum. De Lancy, it turns out, survived her murder attempt. He and Valerie reunite and live happily as man and wife.

The concept of female violence being a mischannelled force is orchestrated most poignantly in one of Braddon's 1863 novels, *John Marchmont's Legacy*. Braddon wrote to Bulwer, at the time of writing the novel, that 'I have tried to draw [...] at least one character more original than any of my usual run of heroes & heroines'.[17] This character, Olivia Marchmont, is one of the era's most extraordinary fictional renderings of the concurrent medicalised images of womanhood. Like her forerunners, Olivia exhibits hysterical symptoms throughout the novel. As with Braddon's earlier texts, also, *John Marchmont's Legacy* appears to agree with the alleged sexual-biological foundations of female violence. Olivia's 'madness', for example, stems from her frustrated desires for her cousin Edward:

> She had loved Edward Arundel with all the strength of her soul; she had wasted a world of intellect and passion upon this bright-haired boy. This foolish, grovelling madness had been the blight of her life. [...] If her life had been a wider one, this wasted love would, perhaps, have shrunk into its proper insignificance: she would have loved, and suffered and recovered; as so many of us recover from this common epidemic. But all the volcanic forces of an impetuous nature, concentrated into one narrow focus, wasted themselves upon this one feeling, until that which should have been a sentiment became a madness.
>
> (p. 86)

Olivia's mental state appears to draw on the supposed 'epidemic', 'volcanic', and excessive nature of hysteria, in addition to the relationship it was believed to have with the narrow lifestyles of women.

As with her earlier texts, however, Braddon also uses such ideas to create a sensational narrative where men gain economic advancement from the pathology of women's passions. Olivia's immoderate desires for her cousin converge into hatred for Edward's chosen bride – her stepdaughter Mary. She subsequently allows Paul Marchmont (Mary's cousin) to imprison Mary in a boathouse and install himself as successor to her estate. Like Valerie de Cevennes, who is a 'pitiful puppet in the hands of a master-field', Olivia's emotions are a 'fitting tool' for those who desire to exploit her:

> Blind and forgetful of everything in the hideous egotism of her despair, what was Olivia Marchmont but a fitting tool, a plastic and easily-moulded instrument, in the hands of unscrupulous people, whose hard intellects had never been beaten into confused shapelessness in the fiery furnace of passion?
>
> (p. 198)

As Olivia is Mary Marchmont's guardian, and Mary stands between Paul and a considerable fortune, it is in the latter's best interests to exploit this vulnerability. He therefore penetrates Olivia's mind and acquaints himself with the cause of her passions:

> He took his dissecting-knife and went to work at an intellectual autopsy. He anatomised the wretched woman's soul. He made her tell her secret, and bare her tortured breast before him; now wringing some hasty word from her impatience, now entrapping her into some admission, – if only so much as a defiant look, a sudden lowering of the dark brows, an involuntary compression of the lips. He *made* her reveal herself to him.
>
> (p. 219, italics in original)

As with the 'uterine' theories of hysteria, this extract makes no distinction between body and mind, as is most apparent in its suggestive use of surgical, post-mortem imagery. The passage is also sexualised, as Paul '*made* [Olivia] reveal herself' and 'bare her tortured breast'. The use of the term 'entrapping her' also underscores how Olivia's sexual, psychological revelations, like Valerie's, become a way in which she is controlled and contained by her male exploiter. Discovering Olivia's secret, Paul is subsequently able to exacerbate her hatred for Mary until she relinquishes her role as guardian, allowing him to exchange his Bohemian obscurity for the Marchmont estate.

Towards the end of the novel, however, the tables are turned as Olivia's passions, like Valerie's, become instrumental in Paul's fall. Believing his wife Mary to be dead, Edward plans to remarry. On hearing of his intended betrothal, Olivia informs him that his wife (who has given birth to his son) is still alive and being held prisoner. In a chapter aptly titled 'The Turning of the Tide', Paul attempts to silence Olivia by claiming that her accusations are the ravings of a madwoman. He says:

> There is no knowing what may be attempted by a madwoman, driven mad by a jealousy in itself almost as terrible as madness. [...] What has

not been done by unhappy creatures in this woman's state of mind? Every day we read of such things in newspapers – deeds of horror at which the blood grows cold in our veins. [...] I come to tell you that a desperate woman has sworn to hinder to-morrow's marriage. Heaven knows what she may do in her jealous frenzy!

(p. 414)

Paul's historically accurate persuasions are short-lived as Olivia, considering herself sane ('mad until today [...] but not mad today'), storms the marriage ceremony with the irrefutable evidence of Mary and her child waiting nearby (p. 423).[18] Like Valerie de Cevennes, Olivia's passions – once the 'fitting tool' of evil, exploitative schemes – now become a formidable obstacle for the novel's villain. As with *The Trail of the Serpent*, *John Marchmont's Legacy* suggests that the intellects of women, when given suitable outlet, are a match for the social pretensions harboured by any man.

Unlike *The Trail of the Serpent*, however, we do not need to rely upon metaphors and implicit suggestions to reach such conclusions. In its characterisation of Olivia Marchmont, *John Marchmont's Legacy* makes a direct connection between the narrow existences of nineteenth-century women and the incubation of insane violence. With the image of the first female physician, Elizabeth Garrett, looming over mid-Victorian society, it is not surprising to discover a reference to Garrett's American colleagues:

The narrow life to which [Olivia] doomed herself, the self-immolation which she called duty, left her a prey to this one thought. Her work was not enough for her. Her powerful mind wasted and shrivelled for want of worthy employment. [...] If Olivia Marchmont could have gone to America, and entered herself amongst the feminine professors of law or medicine, – if she could have turned field-preacher, like simple Dinah Morris, or set up a printing press in Bloomsbury, or even written a novel, – I think she might have been saved. The superabundant energy of her mind would have found a new object. As it was, she did none of these things. She had only dreamt one dream, and by force of perpetual repetition the dream had become a madness.

(pp. 135–6)

As Sally Shuttleworth has argued, this passage reworks the contemporary idea that insanity could be a singular obsession with one object: a monomania.[19] In Olivia's case, the object of her monomania is her cousin. Yet from the same passage we witness the author's discontent with the limited social roles of women. The female monomaniac's insane energies, the novel suggests, are mischannelled ambitions and misspent intellectual activity. When Lavinia Weston, a doctor's wife, attempts to diagnose Olivia's malady as hysteria, the latter disagrees. 'A doctor's wife', Mrs Weston says, may often be useful when a doctor is himself out of place. There are little nervous ailments – depression of spirits, mental uneasiness – from which women, and sensitive women, suffer acutely, and which perhaps a woman's more refined nature alone can thoroughly comprehend. [...] Weston is a good simple-hearted creature, but he knows as much about a woman's mind as he does of an Aeolian harp. [...] These medical men watch us in the agonies of hysteria; they hear our sighs, they see our tears, and in their awkwardness and ignorance they prescribe commonplace remedies out of the pharmacopoeia.

(p. 196)

Olivia replies, 'I am not subject to any fine-ladylike hysteria, I can assure you, Mrs Weston' (p. 197). Lavinia attempts to use hysteria as a common ground between all women – a ground that remains exclusive *to* women. Yet Olivia's rejection of the term reminds the readers that 'hysteria' is itself a label devised by male science. What Olivia suffers from is the *true* female malady: the undervalued energies of a 'brilliant mind'.

Unmotherly glances and sickly sentimentality: Dangerous maternities

In portraying the violence of her most famous female characters, Lady Audley and Aurora Floyd, Braddon's fiction appears to imply that their mothers are accountable for their daughters' actions. In the confession where she declares herself to be 'a madwoman' (p. 340), for example, Lady Audley explains how her insane violence is inherited from her mother:

> My mother was a madwoman. [...] Her madness was an hereditary disease transmitted to her from her mother, who had died mad. She, my mother, had been, or had appeared, sane up to the hour of my birth; but from that hour her intellect had decayed [...]. The only inheritance I had to expect from my mother was insanity!
>
> (pp. 343–5)

Lady Audley later refers to her own madness as 'the hidden taint that I had sucked with my mother's milk' (p. 386). Her self-diagnosed insanity draws on many of the period's notions regarding the role played by heredity in the development of insane violence.[20] Lady Audley's mother, for instance, loses her senses after the birth of her daughter, implying that she experienced puerperal mania. The way in which she transmits insanity to her daughter, via her breast-milk, also echoes the period's concerns regarding wet-nursing and its possible effects on the mental health of babies.

By contrast, Eliza Floyd is held accountable for Aurora's immoderate aggression, not because she gives more than was bargained for, like Lady Audley's mother, but because she gives too little. Like Benja St John's mother, she dies shortly after giving birth, leaving her baby prey to unhealthy influences:

> Aurora shot wither she would, and there was none to lop the wandering branches of that luxurious nature. She said what she pleased; thought, spoke, acted as she pleased; learned what she pleased; and she grew into a bright impetuous being.[21]

As Mrs Alexander, Aurora's aunt, and Lucy Floyd's mother suggests, the absence of a mother had left Aurora 'sadly in need of some accomplished and watchful person, whose care it would be to train and prune those exuberant branches of her nature which had been suffered to grow as they would from her infancy' (p. 50). It is this 'impetuous' disregard of 'proper' boundaries that appears to culminate in Aurora's horsewhipping of the Softy. Indeed, that scene is loaded with images of the heroine as a spoiled child. Mellish, for example, 'as if he had been trying to soothe an agitated child', entreats Aurora to 'go in, go in, my darling girl' (p. 139). Although his parental treatment could be read as an attempt to regain authority (after Aurora's impressive overpowering of the Softy), the use of childish metaphors links Aurora's 'beautiful fury' with the infantile stages of her development; stages, as we have seen, that were unaccompanied by the watchful influence of a mother. As with Lady Audley's mother, therefore, Eliza Floyd (despite her total absence from the text) is held accountable for the violence inflicted by her daughter.

Such also seems to be the central message contained in the earlier novel *The Trail of the Serpent*. Braddon draws on mid-century concerns with child murder to construct the melodramatic story of the text's villain, Jabez North. Jabez, a twin, is cast as a baby into the river Sloshy because his slum-living mother can only afford to raise one of her illegitimate offsprings. He is subsequently rescued by a fisherman and raised by the parish of Slopperton-on-the-Sloshy. His twin, Jim Lomax, is meanwhile raised to the best of his mother's abilities. Jim becomes a poor, honest labourer and Jabez turns out to be a dissident social climber. The didactic message of the novel seems to be that, regardless of its economic status, motherly love is an indispensable part of creating healthy, honest children. It is a message, as we have seen, that Braddon chose to echo in the plot of *Aurora Floyd*.

The idea that the actions of the mother have repercussions on the children is corroborated when Jabez's story is rerun by his own son. As a school usher, Jabez seduces a factory girl who later gives birth to a baby boy. In a chapter ironically entitled 'The Healing Waters', Jabez holds an interview with his mistress and refuses to marry her. She consequently throws herself and her baby into the river. The baby is rescued (though his mother is not) and aptly named 'Slosh'. The river after which he is named is described as follows:

> It has quite a knack of swelling and bursting, this Sloshy; it overflows its banks and swallows up a house or two, or takes an impromptu snack off

a few outbuildings, once or twice a year. It is inimical to children, and has been known to suck into its muddy bosom the hopes of divers families; and has afterwards gone down to the distant sea, flaunting on its breast Billy's straw hat or Johnny's pinafore, as a flag of triumph for having done a little amateur business for the gentleman on the pale horse.

(p. 32)

This Dickensian description employs the period's ideas on the demonic potential of the maternal role. Its characterisation of the Sloshy as overflowing, bursting, and swelling, for example, echoes concurrent constructions of puerperal mania, while references to drowned babies echoes the period's preoccupations with child mortality and infanticide. Its allusions to the river's 'muddy bosom' and 'breast', plus references to sucking, invoke the image of breast-feeding. These are combined with more gruesome, cannibalistic notions of the maternal role as the river 'snacks' on outbuildings and 'sucks' infants in. *The Trail of the Serpent* appears to concur with wider assumptions that there was a thin boundary between maternal care and maternal violence. As with the cases outlined in chapter one, the story of Jabez and his unloved son appears to create links between motherhood and murder.

In her excellent study of child murder, however, Josephine McDonagh has observed how Chartist sympathisers of the 1830s and 1840s represented the trope as a 'political act of sacrifice'.[22] She reveals how the image of the impoverished mother, murdering her baby because she was unable to afford its maintenance, became a poignant, heart-rending signifier of slum misery and social oppression for poor-law commentators. The radical Chartist preacher, Joseph Raynor Stephens, for example, reported in one of his sermons how he

had read the other day of one young woman who took her little child, and, with a bandage, fastened it round her bosom, and plunged herself and her baby into a stream, and as they could not live together, they must die, and trust to God's pity, rather than to man's mercy (great sensation) [...] she must either take herself to the Bastile, and be kept a prisoner all her life, and have the baby taken from her either to be poisoned or strangled, or cut up alive or dead by the damned doctors, or sent abroad to the plantations, – she must do all that, or bind her baby to her broken heart, and together with it plunge into the stream and die.[23]

For Stephens's 'young woman', the double act of infanticide and suicide is the dutiful last resort of a loving mother in an unfeeling and tyrannical social regime. In *The Trail of the Serpent*, Braddon also uses the image of child murder in order to create a more ambivalent attitude towards nineteenth-century class ideology. In a ghastly conversion of the portraits of Ophelia that were concurrently appearing on the nation's gallery walls (which Helen

Small terms an 'Ophelian industry'[24]) the distracted factory girl presents a markedly different portrait of love-madness:

> The woman's baby is fretful, and it may be that the damp foggy atmosphere on the banks of the Sloshy is scarcely calculated to engender either high spirits or amiable temper in the bosom of infant or adult. The woman hushes it impatiently to her breast and looks down at the little puny features with a strange unmotherly glance. Poor wretch! Perhaps she scarcely thinks of that little load as a mother is apt to think of her child. She may remember it only as a shame, a burden, and a grief. She has been pretty; a bright country beauty perhaps, a year ago; but she is a faded, careworn-looking creature now, with a pale face, and hollow circles round her eyes.
>
> (p. 33)

Like Menamenee and Ophelia, whose excessive passions for Roderick and Hamlet lead them to the brink of 'a dismal pool', the girl in this scene is driven to the banks of the Sloshy through her amorous yearnings. Although Braddon's 'poor wretch' does not have the same level of affection for her baby as Stephens's 'young woman', the description of her on the banks of the river is calculated to produce the same level of sympathy. Similarly, whereas Stephens has confidence in this sympathy producing a subsidiary animosity towards the social regime that has led his 'young woman' to the murky waters, Braddon's portrait of the factory girl's suicidal infanticide has the effect of casting Jabez, the man who seduced her, in a very unflattering light.

As Valerie de Cevennes is later driven to crime through Jabez's desire for her wealth, so does the factory girl appear to fall victim to his social ambitions. The interview between the girl and Jabez prior to her infanticide and suicide is symbolically represented as a card game. As in his later bribery of Valerie, which is called 'the game', the factory girl, we are informed, 'has played the only game a woman has to play, and lost the only stake a woman has to lose' (p. 33). Throughout the conversation, Jabez plays with a deck of playing cards:

> He took up the dog's-eared cards on the sticky table before him, and began to build a house with them, such as children build in their play. [...] Jabez's card-house had risen to three stories; he took the dog's-eared cards one by one in his white hands with a slow deliberate touch that never faltered. [...] He counted four sovereigns on the sticky table, and then, adding the sixth story to his card-house, looked at the frail erection with a glance of triumph.
>
> 'And so will I build my fortune in days to come', he muttered.
>
> (pp. 35–7)

Jabez's house of cards, a metaphor for his social aspirations, is, like Luke Mark's inn, described as a 'frail erection' and is built upon the passions of the woman he controls. As with Luke, we could read Jabez as a representative of the Victorian rising class. Born in the slums and eventually accruing millions, he personifies the industrialist's dream of self-made status.

As with Luke's 'frail erection', however, Jabez's fortunes are infected with the taint of destruction. Although the novel's detective, Joseph Peters, orchestrates the villain's downfall, his losses hinge entirely on the actions of the factory girl during the interview prior to her death. Jabez makes the mistake of assuming that the factory girl is driven by pecuniary motives like himself: 'How much do you expect?' he asks her and offers her four sovereigns. Her reaction is both explosive and retaliatory:

> 'I would go to the black river for pity and help rather than to you'. As she said this, she threw the sovereigns into his face with such a strong and violent hand, that one of them, striking him above the eyebrow, cut his forehead to the bone, and brought the blood gushing over his eyes.
>
> (p. 38)

Detective Peters enters the room during the interview and knocks down the cards: 'the house of cards shivered, and fell in a heap on the table' (p. 37). It is noteworthy how the cards display the hysterical symptom of shivering before collapsing. It echoes how Luke's 'frail erection' similarly shakes and totters in the wind. Like Alfred Taylor, who was unmanned by a female assailant while visiting the Charenton, Jabez's misjudgement of the factory girl leads to a similar assault on his masculinity. Besides the suggestive collapse of his 'frail erection', for example, the scar on his eye brands him with a particularly feminine image. Remember how the Softy fantasises about Aurora Floyd's throat being laid open, streaming oceans of blood. It is a menstrual image echoed by the gushing slit in Jabez's forehead. Indeed, the scar is also somewhat scarlet-letter-like in its indication of Jabez's sexual indiscretions. The rebellious violence of Slosh's mother, combined with that of Valerie's later, instigates a chain of events that ultimately culminates in the loss of Jabez's millions and his social pretensions. The scar links Jabez to the sovereign, which was appropriated in a murderous robbery he committed the night before meeting the factory girl. Hence, although the novel reproduces some of the era's associations of maternity with violence, it also explores how these associations have another link with the aspirations of social climbers. Their 'frail erections', moreover, those shivering houses of cards connotative of masculine economic and social achievement, seem to be as pathological as the very women they exploit.

As I explored in chapter one, Victorian mothers were suspected of being capable of inflicting violence on the body of society through less overt means like bringing up children erroneously or transmitting morbid hereditary influences. In his 1979 biography of Mary Braddon, *Sensational Victorian*, Robert Lee Wolff argues that the novelist's later, twentieth-century fictions, which emerged in the wake of Oscar Wilde's exile and the advent of psychoanalysis, demonstrated a thematic concern with the effete male and the role played by maternity in producing that figure.[25] From the early 1860s, however, Braddon's fictions articulate the same concern which, I argue, was drawn from earlier negotiations of heredity and faulty maternal management.

In *Lady Lisle* (1862), for example, Rupert Lisle, a boy-baronet, is loved immoderately by his nervous mother Claribel: 'She was [...] passionately fond of her son, and to him she devoted herself entirely'.[26] Such immoderation, Claribel's second husband believes, has gone a long way towards spoiling the child:

> 'You spoil your child, Claribel', said the Captain, when the boy was gone.
> 'How could I help it? He is all I have had to love'.
> 'He is a pretty boy, but he does not look strong'.
> 'No; he is not strong. That is the one reason why I let him have his own way a great deal. The physicians tell me he must not be opposed. He is such a nervous child'.
>
> (p. 12)

The Lisles, like the St Johns in *St. Martin's Eve*, are a race of men who have succumbed to 'a lingering decline, [a] wasting away'. The family's males have, one by one, died from a 'kind of disease [...] before they had attained their thirtieth year, leaving only sons to inherit the title and property' (p. 22). Nevertheless, the text accounts for the boy-baronet's nervousness in his mother's immoderate pampering and *her* nervous biological legacy:

> [Rupert was] a pale-faced delicate boy of six years of age, resembling his mother both in person and disposition; like her, quiet and unimpulsive, like her unblest with brilliant talents or energy of character.
>
> (p. 22)

With such a compound of debilitating causes, Rupert is clearly ill-equipped to carry the burden of his aristocratic lineage. As the novel narrates:

> It was strange, after this constant recurrence of the ancient name, this wide extension of the grandeur and wealth of the house of Lisle, to come back to Lislewood Park and find the sole owner of so vast a heritage a little boy of seven years old, with a pale sickly face and languid girlish manners. [...] Had all these strong and valiant men left only this feeble, fair-haired child to inherit their wealth and honours? It seemed almost as if the weight of this vast inheritance, falling solely upon a helpless orphan, must surely crush and destroy him. There was something sinister and

unnatural in the child's lonely splendour. [...] The boy-baronet seemed to languish under a load of grandeur, and to sicken of a surfeit of prosperity.

(pp. 26–7)

In its representation of the relationship between Claribel Lisle and her son, and the wider implications this has for Rupert's ancestral role, *Lady Lisle* allows biological and social categories to bleed into each other. The novel suggests, for example, that the idea of 'strong and valiant men' leaving their property to a boy with 'languid and girlish manners' is 'sinister and unnatural', a delineation that supports Victorian claims that nervous inheritances were poisoning the nation's health. The novel's emphasis on the weak and sickly corporeal frame of Rupert, in addition to the idiomatic references to inheritance and excess, suggest that Claribel's 'idoliz[ation]' (p. 38) of the boy-baronet and *her* inheritance of nervousness, have threatened and weakened the Lisle aristocratic ancestry. In keeping with the period's ideas on heredity and the part played by mothers in the nation's health, *Lady Lisle* suggests that a sickly maternal influence can indeed poison, debilitate, and destroy patriarchal structures like the Lisle lineage.

In addition to men who are ill-equipped, physically, to carry the weight of their forefathers' achievements, excessive maternal devotion, in Braddon's fiction, also produces men who appear to be a monstrous infringement of the period's accepted social and gender categories. Braddon's *The Captain of the Vulture* (1862), for example, features the story of the working-class Sarah Pecker and her son. Sarah's child, like Rupert Lisle, is idolised by his mother. 'I had my boy', she tells another character, 'such a beautiful boy, with great black eyes and dark curly hair – and I was happy as the day was long while all went well with him'.[27] Then later, it is added, 'being left alone with [her son], she lay perfectly still for some moments, looking – ah, Heaven only knows with what vague maternal love and yearning! – at the sharp profile of that young face' (p. 282). Sarah's sentimental description of her boy indicates the excessive love she has for him. Years later, the boy, now a man, is portrayed as a gender- and class-transgressing abnormality:

In an easy chair before the open hearth lolled an effeminate-looking young man, in a brocade dressing-gown, silk stockings with embroided clocks, and shoes adorned with red heels and glittering diamond buckles that emitted purple and rainbow sparks in the firelight. He wore a flaxen wig, curled and frizzed to such a degree that it stood away from his face, round which it formed a pale-yellow frame, contrasting strongly with a pair of large restless black eyes and the blue stubble upon his slender chin.

(pp. 97–8)

The description's emphasis on the feminine qualities of Sarah's son is unmistakable: the silk, the embroidery, the jewellery, the wig. As if it was needed, additional evidence can be found in his highly suggestive nickname 'Captain Fanny', which he is given 'on account of his small hands and feet and his lackadaisical ways' (p. 103). Such effeminate traits, however, are highly inconsistent with the stubble that (supposedly) identifies him as a man. Born of humble parents, Captain Fanny parades himself as Sir Lovell Mortimer, a west-country baronet. As such, he not only flouts gender distinctions, but compromises class boundaries as well. Indeed, Fanny is a grown-up version of the biological monstrosities mentioned repeatedly in the period's medical textbooks. Whereas the emotional immoderations of women like Mrs E and Mrs C (mentioned in chapter one) produced babies resembling frogs and bearing other abnormalities, Sarah Pecker's excessive love for her boy has produced a creature that is not easily identifiable as masculine or feminine, working class or aristocratic.

Such ideas appear to drive the mercenary motivations of *Lady Lisle*'s villain, Major Varney. Like Jabez North, Varney is of humble origins but manages to amass a fortune by exploiting a perceived similarity between two of the novels young characters. Echoing the plot of *The Woman in White* (1860), Varney exchanges Rupert with the son of Gilbert Arnold, the baronet's lodge-keeper. Like the latter, James Arnold inherits a sickly disposition from his mother: 'the Arnolds have only one child, a sickly precocious boy, six years old, with light flaxen hair, and a pale sharp face, resembling his mother, and entirely unlike his stalwart dark-complexioned father' (p. 35). As with the likeness between the wealthy Laura Fairlie and the poor Anne Catherick, it is only the rich garments of Rupert that tell him apart from this plebeian waif:

> The long curls of the Baronet, and James Arnold's closely-cropped hair, were of the same flaxen shade. Both the boys had light-blue eyes, pale faces, and sharp but delicate features; but so great was the distinction made by the rich dress and flowing locks of one, and the ungainly garments and close-cut hair of the other, that the careless observer lost sight of the striking resemblance between the children.
>
> (p. 65)

Unlike *The Woman in White*, however, the likeness between Rupert and James is purely coincidental. So complete are the boys' similarities that Major Varney is able to switch the boys with the intention of bribing James once he has come of age. Varney buys James Arnold from his parents and falsifies the death of Rupert, sending him to a Yorkshire boarding school where his childhood memories are disregarded as insane hallucinations. Knowing that Claribel Lisle, Rupert's mother, will realise the fraud if introduced to James straight away, Varney waits years before uniting the mother with her *impostor* son. Typically, Lady Lisle's emotions at this 'reunion' are excessive:

> 'O let me see him! Take me to him, I implore you! Now – this moment – this very moment! The suspense will kill me!'

'My dear madam, I rely upon your Christian forbearance – your self-control. This is not a matter in which impulse can serve us. One rash step might destroy all. Patience and caution are vitally necessary to us. [...] I shall trust entirely to your instinct as a mother. See him, talk to him, examine every feature. Watch every look, and if after that you say to me 'Granville Varney, that young man is my son, Sir Rupert Lisle', I will move heaven and earth to prove the young man's identity to the world, and to reinstate him in his rights.

(pp. 126–7)

What we observe in this passage are mid-Victorian ideologies of self-control set into fictional form. Varney warns Claribel, the immoderate mother, that 'self-control', 'patience', and 'caution' are needed instead of 'impulse'. In so speaking, he reiterates Victorian claims that passions like Claribel's 'instinct[s] as a mother' must be curtailed in favour of temperate moderation. Unsurprisingly, Lady Lisle faints under the weight of her maternal emotions and, on being left alone, Varney utters, 'poor thing! And all this about a pale-faced child. Who would ever think that there was so much sickly sentimentality in the world?' (p. 122) Of course, the word 'sickly' has two overlapping connotations. On the one hand, it defines a form of surfeit and effusiveness, while, on the other, it communicates ideas of pathology and disease. Claribel's immoderate 'sentimentality' for the 'pale-faced child', in mid-Victorian eyes, qualifies for both definitions. As Varney anticipates, Claribel's longing for her son clouds her ability to notice the impostor. Her 'reunion' with the boy, now a man, is a tableau worthy of the period's theatrical melodramas: Claribel 'uttered a faint scream, and rushing to the bed, fell on her knees, and lifting the fair face in her arms, kissed the young man's forehead passionately' (p. 130). In apparent support for the era's ideas on emotion, the aristocratic Lady Claribel is unable to maintain the rules of self-control and caution advocated by Major Varney. Yet, what is significant about Braddon's text is how it sets these ideas against the mercenary schemes of yet another social climber. Varney not only capitalises on Claribel's excessive passions, but he also profits from the perceived likeness between Rupert and James. *Lady Lisle* thus makes complex use of a nineteenth-century ideology. The self-made Varney exploits an apparent breach between the classes in order to advance *himself* socially. As such, his actions echo those of the self-made man. From the bourgeois point of view, aristocrats and the working classes shared a lack of control. The physical deformities testifying to the poor's way of life, for example, were mirrored by those in the upper classes, whose gouty bodies often bore witness to their lack of control. The bourgeois class distinguished itself from such immoderations in order to promote a view of itself as the controlled and successful ruling class of Britain.

The story of James Arnold and Major Varney, however, is, like Jabez North's, a narrative of thwarted social climbing and the inescapability of class destiny. While James exchanges his 'ungainly garments' for the 'rich dress' of Rupert Lisle, the text suggests that there is more to a baronetcy than semiotic exterior. Once he has come of age, James's true mother, Rachel, visits him. His wealthy guests, familiar with the Lisle family history, witness him striking his mother. Although they believe she is an unrelated beggar, they are shocked with how out of key his violence is with the preceding Lisle chivalry:

> 'I call the exposure of to-day a very awful thing, sir', whispered an elderly man to his neighbour at the dinner-table, 'for I take it as a sign of the deterioration in the blood of our great county families. The Lisles, sir, have been accounted the noblest gentlemen in Sussex for upwards of six hundred years, and I can assure you the conduct of that young man to-day was a severe blow to my feelings.'
>
> (p. 210)

James's wife, Olivia, who marries him for his title and fortune, discovers from his injured mother her husband's true identity and class origins:

> 'Why, look at him!' [Olivia] cried, with passionate vehemence, pointing to her husband as she spoke – 'look at him, as he sits there in his stupid drunkenness – more brutal than the oxen that sleep in his fields – lower than the lowest brute in his stables. Good heavens! What a pitiful dupe I must have been to have been deceived by such a thing as that!' She burst into an hysterical laugh as she looked with ineffable contempt at the young man.
>
> (p. 241)

Even Major Varney, the man to whom James owes his appropriated fortunes and station, tells him: 'you are no more fit for society than those who reared you. Though your own cellars are full of the finest wine in England, you are such a sot by nature, that you can't see a few bottles of champagne without getting drunk' (p. 280). In these three statements, the novel draws on the theme of hereditary psychology, which it first introduced in representing Rupert's nervous legacy from his mother. The 'elderly man' interprets James's savagery as a 'deterioration in the blood' of the Lisles, while Major Varney suggests that what James is 'by nature' can never be glossed over. This is literally represented by the return of James's father. Savage and uncouth, Gilbert Arnold eventually kills both Major Varney and his son. Before shooting the former in the face, he cries:

> 'I told you', he shrieked, 'I told you to look out, if ever I came back from the place you sent me to. I told you to beware, and I told you true. I've come back. I've come back through toil, and trouble, and starvation. I've

come back for the one end of my wicked life. I've come back to murder you, and I'll do it!'

(p. 287)

James's father declares, an emphatic five times, that he has 'come back' to ruin his son's, and Varney's, social aspirations. This return of the working-class father ventriloquises the novel's wider inference that such social climbing as James's is an impossibility, as is the eradication of one's congenital heritage. One might easily read this as a conservative suggestion – the claim that social demarcations are inescapable and, once born into a certain class, one is destined to remain there. Yet, when we bear in mind that the vision of cross-class migration formed a significant part of the unwritten laws governing the middle class and its marginalisation of women, *Lady Lisle*'s apparent determination to deny such class mobility can also be read as a complex comment on a mid-Victorian hegemony.

Such thematic preoccupations with the alleged social threat of maternity are also a central feature of Braddon's short story 'Lost and Found'. Published in *Ralph the Bailiff and other Stories* (1864), the text explores the possible dangers of wet-nursing. The aristocratic Gervoise Gilbert and the working-class Humphrey Melwood are both 'wet-nursed by Mrs Melwood, [...] Humphrey Melwood's mother'.[28] In portraying the adult relationship between Gervoise and Humphrey as unnaturally close and homoerotic, Braddon makes full use of mid-nineteenth-century fears that wet-nursing eroded the congenital and biological boundaries between the upper and lower classes. Humphrey observes to his 'foster-brother' (p. 190), for example, that 'there's that between you and me, Master Gervoise, that's stronger than blood, I sometimes think. [...] We slept upon the same breast when we were children together' (p. 197). He adds that 'the difference between our rank can't alter the feelings of our hearts, you know, Mr Gervoise' (p. 197). Such cross-class breast-feeding was common practise during the mid-Victorian period. In *Infant Feeding*, Charles Routh conceded that well-born children are

> sent to the country to wet nurses, for the most part married women, with a baby of their own to suckle besides; and these women keep them during the period usually allotted to suckling, and for some time afterwards, and so bring them up.[29]

In 'Lost and Found', the nursing of Gervoise and Humphrey at the same breast has created an unnaturally intimate relationship between the two men and, as the story progresses, they become two sides to the same character. As with Jekyll and Hyde, Humphrey fulfils the demonic, semiconscious desires of Gervoise. It is a relationship, as we shall see in chapter five, echoed by that of Ozias Midwinter and Allan Armadale in Collins's *Armadale* (1866). Soon after he inherits a peerage, Gervoise is pursued by his working-class, alcoholic wife, Agnes, whom he married when struggling to sustain an artistic career in London. Desiring to be free of his wife in order to marry a wealthy heiress, Gervoise encourages Humphrey, through a grim form of telepathy, to murder Agnes. Humphrey tells him:

> 'Never mind about to-morrow morning, Master Gervoise. There's a long time between this and the hour of your wedding. Something may happen – to – take this woman – out of your way – between this and then'. [...] Gervoise started up out of his chair, and looked at Humphrey Melwood with a strange expression – an expression in which a wild and sudden horror was mingled with a wild and sudden joy.
> 'What do you mean?' he cried, in a half broken voice. 'You don't mean – you don't mean that – '
>
> (p. 239)

The half-finished sentences and pregnant pauses suggest that one half of the foster-brotherhood understands what the other is intending to say without him having to speak. When he later confesses to murdering Agnes, Humphrey implies that there was a non-verbal communication between the two men:

> 'But he asked you?' cried Margery Melwood; 'he tempted you to do it?'
> 'By no word, mother; by neither word nor look. He did not tempt me it was my own love for him that tempted me. But he knew what I was going to do'.
> 'He knew it?'
> 'Yes, mother, as well as I knew the thought that was in my own mind'.
>
> (p. 291)

Typical of Braddon's fiction, 'Lost and Found' is a narrative that figures this unnatural complicity between Gervoise and Humphrey as having firm links with the social ambition of at least one character in the text. In having his wife murdered by Humphrey, Gervoise takes full advantage of the 'telepathic' understanding between his foster-brother and himself, preserving his position as the Earl of Haughton and becoming free to marry the well-dowered Ethel.

These psychological connections between Gervoise and Humphrey, however, are also the means through which the story achieves its moral closure; Gervoise's psychic links with Humphrey become the source of his ruin as well as the source of his fortunes. Although it is Humphrey who murders Agnes, it is Gervoise who carries the full weight of the guilt. He admits later: 'it was my own sin [...] the full burden of it rest[s] upon me' (p. 300). The guilt is characterised as follows:

> The memory of that night before the wedding at Pendon Church was forever present to Gervoise Palgrave's mind; he started from his sleep

sometimes with a shrill hysterical cry, and the cold drops of agony upon his forehead. [...] Then the worst horror of a guilty conscience began. Gervoise Palgrave knew that he was watched; he knew that curiosity was already aroused, and that the scorpion slander would soon lift its venomous head, rampant, unappeasable, to claim its wretched victim.

(p. 278)

As the passage's reference to hysteria indicates, Gervoise's guilt becomes psychosomatic and has 'a fatal effect upon Lord Haughton's physical health. His strength ebbed away' (p. 278). Whereas the psychical connections between Gervoise and Humphrey were originally created through the biological channels of wet-nursing, the situation is now reversed as *mental* guilt becomes a *somatic* malady. As one character observes to Gervoise's second wife:

Your husband is ill, you say? Shall I tell you why he is ill? Shall I tell you the nature of his disease? He is sinking under the burden of a guilty conscience. It is remorse which is sapping at the very roots of his life. Judge for yourself whether it is any common disorder which has stricken him down.

(p. 280)

The Earl's guilt is also linked to the estate he retained by having Agnes killed. Palgrave Chase, his stately country mansion becomes, for him, a Gothic, nightmarish place: 'The Earl of Haughton thought of this place as he might have thought of some black and gloomy mansion in which he had dreamed of wandering in some hideous nightmare vision' (p. 273). Approaching the house for the first time since the murder, he exclaims,

I think that the shadow will never be lifted from the dwellers in yonder house. [...] I have heard it said that no Palgrave has ever known happiness since Rupert Palgrave, the Hanoverian, betrayed his Jacobite brother more than a hundred years ago.

(p. 275)

The estate that Gervoise retained by exploiting the foster-brotherhood between himself and Humphrey is now cursed by the brotherly bond of its previous occupants. Biological links, this passage suggests, cannot erase social differences; whereas the fraternal bond between the Jacobite and Hanoverian brothers failed to reconcile their political conflicts, so the wet-nursing links between Gervoise and Humphrey, the text suggests, will never reconcile their diverse class roots. As Humphrey admits in his confession: 'I suppose the gipsy blood that's in me makes me different' (p. 290). Hence, from Braddon's exploitation of her era's fears regarding wet-nursing, and the belief that it was eroding the boundaries between the classes, there emerges a suggestion that draws on and transforms those concerns. While 'Lost and Found' appears to support the notion that wet-nursing could be a vehicle for transmitting psychological traits, Braddon's short story also suggests that traditional class margins are insurmountable – even by this problematic biological exchange.

Uncultivated waste: Post-menopausal women

In an 1862 article appearing alongside *Aurora Floyd* in *Temple Bar*, Eliza Lynn Linton argued that the 'wasted energies' of ageing 'maidenhood' are a terrible thing. Perhaps, she adds, the French custom of confining unmarried women to a convent is 'not so terrible a system after all; and [that] our own habit of letting our unmarried women ramble uncontrolled through the wildest paths, is scarcely so conducive to happiness as it would seem'.[30] Linton's article drew on the prevalent notion that older women were a coarse leftover. The article in *Blackwood's*, for example, which referred to ageing spinsters as 'uncultivated waste', questioned, from the spinster's perspective,

> have not the wives of England husbands to whisper wisdom into their ears? Why, then, are *they* to be coaxed or lectured by tabby-bound volumes, while we are left neglected in a corner? *Our* earthly career, the Lord he knows, is far more trying – *our* temptations are much greater. [...] We may conduct ourselves, it seems, as indecorously as we think proper.[31]

As cited in chapter one, Eliza Linton extended the 'uncultivated waste' delineation to include married women and mothers who, having reached a certain maturity, became surplus to requirements: 'The happy home grows dull and dead, for its merry ghosts have all departed'.[32] The female role, once considered fertile and sweet, is viewed as becoming dead and decrepit once its halcyon days are over.

Whether married or unmarried, therefore, the post-menopausal woman was seen to become superfluous to the domestic and sexual ideologies of the mid-nineteenth century. It seems that she likewise became surplus to Braddon's creative economy. Like most Victorian novels, none of Braddon's early texts feature a post-climacteric woman in a central role. For Braddon's sensational style, the hysterical passions of younger women like Valerie de Cevennes and Aurora Floyd seemed better suited, and older women are thus edged into the margins of her plots.

Yet, it would be inaccurate to suggest that older women have no place in Braddon's novels. While no mature women play the eponymous central role, the figure is nevertheless an important cog in the novelist's fictional exploration of her era's concept of femininity. In novels like *The Trail of the Serpent*, for example, Jabez North's hideous grandmother, alongside Valerie and the infanticidal-suicidal factory girl, completes an inglorious, three-pronged representation of female biological development. In one of the text's many unbelievable coincidences, Jabez, wandering aimlessly though the slum district of Slopperton-on-the-Sloshy, finds himself face to face with his maternal grandmother:

> [Jabez] strolls through two or three dingy, narrow, old-fashioned streets, till he comes to a labyrinth of tumble-down houses, pigstyes, and dog-kennels, known as Blind Peter's Alley. [...] The alley was a reality, and a dirty loathsome fetid reality [...] a refuge for crime and destitution. [...] Blind Peter has risen to popularity once or twice – on the occasion of a girl poisoning her father in the crust of a beef-steak pudding. [...] Jabez pursued his way past the mouth of Blind Peter – which was adorned by two or three broken-down and rusty iron railings that looked like jagged teeth – when he was suddenly arrested by a hideous-looking woman.
>
> (pp. 74–5)

Like Audley Court, Blind Peter has earned notoriety as the site of murder. As it was alleged against Madeline Smith and Constance Kent, a young girl is reputed to have made the place infamous by murdering one of her nearest relatives. As with Luke's penetration of Lady Audley's chambers, Jabez's 'plunging into the dirty obscurity of Blind Peter' (p. 75), on the 'out*skirts*' of Slopperton, is heavily invested with sexual overtones. The point where Jabez negotiates entering the 'mouth of Blind Peter', which is beset with 'iron railings that looked like jagged teeth', for example, is yet another foreshadowing of the 'vagina dentata' image.[33] As with Luke's poking of the embers, Franklin's penetration of the Shivering Sands, and Roderick's hewing of the monster tree, Jabez's entrance into the slums is committed with eagerness and disgust. The difference between this scene and Braddon's earlier symbolic uses of the penetration metaphor is that Blind Peter is a site inundated with decay, refuse, and waste. Whereas Roderick violates an environment that is green, flush, and fertile, Jabez enters 'a dirty, loathsome fetid reality', awash with 'pigstyes, and dog-kennels'. Later in the text, Jabez, now a millionaire, reencounters his grandmother though this time it is in the more recognisable London slums:

> Heaven forbid that we should follow [him] through all the turnings and twistings of that odoriferous neighbourhood, where foul scents, foul sights, and fouler language abound. [...Jabez] walked very quickly through the pestiferous streets [...] holding his breath and shutting his patrician ears to the scents and the sounds around him. [...He] ascend[s] to the very top of a rickety house, the garrets of which are afflicted with

intermittent ague, whenever there is a high wind. [...] Eight years, more or less, have not certainly had the effect of enhancing the charms of this lady; and there is something in her face to-day more terrible even than wicked old age or feminine drunkenness.

(pp. 292–3)

The Old 'Crone' (p. 86) is once again positioned at the heart of an environment immersed in vice, waste, and disease. Jabez's entrance of the London slums echoes his admission into Blind Peter. He averts his senses ('holding his breath and shutting his patrician ears') at the point of entry. The slum is also represented using pathological, biological registers as the building Jabez enters is 'afflicted with intermittent ague'. Taken in conjunction with the novel's portraits of Valerie and the factory girl, *The Trail of the Serpent*'s representation of Jabez's grandmother completes an extraordinary, triangular portrait of womanhood highlighting how the three milestones in female organic life – maidenhood, motherhood, and old age – were firmly associated with images of sexuality, disorder, and violence for the Victorians.

As with her representations of the Old Crone's younger counterparts, however, Braddon ties the characterisation of the old woman in with the economic ambitions of Jabez. Unlike Valerie and the ill-fated factory-girl, however, the Old Crone not only stands between her grandson and a fortune (by withholding knowledge that he is the son of a Marquis), but turns that information into financial gain for herself. Having threatened to 'lay the whole force of [his] ten very rough fingers upon the most vital part of the grinning hag's anatomy' (p. 83), Jabez is reminded by his grandmother:

Kill me, and you'll never know the secret! – the secret that may be gold to *you* some day, and that nobody alive but me can tell. If you've got some very precious wine in a glass bottle, my dear, you wouldn't smash the bottle now, would you? because, you see, you couldn't smash the bottle without spilling the wine.

(p. 83)

The use of the wine metaphor invokes Jabez's relationship with Valerie who is likewise compared to a glass of 'spilling' Madeira. While the metaphor brings the two women under the light of comparison, however, it also highlights the key differences between them. Valerie has little or no control over her abundant energies, revealing her passionate secrets to the observant Jabez; the Old Crone, by direct contrast, keeps the cork on *her* secrets and is able to capitalise on them to her own advantage. 'I must be paid for that secret in gold', she says, 'yes, in gold. They say that we don't rest any easier in our coffins for the money that's buried with us; but I should like to lie up to my neck in golden sovereigns new from the Mint, and not one light one amongst 'em' (p. 294).

Likewise, in Braddon's *Eleanor's Victory* (1863), two old maids, the De Crespigny sisters, stand between the villain, Launcelot Darrell, and *his* attempt at social climbing. He hopes to be the sole inheritor of his uncle's property, yet the two old ladies never let the aging man out of their sight. As Launcelot's fiancé remarks:

> His two aunts who live at Woodlands are nasty, scheming old maids, and they contrived to keep him away from his great-uncle, Mr. de Crespigny, who is expected to leave him all his money. [...] But those two cantankerous old-maids [...] are nagging at the old man night and day, and they may persuade him at last, or they may have succeeded in persuading him, perhaps, ever so long ago, to make a will in their favour.[34]

Older women, Braddon's novels appear to suggest, are free to pursue their own aspirations of wealth. Such ambitions not only offer men like Jabez and Launcelot no pecuniary advantage, but also, it appears, challenge the pecuniary schemes of the social climber. I am not meaning to argue that, in Braddon's fiction, the old woman stands forth as a paradigm of female independence. Although her self-interest and refusal to be a 'fitting tool' in the hands of men could be read as an enlightened portrait of femininity, we cannot ignore how the same representation concurs with the contemporaneous medical opinion that post-climacteric women often developed grotesque and irrational predilections. Jabez's grandmother's absurd wish to be buried in gold sovereigns, for example, is like Miss Havisham's 'sick fancies' or Christiana Edmunds's apparent obsession with poisoning the infant population of Brighton. 'You think me a very unnatural old woman?' the Old Crone asks Jabez. 'It wouldn't be so strange if I did' (p. 84), he unsurprisingly replies.

In some of her non-fictional, journalistic pieces of the 1860s, however, Braddon does develop a more compassionate attitude towards older women, which one can observe being integrated into her fiction. In an article for *Temple Bar* in 1861, for example, she observes how, in households built around a mismatched marriage, there are 'domestic difficulties, [...] domestic quarrels, [...] anxieties attendant on the health, moral and physical, on the lives and prospects of husband and children' and continues,

> from all, or nearly all, these evils the single woman – the old maid, if you will – is free; and if she misses the near and dear ties, the exclusive protection and tender care which her married sister may (or may not) have found in marriage, she can yet find many objects besides dogs, cats, and parrots – though harmless solace may be won from these – round which to twine the loving tendrils that stretch from her heart, anxious to find something round which to cling tenderly.[35]

As with much of our understanding of Braddon's social opinions, the ambiguous tone of the passage renders its true message an obscure one. Is, for example, its argument in earnest; or is it meant to be flippant and humorous? It is perhaps not insignificant that, at the time the article was written, Braddon was living, unmarried, with John Maxwell, the proprietor of *Temple Bar*. Being herself a spinster, it would not be out of place for Braddon to defend the nation's unmarried women. Even Eliza Linton, who at this time had separated from *her* husband, accounted for the sourness of old maids by arguing that some mitigating circumstance is the cause of bitterness: such women, she writes, are 'thoroughly soured by disappointment [...] wasted energies and disappointed hopes going on [...] for years perhaps'.[36] Despite the fact that she is young and hysterical, these 'wasted energies and disappointed hopes' lie at the centre of Olivia Marchmont's characterisation in *John Marchmont's Legacy*. By the close of the novel, Olivia has become what many Victorian readers would have considered an old maid. Like Miss Ainley and Miss Mann in Charlotte Brontë's *Shirley* (1849), Olivia's life, subsequent to the tempestuous events in the novel, is fully determined by charitable works and routine:

> Day by day she went the same round from cottage to cottage, visiting the sick; teaching little children, or sometimes rough-bearded men, to read and write and cipher; reading to old decrepid pensioners; listening to long histories of sickness and trial, and exhibiting an unwearying patience that was akin to sublimity. Passion had burnt itself out in this woman's breast, and there was nothing in her mind now but remorse, and the desire to perform a long penance, by reason of which she might in the end be forgiven.
>
> (p. 484)

Olivia's unrequited, immoderate love for Edward, the narrative implies, lies at the root of her old maid's existence of nostalgia and routine. Her smouldering passions have been spent and left a worn-out shell, an 'uncultivated waste'. Thus, as with *Shirley* and *Great Expectations*, *John Marchmont's Legacy* is a novel that explores behind the gorgon exterior of the sour old maid. Similar to Miss Mann's emotive confession to Caroline Helstone in Brontë's novel, and Miss Havisham's penitent grovelling to Pip in Dickens's, Olivia Marchmont's story reveals how the source of the routine, systematic, and bitter life of the old maid figure is a 'passion [that] had burnt itself out'.

Besides the fact that Olivia is a widow, the main difference between Braddon's old 'maid' and those of Dickens and Brontë is that whereas the latter two novelists' sympathetic histories are revealed in retrospect, Braddon's runs concurrently with the text. In *The Captain of the Vulture*, however, Braddon utilises retrospective confession in order to evoke reader sympathy for the middle-aged shrew, Sarah Pecker. As with Olivia, Sarah is not an old *maid* as she is twice married and mother to Captain Fanny. She does, however, bear all the hallmarks of the sour and embittered post-climacteric woman. In portraying Sarah's second husband, for example, the novel implies that her influence has had a poisonous, violent, and debilitating effect on him:

> He had been a much livelier man before his marriage, and [...] the weight of his happiness was too much for him – that he was sinking under the bliss of being allied to so magnificent a creature as Mrs. Samuel Pecker, and [...] his unlooked-for good fortune in the matrimonial line had undermined his health and spirits.
>
> (p. 11)

As with Blind Peter's and the Old Crone's effects on Jabez North, Sarah Pecker has a feminising effect on her husband. She is constantly informing other characters, for example, of his delicate, nervous demeanour:

> He's as full of fancies as the oldest woman in all Cumberland; he's always a-seein' of ghosts and hobgoblins and windin' sheets, and all sorts of dismals [...] and unsettlin' his mind for business and bookkeepin'. I haven't common patience with him, that I han't. He can't pass through the churchyard after dark but honest folks that have had Christian burial must needs come out of their graves to look at him, according to his account – as if any decent corpse would leave a comfortable grave for such as *him*'.
>
> (p. 19, italics in original)

Samuel's visit to the graveyard read like a humorous version of Jabez's visits to the slums. Both men are haunted by irrational fears and experience forms of emasculation relating to their associations with older women.

The relationship between Samuel and his wife is explained, however, in a chapter entitled 'Sally Pecker Lifts the Curtain of the Past'. In that chapter, Sarah reveals the cause of her present Xanthippe-like treatment of her spouse. Her first husband, aptly named Masterson, not only treated her brutally, but separated her from the son she loved excessively:

> 'You see me here, miss, with Samuel, having my own way in everything, and managing of him like; and perhaps it's my recollection of having been ill-used myself, and the thought of what a man can be if once he gets the upper hand, that makes me rather sharp with Pecker. You wouldn't believe I was the same woman, if you'd seen me with Masterson. I was afraid of him, Miss Millicent – I was afraid of him!'

The very recollection of her dead husband seemed to strike terror to the stout heart of the ponderous Sarah. She cowered before the fire, clinging to Millicent as if she would have turned for protection even to that slender reed, and glancing across her shoulder, looked towards the window behind her, as if she expected to see it shaken by some more terrible touch than that of the wind and the rain.

(pp. 88–91)

As I indicated in chapter one, post-menopausal women were often perceived to be dangerous because of their alleged obsessions with past grievances. Like Miss Havisham, old women were understood to invoke old complaints as a means of embittering the present. That same idea is drawn upon and transformed by the above passage from *The Captain of the Vulture*. Although Sarah's recollections deform her current marriage to Samuel, the representation of her looking over her shoulder, expecting to see Masterson behind her, is an image that reveals her rancour to be generated from fear. Like Olivia's love for Edward, Sarah's excessive maternal desire has 'burnt itself out', leaving an embittered carcass. Although her love for Captain Fanny is represented as immoderate and pathological (leading, I argued, to his feminisation), the story of Sarah Pecker, like that of Olivia Marchmont, urges the reader to reassess the sourness and the dangers of the post-climacteric woman. In one of Braddon's most sensitive passages, for example, she mitigates Sarah Pecker's tyranny over her second husband as follows:

The worthy Sarah, in common with many other wives, made a point of scrupulously concealing from her weaker helpmate any tender or grateful feeling that she might entertain for him; being possessed with an ever-present fear that if treated with ordinary civility, he might, to use her own words, try to get the better of her.

(p. 91)

Sarah's characterisation is certainly a powerful one, yet perhaps the most central role played by a post-menopausal woman in Braddon's novels of this period is Mrs Powell, chaperone to Aurora Floyd. Mrs Powell is endowed with a typical old-womanish angularity, ugliness, and fadedness: 'She was a woman with straight light hair, and a lady-like droop of the head [...a] poor faded creature' and a 'grim, pale-faced watch-dog' (p. 51). She also demonstrates the systematic routine of old age as she 'had grown mechanically proficient as a musician and an artist; [and] had a certain parrot-like skill in foreign languages' (p. 51). Unlike Sarah Pecker or Olivia Marchmont, however, whose disappointments and fears are introduced subsequent to a portrait of acidity, Mrs Powell's disappointments are exhibited as the source of her sourness from the moment she is first introduced to the text:

[She] was the widow of an ensign who had died within six months of his marriage, and about an hour and a half before he would have succeeded to some enormous property, the particulars of which were never rightly understood by friends of his unfortunate relict. But vague as the story might be, it was quite clear enough to establish Mrs Walter Powell in life as a disappointed woman.

(p. 51)

Whether her expectations were real or fabricated Mrs Powell is characterised as an 'unfortunate' and disappointed woman, more deserving of sympathy than castigation for her bitter demeanour. Yet the reference to her as a 'relict' has a number of possible meanings. The word shares the same roots as 'relic', which supports the idea of Mrs Powell as a martyr to her past, a saintly relic of her foregone days. On the other hand, however, the word also implies that she is an 'uncultivated waste', a 'burnt out' remainder from the days she spent with her husband. The *Oxford English Dictionary* defines 'relict' as an 'object which has survived in primitive form'. As such, and bearing in mind the prominence of evolutionary theories at the time, 'relict' conveys nuances of atavism and degeneration.[37] Indeed, Mrs Powell's story reads like a reversal of the evolving, sympathetic trajectory of Sarah Pecker's story in *The Captain of the Vulture*. As *Aurora Floyd* progresses, the portrait of the ensign's widow reverts from the pathetic image of a woman damaged by disappointment, into that of a spiteful old maid, wilfully inflicting harm on the younger generations. Mrs Powell hates Aurora:

> She hated her as such slow, sluggish, narrow-minded creatures always hate the frank and generous; hated her as envy will forever hate prosperity. [...] If Mrs Walter Powell had been a duchess, and Aurora a crossing-sweeper, she would have still envied her; she would have envied her glorious eyes and flashing teeth, her imperial carriage and generous soul. This pale, whity-brown-haired woman felt herself contemptible in the presence of Aurora, and she resented the bounteous vitality of this nature which made her conscious of the sluggishness of her own.
>
> (p. 133)

Offsetting the barrenness and 'sluggishness' of her own body, the 'bounteous vitality' of Aurora's fertile sexuality is both the cause and indication of Mrs Powell's slide down the evolutionary scale. Such 'petty spites and jealousies' are responsible, according to Braddon's non-fiction, for the 'low standard of feminine cultivation' in the mid-nineteenth century.[38] Mrs Powell's envy converts her into a lower species than the one she is introduced as. Her exit from the novel, for example, is a remarkably different representation to her entrance. Whereas in the latter she is hypersensitive and overeducated, by the time she is dismissed from Mellish Park, she has degenerated into something reptilian:

> All her viperish nature rose against [Mellish] as he walked up and down the room. [...] Mrs Powell descended to a very commonplace locution, and stooped to the vernacular in her desire to be spiteful. [...] Mrs Powell

rose, pale, menacing, terrible; terrible in the intensity of her wrath, and in the consciousness that she had power to stab the heart of the man who affronted her.

(p. 343)

By the closing scenes of the novel, Mrs Powell lives up to the mid-Victorian idea of post-menopausal women as brooding, infectious, and gorgon-like relicts, stabbing at the vitals of society and challenging its progressive proclivities.

Yet, this portrait of Mrs Powell is, I argue, an example of how Braddon's concerns with her vocation, as sensation novelist, influenced her handling of certain issues within the novels themselves. In an article printed alongside *Aurora Floyd*, Robert Buchanan, writing for a journal that was one of the decade's main vehicles for sensation novels, attacked their perceived antithesis, domestic realism. Calling the latter 'a cancer' that 'no Hippocrates or black doctor can lance [...] out', he added that society thus

> chooses to interest herself in trifles light as air, – not in great social problems. She prefers millinery to metaphysics, photography to poetry, crochet to astronomy. She believes romantic affections, grand passions, to be out of date; but she will go into ecstasies in following the details of a little love-affair.[39]

Braddon utilises similar imagery when representing Mrs Powell:

> With her embroidery in full working order, [she] threaded her needles and snipped away the fragments of her delicate cotton as carefully as if there had been no such thing as crime or trouble in the world, and no higher purpose in life than the achievement of elaborate devices upon French cambric.
>
> (p. 308)

Similarly, just as Braddon refers to realism as 'the dullest namby-pambyism' in her letters to Bulwer,[40] so Aurora notices that her own youth and vitality is 'the very opposite of [Mrs Powell's] namby-pamby pale-faced self' (p. 198). Buchanan also likened an unnamed realist novelist (though one might speculate Anthony Trollope to be his subject) to an old maid:

> Wielding a delicate and fragile quill, and attempting to be intensely pure and feminine, he [has] succeeded in writing like an insipid spinster of fifty. There [is] no flesh and blood in his men and women. They [are] simply colourless puppets shivering on the brink of moral evangelism.[41]

As with the differences between Mrs Powell and Aurora, the insipid, passionless, and fragile realist hardly compares, according to Buchanan, to the 'flesh and blood' style of the sensationist, who was unafraid to hold a looking glass to the true passions of humanity. Realists simply contented themselves with the most trivial of domestic 'scandals':

> [Society] is determined to have the looking-glass of fiction simply a looking-glass, in which she can secretly examine her own follies, flaws, beauties. She is content, therefore, with the reflection of her superficial features – the externals and 'realities' of daily life. Consequently few, if any, of our novelists see farther than the domestic parlour and the drawing-room window.[42]

Mrs Powell, Aurora's enemy 'within her pleasant home [...] forever nursing discontent and hatred within the holy circle of the domestic hearth' seems to be similarly occupied in exposing the trivial scandals of domestic life (p. 141). Buchanan's metaphor of the realist standing at the drawing-room window, for example, receives a fictional rendering in *Aurora Floyd* as Mrs Powell pursues Aurora to the house of James Conyers and spies through the drawing room window: 'Mrs Powell, crouching down beneath the open casement, had heard every word. [...] Half forgetful of all danger in her eagerness to listen, she raised her head until it was nearly on a level with the window sill' (pp. 206–7). Suddenly accompanied in her espionage by the Softy, Mrs Powell finds herself in a particularly compromising encounter:

> She recoiled with a sudden thrill of terror. She felt a puff of hot breath upon her cheek, and the garments of a man rustling against her own.
> She was not the only listener.
> The second spy was Stephen Hargraves the 'Softy'.
> 'Hush!' he whispered, grasping Mrs Powell by the wrist, and pinning her in her crouching attitude by the muscular force of his horny hand. [...] Mrs Powell could hear the laborious beating of his heart in the stillness.
> (p. 207)

The links between Mrs Powell and domestic realism, taken in conjunction with this sexualised scene of surveillance, suggests that the realist tendency of peering through the drawing-room window at the '"realities" of daily life' is more compromisingly meretricious than the passions and newspaper stories that occupied the popular novelist.

Braddon thus finds Victorian ideas on female old age a valuable currency. Such imagery allowed her to enter into debates on whether realism or sensation was the better form of writing. This strategy epitomises, more broadly, how images of female violent behaviour provided Braddon with the means to explore her era's obsession with 'getting on' – a theme, as we shall see, that Mrs Henry Wood also took up in her fictions of the 1860s. Dismissed by many of her contemporaries as a populist hack, Braddon's authorial vision is undoubtedly a complex one. Her works frequently converted a misogynistic view of women's minds and bodies into a protracted and fertile consideration of the actions and motivations of the period's ruling class.

4
'Nest-Building Apes': Female Follies and Bourgeois Culture in the Novels of Mrs Henry Wood

The most extensive analysis of Mrs Wood's fiction, in recent years, has been offered by Deborah Wynne. She has shown how, 'as the daughter of a successful glove manufacturer', Wood is 'well qualified [...] to champion in her fiction the tradesman and entrepreneur'.[1] Wood's novels, she concludes, read like fictional testimonials to the glories of middle-class professionalism. Indeed, this 'championing of the middle classes', as she calls it,[2] concurs with some landmark mid-century texts. In his 1859 *Self Help*, for example, Samuel Smiles reminded his readers of the optimistic view that wealth and respectability were achievable through honest hard work and perseverance. According to this highly popular treatise, the barons and earls of old were being gradually replaced by a 'modern', industrial class of up and coming professionals:

> The great bulk of our peerage is comparatively modern, so far as titles go; but it is not the less noble that is has been recruited to so large an extent from the ranks of honourable industry. [...] The modern dukes of Northumberland find their head, not in the Percys, but in Hugh Smithson, a respectable London apothecary.[3]

Such enthusiastic anticipations of bourgeois success, however, are only one side of the mid-Victorian attitudes towards middle-class development. That same year, Darwin published the *Origin of Species* (1859) and, although its overall tone communicated ideas of evolutionary *progression*, a large number of his contemporaries drew on the book's ideas to explore less optimistic views of human development. In 1867, for instance, Henry Maudsley suggested in *The Physiology and Pathology of Mind* that the mid-Victorian preoccupation with 'getting on' was jeopardising the health of the nation's future:

> Perhaps one, and certainly not the least, of the ill effects arising out of the conditions of our present civilisation is seen in the general dread, and disdain, of poverty, in the eager absorbing passion to become rich. The practical gospel of the age, testified everywhere by faith and works,

is that of money-getting; men are estimated mainly by the amount of their wealth, take social rank accordingly, and consequently bend all their energies to acquire that which gains them esteem and influence.[4]

This 'sole aim of getting rich', he added, in a lecture delivered to the Harveian Society of London that same year,

> honestly, if it may be, but if not, still of getting rich – is extremely baneful. But the evil does not end there; the deterioration of nature which the parent has acquired is likely enough to be transmitted as an evil heritage to his children, who continuing the degeneracy, exhibit its effects in a more marked form.[5]

According to Maudsley, there was no such thing as 'self' in the organic network of natural evolution:

> The individual [...] is but a link in the chain of organic beings connecting the past with the future [...]. The present individual is the inevitable consequence of his antecedents in the past, and in the examination of these alone do we arrive at the adequate explanation of him.[6]

Victorian obsessions with *self*-advancement and *self*-help were, according to Maudsley and others, evincing a form of alienation that could become an 'evil heritage' in forthcoming generations. Mrs Henry Wood's 1860s fictions were concurrent with this ambivalent exchange of ideas on the nature of progress. In 1862, as her *Shadow of Ashlydyat* (1864) was running in the *New Monthly Magazine*, and *Verner's Pride* (1863) in *Once a Week*, the latter featured an article entitled 'Nest-Building Apes'. Reviewing an exhibition of stuffed primates at the British Museum, journalist John Hollingshead suggested that the nineteenth-century professional gentleman was little better than a nest-building ape himself:

> It would be so easy to show that certain gorillas are nest-building men, or that certain men are nest-building apes, that we can hardly wonder at the interest taken in our newly-discovered cousins. [...] Few of us can lay our paws upon our hearts and say honestly that we are unworthy of the classification. [...] It may be called by various names, – such as prudence, industry, success, or, property qualification; because language, like figures, is given to us to conceal the truth.[7]

The article then classifies various nest-building apes as political, speculative, clerical, and legal. With emphasis on 'prudence, industry', and 'success', Hollingshead aimed to comment on the ideologies of self-help and the work ethic. Like Maudsley, he suggested that the glorification of progress

Figure 4.1 Unknown artist, 'Nest-Building Apes', *Once a Week*, 19 July 1862, p. 112

had produced abject 'selfishness' in the country's ambitious men: 'They all have one little fault, – selfishness a little too strongly developed; they all believe devoutly in the same worldly-wise maxim, – each one for himself and God for us all. And yet are they not all "men and brethren?"'[8] What we see crystallised here is an illustration of how the Victorian concepts of progress and degeneration were working for and against each other at mid century. In the illustration accompanying 'Nest-Building Apes', for example (Figure 4.1), competitive apes are shown inhabiting nests and wearing professional human clothing. Like the written piece it accompanied, the image highlights the perceived irony that the desire to 'get on' and advance oneself socially is an atavistic process.[9] The left-most ape, for example, carries a sign saying 'no connection with any other establishment'. It indicates that, although science was teaching people how they were part of an ever-changing natural network, the 'self-help' philosophy had, according to writers like Hollingshead and Maudsley, morbid and alienating consequences.

Mrs Henry Wood's fiction of the 1860s reveal, as Wynne suggests, a fascination with the observable rise of the manufacturing classes. Yet Lyn Pykett suggests that the plots of Mrs Wood's novels can be described, in Bakhtinian terminology, as dialogic. As she explains:

> The subversive sub-text of *East Lynne* [...] derives from the way in which it allows (or even requires) its readers to think otherwise contradictory things at once; in other words, from what Bakhtinian theory would describe as its dialogism. One of the most prominent aspects of this dialogism can be seen in the novel's manipulation of point of view, and particularly in the way in which it appears to require its readers to condemn a character which whom they are also supposed to identify and sympathise.[10]

Drawing on Pykett's ideas, I argue that in order to accurately gauge the attitudes shown towards social climbing in Wood's fiction, we need to acknowledge a more ambivalent and uneasy attitude towards professional development within those texts. By discussing Wood's novels in relation to the period's conflicting ideas on progress and degeneration, it is possible to observe how the author used representations of female violence as a vehicle for expressing undecided or ambivalent views towards Smiles's eminent Hugh Smithson.

A man of two wives/a man of two lives: Divided masculinity and domestic ideology in *East Lynne* (1862)

Mrs Wood's 1862 bestseller, *East Lynne*, features no overt act of violence by a woman. The only possible exception is Cornelia Carlyle's emptying of a bowlful of treacle on a man presumptuous enough to propose to her – an act that echoes Xanthippe's actions with a less saccharine substance. Yet, like much of Wood's fiction of the 1860s, *East Lynne* employs imagery associated with female violence in order to explore the role of women as the seeming cause of masculine failure. In an emotionally charged plot, the failure of *East Lynne*'s central family, the Carlyles, appears to hinge, almost entirely, on the ungovernable passions of the wife and mother, Lady Isabel. In this the text appears to support the period's belief in the associations between excessive female passion and the potential for violence. In the following extract, for example, Isabel has just learned how her husband Archibald has been seen 'enjoying a *tête-à-tête* by moonlight' with another woman. Notice how the text characterises Isabel's feelings as explosive and energetic:

> Lady Isabel almost gnashed her teeth; the jealous doubts which had been tormenting her all the evening were confirmed. [...] Had she been alone in the carriage, a torrent of passion had probably escaped her. [...] She was most assuredly out of her senses that night or she never would have listened.
> A jealous woman is mad; an outraged woman is doubly mad; and the ill-fated Lady Isabel truly believed that every sacred feeling which ought to exist between man and wife was betrayed by Mr. Carlyle.[11]

Like the 'smouldering fires' metaphor employed by many of the period's writers to describe the nature of female emotion, Lady Isabel's feelings are portrayed as a 'torrent' that requires an explosive outlet. Unlike Charlotte St John in *St. Martin's Eve* (1866), however, Isabel's torrential passions do not culminate in a direct act of violence (like the former's beating of Benja) but in the adulterous elopement with Francis Levison. This act, as suggested by Barbara, Archibald's second wife, has disastrous consequences for the family. Speaking to Isabel herself, who is by this time disguised as the governess Madame Vine, Barbara tells how

> 'Mr. Carlyle married Lady Isabel Vane, the late Lord Mount Severn's daughter. She was attractive and beautiful, but I do not fancy she cared very much for her husband. However that may have been, she ran away from him'.
> 'It was very sad', observed Lady Isabel, feeling that she was expected to say something. Besides, she had her *rôle* to play.
> 'Sad? It was wicked, it was infamous', returned Mrs. Carlyle, giving way to some excitement. 'Of all men living, of all husbands, Mr. Carlyle least deserved such a requital. [...] Of course the disgrace is reflected upon the children, and always will be; the shame of having a divorced mother – '
> 'Is she not dead?' interrupted Lady Isabel.
> 'She is dead. Oh yes. But they will not be the less pointed at, the girl especially, as I say. [...] I trust you will be able to instil principles into the little girl which will keep her from a like fate'.
> (pp. 321–2)

Not knowing Lady Isabel and Madame Vine to be the same woman, Barbara ironically expects the governess to have a healthier influence on the children. What this passage also reveals is that not only does Isabel's adultery destroy the constitution of the family she leaves behind, but how her actions are assumed to have repercussions for her children in the years to come. Victorian readers would have recognised Barbara's fears as a genuine problem. As I discussed in chapter one, the actions and emotions of mothers were considered crucial to the healthy development of their offspring. Even Samuel Smiles, whose book stressed the importance of independent human agency in bringing about success, recognised the significance of a beneficial upbring. 'The nation', he observed, 'comes from the nursery'.[12]

Thus, in the threat it poses to the nuclear, bourgeois family, Isabel's elopement plays out a hackneyed nineteenth-century narrative: that of the immoderate passions of women destroying what the Victorians valued most. When masquerading as Madame Vine, Isabel is constantly forced to compare her current state (as governess) with that of Barbara, who fulfils the position previously held by her ladyship:

> Terribly indeed were their positions reversed; most terribly was she feeling it. And by whose act and will had the change been wrought? Barbara was now the honoured and cherished wife, East Lynne's mistress. And what was she? Not even the welcomed guest of an hour, as Barbara had been, but an interloper, a criminal woman who had thrust herself into the house; her act, in doing so, not to be justified, her position a most false one.
>
> (p. 343)

In an age that glorified progress and the amassing of wealth, Isabel's lost status becomes a poignant reminder of the destructive potential of uncontrolled emotion. Like the actual women who killed husbands, siblings, and children, Isabel's irrational flight renders her a criminal in her own home. The second half of *East Lynne* is dominated by Lady Isabel's installation of herself as governess to her own children. The narrative draws on the ubiquitous Victorian fear that beneath the respectable surface of the middle-class family there lurked a criminal element – an unforeseen and unknown threat posed by the misleading natures of women. This fear is perhaps explored most deeply in the novel's use of images of child murder. Subsequent to her adultery, Isabel's progress through the narrative leaves a trail of dead children. When leaving Grenoble, the 'continent[al ...] refuge' (p. 223) in which she retreats with Levison and their illegitimate child she is involved in a railway accident that leaves her 'poor baby [...] quite dead' (p. 253). Her return to East Lynne, moreover, triggers a sickly downward spiral for her son William, who eventually dies of consumption. In the following scene her contact with the dying boy is figured as an act of violence:

> Lady Isabel [...] had drawn [William] to her, and was hanging over him in unguarded tenderness, when, happening to lift her eyes, they fell upon Mr. Carlyle. [...] Had Lady Isabel been killing the boy she could not have dropped him more suddenly.
>
> (p. 332)

Isabel's maternal 'tenderness' is represented here as vampirically and 'unguarded[ly] hanging over' the boy. Sally Shuttleworth has revealed how, in Mrs Beeton's *Book of Household Management* (1859), a connection is made between excessive breast-feeding and vampirism. In some cases, Beeton wrote, the mother experiences 'febrile symptoms and hectic flushes, caused by her baby vampire'.[13] As Shuttleworth notes, 'the seemingly innocent picture of a mother asleep with her babe in her arms becomes a scene of uncontrolled debauchery'.[14] I would add that it also becomes one of horror. Like Lady Isabel's 'unguarded' embrace of her son, Beeton's notion of the 'baby vampire' aligns images of uncontrolled violence to those associated with the maternal role.

Immediately after William's death in *East Lynne*, Barbara brings up the subject of child murder:

> Talking about smothering children, what accounts we have in the registrar-general's weekly returns of health. So many children 'overlaid in bed'; so many children 'suffocated in bed'. One week there were nearly twenty, and often there are as many as eight or ten. Mr. Carlyle says he knows they are smothered on purpose.
>
> (p. 473)

It is also probably no coincidence that Isabel elopes with a man known to some characters as Captain Thorn. As Josephine McDonagh has observed, since the publication of Wordsworth's 'The Thorn', a poem about infanticide in *Lyrical Ballads* (1798), images of thorns and thickets have held firm associations with infanticide.[15] Hence, although Isabel's 'torrent of passion' does not result in any *actual* act of violence, *East Lynne* implies that her actions – as driven by her unchecked emotions – have *inherently* destructive consequences for her children.

East Lynne thus echoes mid-Victorian, conformist claims that the control of female emotion is crucial to the health and preservation of the middle-class way of life. Shuttleworth argues that the connections between maternal excess and violence were used in non-fictional texts in order to enhance bourgeois controls over reproduction and guarantee the middle class's privileged position as Britain's ruling class. Indeed, with its fallen aristocrats and successful middle-class characters, *East Lynne* appears to offer a fictional tribute to the triumphs of bourgeois self-control and the failures of upper-class immoderation. While 'promoting the "superior" qualities of the middle-class Barbara Hare' and Archibald Carlyle, Wynne writes, the reader is encouraged to develop a 'covert satisfaction in witnessing the downfall of the aristocratic [Lady Isabel] and Carlyle's triumph over Levison and all other upper-class men'.[16] A significant part of this 'triumph', I argue, depends on Barbara and Archibald's ability to control their feelings. Despite giving way to hysterics earlier in the text, Barbara's chosen method of running the East Lynne household is determined by moderation:

> I never was fond of being troubled with children. [... Some mothers] are never happy but when with their children; they must be in the nursery, or the children in the drawing-room. They wash them, dress them, feed them, rendering themselves slaves and the nurse's office a sinecure. [...The mother] has no leisure, no spirits for any higher training; and as they grow old she loses her authority. One who is wearied, tired out with her children, cross when they play, or make a little extra noise which jars on her unstrung nerves, who says, 'You shan't do this; you shall be still', and that continually, is sure to be rebelled against at last; it cannot be otherwise. [...] I consider it a most mistaken and pernicious system.
>
> (p. 322)

Like the victim of the 'baby vampire', the excessive mothers described by Barbara have their energies sapped by troublesome children. By contrast, *Barbara's* system is one of controlled and moderate affection; and one, moreover, that seems to assure her success as surely as Isabel's abandon guarantees hers.

Similarly, Archibald rarely gives vent to his emotions. Shortly after his first wedding to Isabel, for example, he interrupts her while she is dressing for dinner:

> 'Isabel! Are you there?'
> 'I am waiting for you. Are you ready?'
> 'Nearly. He drew her inside, caught her to him, and held her against his heart.
> There was an explosion the following morning. Mr. Carlyle ordered the pony carriage for church, but his sister interrupted him.
>
> (p. 118)

Observe how the passage appears to elide a sexual encounter between man and wife. Archibald grasps Isabel while she is in a state of undress and immediately afterwards the narrative jumps to the following morning. The narrative's reference to the explosion of the following day appears an orgasmic image, yet the way in which the reader is jolted into the matter-of-fact business of the carriage ride to church helps neutralise any narrative nuances of passion between Archibald and his wife.

When Carlyle later reads that Isabel has been killed in a train accident (a report that turns out to be erroneous), he is able to curtail his shock almost immediately: 'Mr Carlyle stared [...] for a moment, as if his wits had been in the next world. Then he swept the newspaper from before him, and was the calm, collected man of business again' (p. 257). Like Barbara's controlled 'love' for her children, Archibald's ability to sweep aside his emotions seems to guarantee him a successful future. The temperate preservation of middle-class composure is, as Wynne points out, apparently rewarded, while the indulged passions of Levison and Isabel are punished, respectively, with gaol and an unmarked grave.

East Lynne made its appearance at a time when, as we have seen, writers from a range of disciplinary backgrounds expressed discontent with the values of the developing, bourgeois class. Emerging from such an intellectual climate as this, Wood's novel is, indeed, no exception. While the text reproduced, and seemed to validate, the period's ideas on the innate destructive qualities of immoderate women, there is also an implicit narrative wherein the bourgeois lifestyle of Archibald Carlyle is the *true* cause of his family's failure. For example, although Carlyle's ability to circumvent his emotions and become a 'calm, collected man of business' appears to conform to the middle-class code of conduct, this ability to separate business from feeling leads to a complete and destructive lack of understanding between him and Isabel. Pykett has written of sensation fiction that 'men and women are shown as being foreign countries to each other. [...] In such narratives marriage, the presumed site of union and mutual understanding, is revealed as, in fact, a state of mutual isolation, secrecy and misunderstanding'.[17] In *East Lynne*, this is clearly the state of Archibald's marriage to Isabel. As a lawyer, Carlyle is consulted by Barbara with regards to a murder in which her brother is involved. His clandestine meetings with her are ostensibly innocent yet his resolution to keep his private and professional lives separate (by not telling Isabel) leads his wife to suspect he is having an affair. She asks,

'What is it that she wants with you so much, that Barbara Hare?'
'It is private business, Isabel. She has to bring me messages from her mother'.
'Must the business be kept from me?'

(p. 203)

Archibald prevaricates with his answer but it is essentially 'yes'. This lack of complicity between the private and public lives of professional men is well-known as a standard arrangement for the period's families. According to Wemmick, the clerk in *Great Expectations* (1861) whose domestic conditions are completely unknown to his employer, 'the office is one thing, and private life is another'.[18] Although this schizophrenic arrangement appears to work for Wemmick, *East Lynne* questions the effectiveness of such a division. Immediately before the novel began its serialisation in the *New Monthly Magazine*, for example, the periodical featured an essay entitled 'Domestic

Hero Worship'. Signing himself as 'A Proser', its unsigned author outlined the period's domestic iconography:

> [We must] appreciate that spirit of family hero-worship in which the good woman of a household stirs the fire, adjusts the slippers at each side of the tabooed chair, and telegraphs to the lower regions for 'dinner at once', so soon as she perceives the suburban omnibus draw up, for an avatar of the god of her home idolatry, who presently gladdens her admiring eyes, as he gravely measures the six-yard gravel walk which separates his suburban temple from the common world without.[19]

The tone of the piece is meant to be ironic as the writer continues to reveal how the hegemonic nature of the separate spheres ideology often tied women to selfish and impossible men:

> But what is to be said of other home idols, hideous both mentally and corporeally, embodied meannesses, tyrannic compounds of selfishness and savageness, hateful and hated of all the world except the blindly doting wife and deluded children, to whom they stand as representative men, the personification of all that is good and gracious? Is such home idolatry as *this* to be encouraged or endured? – are 'they of a man's household', alone of all the world, to be blind to his deformities, and deaf to his dispraise? To such questions we deliberately say yes! – a thousand times yes! – such cavils of the clear-eyed are not to disturb the sanctity of hero-worship.[20]

The article includes the allegory of a man whose true identity is utterly unknown to 'the wife of his bosom'.[21] When he dies his wife gradually becomes aware of his real, professional nature, which was completely different to what she knew at home.

Similarly, in *Temple Bar*, the magazine that would serialise Mrs Henry Wood's *Lady Adelaide's Oath* in 1866, Eliza Lynn Linton expressed this idea with clearer discontent. Commentating on ancient customs, yet obviously writing on her own culture, she notes:

> The rule is that [women] do not mingle in the outward or political life of the men, but content themselves with bearing children, cooking food, carding wool, scolding the servants, and waiting to be married. [...] Then the fathers and husbands, having carefully trained and moulded this uninteresting race of virtuous possessions, lock the door [...] and turn to the brilliant, educated, sparkling [...] outward society.[22]

Linton then questions whether 'this division of functions and multiplications of persons [is] the best and wisest model of human society possible to be fashioned'.[23] In the customary division of labour, she suggests, men, who vacillate between both (domestic and public) spaces, stand forth as the owners of more than one conflicting identity.

Although Archibald is hardly the deceptive tyrant described in the *New Monthly*, the novel suggests that the lack of communication between him and Isabel (as augmented by his professional status) is a significant factor in the breakdown of his marriage. 'Being a practical, matter-of-fact man', the narrator writes of him, 'it did not occur to him that [Isabel] could be [jealous]'. When they are finally reunited in a tearful deathbed tableau, Archibald asks her

> 'Why did you go?' [...]
> 'Did you not know?'
> 'No. It has always been a mystery to me'. [...]
> 'I thought you were false and deceitful to me; that your love was all given to another; and, in my sore jealousy I listened to the temptings of a bad man, who whispered to me of revenge. It was not so, was it?'
> Mr. Carlyle had regained his calmness – outwardly, at any rate. He stood by the side of the bed, looking down upon her, his arms crossed upon his chest, his noble form raised to its full height.
>
> (pp. 488–9)

Archibald behaves in a way that the reader has come to expect of him. Controlling his emotions, he stands upright, pious, and morally judgemental of the fading Isabel. Despite his claims that Isabel was mistaken in believing him to be 'false and deceitful', the way in which he hides his true feelings in this scene seems to suggest otherwise. Indeed, notice how he and Isabel have exchanged positions. She no longer wears the Madame Vine disguise, yet he now wears that of the 'practical, matter-of-fact man'. The prevailing notion of women as deceitful and misleading is reinterpreted here so that it is the man, not the woman, being the most duplicitous. Witness also how this farewell episode refigures the image of Isabel vampirically arching over her son William. Here Archibald towers over his former wife. The more she becomes downtrodden, the taller he stands; as she grows weaker, he grows stronger. In this the text suggests that, in the system whereby women were very much part of a middle-class ideology of control, self-help, and professionalisation, men were the causes of their *own* failures.

Thus, the contention that *East Lynne* aimed to 'champion the middle classes' is too simplistic; the novel is in fact more complex than this. Although Lady Isabel's excessive, maddening passions are held accountable for the destruction of the Carlyle family, and she is heavily punished for her fall, it is also possible to read *East Lynne* as a text that highlights the shortfalls inherent to bourgeois masculinity.

'Looking back': The mother's influence in *Danesbury House* (1860) and *Mrs Halliburton's Troubles* (1862)

Danesbury House and *Mrs Halliburton's Troubles* are similar novels that deal with issues surrounding the rearing of children and maternal management. *Danesbury House* was Mrs Henry Wood's first full-length novel. Written for the Scottish Temperance League, it aimed to highlight the hazards of excessive alcohol consumption. When John Danesbury's wife is killed in a carriage accident, leaving three children motherless, he marries the vinegary Eliza St George and has two further sons by her. The narrative compares the results of two very different forms of upbringing. The two eldest children, Arthur and Isabel, follow their mother's instruction that 'a child should never be allowed to drink anything' but water.[24] The three younger children, William, Robert, and Lionel (of which the latter two are Eliza's) are meanwhile indulged in their taste for wine and beer. With the exception of Isabel, who marries a viscount, all of the children grow up in middle-class professional employment. Arthur takes over his father's iron works, William trains as an engineer, and Robert and Lionel move to London to join the army and train as a physician respectively. Predictably, Arthur and Isabel seem to 'live happily ever after' due to their abstinence from drink. Because of their predilections for alcohol, however, Lionel and Robert run into violent and disgraceful deaths. The former dies of 'delirium tremens' (insane convulsions caused by drinking) and the latter cuts his own throat. William, who is not Eliza's child but is raised by her, escapes a likewise grisly death due to the hereditary influences of his biological mother and the gruesome examples set by his two younger brothers.

A similar comparison of two methods of upbringing drives the narrative of *Mrs Halliburton's Troubles*. Following the untimely death of her husband, the middle-class Jane Halliburton is forced to work as a glove sewer and raise her children in shabby (though still 'respectable') obscurity. Among all the hard work, Jane teaches her children the value of perseverance. Gathering them around her, she says:

> In all the tribulation that will probably come upon us, the humiliations, the necessities, we must strive for patience to bear them. You do not understand the meaning of the term, *to bear;* but you will learn it all soon. [...] My darling children, let us all strive to bear on steadfastly to that far-off light, ever looking unto God.[25]

In his introduction to a 1968 edition of Smiles's *Self Help*, Lord Thomson of Fleet emphatically wrote: 'what are the lessons to be learned from this book? First and last, PERSEVERANCE'.[26] Indeed, one of the central messages in Smiles's text appears to be the idea, echoed in the above passage from

Mrs Halliburton's Troubles, that happiness and success are more likely to be gained from the uncomplaining endurance of a working life than the indulgence of an easy one. 'On the whole', Smiles writes,

> it is not good that human nature should have the road of life made too easy. Better to be under the necessity of working hard and faring meanly, than to have everything done ready to hand and a pillow of down to repose upon. Indeed, to start in life with comparatively small means seems so necessary as a stimulus to work, that it may almost be set down as one of the conditions essential to success in life.[27]

Because he has experienced this 'necessity of working hard', William Halliburton, Jane's eldest child, emerges as the text's hero and a true gentleman. In direct contrast, the life of Anthony Dare who, like the younger Danesburys has his every whim indulged, ends shamefully and aggressively. As the narrator informs us, 'the Dares had been most culpably indulged. The house was one of luxury and profusion, and every little whim and fancy had been studied. It is one of the worst schools a child can be reared in' (p. 161). Like Eliza Danesbury, Anthony's mother, Julia Dare, makes little attempt to condition her children's moral characters: 'she had taken no pains to train her children: she had given them very little love' (p. 161). Lacking the ethical discipline instilled into the Halliburtons, Anthony seduces the family's Italian governess, Bianca Varsini. When she discovers him attempting to seduce a poor Quaker girl, she murders him by stabbing him in the heart. The narrative therefore seems to comply with Smiles's claim that 'far better and more respectable is the good poor man than the bad rich one – better the humble silent man than the agreeable well appointed rogue who keeps his gig'.[28] Both *Danesbury House* and *Mrs Halliburton's Troubles* put forward a central, didactic, and essentially bourgeois message: avoid excessive partialities and work hard.

In keeping with the non-fictional sources I discussed in chapter one, Wood's novels appear to rely upon the trope of violent femininity in order to underscore this message. The mothers in *Danesbury House* and *Mrs Halliburton's Troubles*, for example, seem to bear the entire weight of responsibility for their children's successes or failures. In his *Physiology and Pathology of Mind*, Henry Maudsley warned against the dangers of indulging children and neglecting their moral education as Eliza Danesbury and Julia Dare do: 'how often one is condemned to see, with pain and sorrow, an injurious education sorely aggravate an inherent mischief'. One such 'injurious education' he identifies as 'a foolish indulgence through which [the child] never learns the necessary lessons of renunciation and self-control'.[29] Although Maudsley's focus in this passage is laid on Victorian education as a whole, he nevertheless held 'silly mothers' to be central to the many calamities that befell a cosseted child.[30] In *Danesbury House* and *Mrs Halliburton's Troubles*, this warning is set into melodramatic and fictional form, especially in scenes outlining the deaths of the most dissipated male characters. After striking his father, for example,

Robert Danesbury retires remorsefully to his bedroom where he is afterwards discovered with razor in hand and his throat cut:

> 'HE HAS COMMITTED SUICIDE', was the dead whisper [of his doctor], 'May the Lord have mercy on his soul!'
> They went in, Arthur nerving himself. The ill-fated maniac – let us call him so! – was lying on the bed in a pool of blood, the razor clasped in his right hand. He was not dead; but ere the lapse of many minutes he would no longer be numbered amongst the living.
> (p. 237)

His mother forces her way into the scene:

> She had the strength of a desperate woman, and struggled with [Arthur]. He soothingly strove to lead her away, but she suddenly raised her foot and kicked open the door, and the scene within was disclosed to her. A long shrill shriek ran through the house, and she fell back into Arthur's arms.
> (p. 238)

Eliza's witnessing of this scene is clearly meant to foreground her culpability. The image of a woman standing besides a bloody corpse was not unfamiliar to mid-Victorian readers whose newspapers were full of reports of sensational cases like the Road Murder. Dying from a broken heart later, Eliza warns William Danesbury to abstain from drink: 'William, be you warned while there is yet time; [...] Do not let me have another lost soul upon my hands!' An unforgiving narrator adds, 'She had ruined her sons, and they, in their turn, had sent her to her grave' (p. 249).

A similar case of the son reaping the fruits of his faulty upbringing occurs in *Mrs Halliburton's Troubles*. Anthony Dare's body is discovered in the early hours of the morning by his parents and the servants:

> Mr. Dare, his own life-blood seeming to have stopped, bent over his son by the light of the candle. Anthony appeared to be not only dead, but cold. In his terrible shock, his agitation, he still remembered that it was well, if possible, to spare the sight to his wife and daughter. Mrs. Dare [...] had run downstairs, and [was] now hastening into the room.
> 'Go back! Go back!' cried Mr. Dare, fencing [her] away with his hands. [...] 'You must not come in! Julia', he added to his wife, in a tone of imploring entreaty, 'go upstairs'.
> (p. 312)

As with Robert's death in the earlier novel, the discovery of Anthony's body is a scene in which the desperate mother forcibly involves herself. Although the governess disrupts the chain of causation between Julia and the death of her son, Mrs Dare is still given full responsibility for the death of Anthony.

In a chapter aptly entitled 'Fruits Coming Home to the Dares', Julia's husband delivers a devastating accusation to his wife:

> Had [the children] been reared more plainly, they would not have acquired those extravagant notions which have proved their bane. [...] Julia, [...] it might have been well now, well with them and with us, had our children been obliged to battle with [...] poverty.
>
> (p. 346)

What is interesting about these episodes is the almost-complete disregard for the possible blame that may be due to other characters. Robert Danesbury, Anthony Dare, Bianca Varsini, and the boys' fathers appear to escape Wood's moralistic narrative focus and responsibility is laid instead upon what Maudsley would term the 'silly mothers'. Taken in conjunction with the successes of temperate male characters, the stories of Robert Danesbury and Anthony Dare appear to echo the period's promotion of bourgeois values through images of female destructiveness. In other words, by depicting violence at the heart of the Danesbury and Dare families, Wood's novels reverberate with the calls for control and industry that were so central to Victorian, middle-class culture.

If, however, the successes or failures of the novel's male characters hinge upon the actions of their mothers, then the texts may also question how far individual hard work and perseverance *are* viable guarantors of success. For example, according to *Danesbury House* and *Mrs Halliburton's Troubles*, the actions of Robert Danesbury and Anthony Dare are essentially impotent against the downward trajectory detonated by their mothers' actions during childhood. Furthermore, the business triumphs of the novels' 'successful' men are likewise firmly associated with the influences of the mothers. In the overworked endings of both novels, for example, the heroes' mothers are figured as crucial to the successes of both characters. In *Danesbury House*, the long-dead Mrs Danesbury is revamped in her son's didactic address to his manufactory workers. 'Some amongst you', he says, 'still remember my mother. [...] And you remember that she was all kindness to you; she would have ever been so, had she lived' (p. 316). Similarly, in *Mrs Halliburton's Troubles*, William, a successful glove manufacturer like Mrs Henry Wood's father, attributes his achievements to the moral lessons taught by his mother:

> What was William thinking of, as he stood a little apart, with his serene brow and his thoughtful smile? His mind was in the past. [...] 'Bear up, my child', were the words his mother had comforted him with: 'only do your duty, and trust implicitly to God'.
>
> (p. 461)

Despite the fact that William Halliburton and Arthur Danesbury (as industrial, middle-class men) stand for progress and success, the images of their mothers, in these final scenes, could signify a form of psychological deadlock. William Halliburton's reveries, for example, are 'in the past' with his mother and Arthur Danesbury is similarly preoccupied with remembering his childhood. Although Smiles cites a number of cases where successful men are similarly concerned with 'looking back upon the admirable example set [...] by [their] mother',[31] *Danesbury House* and *Mrs Halliburton's Troubles* present such 'looking back' as undercutting the most pivotal messages of the self-help philosophy. If the achievements of men are always reducible to the actions of their mothers, then 'self help' is not as powerful a concept as Smiles would have us believe. William Halliburton, for example, was instructed to strive forward, to 'bear on steadfastly'. When the novel closes, however, he is looking backwards; his 'mind [is] in the past'.

This form of psychological stalemate is echoed by what appears to be a *biological* form of sterility in the Danesburys and Halliburtons. In the conclusions of both novels a party is held in honour of their triumphant heroes. A crowd comprising local nobility and grateful factory 'hands' raise their glasses in celebration of Danesbury's and Halliburton's commercial and moral accomplishments. Both men are typically rewarded with marriages to their sweethearts, yet, atypically, Halliburton and Danesbury are not bestowed with children. The 'pitter-patter of tiny feet' is a sound that echoes across the endings of many well-known Victorian narratives – including the most famous sensation novels. Robert Audley and George Talboys, for example, have extended families by the time Lady Audley dies in her foreign asylum; Aurora Floyd's passionate personality is tamed by the arrival of a baby; and Walter Hartright and Franklin Blake are similarly granted children to whom they can bequeath their appropriated heritages. By contrast, Arthur Danesbury and William Halliburton may have advanced themselves socially, but when it comes to advancing their families congenitally, they are effectively powerless. As with the 'Nest-Building Apes', whose desire to 'get on' had forfeited any rewarding and altruistic connections with 'other establishments', success and biology in *Danesbury House* and *Mrs Halliburton's Troubles* appear to be at odds. A man, it seems, may advance himself socially but, in doing so, he jeopardises his position as a healthy member of the procreative race.

Mrs Henry Wood and John Hollingshead (author of 'Nest-Building Apes') were not unique in their suspicions that social success heralded biological sterility. In 1841, for example, Thomas Doubleday offered a very interesting variation on Malthus's ideas on population. Whereas Malthus claimed, at the beginning of the century, that the human race was outgrowing its resources and would therefore be moderated by 'checks' such as famine, disease, and war,[32] Doubleday suggested, in an ambitiously entitled *The True Theory of Population* (1841), that mankind would adapt to such calamities by increasing its numbers. In a post-Darwinian article on 'Infanticide and Abortion', Ewing Whittle quoted the following from Doubleday's book:

> In nature a general law exists for the protection of species, whereby fecundity is stimulated by a condition of depletion, and checked by a condition of repletion; that this law applies equally to the vegetable and animal kingdom; that, as applied to man, this law produces the following results: that in all societies a constant increase is going on amongst the worst fed, and that amongst those well supplied with food and luxuries a constant decrease goes on; amongst those in a medium state, who are tolerably well fed, not over worked and yet not idle, population is stationary.[33]

Doubleday's is a theory that clearly drew on the era's emerging preoccupations with evolution and anticipated the 1859 publication of Darwin's *Origin of Species*. Applied to the state of Victorian society, Doubleday's idea suggested that the hardships experienced by the working classes caused them to flourish, while the increasing levels of luxury generated by the bourgeoisie resulted in a depletion of their numbers. This could explain why Halliburton's and Danesbury's successes do not include the healthy propagation of their families. According to Doubleday, the class that is most at risk from a reproductive gridlock is that in a 'medium state'; that 'not over worked and yet not idle'. In other words, the middle class. In *Mrs Halliburton's Troubles*, in particular, the central family are not as idle as the Dares, yet are not as overworked as the factory workers around them. In addition to the lack of new Halliburton children, the family's biological failures are epitomised by the melodramatic death of William's younger sister Janey. Unlike Anthony Dare's violent and unexpected demise, Janey's consumptive death is a sublime and welcomed resignation:

> 'Oh, mamma, don't keep me!' she said in a strangely thrilling tone; 'don't keep me! I see the light! I see papa!'
> There was a strange light, not as of earth, in her own face, and an ineffable smile on her lip, that told more of heaven. Her arms dropped; and she sank back on the pillow. Jane Halliburton had gone to her heavenly father.
> (p. 185)

When compared to the killing of the wealthy Anthony Dare, Janey's death seems to reinforce the text's apparent central message: that it is better to live and die in a hard-working family than to burn out in an indulged one. Yet, immediately after Janey's death, Anna Lynne (a working-class Quaker girl) asks Mrs Halliburton how her daughter is faring:

> 'Is she better?'
> 'No, Anna. She is dead'.

Jane spoke with unnatural calmness. The child, scared at the words, backed away out at the garden door. [...] Jane was nearly prostrate then. [...] 'Oh, [...] why should it be?' she wailed aloud in her despair and bereavement. 'Anna left in health and joyousness; my child taken! Surely God is dealing hardly with me'.

(p. 186)

This exclamation is inconsistent with her earlier recommendations that her children 'strive to bear on steadfastly to that far-off light, ever looking unto God' (p. 82). By contrasting the health of the working-class girl and the decline of the bourgeois Janey, the novel appears to echo Doubleday's 'true' theory of population. While the working-class lifestyle has caused Anna's health to flourish, the industrious yet middle-class lifestyle of the Halliburtons has created a sickly organisation in Janey resulting, as with her father, in premature death.

Thus, although *Danesbury House* and *Mrs Halliburton's Troubles* appear to confirm existing suspicions that careless mothers inflicted violence on their children through bad maternal management, the novels also explore ways in which the middle-class lifestyle generated the hazards it seemed most eager to overcome. The preoccupations with 'looking back' to the maternal influence, for example, seems to have challenged the forward-facing principles advocated by the self-help ideology. In accordance with contemporaneous ideas on population, moreover, the novels also appear to corroborate existing fears that success was, ironically, an atavistic route ensuring the sterility of the middle class.

'The matrimonial lottery': Choosing a good wife in *Lady Adelaide's Oath* (1867)

In 1866, Mary Braddon ceased contributing to *Temple Bar* in order to concentrate on editing her own journal *Belgravia*. In an attempt to retain the high sales of *Temple Bar*, its editor, George Augustus Sala, commissioned the serialisation of a novel from Mrs Henry Wood who was by then rated alongside Braddon, Collins, and Dickens as one of Britain's best-selling novelists. With a similar title to *Lady Audley's Secret*, the resulting work, *Lady Adelaide's Oath* appeared to fulfil expectations with a murder mystery packed with crime, resurrections from the dead, and ghostly phenomena. In the opening chapters, an unknown assailant seems to push Harry Dane, heir to the wealthy Dane Castle estate, off the edge of a cliff. He actually falls after an argument with his cousin Herbert. The source of their rivalry is their common attraction to the beautiful, but spoiled, Lady Adelaide. Adelaide is the only apparent witness of the accident yet, because of her love for Herbert, she gives a false oath, declaring that she saw nothing. When Harry's body is not found, it is assumed that it has been washed out to sea. He nevertheless survives the fall and is rescued by a passing yacht. Unconscious then amnesic, Harry is taken to America onboard the vessel, thus allowing his family to believe him dead. Within months, his parents die and the estate is passed on to Herbert. As the title of the novel suggests, Lady Adelaide's false oath is situated at the centre of the family's disasters and the ruin of their *primiparæ* heritage.

In the same periodical that *Lady Adelaide's Oath* was serialised, Alfred Austin wrote of Sensation Novelists that 'dead, yet not dead, is one of their favourite resources'.[34] Accordingly, Harry returns from his apparent demise to reclaim his inheritance and reprove Adelaide for not giving a true account of his fall. In a chapter appropriately headed 'Sowing and Reaping', Adelaide admits to Harry:

> I have looked upon myself as your murderer also in a degree: for, had I told at once what I saw, you might have been rescued; and I did not tell it, in my infatuation for Herbert Dane. Ah, how the sin came home to me ere many hours had elapsed! But it was too late then, and I took that oath which has been so fatal to my peace.[35]

As with Eliza Danesbury and Julia Dare, Adelaide's instrumentality in the failures of the Dane estate is figured as an act of murder committed vicariously through another. The 'resurrected' Harry agrees with Adelaide: 'But for your own conduct', he tells her, 'that night's work had never taken place' (p. 427). In *Lady Adelaide's Oath* a woman is once again weighed down by the burden of masculine failure. If, however, a family's estate can be thus brought down by the oath of one woman, it begs the question, how secure or healthy was that 'stronghold' to begin with? This assumes, however, that the connections between Lady Adelaide's oath and the loss of the Dane estate are unbroken. The novel, in fact, not only suggests those links to be interrupted, but does so in such a way that reveals the Dane failure to hinge on the unhealthy organisation of key *male* characters. In a later revision of *The Physiology and Pathology of Mind*, for example, a textbook originally published the same year as *Lady Adelaide's Oath*, Maudsley

> venture[d] to describe, and to place side by side as having near relations to one another, three neuroses – the epileptic, the insane, and the criminal neurosis – each of which has its corresponding psychosis or natural mental character.[36]

These sometimes coexisting conditions, he added, were often the links in a chain of ancestral degeneration. Showing a clear indebtedness to the *Origin of Species*, he noted:

> The sufferer from any one of these neuroses represents an initial form of degeneracy, or a commencing morbid variety, of the human kind, and life to him shall be a hard struggle against the radical bias of his nature,

unless he minds not to struggle and leaves it to the free course of a morbid development.[37]

For the criminal, the epileptic, and the insane individual, therefore, life was a struggle against his own biological organisation. Referring back to *Lady Adelaide's Oath*, her ladyship is not the only participant in the scene of Harry's accident as three men, each displaying symptoms of the degenerative neuroses identified by Maudsley, play key roles in the mystery surrounding the heir's disappearance. The criminal neurotic, for example, is played by Herbert Dane who allows his cousin to plummet and then usurps his estate. Shortly after Harry's fall, the latter's stunned and unconscious body is found by Mitchell, a preventative man whose job it is to patrol the coastline to prevent smuggling. Mitchell had 'earlier in life [...] been subject to epileptic fits' (p. 37). When he discovers Harry he waits 'in lamentable indecision, his brain confused' (p. 38), then finally runs to the nearest coastguard station to report the incident:

> 'He is dead; he is dead!' gasped Mitchell at length. 'I must have assistance for him. If ——'
> Mitchell did not go on; apparently his breath would not let him continue, or perhaps it was his heart. [...] Mitchell opened his lips, but no words came forth, and he suddenly threw up his hands. But for their springing forward and catching him, he had fallen to the ground. [...] Mitchell was in a fit. The fright he had experienced on the beach, or the prolonged and violent exertion of running, or perhaps the two combined, had brought on a similar fit to those he had been subject to in early life.
> (p. 40)

By the time Mitchell recovers, Harry has been washed out to sea. Harry himself plays the third role in his own accident scene. Onboard the yacht, he recovers from his injuries but is overcome with an irrational desire not to inform his parents that he has survived. As he confesses in the 'Sowing and Reaping' chapter, 'my head was confused from the injuries', adding:

> '"Let them think me dead," I said' [...]
> 'But why?'
> 'Ah, why! You may well ask it. Why do we say foolish things in our passionate tempers? I was feeling that the whole world was against me; that Heaven had turned its eyes from me; and it seemed to my bitterness – my selfishness, if you will – very gratifying to resent it'.
> (p. 430)

It is significant how the confession is made in the same chapter that Adelaide's fabricated oath is blamed for the family's failures. With his head in a whirl and his resolve overcome by an illogical whim, Harry could represent the insane neurotic identified by Maudsley. What the novel seems to suggest, therefore, is that the reticence of Harry Dane, as well as that of Mitchell and Herbert Dane, is more responsible for the lost property than Adelaide's oath. The first link in the chain of the Dane degeneration is *not* Lady Adelaide's faulty testimony but a combination of one man's criminality, another's epilepsy, and a third's temporary insanity.

Adelaide's silence on the subject of Harry's fall is just one part of a personality that the novel aims to represent as duplicitous and misleading. Printed alongside the novel in *Temple Bar* was an article that sought to explore the alleged, deceptive natures of women and their effects on the nineteenth-century marriage market. Written by Lucy Coxon and entitled 'A Few Tickets in the Matrimonial Lottery', it claimed that choosing a wife was like taking 'a ticket [...] in the matrimonial lottery'.[38] In an age of 'playing coquettes' and 'private theatricals', all attempts to select a good wife were essentially a matter of chance:

> 'Take my advice, my boy', an elderly widower, and old friend of mine, used to say to his son, 'and don't marry in a hurry or with your eyes shut'. [...] Capital advice, no doubt, but [...] as long as female beauty, fascination and wily cleverness exist, it is useless to preach or give rules to men on the important business of choosing a wife. A lovely face, a perfect figure, the many and nameless snares of a clever woman's tact and flattery will in a moment cast to the winds the divine eloquence of a Taylor or the persuasive elegance of an Addison or a Steele.[39]

This perceived fear of getting caught in the 'snares of a clever woman's tact' formed the crux of a similar article published in the same magazine two years later. In 'Girl's Brothers', William Black advised his male readers to study their sweethearts' brother as 'he will betray the weak points of the bringing-up, notions, and temper of the whole family. [...] In the case of the brother there are no pretty feminine disguises to conceal the true state of affairs'.[40] Although these ideas seem to be isolated opinions, they actually emerged from wider concerns on how marital choices effected the nation's health. In particular, medical treatises often featured advice on the necessities of a good, well-balanced love match. In his *Responsibility in Mental Disease* (1874), Maudsley wrote:

> When we observe what care and thought men give to the selective breeding of horses, cows, and dogs, it is astonishing how little thought they take about the breeding of their own species: perceiving clearly that good or bad qualities in animals pass by hereditary transmission, they act habitually as if the same laws were not applicable to themselves; as if men could be bred well by accident. [...] When will man

learn that he is at the head of nature only by virtue of the operation of natural laws? When will he learn that by the study of these laws and by deliberate conformity to them he may become the conscious framer of his own destiny?[41]

A man of morose disposition, he added, ought to marry a woman with a happy temperament in order to produce children who have both of those qualities in a healthy, well-balanced degree. 'Failure in this aim', he warned, 'is punished by manifest degeneration and disease'.[42] The ability to make a good marriage was seen as the self-help concept in its most attainable form. Choosing a worthy wife, it seems, was the easiest method of authoring one's own destiny plus that of future generations.

Yet, according to the non-fictional pieces in *Temple Bar* and *Lady Adelaide's Oath*, making the right choice was not that straightforward. 'The whole affair is a lottery', claimed Coxon, 'in which success as often attends the bold and desperate player as him who draws his lot by line and rule guided by all the laws of chance and propriety'.[43] Sharing Maudsley's imagery, she adds, 'when a hasty match turns out badly, the downfall is generally sudden and speedy'.[44]

Accordingly, Lady Adelaide, as a deceptive woman, is a characterisation that draws on such fears in order to confirm, explore and, finally, through the internal contradictions of the text, negate them. As a woman who demonstrates hysterical symptoms, Lady Adelaide is a bad candidate for marriage if we judge her by standards established by the period's medical writers. During a hysterical paralysis, for example, she is described as 'panting, trembling, crying still, unable to support herself [...]. She fell into a chair in strong hysterics. The wondering servants removed her cloak; ran for smelling salts, for water' (pp. 32–3). Such changeability of temper as this, observed the writer of 'Girl's Brothers', was precisely the reason why it became necessary to observe women's male relatives: women's constitutions were constantly transforming and misleading. These 'minute shades of discrepancy', Black writes, 'form a sort of psychical kaleidoscope perpetually offering new combinations'.[45] Despite continuing to display such fractured traits, and being considered 'as wild as a March hare' by the novel's more observant characters (pp. 115–6), Adelaide receives a marriage proposal from the particularly dull-witted Squire Lester. She accepts his offer and, as warned by Maudsley and Coxon, ruins the family. As Lester's grown-up son Wilfred observes, 'It was a dark day for me and [my sister] when my father married her' (p. 318). Again, in the 'Sowing and Reaping' chapter, Harry Dane lays the ruin of the Lester estate on Adelaide's shoulders. Speaking of the Squire, Adelaide admits that 'he has been an indulgent husband':

'Very much so, I hear', returned Lord Dane. 'More indulgent than he has been to [his] children'.

The severe, honourable Dane face was bent upon her, and her own flushed, with a burning flush. If the treatment she had pursued towards those children never came home to her before, it came now in all its sin and shame.

(p. 428)

Adelaide is not being criticised here for *indulging* the Lester children as Eliza Dane and Julia Dare do, but for spending the money with which they might have indulged themselves had they been so inclined. Thus, through her uncommunicativeness on the one hand, and her hysterical, duplicitous nature on the other, Adelaide's conscience is heavily burdened with the ruin of two family estates. It follows, therefore, that her story seems to confirm the mid-Victorian view that a good marriage is crucial to reproductive health, and the essentially deceptive natures of women rendered the possibility of making such a good match very difficult.

The marriage of Adelaide and Lester is contrasted to that of Lester's son Wilfred and his wife Edith. This parallel suggests that there is more to a marriage than the initial choice of partner. As with his father's disastrous wedlock, Wilfred's union to Edith is a failure. Because Edith is dowerless and Adelaide has bankrupted his family, Wilfred is not given his father's consent. When he marries Edith clandestinely, the Squire furiously disowns him. In apparent agreement with the non-fictional advice against 'marrying in haste',[46] Wilfred's marriage is poverty-stricken, miserable, and sterile. The extent of the misery is embodied in the character of the sickly Edith herself:

Had [Wilfred] been more observant, he might have seen that something was troubling his wife in an unusual degree. She sat on the sofa, reclining her head on the opposite arm to where Wilfred was sitting. A fair, fragile girl she looked – her features painfully delicate, her blue eyes unnaturally bright, her light hair taking a tinge of gold in the sunlight. She wore a white wrapper, or dressing-gown, which made her appear still more of an invalid. [...] Wilfred's] heart [was] aching for his wife's sake, his spirit terribly rebellious against his father and Lady Adelaide.

(pp. 314–5)

Lady Adelaide is once again the locus of blame. Here, her figurative shadow arches over the failing Edith, vampirically drawing out her lifeblood. Yet, it soon becomes apparent that the *main* cause of Edith's wasting is her husband's behaviour. He is loving and kind to his wife but his involvement in poaching and burglary appears to sap her energy. In the following scene, for example, Edith's suspicions exhaust her. She asks:

'Where did you go last night, Willy?'
Mr. Wilfred Lester took a momentary and rapid glance at the speaker. Something in the tone of the voice rather startled his conscience.

'Where did I go last night? Nowhere in particular that I remember. [...] I was out and about talking to one and another'.

'So you always say, Wilfred', and the girl's tone dropped to one of dread, and she seemed to shiver as she spoke. 'You had your gun with you'. [...] The emotion had exhausted her feeble strength, and she lay down on the sofa, white, sad, and only half-convinced.

(pp. 313–5)

As if to leave little doubt, their servant observes that should Wilfred be arrested for his crimes, 'it will just kill his wife; she'd be in the churchyard in a week' (p. 395). Emma Liggins writes of Mrs Henry Wood's fiction that it 'advocates the practice of good household management but implies that women's domestic authority may not be sufficient to moderate men's behaviour'.[47] While this is supported by Wilfred and Edith's marriage, *Lady Adelaide's Oath* also suggests that 'men's behaviour', as well as women's, has a large impact on whether or not a marriage will be healthy. It is not the woman who is the deceptive and dangerous half of *this* marriage but the man. The roots of Wilfred and Edith's marital failures, as with Archibald and Isabel Carlyle's, is the husband's inability to be truthful to his wife.

Like much of Mrs Henry Wood's fiction, therefore, *Lady Adelaide's Oath* is a complex and contradictory narrative that draws on many of the gender debates preoccupying the mid-Victorian population. Whereas *Danesbury House* and *Mrs Halliburton's Troubles* explored the roles of mothers in relation to the self-made culture of the nineteenth-century, *Lady Adelaide's Oath* investigates the wives. The novel appears to appropriate and confirm prevailing ideas on the deceptive and destructive natures of women and also, it seems, advocates the contemporary preoccupation with carefully appraising marital choices. Yet, the intricate narrative structure of the text raises key problems with this argument. The involvement of troubled male characters – in Harry Dane's accident and Wilfred Lester's marriage – suggests that the failures of the Dane and Lester dynasties also have a lot to do with the innate, self-destructive tendencies of men.

'Evil heritages': Superstition and morbid heredity in *The Shadow of Ashlydyat* (1864)

As with much of Mrs Henry Wood's fiction, *The Shadow of Ashlydyat* is narrated around the failure of a wealthy family estate. The Godolphins are an ancient race of working bankers who have lived at Ashlydyat, 'a cranky old house full of nothing but passages',[48] for centuries. A highly superstitious family, their ancestral history is thick in myth and tradition. In particular, it is their belief that, in order for them to prosper, every head of the Godolphin family must inhabit the estate. According to one of the Godolphin women, 'the belief was; nay the tradition was; that so long as a reigning Godolphin held by Ashlydyat, Ashlydyat would hold by him and his' (p. 241). In the opening stages of the novel, however, the current head of the family, Sir George, breaks the chain by agreeing to live in his wife's glorious summerhouse, 'Lady Godolphin's Folly':

> 'We will reside there, and let Ashlydyat', said Lady Godolphin to her husband.
> 'Reside at the Folly! Leave Ashlydyat!' he repeated, in consternation. 'It could not be'.
> 'It will be', she answered, with a half self-willed, half-caressing laugh.
> (p. 18)

In accordance with the legend, Sir George's leaving of Ashlydyat heralds the family's downfall. Mr and Mrs Verrall, the house's new tenants, introduce Sir George's son (George) to gambling and, in order to repay his massive debts, George embezzles the family's fortune. The Ashlydyat myth thus appears to have been fulfilled: 'As it had been foretold, (so ran the prediction) ages before: When the chief of Ashlydyat should quit Ashlydyat, the ruin of the Godolphins would be near. And it had proved so' (p. 443).

As with Lady Adelaide's apparent culpability in the failures of the Dane and Lester families, therefore, the loss of the Godolphin fortune seems to hinge entirely on the actions of Lady Godolphin. It is her folly, after all, a 'self-willed' resolution to live in her summerhouse, that forges the first link in a chain of destruction. According to Charles Wood, the author's son and biographer, his mother 'had hesitated between this title [*The Shadow of Ashlydyat*] and *Lady Godolphin's Folly*, though much preferring the one she adopted'.[49] This alternative title shows how Wood herself considered Lady Godolphin's Folly to be central to the story of the Godolphins' ruin. Her decision to adopt *The Shadow of Ashlydyat* as a title, however, reveals a tension that runs throughout the novel itself. Is the Godolphin downfall the result of Lady Godolphin's follies, the text inquires, or is it really caused by a central flaw, a shadow even, in the family's economic and biological heritages?

The Godolphins provide a good example of what Smiles called the 'modern peerage'. Recruited 'from the ranks of honourable industry' instead of a long line of idle aristocratic ancestry,[50] the Godolphins can 'trace themselves back to the ages of the monks. But of no very high ancestry boasted they; no titles, places, or honours; they ranked amongst the landed gentry as owners of Ashlydyat, and that was all' (p. 13). The Godolphins are a race of 'Hugh Smithsons', the persona Smiles used to represent the man who had *built* an empire rather than inherited one. Ashlydyat, the narrator informs us, is the Godolphins' 'pride, their stronghold, their boast' (p. 13). As already noted, however, this achievement is apparently destroyed by the whims of a single woman. Yet, it is not my argument that this reveals an overall weakness in male professional achievements. It seems, for instance, that if a 'stronghold' like Ashlydyat can be destroyed by the follies of one woman, then the estate could not have been all that sturdy to begin with.

Like *Lady Adelaide's Oath*, however, *The Shadow of Ashlydyat* suggests that more is needed in order to bring a patriarchal dynasty to its knees completely. Lady Godolphin's Folly does not destroy the Godolphins wholly by itself, but triggers a disastrous chain of events that eventually culminates in the collapse.

Of course, this also means that if her ladyship's folly is just one factor in a series of disasters then the chain of causation between her actions and the family's ruin is interrupted. Revealing its chronological synchronicity with emerging discourses on evolution and hereditary psychology, for example, the novel also reveals how the failure could be caused by the family's inability to adapt to the modern world. As Henry Maudsley suggested, using Darwinian and Lamarckian terminology:

> As it is with the origin and the decay of instincts among animals, so it is with the development and the decadence of these ancestral nervous substrata: conditions of life suited to their activity will stimulate them into action and will foster also the development of new adaptive tendencies with their appropriate substrata; conditions of life unsuited to their activity will cause by degrees the waning and the ultimate disappearance of old tendencies with their substrata.[51]

Amidst the dense, repetitive language it is possible to read Maudsley's belief in the importance of adaptation, as drawn from earlier theories on evolution and applied to questions of human descent. According to Maudsley, a family, like a zoological strain, needs to adapt to social and environmental changes if it is to avoid becoming obsolete. Lady Godolphin's building of her own home with her own money may be drawing on the 'modern' state of Victorian marital law. Following the Matrimonial Causes Act of 1857, women like Lady Godolphin had more control over the money they brought into a marriage. This modern financial liberty is highly inconsistent with the submissiveness of previous Godolphin wives. The first ever Godolphin, for example, murdered his unfortunate spouse:

> [He] killed her by gradual and long-continued ill-treatment. [...] He wanted her out of the way that another might fill her place. He pretended to have discovered that she was not worthy: than which assertion nothing could be more shameful and false, for she was one of the best ladies ever created. She was a De Commins, daughter of the warrior Richard de Commins, who was brave as she was good. She died; and the Wicked Godolphin turned her coffin out of the house.
>
> (p. 238)

Hearing 'of his child's death, [De Commins] hastened to Ashlydyat' where he was murdered by Godolphin (p. 239). Before he died, however, De Commins, gasping for breath, 'cursed the Godolphins, and prophesied that the shadow of his daughter's bier, as it appeared then, should remain to bring a curse upon the Godolphins' house for ever' (p. 239). Although the story is one of unjustified and unreasonable victimisation, the modern Godolphins are not ashamed of the history but proud of it. A pride, moreover, that blends with the gratification they feel for their estate: 'People thought that the Godolphins loved [Ashlydyat] from its associations and traditions; from the very fact that certain superstitions attached to it' (p. 13). Lady Godolphin's 'self-willed' decision to live elsewhere is thus inconsistent with the family's ancestral traditions, which seemingly required the Godolphin women to submit to the wills of their husbands. The family's ruin could therefore be viewed as extinction caused by their inability to adapt to mid-nineteenth-century changes – especially those endowing women with their own forms of self-help.

In believing in a superstition like the Ashlydyat curse, the Godolphins are, according to Victorian scientific standards, ill-equipped to deal with the pressures of the nineteenth century. The legend of the Shadow is told mainly through dialogues of female characters, suggesting that the myth is kept alive and bequeathed by the family's women. Yet, it is Godolphin men that see the Shadow and, when they do, experience a mental conflict between their progressive proclivities and the inexplicable superstition. In the following scene, for example, the Shadow is observed by Thomas Godolphin (Sir George's eldest son and heir) and his friend Lord Averil:

> You and I are rational beings, Averil, not likely to be led away by superstitious folly: we live in an enlightened age, little tolerable of such. And yet, here we stand, gazing with dispassionate eyes at that Shadow, in full possession of our sober judgement. [...] The Shadow of Ashlydyat is ridiculed from one end of the country to another; spoken of – when spoken of at all – as an absurd superstition of the Godolphins. But there the shadow is: and not all the ridicule extant can do away with the plain fact, I see it: but I cannot explain it.
>
> (pp. 267–8)

An authorial enunciation is made, earlier in the novel, to defend the narration of such superstitious subject matter:

> Foolish superstitions, you will be inclined to call them, as contrasted with the enlightenment of these matter-of-fact days – I had almost said these days of materialism. [...] Whence the shadow came, whether it was ghostly or earthly, whether those, learned in science and philosophy, could account for it by nature's laws, whether it was cast by any gaseous vapour arising in the moonbeams, I am unable to say. If you ask me to explain it, I cannot: if you ask, why then do I write about it, I can only answer, because I have seen it. I have seen it with my own unprejudiced eyes.
>
> (pp. 13–5)

In both extracts, the 'superstitious folly' of the Ashlydyat legend is highly incongruent with the 'enlightened', scientific awareness of the 'matter-of-fact [...] days of materialism'. At the very least, it seems that believing in the curse is a dated opinion, highly out of key with the forward-facing tenacity of the nineteenth century. It is hardly surprising, therefore, that the family becomes extinct. Superstition appears to be, like Danesbury and Halliburton's thoughts of their mothers, a form of looking back – a type of cognitive atavism. Believing in 'the supernatural', warned Maudsley,

> will not help but hinder intellectual development, will not strengthen but weaken moral character. By holding notions which are not founded on reason and cannot be reasoned about [...] the mind goes counter to the very principles of its intellectual being, undermines its own foundations, proceeds with a fundamental inconsistency declaring itself in every phase of its growth.[52]

Superstition was counter-productive – an intellectual flaw passed from generation to generation. Set in this discursive context, the failures of the Godolphin race might be the result, not of Lady Godolphin's Folly only, but the 'superstitious folly' of the men, a possessive clinging to ancient allegories that are outdated.

This perceived importance of ancestral influence was not unrecognised by Samuel Smiles who, in *Self Help*, paused in his promotion of individual hard work to insist upon the rule of consequence:

> Man is a fruit formed and ripened by the culture of all the foregoing centuries; and the living generation continues the magnetic current of action and example destined to bind the remotest past with the most distant future. No man's acts die utterly; and though his body may resolve into dust and air, his good or his bad deeds will still be bringing forth fruit after their kind, and influencing future generations for all time to come.[53]

Pessimistic though this passage may seem, Smiles's warning regarding the results of ancestral actions is actually more optimistic than the cautionary messages we find in the writings of Maudsley and Mrs Wood. Smiles, for example, limits unhealthy consequences to actions that might be viewed as dissolute. Wicked Godolphin's murderous exploits are thus a good example of the 'bad deeds' Smiles perceived as damaging subsequent generations. By contrast, Maudsley believed that some acts might be well intentioned and *still* have unhealthy results for our descendants. For example, he believed, as previously noted, that the pursuit of success and financial security was a cause of atavism (the 'nest-building ape' syndrome). This suspicion is also played out by the Godolphins in Wood's novel. When Lady Godolphin first moves into Ashlydyat as a new bride she is surprised by the family's isolation from the rest of society: 'She was a woman who had no resources within herself, who lived but in excitement, and Ashlydyat's quietness overwhelmed her with *ennui*. She did not join in the love of the Godolphins for Ashlydyat' (p. 17, italics in original). This may provide an overt condemnation of Lady Godolphin, but it also connotes the family's alienation which, as a modern woman, she finds oppressive. The mansion is a remote fortress, cut off from the rest of society and standing amidst a barren landscape:

> At the extremity, opposite the ash-trees, there arose a high archway, a bridge built of grey stone. It appeared to have formed part of an ancient fortification, but there was no trace of water having run underneath it. Beyond the archway was a low round building, looking like an isolated windmill without sails. It was built of grey stone, and was called the belfry: though there were as little signs of bells ever having been in it, as there was of water beneath the bridge. The archway had been kept from decay; the belfry had not. [...] Immediately before the archway, for some considerable space, the ground was entirely bare. Not a blade of grass, not a shrub grew on it. Or, as the story went, *would* grow.
>
> (pp. 14–5, italics in original)

Like Satis House in *Great Expectations*, Ashlydyat is an estate of isolation, decay, and sterility. The passage's foregrounding of decrepit objects and the sense of 'bygone days' suggest that the Godolphins are fast approaching extinction. The fortress-like qualities of Ashlydyat ensure the property's alienation and might as well be a sign bearing 'no connection with any other establishment' like the nest-building apes portrayed by Hollingshead. The barrenness of the estate also concurs with prevailing scientific opinions on unsuccessful or counterproductive breeding. According to Maudsley, 'nature puts the ban of sterility on the morbid type, and thus manifests her resolve that man shall not continue a lower kind'.[54] As a race of men whose ambition has led to isolation and sterility, the Godolphins are a family that falls into this category of a 'morbid type'.

It is significant that 'nature puts the ban of sterility' upon their race by rendering them incapable of producing male heirs. Sir George's eldest son dies as a bachelor, leaving George, the gambler, the only propagator of the family. He marries the beautiful Maria Hastings who, six years into the marriage, is described as follows:

> Standing on the covered terrace outside the dining-room at the bank, in all the warm beauty of the late lovely spring morning, surrounded by luxuriant shrubs, by the perfume of flowers, the green lawn stretching out before her [...] was Maria Godolphin. [...] Six years and a half, turned, it is, since her marriage took place, and the little girl whom Maria is holding

by the hand is five years old. Just now Maria's face is all animation [...] but if you saw her at an unaccompanied moment, her face in repose, you might detect an expression of settled sadness in it. It arose from the loss of her children. Three had died in succession, one after the other; and this one, the eldest, was the only child remaining to her.

(p. 183)

This extract begins with an influx of fertile imagery, with 'luxuriant shrubs' and fragrant flora, yet as the passage continues, the fecundity gradually wanes – degenerates even – as Maria's reproductive failures are outlined. Her surviving child has inherited her mother's frailty:

A wondrously pretty little girl, her naked legs peeping between her frilled drawers and her white socks; with the soft brown eyes of her mother, and the Saxon curls of gold of her father. With her mother's eyes the child had inherited her mother's gentle temperament. [...] She had been named Maria; but the name, for familiar use, was corrupted into Meta: not to clash with Maria's.

(p. 183)

If Meta has inherited her mother's biological state, then the Godolphins seem to have reached their end. Like Maria's temperament, the transmission of her name is something that needs to be avoided; the name 'Meta' is the mother's inheritance 'corrupted' and tainted by the time it reaches her offspring. The novel aims to represent Maria as a poor breeder and George Godolphin seems to have drawn a bad lot in the matrimonial lottery. Maria's inability to produce healthy children begins with a miscarriage she has during her long wedding tour. Noticing a change in Maria at that time, Mrs Verrall asks her, 'what have you done with your roses?'

Maria's 'roses' came vividly into her cheeks at the question. 'I am not in strong health just now', was all she answered.
George smiled. 'There's nothing serious the matter, Mrs Verrall', said he. 'Maria will find her roses again after a while'.

(p. 172)

When Maria returns home to England, she is no longer 'in a condition' and explains why to her mother:

'My dear, you have been ill, George wrote me word. How did it happen? We were so sorry to hear it'.
'Yes, we were sorry too', replied Maria, her eyelashes resting on her hot cheek. 'It could not be helped'.
'But how did it happen?'

'It was my own fault: not my *intentional* fault, you know, mamma. It occurred the day after we reached Homburg. I and George were out walking and we met the Verralls. We turned with them, and then I had not hold of George's arm. Something was amiss in the street, a great mass of stones and earth and rubbish; and, to avoid a carriage that came by, I stepped into it. And, somehow, I slipped off. I did not appear to have hurt myself: but I suppose it shook me'.

(pp. 179–80, italics in original)

Maria's fall, however, is just one possible explanation for the miscarriage. Her accident occurs just as she discovers the full extent of her husband's gambling addiction. 'Good heavens, Maria!' George notices, 'how ill and tired you look!' He continues,

'What are you thinking of? What is the matter?'
Maria changed her position. She let her head slip from the easy-chair on to his sheltering arm. 'Mrs Verrall frightened me, George. Will you be angry with me if I tell you? She came in this evening, and she said you and Mr Verrall were losing all your money at the gaming-table'.

(p. 177)

Bearing in mind how medical treatises featured stories of women whose babies turned out to be monstrosities following shocks like this during pregnancy, George and Maria appear to have escaped lightly with the miscarriage. Although Maria believes her fall to be the true reason for her failed pregnancy, the chapter suggests that George's gambling may have been instrumental in the loss. Like Edith Lester in *Lady Adelaide's Oath*, Maria's frail constitution, which makes her a weak breeder, has more to do with her husband's dissipated habits than any inherent pathology. Certainly, when it comes to George's embezzlement, the links between a husband's dissolution and his wife's infirmities are drawn with greater clarity. In one of her characteristic addresses to the reader, Mrs Henry Wood explains why she does not outline the fiscal technicalities of George's fraud:

We have only to look to the records of our law courts – criminal, bankruptcy, and civil – for examples. [...] It is rather with what may be called the domestic phase of these tragedies that I would deal: the private, home details; the awful wreck of peace, of happiness, caused *there*. The world knows enough (rather too much, sometimes) of the public part of these affairs; but what does it know of the part behind the curtain? – the, if it may be so said, inner aspect?

(p. 348, italics in original)

Although this passage implies that the 'public part of these affairs' and the 'part behind the curtain' are essentially separate spheres of experience, the novel actually reveals a high level of interaction between the 'professional' lives of men and the private lives of women. Again, using the highly suggestive term 'folly', the narrator melodramatically exclaims:

> Oh! if these miserable ill-doers could but bear in their own person all the pain and shame! – if George Godolphin could but have [...] expiated all his folly alone! But it could not be. It never can or shall be. As the sins of the people in the Israelitish camp were laid upon the innocent and unhappy scape-goat, so the sins which men commit in the present day are heaped upon unconscious and guileless heads. As the poor scape-goat wandered away with his hidden burden into the remote wilderness, away from the haunts of man, so do these other heavily-laden ones stagger away with their unseen load, only striving to hide themselves from the eyes of men – anywhere – in patience and silence – praying to die.
>
> Every humiliation which George Godolphin had brought upon himself – every harsh word cast on him by the world – every innate sense of guilt and shame which must accompany such conduct, was expiated by his wife. Yes, it fell worst upon her [...because] she was part and parcel of himself.
>
> (p. 384)

Here we see a complex and ironic relationship between the emotional lives of women and the professional lives of men. The allegedly sickly bodies of women like Maria Godolphin and Edith Lester and the dangerous 'follies' of women like Lady Adelaide and Lady Godolphin appear to screen the male population's culpability for its own failures. The professional and private are, as Mrs Wood suggests, 'part and parcel' of each other. This is observable in how the failures of George's 'professional' life results in a sterile deadlock in his emotional, private life with Maria. 'In no way', the novel suggests, 'was Maria fitted to cope with this' (p. 384). It is not long after the embezzlement, therefore, that she dies from what her doctors diagnose as 'nervousness' (p. 448). Her illness is similar to Caroline Helstone's decline in Charlotte Brontë's *Shirley* (1849), although Caroline recovers from her malady. It is a form of wasting away caused by the internalisation of worry. Maria 'bur[ies] the load of her care' (p. 346) and 'cloak[s] all too well her mental agony' (p. 338). The novel continues:

> Down deep in her heart she thrust that dreadful revelation of [George's] falsity, and strove to bury it as an English wife and gentlewoman has no resource but to do. Ay! To bury it; and to keep it buried! Though the concealment eat away her life.
>
> (p. 382)

Whereas Caroline Helstone's malady is a solitary experience, however, Maria's digestion of *her* sorrows is terminal for both her and the entire Godolphin cohort. In accordance with some concurrent medical ideas,

Maria's tragic story suggests that the failures of the 'modern peerage' are the result of pathologies harboured in the male professional realm.

Mrs Henry Wood's decision to change the title from *Lady Godolphin's Folly* to *The Shadow of Ashlydyat* seems likely, therefore, to have been more than just the moment's hesitation suggested by her son. The word 'shadow' has specific meanings in both a superstitious and medical context. Supernaturally, a shadow can denote an apparition, a phantom, which is the ostensible interpretation forwarded by the text. Medically, however, the term can also imply a central flaw like, for example, the 'hidden shadows' of insanity explored in the next chapter. As Maudsley's theories on the pathological effects of superstitions indicate, these two, ghostly and medical, connotations are not entirely unrelated. In *The Shadow of Ashlydyat* the curse of the Godolphins does become a cause of biological weakness; the family's belief in the legend ill-adapts them for the 'days of materialism'. From an exclusively medical point of view, however, the shadow also suggests that the 'getting on' obsessions of the family's ancestors (which, in the case of the first Godolphin, knew no ethical bounds) have become a central flaw in the race's congenital heritage. It seems hardly coincidental that Thomas Godolphin dies from an inherited bronchial disease. As Maudsley pointed out, hereditary lung and brain disorders were not unrelated:

> There are unquestionably very close relations between these two diseases; not only is one fourth of the deaths in asylums due to phthisis, but tubercle is often found in the bodies of the insane who have died without ever having been though to have tubercle.[55]

Like George Godolphin's gambling habits, therefore, Thomas's faulty lungs are a likely result of the 'sins' of his forefathers casting a sickly shadow over the health of the present generation. The novel's title change might therefore signify how, within the text itself, a change in culpability is made from Lady Godolphin's destructive follies to the Shadow of Ashlydyat – a central defect, an 'evil heritage', in the family's biological constitution.

A moth in the upturned tumbler: The control and display of passion in *Verner's Pride* (1863)

Mrs Henry Wood's fifth novel, *Verner's Pride*, is a text that reveals, more obviously than the stories hitherto discussed, why certain women were figured (by the male population) as dangerous epicentres of familial destruction. In the final section of this chapter, I want to argue that, through the characterisation of its central male character Lionel Verner, *Verner's Pride* reveals how the concept of possessing and controlling irrational, dangerous women was central to the definition and construction of a masculine, bourgeois identity in the mid-nineteenth century.

From an early age, Lionel is led to believe that he will inherit his uncle's substantial estate. Built around a Gothic mansion called 'Verner's Pride', the property is an obvious signifier of the head Verner's masculine and professional acumen. Lionel's grandfather 'erected this [house], calling it "Verner's Pride". An appropriate name. For if ever a poor human creature was proud of a house he has built, old Mr. Verner was proud of his – proud to folly'.[56] The house's current owner, Stephen Verner,

> kept it no secret that his nephew Lionel was to be his heir; and, as such, Lionel was universally regarded on the estate. 'Always provided that you merit it', Mr. Verner would say to Lionel in private; and so he had said to him from the very first. 'Be what you ought to be – [...] a man of goodness, of honour, of integrity; a *gentleman* [...] – and Verner's Pride will be yours. But if I find you forget your fair conduct, and forfeit the esteem of good men, so surely will I leave it away from you.
> (pp. 3–7, italics in original)

This emphasis on the word '*gentleman*' is clearly responsive to the period's discursive climate as, written in the early 1860s, *Verner's Pride* closely followed a number of texts, including *Great Expectations* and *Self Help*, that offered protracted analyses of the nature of the 'proper' gentleman. In a chapter entitled 'Character: The True Gentleman', for example, Smiles noticed how 'it is a grand old name, that of Gentleman, and has been recognised as a rank and a power in all stages of society'.[57] Like Dickens, Smiles was eager to show how 'riches and rank have no necessary connexion with genuine gentlemanly qualities'.[58] The way in which Stephen Verner binds Lionel's gentlemanly 'conduct' with the vast property, however, would suggest otherwise. When Stephen suspects Lionel has been involved in the disgrace and suicide of the young, working-class Rachel Frost, he wills the estate upon his stepson, John Massingbird or (should *he* die) his younger brother Frederick. Witnessing the amendments to the will, Stephen's physician, Dr West, persuades his daughter Sibylla to abandon her engagement to Lionel and marry Frederick who has shown an interest in her and is now closer to the Verner estate than her chosen lover. Still incognisant of their rights to Verner's Pride, John, Frederick, and his new wife Sibylla emigrate to Australia. When he is dying, however, Stephen regrets disinheriting Lionel and writes a codicil amending his previous last testament. Dr West, witnessing the signing of the alteration, steals the codicil so that the property remains with the Massingbirds. Accordingly, when Stephen dies, Lionel is forced to leave the house. When an attempt is made to contact the Massingbirds, however, it is discovered that the brothers are dead: John from a fever and Frederick killed by highwaymen. Verner's Pride is consequently restored to Lionel and so is Sibylla. Returning home widowed, she is proposed to by Lionel in 'a moment's delirium' (p. 184). Wood employs her favourite 'dead but not dead' strategy and John Massingbird reappears. He only concocted his death in order to avoid his debtors. Verner's Pride is once again taken from Lionel and, likewise, so is Sibylla who dies of inherited tuberculosis. When Dr West leaves the country because of a scandalous liaison with one of his female patients, the stolen codicil is recovered and Lionel again reclaims the estate. As one character remarks to Lionel's brother, 'what an extraordinary course of events seems to have taken place with regard to Verner's Pride! [...] Now your brother's, now not his; then his again, then not his! I cannot make it out' (p. 490). Indeed, one thing that the novel aims to show is that property is an itinerant thing and its ownership fundamentally unstable. The same might also be said of Sibylla. She is engaged to Lionel, marries Frederick, weds Lionel when Frederick dies, and finally dies herself. When Verner's Pride is eventually restored to Lionel, after his wife's death, we half expect Wood to resort to her 'dead but not dead' proclivities in order to restore Sibylla to Lionel also.

In life, Sibylla is portrayed as a highly sexual and dangerous woman. When she is first introduced to the reader, for example, the narrator gives specific emphasis to her exploitation of appearances:

Had you, with [a] critical eye, scanned the young lady, you would have found that of real beauty she possessed little. A small, pretty doll's face, with blue eyes and gold-coloured ringlets; a round face, betraying nothing very great, or good, or intellectual; only something fascinating. Her chief beauty lay in her complexion; by candlelight it was radiant and lovely, a pure red and white, looking like wax-work. A pretty, graceful girl she looked; and, what with her fascinations of person, of dress, and of manner, all of which she perfectly well knew how to display, she had contrived to lead more than one heart captive and to hold it fast in chains.

(p. 72)

Staring at her reflection in a mirror, Sibylla is interrupted by Lionel and pretends to have been watching a captive moth:

'I was looking at this', pointing to an inverted tumbler on the mantlepiece. 'Is it not strange that we should see a moth at this cold season?' [...] Did he see through the artifice? Did he suspect that the young lady had been admiring her own pretty face, and not the moth? Not he. Lionel's whole heart had long ago been given to that vain butterfly, Sibylla West, who was gay and fluttering, and really of little more use in life than the moth. [...] Sibylla did not love him. The two ruling passions of her heart were vanity and ambition. [...] She did not encourage him very much; she was rather in the habit of playing fast and loose with him; but that only served to rivet more tightly the links of his chain.

(pp. 72–3)

These descriptions of Lionel and Sibylla's relationship clearly draw on the Victorian idea, much explored in *Lady Adelaide's Oath*, that choosing a wife was a dangerous matter of chance. Sibylla's beauty and suitability for marriage are both constructed as a question of 'artifice'. The scene's metaphorical use of the moth is an interesting stylistic choice. On the one hand, Sibylla is figured as a moth disguised as a butterfly, yet, on the other, Lionel is like a captive insect drawn towards a flame. In this representation, Sibylla has much in common with the women of Braddon's fiction, especially Lady Audley, who is also portrayed as deceptive, intoxicating, and dangerous. Like Sir Michael and Robert Audley, Lionel is characterised as being held 'fast' in 'the chains' of Sibylla's mesmerizing, artificial beauty.

Verner's Pride makes more obvious references to Sibylla's sexuality as dangerous in a scene where she entices Lionel into proposing marriage for a second time:

> Standing there before the fire, her young, slender form habited in its black robes, was Sibylla. [...] Her head was uncovered, and her fair curls fell on her brilliant cheeks. It has been mentioned that her chief charm lay in her complexion: seen by candle-light, flushed as she was now, she was inexpressibly beautiful. A dangerous hour; a perilous situation for the still wounded heart of Lionel Verner.
>
> (p. 184)

In keeping with many mid-Victorian representations of women, this depiction of Sibylla blurs any distinctions between sexuality and danger. Her 'slender form' and 'uncovered' hair, for example, are rendered all the more 'beautiful' because of their proximity to the flames, which, again, invoke the image of Lady Audley whose hair is described as a 'tangled mass that surrounded her forehead like a yellow flame'.[59] As in the scene where Lady Audley burns Luke's inn, Sibylla is described as 'flushed'. She has all the explosiveness of the women discussed in chapter one, whose blood rushes were thought to augment explosive, psychosomatic conditions. Her death, therefore, is not an apathetic wasting away like Maria Godolphin's but a 'burning out' of energy caused primarily by her jealousy of Lionel's relationship with another female character.[60] In a scene that would be echoed by Charlotte St John's passionate beating of Benja in *St. Martin's Eve* (1866), Sibylla aggressively confronts her husband over his alleged extramarital connection:

> What precisely happened, Lionel could never afterwards recall. [...] Lionel remembered little more until he saw Sibylla lying back, gasping, blood pouring from her mouth. [...] Words that burnt into the brain of Sibylla Verner [had] turned the current of her life's pulses. [...] Fighting her hands on the empty air, fighting for breath or for speech, so she remained for a passing moment: and then the blood began to trickle from her mouth. The excitement had caused her to burst a blood vessel.
>
> (pp. 424–5)

Sibylla's passion, like that of Charlotte St John and many of Braddon's dangerous women, is figured in biological terms. Although in this case her aggression is caused by the alleged misdeeds of her husband, Sibylla's paroxysm concurs with contemporaneous descriptions of female passion as physical and explosive. For Sibylla, vehement words are portrayed as blood 'burst[ing]' to the surface and her passions are figured as having a debilitating effect upon her husband. As we have seen, he is portrayed as being held fast in her chains; a captive moth to her flame.

Yet, looking back at the latter metaphor, we could also interpret it as representative of Sibylla and how *she* could be, metaphorically, the moth in an upturned tumbler. It soon becomes apparent, for example, that, during their short marriage, Sibylla's irrational temper is something Lionel values. This is perhaps best exemplified in a brilliant scene, worth citing at length, where Sibylla becomes afraid of a thunderstorm:

> Up she started at the sound of [Lionel's] voice, and flew to him. There lay her protection; and in spite of her ill-temper and her love of aggravation, she felt and recognised it. Lionel held her in his sheltering arms, bending her head down upon his breast, so that she might see no ray of light: as she had been wont to do in former storms. [...] He stood patiently holding her. Every time the thunder burst above their heads, he could feel her heart beating against his. One of her arms was around him; the other he held. He did not speak: he only clasped her closer every now and then, that she might be reminded of her shelter. [...] She lifted her head from its resting-place. Her blue eyes were bright with excitement, her delicate cheeks crimson, her golden hair fell around her. [...] Lionel held her to his side, his arm still round her. She trembled yet; trembled excessively; her bosom rose and fell beneath his hand. [...] In these moments, when she was gentle, yielding, clinging to him for protection, three parts of his old love for her would come back again.
>
> (pp. 307–9)

As with the elided sex scene in *East Lynne*, the storm appears to be a euphemistic way of outlining a sexual encounter between husband and wife. Notice, for example, how the bodies of the two are entwined. The scene is awash with beating hearts, shivering frames, and heaving bosoms. The connection between the two also highlights an unmistakable distribution of power. Under the pretext of protecting Sibylla, Lionel has an opportunity of demonstrating some dominance over her. With the emphasis on her golden locks and crimson countenance, the reader is reminded of previous scenes in which Sibylla played the dangerous and intoxicating siren. The role played by *Lionel* in those earlier encounters, the captive moth to the flame, is clearly different to the way he now towers over his wife, enveloping her with his own body. Rather than incapacitating and deluding Lionel, Sibylla's passion now allows her husband to fulfil a domineering role.

This is also evident in the financial state of Lionel and Sibylla's affairs. Despite her fear during the storm, Sibylla does not forget to hide a letter she was writing to her creditors:

> In spite of the sudden terror which overtook her, she did not forget to put the letter – so far as it had been written – safely away. It was not expedient that her husband's eyes should fall upon it: Sibylla had many answers to write now to importunate creditors.
>
> (p. 308)

As with Lady Adelaide, Sibylla is an over-extravagant woman whose expenditure seems to draw the lifeblood out of the Verner estate.[61] Although, unlike Adelaide, Sibylla does not ruin the Verners, 'her extravagance was something frightful, and Lionel did not know how to check it' (p. 240). Female extravagance, a favoured theme in Wood's fiction, is figured in this novel as another one of Sibylla's excesses. Like her temper, it appears to challenge Lionel's authority but ends up reasserting it. According to Smiles, for example,

> there are many tests by which a gentleman may be known; but there is one that never fails – How does he *exercise power* over those subordinate to him? How does he conduct himself towards women and children? [...] The discretion, forbearance, and kindliness with which power in such cases is used may indeed be regarded as the crucial test of gentlemanly character.[62]

It follows that the more 'discretion and forbearance' a man shows towards his family, the more 'gentlemanly' his character appears. The more excessive a wife like Sibylla is allowed to become, the more kindly and gentlemanly a husband like Lionel can appear. Lionel himself admits, 'when I married Sibylla, I took her with her virtues and her faults; and I am ready to defend both' (pp. 381–2) – an admission that barely corresponds with the image of him as a 'moth to the flame'. As with his vast mansion, therefore, Sibylla seems to be part of the stronghold that defines him as a gentleman.

This is also evident with reference to Lionel's relationship with certain working-class characters. In addition to 'Nest-Building Apes', *Verner's Pride* was printed alongside a run of articles in *Once a Week* exploring the living conditions of Britain's rural poor. In one essay, entitled on 'How to Deal with Our Rural Poor', the well-to-do female writer describes her encounters with the poor inhabitants of her husband's estate:

> [The] cottages were low, miserable places. [...] Most of them consisted of one room on the ground floor, with one above, reached by a narrow ladder, and a 'lean-to' behind. It was a service of difficulty to visit the sick.[63]

Such conditions, she adds, have led to a proliferation of illegitimacy:

> In making my calls and ascertaining exactly of how many each family consisted, I was truly shocked to find the number of, what they were

pleased to call, love children, and the very lenient view taken of lapses of male and female chastity. [...] I showed my disapproval of all such proceedings by omitting to invite any such delinquents to our tea-drinkings, and by giving no caudle to such damsels as returned to the paternal abode under disgraceful circumstances.

Neither parents nor children seemed to view this great sin as they ought.[64]

One can only imagine the disappointment felt by those not invited to the essayist's tea-drinkings. In *Verner's Pride*, Mrs Henry Wood has descriptions of the rural poor and uses similar images. Lionel's brother Jan, for example, is a physician. Describing his entrance into the lodgings of the illegitimately pregnant Alice Hook, the narrator inquires,

did you ever pay a visit to a room of this social grade? If not, you will deem the introduction of this one highly coloured. Had Jan been a head and shoulders shorter he might have been able to stand up in the lean-to attic, without touching the roof. On a low bedstead, on a flock mattress, lay the mother and two children, about eight and ten. [...] Opposite, on a straw mattress, slept three sons, grown up, or nearly so; between these beds was another straw mattress where lay Alice and her sister, a year younger: no curtains, no screens, no anything. All were asleep, with the exception of the mother and Alice: the former could not rise from her bed; Alice appeared too ill to rise from hers. Jan stooped and entered.

(p. 288)

As with the non-fictional articles in *Once a Week*, *Verner's Pride* portrays the bold, middle-class visitor as stooping (physically and metaphorically) in order to enter the working-class home. Both texts reveal concerns as to how to treat paupers medically and view their cramped conditions as responsible for the propagation of illegitimacy. The narrator notices how Alice Hook's home 'is not a pleasant room to linger in, so we will leave Jan to it' (p. 288). Before our attention is discreetly redirected, however, we observe enough to understand why the narrator is reluctant to linger. In keeping with Thomas Doubleday's theories on working-class struggling as amplifying their breeding capacities, the description of Alice Hook's family suggests that the poor were procreating excessively. The working-class characters of the novel thus appear to have something in common with Sibylla: both seem to symbolise excessive sexuality and passion. Jan's encounter with the poor also reflects Lionel's relationship with his wife. As a middle-class, observant figure, Jan adopts a higher moral ground. The excesses of the poor justify his self-delegated position of superiority. It reflects how Lionel's encounters with his wife's uncontrollable temper allow him to adopt the loftier position.

All of these ideas are interestingly brought together in an episode in which Lionel attempts to control a riot of angry women. The scene occurs shortly after the death of Lionel's benefactor and the loss of Verner's Pride. Under the control of Fred Massingbird's manager, the estate's workers are unjustly paid in tokens for a local shop, with whose owners the manager has struck a deal. When the shop attempts to sell the workers contaminated offal, their wives gather outside the store in protest:

> Not a peaceable crowd evidently, although it was composed for the most part of the gentler sex; but a crowd of threatening arms and inflamed faces, and swaying white caps and noisy tongues. [... Lionel enters the scene.] They drew aside when they saw who it was. In their passions – hot and angry then – perhaps no one, friend or enemy, would have stood a chance of being deferred to except Lionel Verner. [...] The particular grievance this morning, however easy to explain, was somewhat difficult to comprehend, when twenty tongues were speaking at once; and those, shrill and excited. [...] Excited women, suffering under what they deem a wrong cannot be made quiet: you may as well try to stem a rising flood. Lionel resigned himself to his fate, and listened: and at this stage in the affair a new feature struck his eye and surprised him. Scarcely one of the women but bore in her hand some uncooked meat. Such meat! Lionel drew himself and his coat from too close proximity to it.
>
> (pp. 118–9)

As with the representation of Sibylla, the novel's portrait of the mob of angry women, reminiscent of the rebellious female crowds in *A Tale of Two Cities* (1859), features 'inflamed faces' and a heated, volcanic flood of energy. In this scene, the women also threaten that the manager might 'get burned up some night in his bed' (p. 122), which clearly echoes the fiery hysterics of Lady Audley and Bertha Rochester. The image of these irrational women brandishing contaminated offal is also in keeping with Victorian perceptions of femininity as essentially corporeal and polluted. It is an image used years later by Thomas Hardy in his portrayal of Arabella, the *femme fatale* of *Jude the Obscure* (1899). Arabella first introduces herself to Jude by flinging a 'pig's pizzle' at him. There is the likelihood that the rioter's meat in *Verner's Pride* ('such meat!') is also animal genitalia. Despite the disconcertion this causes Lionel, he adopts the role of peacekeeper and manages to dispel the crowd temporarily. Yet, because he no longer owns the estate, he is unable to resolve the situation completely. As another character reminds him, 'you have no right to interfere' (p. 123). This appears to deliver a serious challenge to his sense of masculine selfhood. Shortly after his 'control' of the female mob he has a psychosomatic breakdown: 'Lionel's voice faltered. An awful pain – a pain, the like of which he had never felt – had seized him in the head. He put his hand up to it, and fell' (p. 124). With the loss of Verner's Pride and his encounter with the mob, Lionel experiences a form of psychological abstraction – a loss of selfhood:

> Whether it was sun-stroke, or whether it was but the commencement of a fever, which had suddenly struck him down that day, certain it was, that a violent sickness attacked him, and he lay for many, many days – days and weeks [...] between life and death. Fever and delirium struggled with life which should obtain the mastery.[65]

Although Lionel diagnoses his condition as sunstroke, his malady bears all the hallmarks of hysteria. When he overcomes the fevered delirium, for example, the malady becomes more ornamental than real. As Frederick Skey complained in his lectures on hysteria:

> People without compulsory occupation, who lead a life of both bodily and mental inactivity – people whose means are sufficiently ample to indulge in, and who can purchase, the luxury of illness, the daily visit of the physician, and, not the least, the sympathy of friends – these real comforts come home to the hearts of those ornamental members of society who are living examples of an intense sensibility, whether morbid or genuine, who can afford to be ill, and will not make the effort to be well. [...] A poor man cannot afford this indulgence, and so he throws the sensations aside by mental resolution.[66]

In Wood's novel, Jan Verner, Lionel's physician brother, utters something remarkably similar:

> It's stewing and fretting indoors, fancying themselves ill, that keeps folks back. [...] What you have to do is to rouse yourself, and believe you are well, instead of lying up here. My mother was angry with me for telling her the same, but didn't she get well after it? Look at the poor! They have their illnesses that bring 'em down to skeletons; but when did you ever find them lie up, after they got better! They can't; they are obliged to go out and turn-to again; and the consequence is they are well in no time.
> (p. 128)

Observe how Lionel's condition aligns him to his mother, who suffers from a similar malady. Additionally, Jan implies that Dr West, 'keeps his patients dilly-dallying on, when he might get them well in no time', yet 'he can't grumble at me', he adds to Lionel, 'for doctoring *you*' (p. 128, italics in original). The term 'doctoring' carries additional connotations of castration and therefore suggests that, in succumbing to a malady that was seen by the Victorians to be essentially feminine, Lionel experiences a serious challenge to his 'manhood'.

Skey and Jan's representations of the poor as unable to indulge in ornamental illnesses like Lionel's is carried even further when Lionel visits the home of one of the estate workers. Like Jan's visit to Alice Hook, Lionel stands on the threshold of (the appropriately named) Grind's home contemplating the miseries within:

> On the side of the kitchen, opposite the door, was a pallet-bed stretched against the wall, and on it lay [...] Grind, dressed. It was a small room, and it appeared literally full of children, of encumbrances of all sorts. [...] The children were in various stages of *un*dress. [...] But that Grind's eye had caught his, Lionel might have hesitated to enter so uncomfortable a place.
> (p. 135, italics in original)

Again, the scene is burdened with nuances of over-abundance and sexuality as it is 'full of' encumbrances and half-naked children. This time, however, the middle-class visitor is unable to adopt a high moral stance. Grind, who is sick with 'ague' (p. 135), is unwilling to dilly-dally in his illness but works through it. 'Yesterday', he tells Lionel, 'I got down to the field and earned what'll come to eighteenpence':

> 'Do you mean to say you went to work in your present state?' asked Lionel. [...] 'Don't you think it would be better if you gave yourself complete rest, not attempting to go out to work until you are stronger?'
> 'I couldn't afford it, sir. And as to it's being better for me, I don't see that. If I can work, sir, I'm better at work. I know it tires me but I believe I get stronger the sooner for it. [...] Folks get more harm from idleness than they do from work'.
> (pp. 136–7)

Frederick Skey and Jan Verner would agree. Grind's example, which Wood recommends 'many a rich man might have taken pattern by' (p. 136), not only echoes their contentions that illness prevailed in those who could 'afford it', but also reverberates with the Smilesian promotion of work as the curer of all ills. 'Nothing', exclaims Smiles, 'can be more cheering and beautiful than to see a man combating suffering by patience, triumphing in his integrity, and who, when his feet are bleeding and his limbs failing him, still walks upon his courage'.[67] Lionel Verner is not slow in learning from Grind's example:

> 'What a lesson for me!' he involuntarily exclaimed. 'This poor half-starved man struggling patiently onward through his sickness; while I, who had every luxury about me, spent my time repining. What a lesson! Heaven help me to take it to heart'.
> (p. 138)

Lionel does take it to heart and soon recovers.

Verner's Pride's consideration of the relationship between class, gender, and power is thus a complex and contradictory investigation. Although the novel recognises how women and the poorer classes inhabited the same marginal positions in relation to the middle-class male, and also how notions of sexual excess were employed to enforce controls over both groups, Wood's text nevertheless closes with the ideological message that industry was the key to health and success. *Verner's Pride* is a text as intricate as the popular discussions it emerged alongside. While it seems to confirm the essentially passionate and excessive natures of women, it also highlights how central such 'fears' were to the construction of the 'gentlemanly' ideal.

According to Charles Wood's hagiographic biography of his mother, Mrs Wood suffered from an undiagnosed, psychosomatic malady in 1862. Her physician, Dr Hetley, 'could tell what it was not [but] could not be sure what it was'.[68] As 'books of science were [the] delight' of Wood's husband,[69] he owned an extensive collection of texts on medicine. Mrs Wood consulted them in order to discover the true nature of her illness. Mr Wood and Dr Hetley were not pleased with her conduct:

> Her husband gently remonstrated with her for referring to medical works in her present state. [...] Dr. Hetley looked grave, [...] 'It is a mistake to take up these books', he said, [...] 'Mr. Wood must keep his books under lock and key; they are only for such men as he and I, who can go to the root of these matters. You must promise me never to meddle with them again'.[70]

The biographer's dismissive representation of his mother superficially consulting her husband's medical library is hardly consistent with the ways in which her novels examined some of the period's key scientific and cultural developments. Mrs Wood's fiction, although often ambiguous and convoluted, frequently goes 'to the root of these matters' and suggests that its author did more than just 'meddle' with her husband's library. In particular, her novels draw on the period's fascinations with middle-class gentlemanliness and violent femininity in order to question astutely the intricate relationship between these two ideas. Many of her books attest to the fact that there is a hidden, smouldering energy within *all* women and that it posed an omnipresent threat to the nuclear family. Yet her stories also reveal some awareness of how such images could supply the male population with a platform on which to display their professed glories. Moreover, the complex and multi-layered nature of Mrs Wood's plots permit them to hold more than one possible explanation for their events. In keeping with the period's uneasy views on bourgeois progress, Mrs Wood's fictions portray the respectable gentleman as his own worst enemy. His desire to get on in life seems to have rendered him inert, sterile, and alienated. He is, we might argue, a nest-building ape. He has 'no connection with any other establishment' and, through his forward-facing obsessions, has jeopardised the health of the nation's future.

5
Hidden Shadows: Dangerous Women and Obscure Diseases in the Novels of Wilkie Collins

Since the early 1980s many literary critics have held firmly to the assumption that Collins's best-known works are subversive because they question the links between appearance and reality.[1] Yet, as my preceding chapters have aimed to show, if the main effect of Collins's fiction was to reveal how hidden energies lurked beneath false appearances, his works could hardly claim to be subversive or innovative because the concept of 'outward show' not correlating with 'inner realities' was already a ubiquitous Victorian idea. Studies like Gilbert and Gubar's *Madwoman in the Attic* (1979) have established how such ideas were pivotal to nineteenth-century conceptualisations of femininity. As an example, William Black earnestly warned the male readers of *Temple Bar* against female flirts in 1869. 'Let all men beware', he ominously advised, of 'the typical flirt – the vampire who lives upon the hearts of men. [...] This terrible woman [...] generally comes in the most innocent guise – generally that of a little, soft, big-eyed girl'.[2] Collins's fiction was not unique in representing a non-correlative relationship between appearance and reality. Instead, it appears to have drawn upon a widespread concept that was often used to substantiate the era's most oppressive gender norms as well as to question them. Modern studies that aim to demonstrate how Collins 'lifts the veneer' of nineteenth-century respectability thus reproduce a Victorian binary that, I argue, the author sought to exploit and unravel. Jenny Bourne Taylor is more accurate in her suggestion that Collins used ideas that were already in place. Sensation novels in general, she argues, '*drew on* and broke down distinct methods of generating strangeness within familiarity, of creating the sense of a weird and different world within the ordinary, everyday one'.[3]

At the height of Collins's success in 1862, the *Cornhill* claimed that science had played a particularly significant role in this growing sense of appearance as a deceptive veneer. Through science, it remarked, 'man [...] concedes that the world is not what it seems' and continued,

> the world becomes doubled to us: it is one world of things perceived; one unperceivable. [...] In short, all nature grows like an enchanted garden;

a fairy world in which unknown existences lurk under familiar shapes, and every object seems ready, at the shaking of a wand, to take on the strangest transformations. [...] The most solid substances become mere appearances, and we feel ourselves separated from the very reality of things by an impenetrable barrier.[4]

Although this article does not mention mental science directly, psychology, it seems, aimed to convince its followers that 'unknown existences lurk[ed] under familiar shapes'. In 1860, for instance, the same year that *The Woman in White* was published, psychologist Forbes Winslow published a lengthy and eccentric volume *On the Obscure Diseases of the Brain and Disorders of the Mind*. Along with his *Lettsomian Lectures on Insanity* (1854), *Obscure Diseases* was one of the few psychological treatises included in Collins's personal library.[5] In his preface, Winslow claims that *Obscure Diseases* aims to offer 'the unitiated, as well as those who are medically educated',[6] a guidebook for detecting easily overlooked signs of 'obscure', 'insidious', and dangerous mental conditions:

> Lamentable instances of insanity, suicide, homicide, and murder, are matters of daily occurrence, springing out of unobserved and neglected affections of the brain and mind.
> It is with the view of exciting a deeper interest in and of awakening a profounder and more philosophical attention to this important subject that these pages have been penned.[7]

In order to justify such aims, Winslow suggested that nobody was exempt from the onset of insanity. He utilises imagery familiar to readers of Gothic fiction when he inquires,

> who has not occasionally had a demon pursuing with remorseless impetuosity his every footstep, suggesting to his ever-active and often morbidly-disturbed and perverted imagination the commission of some dark deed of crime, from the conception of which he has at the time recoiled with horror? Is there any mind, pure and untainted, which has not yielded, when the reason and moral sense have been transiently paralysed and God's grace ceases to exercise an influence over the heart, to the seduction of impure thought, lingered with apparent pleasure on the contemplation of physically unchaste images or delighted in a fascinating dalliance with criminal thoughts?[8]

As with the depictions of the Creature in *Frankenstein* (1818) and Robert Mannion in Collins's *Basil* (1852), insane and 'criminal thoughts' are figured in this passage as a demonic 'other' stalking the footsteps of the individual. It is an extraordinary image through which Winslow attempted to warn his readers that nobody was exempt from irrational cerebral phenomena. 'Is not every bosom', he asks, 'polluted by a dark, leprous spot, corroding ulcer, or portion of moral gangrene?'[9] He answers his own rhetorical question in the affirmative and, citing the words of fellow psychologist John Abercrombie, cautions the reader to watch himself and those closest to him with the strictest scrutiny: 'Hence the supreme importance of cultivating in early life the habit of looking within, the practice of rigidly questioning ourselves as to what we are, and what we are doing'.[10]

Although, unlike many of his colleagues, Winslow appears to represent these ideas as having no specific gender implications, his textbook's most striking examples of people who have fallen prey to their 'inner demons' are women. One of his most disturbing case histories, for example, is that of an American woman who suddenly decapitated her husband with an axe. Unbeknown to herself and her family, she had long been harbouring murderous propensities that reached their zenith one morning. This is her own account of that day's events:

About daybreak I got up and built a fire. Something appeared to tell me there was dreadful work to be done. I was very much agitated when the thought came into my head that I must kill him. [...] I felt that I must kill him to save myself. I accordingly went to where the children lay, and drew out a broad axe from under their bed that he had borrowed from a neighbour. I went right to his bed, with the axe in my hand, trembling like a leaf. He was lying on his right side, with his neck bare, and I immediately struck him the one fatal lick across the neck. He kind o' struggled, and partly raised himself to his knees, and wakened the children, a-dying. My daughter came running to me in a fright, and took the axe out of my hands, screaming that I had murdered father, and sprang to him and kissed him on his forehead, crying – 'Oh! he's my poor, poor father'.[11]

Winslow gives no extenuating circumstances for the woman's actions but presents them as utterly without cause or warning. Taken in conjunction with the murder cases that Winslow was involved with, like Mary Ann Brough's, such narratives promoted 'the supreme importance' of not only 'looking within' oneself, but of surveying others as well, especially women.

This perceived necessity for watching the female population seems to have been reinscribed in most of the novels produced by Collins in his forty-year career. In an 1858 edition of *Household Words*, Collins commented, under the narrative guise of 'A Charming Woman', on the lack of convincing female villains in literature: 'I find, for instance, that the large proportion of the bad characters in [...] otherwise very charming stories are always men. As if women were not a great deal worse!' It continues:

Let all rising young gentlemen who are racking their brains in search of originality [in writing fiction] take the timely hint which I have given them in these pages. Let us have a new fictitious literature, in which not only the Bores shall be women, but the villains too.[12]

Despite its deliberate irony, the article seems to have provided a manifesto for Collins's long-standing literary objectives. He chose to reprint the essay as part of an 1863 collection of articles and short stories entitled *My Miscellanies*. Comprised of contributions to *Household Words* and *All the Year Round*, the text has been unjustly neglected by modern scholars. It provides a unique register of the kinds of issues that Collins saw as deserving reiteration and preservation in book form. One of these issues, it seems, was the representation of violent women in literature.

From Collins's own historical novel *Antonina, or the Fall of Rome* (1848) up to his penultimate work, *The Legacy of Cain* (1889), he frequently returned to the idea of violent or dangerous womanhood. Academics are divided on whether the author's interest in such women was an open-minded or conservative preoccupation. Lillian Nayder, for example, believes that 'by highlighting the dangers of female nature', Collins 'reinscrib[es] the social norms and stereotypes that he sets out to critique'.[13] Alexander Grinstein supports her idea. He has contested that Collins's portrayals of violent women are an 'opportunity to describe women in the most uncomplimentary of terms' and that they reveal the author's 'contempt and hatred of the female sex'.[14] In contrast, Virginia Morris believes that Collins's use of 'criminal women' is 'bold' and 'deliberately challeng[ing to] the conventions of middle-class Victorian society'.[15] Yet, it seems that both these views are too narrow. Collins drew on an existing understanding of appearances as deceptive in order to investigate the allegation that all women harboured insanely violent possibilities. In so doing, his novels reveal a lot about the intrinsic problems of masculinity.

'What could I do?': *The Woman in White* (1860)

Throughout *The Woman in White*, Walter Hartright's detective work has much in common with the perceived analytical skills of nineteenth-century psychiatrists. Following his early encounters with Anne Catherick, he develops an obsession with tracking her down and deciphering the mysteries of her identity. 'The way to the Secret', he writes, 'lay through the mystery, hitherto impenetrable to all of us, of the woman in white'.[16] As a man searching for an elusive figure that, for him at least, typifies lunacy, Hartright appears to emulate the psychologists' preoccupation with 'penetrat[ing] behind the curtain' and unravelling the signs of insanity thought indiscernible to the unspecialised observer. Winslow writes:

> To the unskilled, untutored and untrained eye the disease is, in its early stages, occasionally altogether invisible. Even to the practised apprehension of the experienced physician it is almost indiscernible, or at least of a dubious and uncertain character.[17]

The same notions are echoed in *The Woman in White* when Collins describes Hartright's position in relation to Anne. Like an obscure cerebral disease, she frequently evades the grasp of men searching for her. Hartright admits, for instance, that 'like a Shadow she first came to me, in the loneliness of the night. Like a Shadow she passes away, in the loneliness of the dead'.[18] To the 'untrained eyes' of the Cumberland locals, moreover, she is virtually invisible: 'They were quite unable to describe her, and quite incapable of agreeing about the exact direction in which she was proceeding when they last saw her' (p. 83). At one point in the text, Count Fosco even refers to her as 'our invisible Anne' (p. 339). The search for the novel's eponymous central figure thus appears to echo, in a Gothic tale of mystery and suspense, the era's scientific preoccupations with pursuing elusive cerebral disorders.

Yet, during his search for Anne Catherick, Walter's penetrative gaze gets redirected onto himself. In the following passage, for example, Marian has just discovered a letter written by Anne Catherick. Hartright wonders whether Anne is 'deranged':

> Those words and the doubt which had just escaped me as to the sanity of the writer of the letter, acting together on my mind, suggested an idea, which I was literally afraid to express openly, or even to encourage secretly. I began to doubt whether my own faculties were not in danger of losing their balance. It seemed almost like a monomania to be tracing back everything strange thing that happened, everything unexpected that was said, always to the same hidden source and the same sinister influence.
>
> (p. 80)

Like Robert in *Lady Audley's Secret* (1862), who wonders whether Lady Audley is truly the mad adventuress he suspects her of being or whether it is *he* who is insane, Walter's consideration of Anne Catherick's sanity leads him to question how far the process of psychological diagnosis is *itself* an unbalanced mental fixation. Bearing in mind the similarities Hartright shares with nineteenth-century psychiatrists, it seems, therefore, that *The Woman in White* questions the usefulness of the burgeoning psychological profession, while using its imagery and ideas. This concept of the psychiatric diagnosis as being itself a form of mental aberration was not exclusive to the plot of *The Woman in White*. For example, following his defence of George Victor Townley on the grounds of insanity in 1864, Winslow was accused, most acerbically by the *Glasgow Medical Journal*, of having the symptoms he was employed in uncovering and treating. The journal wrote, for instance, that the disorders Winslow purportedly discovered were, firstly, the stuff of his own invention, and, secondly, symptomatic of his own mental imbalances:

> With the fullest conviction of our sanity, we should dread – or hopefully look forward to, as the case might be – an hour's interview with this great

flaw-finder; for either in our moral or in our mental constitution he would discover some screw loose, and by gently moving it backwards and forwards, would naturally find it looser and looser. [...] It is scarcely our business to speculate as to the origin of these comprehensive theories of the mind of the distinguished physician in question; but it may not be irrelevant to go as far as to assume, that when a man is constantly examining cases of real or supposed insanity, a period arrives when his judgement is in a certain manner affected by the continual practice which he has to undergo. [...] Dr. Winslow is fast arriving at a very literal application of the phrase, 'A mad world, my master'. Constant ministering to diseased minds appears to be super-inducing with him a belief that most minds, if there be but an opportunity of probing them, will turn out unsound. He is by no means the first physician devoted to this branch of medical inquiry in who a tendency of this nature has manifested itself; but it must be confessed that it has rarely been carried to a greater and more bewildering height.[19]

Thus, Hartright's suspicion that by tracing everything to the same 'hidden source' he is experiencing a species of monomania actually concurs with a prevailing Victorian apprehension that the process of detecting obscure mental disorders was itself a psychopathological obsession. This, I argue, is the context through which we might best understand the gender dynamics of Collins's best-known book. What appears to be a search for the hidden improprieties of female identity actually lays bare the latent horrors of the *male* psyche.

When Hartright first meets Anne Catherick on the road to Hampstead his fears are largely unnecessary and exaggerated. Long before he discovers that Anne has escaped from an asylum, she has the ability to make his blood run cold:

In one moment, every drop of blood in my body was brought to a stop by the touch of a hand laid lightly and suddenly on my shoulder from behind me.

I turned on the instant, with my fingers tightening round the handle of my stick.

There, in the middle of the broad, bright high-road – there, as if it had that very moment sprung out of the earth or dropped from the heaven – stood the figure of a solitary Woman, dressed from head to foot in white garments; her face bent in grave enquiry on mine, her hand pointing to the dark cloud over London, as I faced her.

I was far too seriously startled by the suddenness with which this extraordinary apparition stood before me, in the dead of night and in that lonely place, to ask what she wanted.

(p. 20)

Although he is confused over 'what sort of a woman she was, and how she came to be out alone in the high road, an hour after midnight' (p. 21), Walter is nevertheless sure that Anne is either an escaped lunatic or a prostitute. 'What had I done?' he asks,

> assisted the victim of the most horrible of all false imprisonments to escape; or cast loose on the wide world of London an unfortunate creature, whose actions it was my duty, mercifully to control? I turned sick at heart when the question occurred to me.
>
> (pp. 28–9)

Although it is arguable that Hartright is disturbed by meeting a possible lunatic or prostitute, his fear could also stem from his own sexualised response to the woman in white. In accepting responsibility for an 'unfortunate creature' he has effectively unleashed on an unsuspecting public, it is not difficult to notice key similarities between him and Frankenstein. Both men appear to release (what are believed to be) unreasoning beings into the world. Yet, there is also a shared imputation that the dangers of these 'beings' are the products of their creator's own invention. Whereas Frankenstein physically sets about building a monster, Hartright's demonic creation is built with more subtle and complex psychological tools. For him, Anne Catherick is a figurative mirror in which he sees the most unnerving aspects of his own identity. His wonderings on Anne's identity, for example, constantly lead him to question his own character:

> We set our faces towards London, and walked on together in the first still hour of the new day – I, and this woman, whose name, whose character, whose story, whose objects in life, whose very presence by my side, at that moment, were fathomless mysteries to me. It was like a dream. Was I Walter Hartright? [...] I was too bewildered – too conscious also of a vague sense of something like self-reproach – to speak to my strange companion for some minutes.
>
> (p. 23)

Like Franklin Blake's search into the 'fathomless depths' of the Shivering Sands, Hartright's contemplation of the 'fathomless mysteries' of the woman in white brings forth the realisation that there are improper, latent depths to his own character. In the scene where he and Anne first meet, for instance, both characters become aware of Anne's vulnerability. She is, after all, a solitary woman who approaches a male stranger, in the dark, miles from anywhere. Her whiteness becomes suggestive, therefore, of her openness to violation: 'Promise not to interfere with me', she implores Walter 'with a pleading fear and confusion', 'say you won't interfere with me, will you promise?' (pp. 22–3). The two potential connotations of the word 'interfere' (as obstructing her means of escape and molestation) create a fitting innuendo. Like his companion, Hartright also recognises Anne's defencelessness:

> What could I do? Here was a stranger utterly and helplessly at my mercy – and that stranger a forlorn woman. No house was near; no one was passing. [...] I trace these lines, self-distrustfully, with the shadows of after-events darkening the very paper I write on; and I still say, what could I do? [...] She came close to me, and laid her hand, with a sudden gentle stealthiness, on my bosom – a thin hand; a cold hand (when I removed it with mine) even on that sultry night. Remember that I was young; remember that the hand which touched me was a woman's. [...] Oh me! and I tremble, now, when I write it.
>
> (pp. 22–3)

After subsequent events that reveal how Anne was wrongly incarcerated, it seems odd that the narrating Hartright still trembles when describing his encounter with the woman in white. It implies that his fears are generated from a realisation within himself. The above citation, for example, suggests that this is related to an awakening sense of his own sexuality and the dangerous potential it poses. The woman in white first appears at the moment Hartright is wondering what Laura Fairlie and Marian Halcombe look like:

> I had mechanically turned in this latter direction, and was strolling along the lonely high-road – idly wondering, I remember, what the Cumberland young ladies would look like – when, in one moment, every drop of blood in my body was brought to a stop by the touch of a hand laid lightly upon my shoulder.
>
> (p. 20)

One of these 'young ladies', Laura, appears to materialise in the form of her ghostly half-sister. At the very instant Hartright is indulging in amorous contemplations of the Cumberland young ladies, one of the objects of his reveries appears to become manifest and makes his blood run cold. John Kaye noted in an 1862 issue of the *Cornhill*, 'what fearful turmoils of the mind there were, what fears, what fightings, on that terrible bridge which unites the opposite banks of boyhood and manhood'.[20] It is not a bridge, however, but a high road that leads the way (or not, as it may be) to manhood for Hartright. It is on this road that he encounters the enigmatic woman in white and the dangerous possibilities of his own heterosexual desire. His frenetic question 'what could I do? [...] what could I do?' may be read, therefore, not only as an attempt to justify his helping a deranged woman, but as a consideration of what the situation could have enabled him to do to his defenceless companion. What could he have done, he seems to ask himself, when he had the opportunity? What were his capabilities? In coming face to face with a woman 'utterly and helplessly at [his] mercy', with 'no house [...]

near' and 'no-one [...] passing', he is struck by the awareness that this was a meeting that *could* have led to his violating Anne Catherick. It is this realisation that I interpret as causing his blood to run cold and the narrator's pen to tremble. I suggested above that Anne's white costume could indicate her openness to violation; it seems hardly coincidental, therefore, that when the narrator recounts the scene, his 'self-distrust[...] darken[s] the very paper [he] write[s] on'. Staining the page appears to fulfil the young Hartright's fantasies of defilement. Anne Catherick becomes a blank canvass onto which he projects the dangers of his own nature. Henceforth, she becomes – for him – the object of a horrified, introspective realisation.

Anne also appears to be connected to the innermost fears of the novel's central villain. Because Sir Percival Glyde is killed in a vestry fire, and is therefore unable to narrate his own version of events, his motivations, desires, and fears are mainly discernible through other characters' accounts of them and the dialogues he shares with others. In the scene where Marian spies on Glyde and Fosco, for example, Glyde reveals how he considers Anne a danger to his social position:

> 'I had done my best to find Anne Catherick, and failed'.
> 'Yes; you did'.
> 'Fosco! I'm a lost man, if I *don't* find her'.
> 'Ha! Is it so serious as that? [...] Yes!' he said 'Your face speaks the truth this time. Serious indeed'.
>
> (p. 21, italics in original)

Glyde suspects that Anne knows he is illegitimate and ineligible for the Blackwater estate: 'I'll let out your Secret', she threatens him, 'I can ruin you for life, if I choose to open my lips' (p. 549). Whereas for Hartright, Anne's whiteness represents her susceptibility to his sexual urges, for Glyde it is a mocking reminder of his own blank identity. For the 'villain', as for the 'hero', the bastard fugitive of the story reflects the male's inner source of psychological conflict: in Glyde's case, his lack of a legitimate selfhood and, in Walter, the dangers posed by his errant sexual impulses.

Glyde's concern that Anne knows his secret, nevertheless, remains a fictive product of the Baronet's paranoid imagination. Mrs Clements, the farmer's wife with whom Anne lodges insists on how Anne is 'harmless [...] – as harmless, poor soul, as a little child' (p. 94). Similarly, Anne's own mother tries unsuccessfully to persuade Glyde that her daughter knows nothing. She tells Walter:

> I told him that she had merely repeated, like a parrot, the words she had heard me say, and that she knew no particulars whatever, because I had mentioned none. I explained that she had affected, out of crazy spite against him, to know what she really did *not* know.
>
> (p. 550, italics in original)

Notwithstanding, Glyde insists on 'shutting [Anne] up' both physically and verbally (p. 550). As with Hartright, the 'dangers' of the woman in white are the bogus inventions of the baronet's obsessive mind. Glyde's paranoia speaks more about the hidden flaws of his own identity. The woman in white once more becomes a blank page onto which the male pursuer projects fears and suspicions generated from within himself.

When Anne Catherick dies, and her influence is removed from the plot's complicated set of events, the compulsive searches of Glyde and Hartright focus instead upon the marriage registers. The search for these documents takes place in a scene where the two men come closest to meeting. In 'life', they never actually meet – as, it seems, it would be impossible for Jekyll and Hyde to do. If we imagine the novel as a play, one actor could easily play the parts of 'hero' and 'villain'; both characters are never 'on stage' at the same time.[21] When Hartright meets a clerk in a dark lane near the church, the latter mistakes him for Sir Percival Glyde who has left immediately before:

> 'I beg your pardon, Sir Percival ——' he began.
> [Hartright] stopped him before he could say more.
> 'The darkness misleads you', [he] said, 'I am not Sir Percival'.
>
> (p. 525)

Ironically, the fact that Hartright and Glyde are never together suggests that they are indistinguishable. The factor that unites them most forcibly is the way the marriage registers provide, like Anne Catherick, an index to the most unseemly aspects of both men's identities. Glyde's desperate attempt to avail himself of the documents echoes his attempt to find the woman in white in order to keep his secret hidden. For Hartright, however, they become, like Anne Catherick, a medium through which his sexual urges find expression. There are telling similarities, for example, between the following passage and his first meeting with Anne on the London high road:

> My heart gave a great bound, and throbbed as if it would stifle me. I looked again – I was afraid to believe the evidence of my own eyes. [...] My head turned giddy; I held by the desk to keep myself from falling. [...] This was the Secret, and it was mine! A word from me; and house, lands, baronetcy, were gone from him for ever – a word from me, and he was driven out into the world, a nameless, penniless, friendless outcast! The man's whole future hung on my lips – and he knew it by this time as certainly as I did!
>
> (p. 521)

These are hardly the sensations of an objective detective. As in his earlier encounter with Anne, Hartright experiences a sporadic heartbeat, spinning head, and he distrusts his own senses. The most significant similarity between the two scenes, however, is the covert satisfaction he feels at having another person completely under his control. Like his earlier recognition of Anne as 'helplessly at [his] mercy', he becomes elated over the possibility of having Glyde's 'whole future [hanging] on [his] lips'. In the vestry fire, Hartright's sexual tensions appear to reach the climax they have been working towards ever since the night he first met Anne Catherick. Immediately prior to the conflagration he admits that 'my head [was] in a whirl, and my blood throbb[ed] through my veins at fever heat' (p. 522). Soon afterwards, the corpse of Glyde lay at his feet: 'I looked up, along the cloth; and there at the end, stark and grim and black, in the yellow light – there, was his dead face. So, for the first and last time, I saw him' (p. 532). The Baron's violent death seems to reconfigure images used, throughout the text, to explore the volcanic, sexual urges of Hartright. Observe, for example, how the description of Glyde's dead body underscores its blackness whereas before, the text had emphasised Anne's whiteness. Metaphorically expressed, the defilement of the woman in white has been fulfilled through the death of Glyde. The whiteness has been blackened. Once again, *The Woman in White* suggests that male explorations of elusive, hidden, and apparently 'dangerous' elements (such as Anne Catherick's alleged insanity and the secrets of the marriage registers) reveal more about the male investigator and the inglorious parts of his own psyche.

The concept of women as misleading and inherently destructive is one that appears to infect male characters' perceptions of all women in the text. Collins highlights this by linking Anne, the novel's ghostly representative of disorder, to all of the story's key female characters. When Walter first meets Marian, for example, his feelings replicate those he experienced on the London high road:

> The instant my eyes rested on her, I was struck by the rare beauty of her form, and by the unaffected grace of her attitude. Her figure was tall, yet not too tall; comely and well-developed, yet not fat. Her head set on her shoulders with an easy, pliant firmness; her waist, perfection in the eyes of a man, for it occupied its natural place, it filled out its natural circle, it was visibly and delightfully undeformed by stays. [...] She turned towards me immediately. The easy elegance of every movement in her limbs and body as soon as she began to advance from the far end of the room, set me in a flutter of expectation to see her face clearly. She left the window – and I said to myself, The lady is dark. She moved forward a few steps – and I said to myself, The lady is young. She approached nearer – and I said to myself (with a sense of surprise which words fail me to express), The lady is ugly! [...] Never was the fair promise of a lovely figure more strangely and startlingly belied by the face and head that crowned it. [...] To see such a face as this set on the shoulders that a sculptor would have longed to model – to be charmed by the modest

graces of action through which the symmetrical limbs betrayed their beauty when they moved, and then to be almost repelled by the masculine form and masculine look of the features in which the perfect figure ended – was to feel a sensation oddly akin to the helpless discomfort familiar to us all in sleep, when we recognise, yet cannot reconcile the anomalies and contradictions of a dream.

(pp. 31–2)

Once the reader has completed the novel, he or she learns how Anne is connected to Marian through a triangular form of sisterhood completed by Laura. In this passage, however, Marian is aligned to the woman in white through her disconcerting influence on Walter. Like Anne, she dislodges any kinship between appearance and reality as her beautiful form is 'belied' by the ugly face that crowns it. When encountering Anne, Hartright panics over 'what sort of woman she was' and distrusts his own senses. In first meeting Miss Halcombe, he is similarly struck with 'helpless discomfort' when her masculine face does not match up to her figure. Notice also how his contemplations are once again driven inward. The description of his encounter with Marian concludes with feelings like those 'anomalies and contradictions' associated with dreaming. As with the meeting with Anne Catherick, the encounter with Marian involves contemplating the anomalous and contradictory phases of his own selfhood.

It is with Laura Fairlie, however, that Anne Catherick shares the most obvious similarities. Numerous critical studies of the text have explored the possible significance of the likeness between Laura and Anne,[22] yet few have shown any reluctance to accept this similarity at face value. Like most opinions offered in the novel, we have only the narrators' testimonies to rely on. Is the resemblance between Laura and Anne 'real', we might therefore inquire, or is it constructed as another fictive production of the novel's disturbed masculine psyches?

For both Glyde and Hartright, the likeness between the two women is expressed most dramatically in scenes where obsessive – monomaniacal even – desires are exercising a powerful dominion over their thoughts. In the overheard dialogue between Glyde and Fosco the conversation appears to move seamlessly from issues of property and inheritance to the likeness between the two women:

'Well, Percival', [Fosco] said; 'and, in the case of Lady Glyde's death, what do you get [...]?'
'If she leaves no children ——'
'Which she is likely to do?'
'Which, she is not the least likely to do ——'
'Yes?'
'Why, then I get her twenty thousand pounds'.

'Paid down?'
'Paid down'. [...]
'I must know how to recognise our invisible Anne. What is she like?'
'Like? Come! I'll tell you in two words. She's a sickly likeness of my wife. [...] Fancy my wife, after a bad illness, with a touch of something wrong in her head – and there is Anne Catherick for you'.

(p. 333, p. 339)

The admission that Laura is unlikely to bear children is clearly meant to imply that her marriage to Glyde is unconsummated. Indeed, for Percival, Laura seems to be, first and foremost, the locus of mercenary desire. His sole reason for marrying her is to access her copious inheritance. Similarly, Walter's recognition of the resemblance between Anne and Laura occurs shortly after his first disturbed encounter with Anne. He notices an 'impression, which, in a shadowy way, suggested to [him] the idea of something wanting. [...] Something wanting, something wanting – and where it was and what it was, [he] could not say' (pp. 50–1). He eventually discovers, however, that the 'something wanting' is a resemblance between Miss Fairlie and the woman in white. The moment of revelation occurs when Laura is looking especially alluring:

Miss Fairlie glided into view on the terrace. [...] My eyes fixed upon the white gleam of her muslin gown and head-dress in the moonlight, and a sensation, for which I can find no name – a sensation that quickened my pulse, and raised a fluttering in my heart – began to steal over me. [...] All my attention was concentrated on the white gleam of Miss Fairlie's muslin dress. [...] A thrill of the same feeling which ran through me when the touch was laid upon my shoulder in the lonely high-road, chilled me again.

There stood Miss Fairlie, a white figure, alone in the moonlight; in her attitude, in the turn of her head, in her complexion, in the shape of her face, the living image, at that distance and under those circumstances, of the woman in white! [...] That 'something wanting' was my own recognition of the ominous likeness between the fugitive from the asylum and my pupil at Limmeridge House.

(pp. 59–61)

Hartright then admits to Marian that 'to associate that forlorn, friendless, lost woman, even by an accidental likeness only, with Miss Fairlie, seems like casting a shadow on the future of the bright creature who stands looking at us now' (p. 61). Dressed in a white dress and steeped in moonlight, Laura appears the very epitome of sexualised femininity. Hartright's ominous psychosomatic symptoms (the quickened pulse, the fluttering heart, the same 'thrill' he felt on the high road) return along with his recollections of Anne Catherick. The psychological 'return' of the woman in white heralds the return of Hartright's unbalanced neuroses:

> 'Call her in, out of the dreary moonlight', [he urges Marian...]
> 'Mr Hartright, you surprise me'. [She replies], 'Whatever women may be, I thought that men, in the nineteenth century, were above superstition'.
> 'Pray call her in!' [he urges].
>
> (p. 61)

As in his encounter with Anne Catherick, he unconsciously asks himself, 'what *could* I do?' We might view him as becoming aware of the violent threat his own psychical urges have for Laura – what he later suggestively calls a 'dangerous intimacy' (p. 63). In his first scenes with Laura he admits to the reader that the 'something wanting' in Miss Fairlie was his '*own* recognition of the ominous likeness'. The similarity is thus not an irrefutable fact, but Walter's *own* impression. An 'impression', moreover, that is related to an unhealthy obsession with the stranger on the high road.

Hence, although *The Woman in White* is a novel that appears to complicate and explore the nature of femininity through the characterisation of Anne Catherick and her links with key female characters, the enigmatic central figure could also be interpreted as revealing more about the distorted nature of masculinity. Her 'encounters' with Walter Hartright and Sir Percival Glyde, for example, highlight how the latter's personality is dominated by fears of loss of wealth and status, while the former's mind is haunted by the dangerous possibilities posed by his own sexuality.

'In a glass darkly': *No Name* (1862)

When Norah and Magdalen Vanstone lose their parents, property, and identities in the early stages of *No Name*, their governess – Miss Garth – considers what hidden parts of their natures the calamity might bring forth. She wonders:

> Does there exist in every human being, beneath that outward and visible character which is shaped into a form by the social influences surrounding us, an inward, invisible disposition, which is part of ourselves; which education may indirectly modify, but can never hope to change? [...] Are there, infinitely carrying with each individual, inbred forces of Good and Evil in all of us, deep down below the reach of mortal encouragement and mortal repression – hidden Good and hidden Evil, both alike at the mercy of the liberating opportunity and the sufficient temptation? Within these earthly limits, is earthly Circumstance ever the key; and can no human vigilance warn us beforehand of the forces imprisoned in ourselves which that key *may* unlock?[23]

Consisting of a series of lengthy rhetorical questions, this extract echoes the written style used by Forbes Winslow in his treatise on obscure diseases and raises a number of pertinent questions. Winslow similarly asks whether 'hidden [...] forces' operated 'beneath that outward and visible character', evading 'human vigilance' and offering no warning of their possible eruption. Miss Garth develops an obsession (also consistent with medical literature) with uncovering the true nature of Norah and Magdalen's personalities:

> Searching, as in a glass darkly, into the two natures, she felt her way, doubt by doubt, from one possible truth to another. It might be, that the upper surface of their characters was all that she had, thus far, plainly seen in Norah and Magdalen. [...] It might be, that under the surface so formed – a surface which there had been nothing, hitherto, in the happy, prosperous, uneventful lives of the sisters to disturb – forces of inborn and inbred disposition had remained concealed, which the shock of the first serious calamity in their lives had now thrown up into view.
>
> (pp. 146–7)

The governess convinces herself that such has to be the case and focuses specifically on Magdalen's 'inbred disposition':

> What if there were dangerous elements in the strength of Magdalen's character – was it not her duty to help the girl against herself? [...] 'Oh!' she thought bitterly, 'how long have I lived in the world, and how little I have known of my own weakness and wickedness until to-day!'
>
> (p. 147)

Miss Garth is trying on the role of psychologist here, and, like Hartright, her thought processes reveal more about *her* than the object under consideration. The focus of her speculations gradually shifts and narrows; beginning with human nature in general ('does there exist in every human being [...]?'), to focus on the Vanstone sisters, then just on Magdalen, and finally onto herself ('how little I have known of my own weakness and wickedness'). Like Glyde and Hartright's search for Anne Catherick, Garth's investigations into the alleged 'dangerous elements' of Magdalen and Norah become an act of looking 'in a glass darkly'.[24] By peering beneath the 'surface' of the young women's characters (particularly Magdalen's), she discovers evidence of her own alleged 'weakness and wickedness' (which she sees as her suspicions of the hitherto faultless Magdalen). In this episode the novel crystallises its wider use of the dangerous womanhood theme. Like Garth's deliberations, the plot acknowledges two sisters yet focuses on one of them: Magdalen. Through this portrait, Wilkie Collins explores his own culture's obsessions with detecting the proposed 'hidden dangers' of femininity. As with Miss Garth, the dangerous adventuress holds up a 'glass darkly' to her observers, revealing a set of grotesque biases and irregularities central to the diagnostic gaze.

Like Walter Hartright, Magdalen is on the cusp of sexual maturity when she is first introduced to the reader. Bursting into the narrative with an energetic flurry of excitement, she is described as follows:

> She bloomed in the full physical maturity of twenty years or more – bloomed naturally and irresistibly, in light of her matchless health and strength. Here, in truth, lay the mainspring of this strangely-constituted organization. Her headlong course down the stairs; the brisk activity of all her movements; the incessant sparkle of expression in her face; the enticing gaiety which took the hearts of the quietest people by storm – even the reckless delight in bright colours, which showed itself in her brilliantly-striped morning dress, in her fluttering ribbons, in the large scarlet rosettes on her smart little shoes – all sprang alike from the same source; from the overflowing physical health which strengthened every muscle, braced every nerve, and set the warm young blood tingling through her veins, like the blood of a growing child.
>
> (p. 14)

This passage portrays a fertile, sexually charged woman through a series of suggestive biological metaphors. References to Magdalen as blooming, for example, are clearly meant to convey ideas of organic fecundity, while the implicit allusions to her over-abundant sexual energies ('overflowing physical health [...] the warm young blood tingling through her veins [...] the scarlet rosettes') identify her as a character with a high level of carnal energy. Typical of the period, however, these images of female biology are accompanied by more menacing ideas of excess. The passage is beset with adjectives that appear to portend danger such as 'reckless', 'incessant', 'headlong', and 'overflowing'; Magdalen also takes other people 'by storm' and her organisation is described as 'strangely-constituted'. Her introduction to the text reveals, even before she sets out on what Margaret Oliphant called a 'career of vulgar and aimless trickery and wickedness',[25] how the sexual(ised) female bore mixed images of desire and disgust in Victorian eyes. In describing Magdalen's face, for example, the narrator depicts lips with 'the true feminine delicacy of form' and 'cheeks [with] the lovely roundness and smoothness of youth', yet combines these with a masculine ugliness: 'but the mouth was too large and firm, the chin too square and massive for her sex and age' (pp. 13–4). This clearly echoes Hartright's first perception of Marian Halcombe, whose voluptuous feminine form jarred with her ugly, masculine physiognomy. Beneath Magdalen's 'exuberant vitality', moreover, there lurks a 'seductive, serpentine suppleness' – a description that foregrounds her female sexuality.

According to Eneas Sweetland Dallas, such 'suppleness' and 'extraordinary mobility' (p. 14) of feature were key to deceiving 'scientific' observations of character. During *No Name*'s serialisation in *All The Year Round*, Dallas contributed to the *Cornhill* (the magazine that would later run *Armadale* from November 1864 to June 1866) two essays on the subject of physiognomy.[26] Interest in physiognomy had waned since the days of John Caspar Lavater but, according to Dallas, the advent of photography would give the subject new life: 'The faithful register of the camera, supplying us with countless numbers of accurate observations, will now render that an actual science which has hitherto been only a possible one'.[27] The wave of psychological interest in obscure mental disease may also have influenced the renaissance of a 'science' that, according to Dallas, had aimed to 'see [...] through a man at a glance' and 'put a window on every heart'.[28] Dallas seemed to complement Collins's portrait of Magdalen by suggesting that mobile facial features were the most deceptive: 'The truth is, that sometimes there is a show of contradiction between the solid and the mobile parts of the body, between the bony structure and the fleshy tissue'.[29] As mobile components of the countenance, he adds, the eyes and lips provide misleading and inconclusive physiognomic evidence. As more solid structures, the brow and chin offer true windows to the soul. In her early scenes, Magdalen is seemingly set up, like the physiognomist's subject, as an object of scrutiny:

> By one of those strange caprices of Nature, which science leaves still unexplained, the youngest of Mr. Vanstone's children presented no recognizable resemblance to either of her parents. [...] All varieties of expression followed each other over the plastic, ever-changing face, with a giddy rapidity which left sober analysis far behind in the race.
>
> (pp. 13–4)

As the target of 'sober analysis' and scientific erudition, Magdalen becomes, in this scene, like a laboratory specimen – a 'specimen', moreover, that confounds and eludes the methodical investigation it seems to encourage. This tension is exemplified in the composition of Magdalen's face. Like Dallas's physiognomic subject, her eyes are 'incomprehensibl[e]' and 'discordant', while her chin is solid and 'square' (pp. 13–4) – traits Dallas believed to be 'signs of stability and persistence; [...and] steadfastness, verging on obstinacy'.[30] Magdalen's countenance, with its mobile and dextrous deceptiveness overlaying solidity and resoluteness, epitomises both her later role as actress and the duality with which the Victorians viewed their women. In *No Name* she adopts a number of personalities and costumes, playing, in turn, the parts of spinster, old maid, wife, and servant, thus parallelling Victorian classifications of women as spinsters, married women, mothers, and old maids. As discussed in chapter one, however, the concept of women as explosive and inherently flawed was one aspect of women's nature that was seen to be consistent with all of these facets of female identity. Magdalen's obsessive crusade towards regaining her father's fortune is the one immovable part of her character that lurks beneath every persona she adopts. This reflects the contemporary conceptions of women as essentially deceptive and capable of harbouring dangerous and resolute intentions. After the Vanstone calamity, the novel projects this image across a series of melodramatic and exaggerated tableaux that question and destabilise the dynamics of the observer/observed relationship.

One such sequence is Magdalen's first attempt at deception outside the arena of provincial theatre. In an attempt to discover the forthcoming plans of Noel Vanstone, she disguises herself as her old-maid governess Miss Garth and conducts an interview with Noel and his housekeeper Mrs Lecount. In creating her Miss Garth disguise, Magdalen 'deliberately disfigure[s] herself' (p. 268) by adopting stereotypical signifiers of female old age. In addition to wearing a grey wig and a dull brown dress, she applies 'false eyebrows (made rather large, and of hair darker than the wig)' and 'change[s] the transparent fairness of her complexion to the dull, faintly opaque colour of a woman in ill-health. The lines and markings of age followed next' (p. 268). She wears padding 'to hide the youthful grace and beauty of her back and shoulders' and, finally,

> she sprang to her feet, and looked triumphantly at the hideous transformation of herself reflected in the glass. [...] Nobody who now looked at Magdalen could have suspected for an instant that she was other than an ailing, ill-made, unattractive woman of fifty years old at least.
> (pp. 268–9)

In her old-maid costume, Magdalen is the ultimate antithesis of the youthful and exuberant woman to whom we are first introduced. Following contemporaneous ideas on aged female appearance, she attempts to make herself look more masculine, worn, sickly, and ugly. Yet, also in keeping with the era's ideas on female senescence, Magdalen retains an explosive interiority. She feels, for example, 'a horror of the vile disguise that concealed her; [and] a yearning to burst its trammels' (p. 272) and, when she is speaking to Noel incognito, the smouldering fires, it seems, are vented temporarily:

> Once more, her own indomitable earnestness had betrayed her. Once more, the inborn nobility of that perverted nature had risen superior to the deception which it had stooped to practise. The scheme of the moment vanished from her mind's view; and the resolution of her life burst its way outward in her own words, in her own tones, pouring hotly from her heart.
> (p. 291)

Although the text constructs Magdalen's volcanic passions as a betrayal of the old-maid exterior, the image actually draws on the nineteenth-century belief that a destructive energy resided beneath every woman's artificial appearance. This could explain why Noel's reaction to the above outburst consists of fear rather than a realisation of Magdalen's true identity: 'Had his fears left him sense enough to perceive the change in her voice? No' (p. 291). Possibly accustomed to the warnings of medical writers, Noel Vanstone would not have perceived 'Miss Garth's' irrational outburst as atypical female behaviour.

As if to highlight this fact, the novel frequently puts the disguised Magdalen adjacent to Mrs Lecount – Noel's brilliant and formidable housekeeper. Over the course of their encounters, the text draws clear similarities between the two women. For example, like Magdalen, Mrs Lecount's appearance is constructed to deceive:

> [Magdalen] found herself in the presence of a lady of mild ingratiating manners; whose dress was the perfection of neatness, taste and matronly simplicity; whose personal appearance was little less than a triumph of physical resistance to the deteriorating influence of time. If Mrs. Lecount had struck some fifteen or sixteen years off her real age, and had asserted herself to be eight-and-thirty, there would not have been one man in a thousand, or one woman in a hundred, who would have hesitated to believe her.
>
> (p. 275)

In standing face to face with Lecount, Magdalen, in her disguise, encounters a mirror image of 'herself'. Whereas Magdalen had sought to add years to her appearance, Lecount's disguise aims to remove them from hers. This 'matching' of the two women is felt by Magdalen herself, whose 'first glance at this Venus of the autumn period of female life, more than satisfied her that she had done well to feel her ground in disguise, before she ventured on matching herself against Mrs. Lecount' (p. 276). Also like Magdalen, Lecount's external appearance and internal character do not correspond. In addition to having a certain 'something in the expression of her eyes', references to Lecount's 'fair and smiling surface' (p. 276) link her to the hideous aquarium she keeps:

> On the table stood a glass tank filled with water; and ornamented in the middle by a miniature pyramid of rock-work interlaced with weeds. Snails clung to the sides of the tank; tadpoles and tiny fish swam swiftly in the green water; slippery efts and slimy frogs twined their noiseless way in and out of the weedy rock-work – and, on top of the pyramid, there sat solitary, cold as the stone, brown as the stone, motionless as the stone, a little bright eyed toad.
>
> (p. 274)

With its 'slippery efts and slimy frogs' twining beneath the surface, the aquarium is an apt metaphor for both its owner and, more generally, wider ideas on the nature of women. When Lecount leaves Magdalen alone with the tank, the latter notices the connection between the aquarium and its owner:

> Left by herself, Magdalen allowed the anger which she had suppressed in Mrs. Lecount's presence to break free from her. For want of a nobler object of attack, it took the direction of the toad. The sight of the hideous little reptile sitting placid on his rock throne, with his bright eyes staring impenetrably into vacancy, irritated every nerve in her body. She looked at the creature with a shrinking intensity of hatred; she whispered at it maliciously though her set teeth. 'I wonder whose blood runs coldest', she said, 'yours, you little monster, or Mrs. Lecount's? I wonder which is the slimiest, her heart or your back? You hateful wretch, do you know what your mistress is? Your mistress is a devil!'
> The speckled skin under the toad's mouth mysteriously wrinkled itself, then slowly expanded again, as if he had swallowed the words just addressed to him. Magdalen started back in disgust from the first perceptible movement in the creature's body, trifling as it was.
>
> (p. 279)

This section clearly recycles the era's hackneyed idea that a hideous, 'unseen' energy lurked behind the 'ordinary' façade of female existence. The 'smouldering fires' image reappears, for example, at the top of the passage, as Magdalen gives vent to the 'suppressed' passions she has kept concealed in Lecount's presence. The object of her wrath, the 'hideous little reptile', is compared to Mrs Lecount's hideous and slippery soul. The effect produced is a sense that Magdalen, Mrs Lecount, and the aquarium all share a hideous 'something' loitering beneath their surfaces.

It is the reworking of such images that has led scholars like Lillian Nayder to perceive Wilkie Collins as having a 'misogynistic conception of woman's sexual power'.[31] According to Jenny Bourne Taylor, however, the encounter between stereotypes (like Lecount) and melodramatic, exaggerated forms of those stereotypes (like Magdalen) actually served to highlight the absurdity of the 'conventional'.[32] In contrast to Nayder, and extending Taylor's idea, I argue that the encounter between Lecount and Magdalen exposes similarities between certain branches of scientific investigation and the supposedly hideous realities they were preoccupied with observing. Lecount's aquarium, for instance, not only symbolises the ghastly interiority of her personality, but also represents science. As she tells Magdalen:

> My dear husband – dead many years since – formed my tastes, and elevated me to himself. You have heard of the late Professor Lecomte, the

eminent Swiss naturalist? I am his widow. [... He] permitted me to assist him in his pursuits. I have only one interest since his death – an interest in science. Eminent in many things, the Professor was great at reptiles. He left me his Subjects and his Tank. I had no other legacy. There is his Tank.

(p. 280)

Although she is a woman, Mrs Lecount embodies the masculine world of science. According to Captain Wragge, 'Mrs. Lecount's one weak point, if she has such a thing at all, is a taste for science, implanted by her deceased husband, the Professor' (p. 323). Prefiguring the sentiments of the vivisectionist Dr Benjulia in Collins's *Heart and Science* (1883), Mrs Lecount exclaims:

'Properly understood, the reptile creation is beautiful. Properly dissected, the reptile creation is instructive in the last degree'. She stretched out her little finger, and gently stroked the toad's back with the tip of it. 'So refreshing to the touch', said Mrs. Lecount. 'So nice and cool in this summer weather!'

(p. 280)

Lecount's observations move seamlessly from the experimental to the sensual. Soon after discussing the merits of dissecting reptiles from a scientific viewpoint, she suggestively fingers one of them and experiences satisfaction in doing so.

No Name was written at a time when gynaecologists and obstetricians obtained a problematic place in medicine. Their advent was not unclouded by suspicions that practitioners experienced a covert satisfaction from their work; such fears would reach their zenith in 1866 with the disgrace of clitoridectomy advocate Isaac Baker Brown. References to gynaecological procedures were obviously unacceptable in a work of fiction at that time, yet perhaps the most obvious allusion to the medical treatment of women in *No Name* comes when Lecount lifts Magdalen's skirts in order to obtain evidence of her true identity. While Magdalen is speaking to Noel, Lecount pretends to leave the room but, instead of departing, she

noiselessly knelt down behind Magdalen's chair. Steadying herself against the post of the folding-door, she took a pair of scissors from her pocket, waiting until Noel Vanstone (from whose view she was entirely hidden) had attracted Magdalen's attention by speaking to her; and then bent forward with the scissors ready in her hand. The skirt of the false Miss Garth's gown – the brown alpaca dress, with the white spots on it – touched the floor, within the housekeeper's reach. Mrs. Lecount lifted the outer of the two flounces which ran round the bottom of the dress, one over the other; softly cut away a little irregular fragment of stuff from the inner flounce; and neatly smoothed the outer one over it again, so as to hide the gap.

(p. 292)

Lecount's collection of evidence reads like a surgical procedure. She 'softly cut[s]' the material of Magdalen's dress and attempts to hide the scar. In *On the Curability of Certain Forms of Insanity* (1866), Baker Brown described clitoridectomy (which he saw as a viable cure for most forms of mental impairment in women) as follows: 'The patient having been placed *completely* under the influence of chloroform, the clitoris is freely excised either by scissors or knife – I always prefer the scissors'.[33] Magdalen is completely unaware of the 'operation' performed by Mrs Lecount. Both Ornella Moscucci and Mary Poovey have shown how, in nineteenth-century gynaecological and obstetrical procedures, it was considered 'proper' that women should be incognisant (if possible) of the procedures performed upon them. Moscucci shows, for example, how important it was considered for women to avoid eye contact with their accoucheurs,[34] and Poovey demonstrates how, through the use of chloroform, practitioners were able to exclude their patients from surgical and non-surgical procedures upon their bodies.[35] Talking to her cousin, while an operation is being performed beneath her skirts, Magdalen demonstrates the same level of unawareness and passivity required from the patient of a nineteenth-century gynaecologist.

Like the era's medical attempts to understand female psychology through a focus on somatic processes, Mrs Lecount hopes that the specimen she obtains from Magdalen will form a direct link to the real Miss Vanstone – the woman beneath the disguise. Holding the fragment of alpaca, for example, she boasts to Magdalen: '"I hold you in the hollow of my hand!" [...] with a fierce hissing emphasis on every syllable' (p. 294, italics in original). The hissing sibilance reminds the reader of her reptilian qualities. So too does the evidence she obtains from Magdalen. Taken from a 'brown alpaca dress, with white spots on it' its appearance mirrors that of the toad's 'brown' and 'speckled' skin. Remember how the toad's skin represented the slimy interiority of its mistress; likewise, the scientific investigations of Lecount seem to have uncovered a link to the professed hideous interiorities of Magdalen's/ Miss Garth's nature.

Mrs Lecount's appropriation of the alpaca specimen, however, seems largely unnecessary, as she is able to identify Magdalen without its assistance later in the story. The actress's next disguise is that of the young spinster, Miss Bygrave. Because she is trying to seduce Noel into marrying her, Magdalen's costume, this time, consists of being 'charming', 'fresh', not 'too pale', or 'too serious' (p. 356). As always, however, Magdalen Vanstone, and her monomaniac obsession with her father's lost fortune, lurks underneath the Bygrave persona. Noticing a growing intimacy between the young spinster and Noel, Mrs Lecount

> employed every artifice of which she was mistress to ascertain [Miss Bygrave's] true position in Noel Vanstone's estimation. She tried again and again to lure him into an unconscious confession of the pleasure which he felt already in the society of the beautiful Miss Bygrave; she twined herself in and out of every weakness in his character, as the frogs and efts twined themselves in and out of the rock-work of her Aquarium.
>
> (p. 374)

Failing to get a confession from Noel, Lecount thinks intensely on the subject:

> She was positively determined to think, and think again. [...] There was something vaguely familiar to her in the voice of Miss Bygrave. [...] Were the members of this small family of three [Magdalen, Captain Wragge, and his wife masquerading as the Bygraves], what they seemed on the surface of them?
>
> (p. 375)

With that question in mind, she goes to bed:

> As soon as the candle was out, the darkness seemed to communicate some inexplicable perversity to her thoughts. They wandered back from present things to past, in spite of her. They set the Aquarium back in its place on the kitchen table, and put the false Miss Garth in the chair by the side of it, shading her inflamed eyes from the light. [...] The next instant [Lecount] started up in bed; her heart beating violently, her head whirling as if she had lost her senses. With electric suddenness, her mind pieced together its scattered multitude of thoughts, and put them before her plainly under one intelligible form. In the all-mastering agitation of the moment, she clapped her hands together, and cried out suddenly in the darkness:
> 'Miss Vanstone again!!!'
>
> (p. 376)

Like a true scientist Mrs Lecount 'think[s], and think[s]' at a problem until she arrives at a eureka moment. Although her conclusion is correct, her method of reaching it is hardly one of unqualified objectivity. An 'inexplicable perversity [of] her [own] thoughts' and memories from her past, for example, are entwined with the chain of associations that lead to her discovery. As such, her breakthrough is heavily weighted with elements from her own consciousness. Her conclusion is like Franklin Blake's discovery of the nightdress in *The Moonstone* (1868): a discovery revealing as much about the investigator, as it does the investigated. In his *Lettsomian Lectures*, Winslow admitted that the medical profession was a frequent prey to false conclusions:

> In the study of medicine, perhaps more than in any other science, we are particularly exposed to the danger of accepting false facts, or being seduced by specious and hasty generalizations, and led into error by deducing general principles from the consideration of a few particulars – the bane of all right and sound reasoning – the foundation of all bad philosophy.[36]

Later in *No Name*, Lecount's biases cause her to reach *incorrect* conclusions as both she and Noel suspect that Magdalen is a potential murderess. In order to expose her true identity, Lecount produces the alpaca specimen and hopes to match it with the original dress in Magdalen's closet. Like Phoebe and Luke's penetration of Lady Audley's private chambers, Noel and Lecount's investigation of Magdalen's personal spaces bears all the hallmarks of a sexual and clinical violation:

> Evidences of Magdalen's natural taste and refinement were visible everywhere, in the little embellishments that graced and enlivened the aspect of the room. The perfume of dried rose-leaves hung fragrant on the cool air. Mrs. Lecount sniffed the perfume with a disparaging frown, and threw the window up to its full height. 'Pah!' she said, with a shudder of virtuous disgust – 'the atmosphere of deceit! [...] Open the wardrobe, Mr. Noel', she said. 'I don't go near it. I touch nothing in it, myself'.
> 'I'll do it as well as I can', he said, 'My hands are cold, and my head feels half asleep'. [...] He was obliged to search in the inner recesses of the wardrobe. [...]
> 'You will see a double flounce running round the bottom of [the alpaca dress]. Lift up the outer flounce, and pass the inner one through your fingers inch by inch'. [...]
> He passed the flounce slowly through his fingers.
> (pp. 546–7)

Lecount then produces the fragment of fabric, which Noel matches to a blank space in the dress he is touching. He gasps '"save me!" [...] in a hoarse, breathless whisper. "Oh, Lecount, save me!"' (p. 547). His characteristically fearful response presumes that, because his wife's external and internal personas do not match, she is a danger to him. The conviction is only strengthened when Mrs Lecount, searching Magdalen's closet for smelling salts, discovers a bottle of laudanum:

> The labelled side of the bottle was full in view; and there in the plain handwriting of the chemist at Aldborough, was the one startling word, confronting them both – 'Poison'.
> Even Mrs. Lecount's self-possession was shaken by that discovery. She was not prepared to see her own darkest forebodings – the unacknowledged offspring of her hatred for Magdalen – realized as she saw them realized now. [...] There the bottle lay, in Magdalen's absence, a false witness of treason which had never entered her mind – treason against her husband's life!
> (p. 549)

Like Lady Audley's chambers, Magdalen's bedroom and closet metonymically represent her body. In the deepest recesses of those spaces, Lecount and Noel discover what they believe to be evidence of Magdalen's potential aggression. The scene draws on the ever-present, Victorian idea that at the heart of every woman there resides a deadly, toxic energy. The discovery of the laudanum, however, could also act as an illustration of how persuasive preconceived suspicions can be. The reader is aware that the poison was not bought to kill Noel, but as a means through which Magdalen could commit suicide. The chemist who originally sold the poison to Magdalen thought it was a remedy for toothache. Neither of these explanations for its possession, however, are anticipated by Noel or Lecount when they make the discovery. In accordance with the contemporaneous penchant for believing all women to be potential murderesses, Noel and Lecount presume that Magdalen must have murderous intentions. The reader knows, however, that the poison (as murder evidence) is evidence of their own invention. As Lecount correctly observes, the bottle represents her '*own* darkest forebodings [...] realized'.

Magdalen's third and final act of dissemblance in *No Name* involves disguising herself as a servant in the house of her relative, Admiral Bartram. In these scenes she hopes to recover a document that will entitle her to repossess her father's fortune. As with her entrances into Noel's home as the Misses Garth and Bygraves, Magdalen's admission into Bertram's house is like Lady Isabel's exploits in *East Lynne* (1862). Like the Trojan horse, the 'criminal' woman appears to circumvent male defences through the use of disguise.

In a short story entitled 'A Queen's Revenge' (1858), Collins explicitly represents this threat as a form of reverse penetration. Originally published in *Household Words*, Collins chose to reprint the story as part of *My Miscellanies*. 'A Queen's Revenge' tells the story of Christina, Queen of Sweden, who, in the seventeenth century, misused her powers to kill her infidel lover, Marquis Monaldeschi. In his *Obscure Diseases*, Winslow recounts the very same story as an example of how real, historical 'tyrants, REGAL and DOMESTIC' could be reinterpreted as of 'unsound mind'.[37] As with Magdalen Vanstone, the deceptiveness of Christina's external appearance is something that Collins's short story emphasises:

> The Queen let [Monaldeschi] go on talking without showing the least sign of anger or impatience. Her colour never changed; the stern look never left her countenance. There was something awful in the clear, cold, deadly resolution which her eyes expressed while they rested on the Marquis's face.[38]

Like the blank page of the marriage register in *The Woman in White* and the 'something wanting' of Laura Fairlie, absence, in this description of Queen Christina, suggests an awful presence. Her passions seem all the more explosive because they are invisible to the naked eye. In both Winslow's and Collins's texts, Christina's emotions imbue her with the male role of penetrator. I have already discussed, in reference to Braddon's *Aurora Floyd* (1863), how a riding-whip might be construed as a symbolic phallus. It is interesting, therefore, that Christina does not kill Monaldeschi herself, but instructs her guards to do so by signalling to them with her riding-whip:

> She pointed, while she spoke, to the Marquis Monaldeschi with a little ebony riding-whip that she carried in her hand. 'I offer that worthless traitor all the time he requires – more time than he has any right to ask for – to justify himself if he can'. [...] She made a sign with her ebony riding-ship to the men with the drawn swords, and they retired toward one of the windows of the gallery.[39]

The Marquis is unable to exonerate himself and 'her Majesty beckoned the men back again with the whip'.[40] As in *Aurora Floyd*, where Aurora beats the Softy with her 'emerald-set toy', the female handling of a riding-whip connotes a reversal of conventional gender roles. The killing of the Marquis, moreover, reads like a sexual violation:

> [A guard] seized Monaldeschi, pressed him back against the wall at the end of gallery [...] and [...] struck at the Marquis's right side with his sword. Monaldeschi caught the blade with his hand, cutting three of his fingers in the act. At the same moment the point touched his side and glanced off. Upon this, the man who had struck at him exclaimed, 'He has armour under his clothes!' and at the same moment stabbed Monaldeschi in the face. As he received the wound, he turned round [...] and cried out loudly.[41]

It is worth noticing how one guard forces the Marquis up against a wall and suggestively 'touches his side' with his sword. As a sexual fornicator, Monaldeschi – once the penetrator – is now the penetrated; the fact that he is wearing armour heightens the sense of invasion. Calling this culling 'an incredible act of frightful cruelty', Winslow emphasised the difficulties the guards faced in breaking through the armour:

> In the vigour of manhood and of health, [Monaldeschi] was loth to die, and he besought his life with tears; but the [Queen] was inexorable. She gave him time to confess, and some soldiers were ordered to fall upon him with their swords and dispatch him. This they had some difficulty in accomplishing as he wore steel armour underneath his doublet.[42]

What is seen to make Christina so 'atrocious' in these narratives is her ability to penetrate her lover. Through her formidable arsenal (her riding-whip and henchmen's swords) she brutally reverses traditional gender behaviour. This is, unsurprisingly, a disturbing prospect for the male reader, whose privileged position in society has delegated him as the wielder of weaponry and women as passive submitters.

Such fears of reverse penetration seem to be confirmed by the closing scenes of *No Name*. When Admiral Bartram's house has retired, Magdalen creeps from her room and steps out of her maid's disguise to search the Banqueting-Hall for the document that will reinherit her. Like Lecount, she seems to be a woman fulfilling the masculine role of scientist as her 'experiment was made on the cabinet [...] devoted to specimens of curious minerals, neatly labelled and arranged' (p. 659). Like Franklin Blake's investigation of the Shivering Sands, her search appears to be conducted into a living and breathing atmosphere:

> She advanced boldly [...] and met the night-view of the Banqueting-Hall face to face.
> The moon was surrounding the southern side of the house. [...] The ceiling was lost to view; the yawning fireplace, the overhanging mantelpiece, the long row of battle-pictures above, were all swallowed up in night. [...] The soothing hush of night was awful there. The deep abysses of darkness hid abysses of silence more immeasurable still.
> (pp. 664–5)

Like the Sands, the Banqueting-Hall (significantly endowed with capital letters) has 'deep' and 'immeasurable' 'abysses' that seem very corporeal. The Hall has a 'face' and yawns and swallows like a living organism. Another similarity between the Hall and the Shivering Sands can be found later (fittingly on page 666 of the Oxford edition) when the narrative portrays the former as 'shudder[ing] with the terror of a sound' (p. 666). Like Blake, Magdalen experiences a mixture of desire and disgust during her investigations. In searching for the document, she is fulfilling her obsession with regaining her fortune. She is, the text suggests, 'haunted day and night by the one dominant idea that now possessed her' (p. 662), yet when she is closest to satisfying this desire, an 'all-mastering hesitation, an unintelligible shrinking from some peril unknown, seize[s] her on a sudden' (p. 663). She searches for the object she desperately craves with a paradoxical 'horror of looking' (p. 666).

The scene thus appears to confirm fears regarding the intrusive and gender-distorting nature of dangerous women as Magdalen, once the penetrat*ed* object of Lecount's experiments, now becomes the penetrat*or* – infringing the private spaces of Admiral Bartram. Yet, like Queen Christina, Magdalen's exploits reveal how the melodramatic actions of the 'violent' woman reiterate the 'ordinary' actions of the male population. In her investigation of the Banqueting-Hall, for example, her actions are parallelled – almost directly – by Admiral Bartram himself who is 'walking in his sleep' (p. 667). Like Blake's somnambulistic theft of the Moonstone, Bartram's sleepwalking is caused by his worries regarding the document Noel has entrusted him with. In this state he searches the cabinet, as Magdalen does, and removes the deed. Magdalen follows him:

> She took up the candle, and followed him mechanically, as if she too were walking in her sleep. One behind the other, in slow and noiseless progress, they crossed the Banqueting-Hall. One behind the other, they passed through the drawing-room.
>
> (pp. 668–9)

It seems as though one character is the shadow of the other as their forms replicate each other's movements. In a state of somnambulism augmented by his concerns, the Admiral is a walking embodiment of his fears. The way in which the adventuress behaves like his shadow therefore suggests that the dubious female figure is an image cast by men's self-reflective suspicions. It is an idea that ties in with the notion, explored in *The Woman in White*, that female dangers are the fabrication of unbalanced, masculine fixations.

In her penetrative and deceptive encroachment of male spaces, Magdalen imitates the 'ordinary' work of men – especially, it seems, scientists. Lecount's links with her hideous zoological specimens may say a lot about her own misleading and slippery character, but they also connect her inglorious personality to the scientific world she married into. *No Name* warns its readers that they need to watch women carefully, yet the complex narrative structure also seems to hold up a 'glass darkly' to the faults and problems of the male observer.

'The shadow of a woman': *Armadale* (1866)

In *Armadale* Collins develops on this concept of the 'dangerous' woman as a shadow of masculine neuroses. In particular, the novel presents a very interesting doubling between Ozias Midwinter and Lydia Gwilt. In the literal and figurative marriage of these two characters, Collins's novel offers a complex exploration of how 'crimes' by dangerous women could be created and driven by the self-reflective fears of men like Midwinter.

In keeping with the decade's emerging debates on morbid psychological inheritance, *Armadale* opens with Ozias's father's forebodings that the consequences of his actions (especially the murder of Allan's father) will be reaped by his son. In a confessional letter, dictated for his son on his deathbed, he admits,

> I look into the Book which all Christendom venerates; and the book tells me that the sin of the father shall be visited on the child. I look out into the world; and I see the living witness around me to that terrible truth. I see the vices which have contaminated the father, descending, and contaminating the child; I see the shame which has disgraced the father's name, descending and disgracing the child's. I look in on myself – and I see My Crime, ripening again for the future in the self-same circumstance which first sowed the seeds of it in the past; and descending, in inherited contamination of Evil, from me to my son.[43]

His fears are consistent with psychology's belief that 'there is in existence a large amount of crime closely connected by hereditary predisposition and descent with diseased mind'.[44] Echoing the biblical reference used in *Armadale*, Henry Maudsley wrote:

> The sins of the father are visited upon the children. [...] Deep in his inmost heart everybody has an instinctive feeling that he has been predestined from all eternity to be what he is, and could not, antecedent conditions having been what they were, have been different.[45]

Accordingly, Ozias's father questions how much of his son's fate has been mapped out by his own actions: 'My son!' he exclaims, 'the only hope I have left for you, hangs on a Great Doubt – the doubt whether we are, or are not, the masters of our own destinies' (p. 55). In case his forebodings are wrong, however, and 'moral free will can conquer mortal fate' (p. 55), Ozias's father outlines a number of instructions through which the deadly legacy might be avoided. These include, most notably, the stipulation that Ozias avoids Allan Armadale and Lydia Gwilt:

> Avoid the widow of the man I killed – if the widow still lives. Avoid the maid whose wicked hand soothed the way to the marriage – if the maid is still in her service. And more than all, avoid the man who bears the same name as your own. [...] Never let the two Allan Armadales meet in this world: never, never, never!
>
> (pp. 55–6)

Armadale anticipates issues that Collins considered with much more blatancy in his penultimate work *The Legacy of Cain* (1889). In the later novel Collins aimed to demonstrate that, while heredity was a strong factor in the development of criminal impulses, such forces could be overcome by the better parts of human nature. On the closing page of that work Collins writes:

> The doctrines of hereditary transmission of moral qualities must own that it has overlooked the fertility (for growth of good and for growth of evil equally) which is inherent in human nature. There are virtues that exalt us, and vices that degrade us, whose mysterious origin is, not in our parents, but in ourselves.[46]

Accordingly, Eunice Gracedieu, the daughter of a hanged murderess, manages to overcome her inherited passions, which the text calls her 'lurking hereditary taint',[47] and resists murdering her step-sister in the nick of time.

For Ozias Midwinter, the struggle is much more difficult. *His* taint does manage to overcome him but only through the complex relationship he has with Lydia Gwilt. He begins life with what Maudsley terms 'an enemy in his camp, a traitor in his own nature'[48] and, being made aware of this by his father's letter, employs the kind of self-vigilance recommended by Winslow in *Obscure Diseases*. Soon after reading his father's ominous missal, for example, he irrationally asks Mr Brock, his clergyman friend, 'is my father's crime looking at you out of *my* eyes? [...] Has the ghost of the drowned man followed me into the room?' (p. 103, italics in original). Like Maudsley's individual, who has an enemy in his own camp, Ozias, it seems, must wrestle against his own nature:

> I felt the horror that had crept over [my father] in his last moments, creeping over me. I struggled against myself, as *he* would have had me struggle. I tried to be all that was most repellent to my own gentler nature.
> (p. 120, italics in original)

The narrator adds that 'the cruel necessity of self-suppression was present to his mind' (p. 122). Yet, notwithstanding these fears, Ozias (with the aid of Mr Brock) attempts to reject his father's Pagan fatalism in favour of the more Christian idea that the son's life might be spent atoning for his father's sins:

> What is it appointed me to do – now that I am breathing the same air, and living under the same roof with the son of the man whom my father killed – to perpetuate my father's crime by mortally injuring him? or to atone for my father's crime by giving him the devotion of my whole life?
> (pp. 122–3)

This passage's combination of the father's fatalism with a more level-headed interpretation is characteristic of how the text consistently juxtaposes the idea of predestination with more 'rational' explanations. Despite the fact that *Armadale* creaks with coincidences that appear to verify the fatalistic forebodings of the father, episodes in which the legacy appears to be most active often contain a more logical reason for certain ill-omened events.

On numerous occasions, for example, the text seems to allege that the 'morbid inheritance' of Ozias's father is only ever 'morbid' in light of Midwinter's obsession with it. In *Obscure Diseases*, Winslow warned against the dangers of allowing the mind to 'dwell' on such matters. In the following passage, in particular, he could be describing Ozias's mental state:

> Instead of making an effort to crush this feeling, he allows – in fact, forces – his mind to dwell upon it; the idea pursues him in his walks, haunts him in his waking thoughts, and exercises a fearful ascendancy over him during the darkness of the night. The mind eventually becomes so absorbed in the idea, that the bitter, angry feeling which, in the first instance, was insignificant and amenable to control, seizes hold of the mind, and influences and distorts every idea and action.[49]

Again, the image of the demon wraith pursuing the individual's thoughts and movements invokes key persecution tableaux from nineteenth-century popular fiction. Winslow revises earlier theories on monomania where single ideas were thought to infect and influence every thought and action of the individual, leading him or her into behaviour that he or she was unconscious of and powerless to avoid. 'The self-created delusion', Winslow argues, 'may [...] obtain a fearful dominion over the mind, and actually lead to the commission of criminal acts'.[50] A similar notion was explored by another psychological text in Collins's library. In *Psychological Inquiries* (1854), Sir Benjamin Brodie claimed that

> a gentleman of my acquaintance, of a very sensitive and imaginative turn of mind, informed me that, not infrequently, when he had had his thoughts intensely fixed for a considerable time on an absent or imaginary object, he had at last seen it projected on the opposite wall, though only for a brief space of time, with all the brightness and distinctness of reality.[51]

According to Brodie and Winslow, therefore, obsessions can become (or seem to become) reality. This is, I argue, the driving force behind many of the foretold sequences in *Armadale*. Ozias's obsession with his father's criminal legacy produces the situations that the former fears the most. The father's legacy works its fulfilment without superstition or coincidence. What is more, Lydia Gwilt becomes a key mediator between Ozias's obsessions and their realisation.[52]

Perhaps the most obvious example of how persuasive and officious Ozias's obsessions can become is to be found in his interpretation of Allan's dream. While onboard the wreck of *La Grâce de Dieu*, the vessel on which his father was murdered, Allan dreams what seems to portend three future episodes from the narrative. Firstly, he dreams he will encounter the 'Shadow of a Woman', then, that he will have a quarrel with the 'Shadow of a Man', resulting in the breaking of a porcelain ornament, and, finally, in the presence of both these shadows, he will be given a drink that causes him to lose consciousness. Although, at the time of the dream, it is impossible for Ozias to know how it will be fulfilled, he is convinced that it is evidence of his father's warnings. As Allan boisterously informs Mr Hawbury, the medical man he and Ozias are lodging with at the time, 'What do you think? – [Midwinter] will have it that my dream is a warning to me to avoid certain people; and he actually persists in stating that one of those people is – himself!' (p. 169). Allan implores Hawbury, as a 'professional man' (p. 169), to give Ozias a more rational explanation for the dream's events. Hawbury does so by showing how the dream actually replicates the latter's experiences from the preceding day. According to Jenny Bourne Taylor, the episode exploits contemporaneous ideas on clairvoyance. 'Clairvoyance' was defined at the time as a telepathic confluence between two minds as well as a form of prescience.[53] Allan's dream thus appears to appropriate the fears occupying *Ozias's* mind and to forecast future events. Hawbury's interpretation, however, could actually be correct; Allan's dream does replicate recent experiences and one reason why its main visions are fulfilled is that Ozias's obsessions drive them towards realisation.

When Ozias discovers that Allan has employed a spy to watch Lydia Gwilt, for instance, whom the latter intends to marry, he loses his temper and his father's passions appear to resurface: "Explain!" cried Midwinter, his eyes aflame, and his hot Creole blood rushing crimson into his face' (p. 479). Allan's dim-witted explanation, however, only 'heap[s] fuel on the fire' (p. 480), resulting – as predicted by the dream – in a Statuette being broken:

> [Ozias] had drawn back along the wall, as Allan advanced, until the bracket which supported the Statuette was before instead of behind him. In the madness of his passion, he saw nothing but Allan's face confronting him. In the madness of his passion, he stretched out his right hand as he answered and shook it threateningly in the air. It struck the forgotten projection of the bracket – and the next instant the Statuette lay in fragments on the floor.[54]
>
> (p. 481)

Predictably, Ozias connects the incident with Allan's dream: 'The horror of the night on the Wreck had got him once more, and the flame of his passion was quenched in an instant. "The Dream!" he whispered, under his breath, "The Dream again!"' (p. 482). It is Ozias's *own* actions, however, that break the Statuette. At the moment his passions become a form of 'madness', and his father's murderous work comes closest to being repeated, a part of Allan's dream gets fulfilled. It seems significant that the bracket holding the ill-fated figurine is called a 'projection'. It is a term that would later be used by twentieth-century psychologists (especially Freud) to refer to the mental strategy whereby thoughts and emotions are displaced onto physical objects or people (as, for example, Glyde and Hartright's fears get projected onto Anne Catherick). Remember how, in his *Psychological Inquiries*, Brodie describes a man who had seen his obsessions 'projected on the opposite wall'. In *Armadale*, Ozias's obsessions with his own (alleged) morbid inheritance drive him, involuntarily, to break the Statuette. Notice, for example, how Midwinter's passions are 'quenched in an instant' as soon as the ornament is smashed. The violence that was meant for Allan, it seems, has been diverted onto the figurine.

One of Allan's other oneiric visions, 'The Shadow of a Woman', also seems to reach its fulfilment through the unconscious agency of Ozias. As with the hereditary 'taint in the blood' described by many of the era's medical texts, Lydia is often described through similar symbolism of toxic and deadly infection. In an essay on *Armadale*, Jessica Maynard has demonstrated how the characterisation of Lydia exploits scientific and popular Victorian ideas of contamination. She argues that Lydia's

> dalliance with poisons has a counterpart of sorts in the catastrophic potential of her personal appearance, which repeatedly numbs and incapacitates the male viewer. The overall effect of the novel is to cast her not merely as poisoner (though this is never proved), but as source of poison too.[55]

In addition to intoxicating and immobilising several male characters, Lydia's venomous progress through the narrative also appears to cause what Ozias notices as a 'succession of deaths' (p. 125). She operates like a biological disease, working her/its way through the novel's unsuspecting population. As such, her characterisation corresponds with one of the period's key methods of representing women's violence. Soon after *Armadale* completed its run in the *Cornhill*, for example, the magazine featured an article by M. E. Owen entitled 'Criminal Women'. Appearing soon after Collins's portrait of female villainy within a primarily middle-class setting, the essay seems eager to relocate female criminality in the working classes. 'As a rule', it observes, 'educated women are not known in prison'.[56] Yet, in keeping with the themes explored in Collins's novel, Mrs Owen apparently agrees that the criminal woman was a disease. Such women, she says, are 'one of the sores of the body politic' and, through their roles as mothers, they exert a noxious influence on society:

> How is it that we have a class of women amongst us who poison the springs of their home life – who bring forth children to follow in their

steps – whose influence helps so largely to degrade our streets, to fill our gaols, and whose cost, consequently, to the country is considerable? [...] A female infant, the offspring of depraved and diseased parents, comes into the world. With its mother's milk it imbibes the poison that results from dram-drinking.[57]

Like the prostitute, from whom she was often indistinguishable, the criminal woman – according to Mrs Owen – contaminated and destroyed the central buttresses of nineteenth-century culture. This is a fear that Collins exploited for his portrayal of Lydia Gwilt, yet, by linking her with the *hereditary* influences of nefarious father figures, *Armadale* also demonstrates how, for the Victorians, dangerous women came to represent the most unsettling elements of *masculine* culture. For Ozias Midwinter, in particular, Lydia becomes the walking embodiment of his father's evil inheritance. When he first hears of Lydia's visiting Allan's mother, for example, 'the horror of his hereditary superstition [crept] over him again' (p. 124) and he asks: '*Is* there a fatality that follows men in the dark? And is it following *us* in that woman's footsteps?' (p. 125, italics in original). Like Frankenstein's relationship with his monster, Lydia becomes Ozias's Shadow – a fearful doppelganger manifesting the most dangerous aspects of his own character. According to his own admissions, these are the inherited, murderous proclivities of his father. Throughout *Obscure Diseases*, Forbes Winslow often returned to the metaphorical idea of insanity as a shadow. It was a method through which he could emphasise the insidious and fleeting nature of mental alienation:

Alas! we should be closing our eyes to the truth if we were to ignore the existence of such, thank God, perhaps only temporary, paroxysmal, and evanescent conditions of unhealthy thought, and phases of passion which occasionally have been known to cast their withering influence and death-like shadow over mind, blighting, saddening, and often crushing the best, kindest, and noblest human natures.[58]

Soon after this section, Winslow refers to 'the dawning, obscure, faint tints, shadowy outline of approaching insanity'.[59] In *Armadale*, Lydia is constantly depicted as Ozias's shadow. As noted above, she is portrayed as 'the shadow of a woman' in Allan's dream and, when he and Ozias first encounter her, she is a shadowy silhouette standing on the margins of a reservoir. With the dream ever present in his mind, Ozias is not slow to connect Lydia with the Shadow in his friend's dream:

On the near margin of the pool, where all had been solitude before, there now stood, fronting the sunset, the figure of a woman. [... Ozias] opened the narrative of the Dream, and held it under Allan's eyes. His finger pointed to the lines which recorded the first Vision; his voice sinking lower and lower, repeated the words: – [...]

'The darkness opened and showed me the vision – as in a picture – of a broad, lonely pool, surrounded by open ground. Above the farther margin of the pool I saw the cloudless western sky, red with the light of sunset.

'On the near margin of the pool there stood the Shadow of a Woman'.

(pp. 320–1)

Ozias's father warned his son that the murder would 'darken all your young life at its outset with the shadow of your father's crime' (p. 56). Through Lydia, it seems, the legacy has been fulfilled as 'the shadow of [the] father's crime' becomes 'The Shadow of a Woman'.

All of this shadow imagery recalls central episodes in Mrs Wood's *The Shadow of Ashlydyat* and Collins's *No Name*. Like the Shadow on the Godolphin estate, Lydia is figured as the epitome of the forefather's deadly, congenital legacy. Like Magdalen Vanstone when she pursues Admiral Bartram through his Banqueting-Hall, also, *Armadale* shows how the 'dangerous' woman might be a shadow cast by the psychopathic male himself. A shadow, it is worth noting, is essentially an 'unreal' phenomenon that only ever exists in relation to the object generating it. In his portrait of the relationship between Ozias and Lydia, Collins seems to draw on this idea to suggest that the 'villainess' is a danger generated and driven by the obsessions of men.

Maynard has asked the pertinent question, 'where [...] is the crime? There is no necessary connection between [Lydia's] material presence and these deaths'.[60] With the exception of her first husband's murder, which takes place prior to the novel's 'current' sequences, Lydia is actually guilty of killing no one in *Armadale*. The deaths of Allan's mother, uncle, and cousin (the 'succession of deaths' noticed by Ozias) are only circumstantially connected to Lydia's presence. Her 'influence' over these deaths is noticed first and foremost by Midwinter and based upon the conjectures of a mind already obsessed with her dangerous potential. Indeed, these are crimes that feature an act without intention; in legal terminology, the *actus reus* without *mens rea*. As a man who had legal training, Collins would have been aware that a proper, legally defined, crime consisted of two interlinking elements: *actus reus* (the action – for example, pointing a gun and pulling the trigger) and *mens rea* (the intention to perform that action). Without both of these elements, a criminal conviction in British law was (and still is) unsustainable. Therefore, Lydia's supposed killing of Allan's relatives, which feature an *act* without the *intention*, do not, in the eyes of the law, make her a murderess. By direct contrast, however, her next three 'crimes' are the exact reverse: attempted murders, featuring the *mens rea* (properly 'malice aforethought' in murder cases) but failing in their commission (thus lacking the *actus reus*). These three *attempted* murders are, moreover, like the breaking of the

Statuette: unconsciously choreographed by the fears of Ozias. In short, Midwinter commits (or attempts to commit) the violence his father forewarned through the agency of Lydia Gwilt.

Ozias's love affair with Miss Gwilt appears inseparable from an increasing animosity he feels for Allan. In the following citation, Ozias, newly returned from London, encounters Lydia on the road to Allan's house. There are a number of key similarities between this encounter and Walter Hartright's meeting with Anne Catherick on the London high road:

> The magnetic influence of her touch was thrilling through him while she spoke. [...] A man exceptionally sensitive, a man exceptionally pure in his past life, he stood hand in hand in the tempting secrecy of the night, with the first woman who had exercised over him the all-absorbing influence of her sex. At his age, and in his position, who could have left her? The man (with a man's temperament) doesn't live who could have left her.
>
> (p. 461)

Lydia admits, like the woman in white, 'I am so friendless, I am so completely at your mercy!' (p. 465) and, as in the earlier novel, their meeting reveals Ozias's position as a young man in the throes of sexual alertness. Over the page, Collins employs clichéd ideas on the seductive irresistibility of women like Lydia:

> Perfectly modest in her manner, possessed to perfection of the grateful restraints and refinements of a lady, she had all the allurements that feast the eye, all the Siren-invitations that seduce the sense – a subtle suggestiveness in her silence, and a sexual sorcery in her smile.
>
> (p. 462)

The stylistic use of sibilance is clearly meant to invoke well-worn images of paradise lost and women as serpentine temptresses. As in *The Woman in White*, however, idioms of sexual awakening in the scene are linked to the man's increasing awareness of his own unhealthy character traits. It is hardly coincidental, for example, that episodes including Ozias's alleged love for Lydia, are also scenes in which he becomes aware of his deep-rooted hostility towards Allan: 'For the first time since they had known each other, his interests now stood self-revealed before him as openly adverse to the interests of his friend' (p. 463). Also, like the hereditary taint in his blood, the 'enemy in his own camp', which Ozias is painfully aware he needs to control, his 'love' for Lydia becomes something he seems eager to avoid: 'Midwinter struggled against the fascination of looking at her and listening to her. [...] He was trembling, and she saw it' (p. 462, p. 465). Like Hartright's meeting with Anne Catherick, therefore, the encounters between Ozias and Lydia bring forth the former's psychological demons and, like the woman in white, Lydia becomes a site of projected masculine fears. As Lydia herself admits, there is a 'strange, strange sympathy' between her and Ozias (p. 465); and, the trembling, pugnacious sensations experienced by him are hardly explicable as 'ordinary' courtship passions.

Lydia's first murder attempt against Allan reveals these connections between the villainess's actions and Ozias's semiconscious desires. She laces Allan's lemonade with laudanum and brandy and, because he is allergic to the latter, he faints before drinking any of the poison. Soon afterwards, Ozias notices how the event echoes one of the events in Allan's dream:

> There is a curse on our lives! there is a fatality in our footsteps! Allan's future depends on his separation from us [that is, Ozias and Lydia] at once and for ever. Drive him from the place we live in, and the air we breathe. Force him among strangers – the worst and wickedest of them will be more harmless to him than we are!
>
> (p. 683)

It is noteworthy how Ozias and Lydia are united in this passage as 'we'. Their influence on Allan has become a dangerous double act. Ozias's fears that he will harm Allan are almost realised through the agency of Lydia. Summing up the event, Midwinter says to Lydia,

> I approached you, and said the lemonade took a long time to make. You touched me, as I was walking away again, and handed me the tumbler filled to the brim. At the same time, Allan turned round from the window; and I, in my turn, handed the tumbler to *him*.
>
> (p. 680, italics in original)

The attempted murder seems to be the result of Ozias's passions, rather than Lydia's. Although it is not my intention to argue that Ozias *intends* to kill Allan, it seems that *he* has the *mens rea* (the mental processes that lead up to the commission of a crime) and Lydia performs the *actus reus*. They are like Gervoise Gilbert and Humphrey Melwood, in Braddon's 'Lost and Found' (1864), who share culpability for the murder of Agnes Gilbert. Or, similarly, like Jekyll and Hyde in that one identity fulfils the latent, demonic desires of another. Lydia explains:

> In a tone that I now heard, and with a look that I now saw, for the first time [Ozias said],
>   'You didn't suppose, Allan, [...] that a lady's temper could be so easily provoked'.

The first bitter word of irony, the first hard look of contempt, I had ever had from him! And Armadale the cause of it!

My anger suddenly left me. Something came in its place, which steadied me in an instant, and took me silently out of the room.

(p. 676)

It seems that Lydia appropriates Ozias's inherited animosity for Allan. Observe the way her own anger is replaced with a certain 'something'. This could be Ozias's capability of killing his friend. The 'lady's temper' of this scene seems to be the arsenal with which Ozias's obscure, murderous passions work their predestined fulfilment.

This process is even more obvious in Lydia's second attempt to murder Armadale. Through her rogue husband, Manuel, Lydia has Allan nailed into a sinking yacht. In the nick of time, Manuel feels compunction and warns his victim of the plot to kill him. 'I can't find it in my heart', he writes to Allan in a secret note, 'not to give you a chance for your life':

Don't be alarmed when you hear the hammer above. I shall do it, and I shall have short nails in my hand as well as long, and use the short ones only. Wait till you hear the boat with all of us shove off, and then prize up the cabin hatch with your back.

(p. 730)

This abortive murder attempt duplicates, almost exactly, the murder committed by Ozias's father. The key difference is that Allan survives where his father does not. In the letter to his son, Ozias's father admits how, like Manuel, he had bolted the cabin door of a sinking ship on Allan's father:

The devil at my elbow whispered, 'Don't shoot him like a man: drown him like a dog!' He was under water when I bolted the scuttle. But his head rose to the surface before I could close the cabin door. I looked at him, and he looked at me – and I locked the door in his face.

(p. 51)

This is the crime that Ozias's father fears will be replicated by his son: 'I see danger in the future, begotten of the danger in the past [...] crime that is the child of *my* crime' (p. 54, italics in original). When Allan is nailed into the sinking yacht, it seems that the forebodings have been validated.

Lydia's third and final attempt to murder Allan offers a clear indication of the ways in which Ozias has covertly inflicted violence on his friend throughout the text. Under false pretences, Lydia lures Allan to Dr Downward's Sanatorium, an institution for the treatment of nervous disorders. In the portrait of Downward's clinical techniques and his institution, we find echoes of the mid-Victorian belief that obscure diseases ought to be cured by 'obscure' remedies.[61] Winslow wrote, for example, that

> if the practitioner is judicious in his inquiries he may generally succeed in effecting his object without inducing the patient, in the slightest degree, to suspect the purport of his visit. In a few cases, the physician may administer remedial agents, and succeed in warding off an attack of insanity, without conveying an intimation of the suspicions which exist as to the person's state of mind.[62]

Downward seems to subscribe to Winslow's theory of keeping the patient in the dark regarding the full extent of his (or her) prognosis and treatment. 'Moral treatment', Downward says, 'soothes, helps, and cures [the patient], without his own knowledge' (p. 772). His Sanatorium thus includes clandestine methods of locking its patients into their rooms, opening and closing their windows, and administering medicine.

It is through these 'obscure remedies' that Lydia commits her final act of violence. While he gives a crowd of women a tour of the institution, Downward surreptitiously informs Lydia how she might murder Allan. He says:

> 'I noiselessly fumigate one [patient]; I noiselessly oxygenise the other, by means of a simple Apparatus fixed outside in the corner here'. [...]
>
> With a preliminary glance at Miss Gwilt, the doctor unlocked the lid of the wooden casing, and disclosed inside nothing more remarkable than a large stone jar, having a glass funnel, and a pipe communicating with the wall, inserted in the cork which closed the mouth of it. [...] Without a word passing between them, she had understood him. She knew as well as if he had confessed it, that he was craftily putting the necessary temptation in her way, before witnesses who could speak to the superficially-innocent acts which they had seen, if anything serious happened. [...]
>
> 'Armadale will die this time', she said to herself. [...] 'The doctor will kill him by my hands'.
>
> (p. 774)

The final sentence of this extract offers a pertinent demonstration of the way in which Lydia fulfils the dangerous propensities of the novel's male characters. As with Ozias, Lydia becomes the agent of Downward's intention to kill. Ironically, the scene also reveals how the anticipation of irrational behaviour can become self-fulfilling. The tools intended to *cure* mental disorders (such as homicidal mania, for example) become the arsenal through which such motivations are realised. It is a reflection of how, throughout the narrative, Ozias's fears of his innate criminal tendencies create and propel the very consequences he is most afraid of. This is an idea that relates back to Magdalen Vanstone's laudanum in *No Name*. There is a fine line, that novel suggested, between medicine and poison; a fact, it seems, that is repeated by Dr Downward:

> 'Do you see that bottle?' he said; 'that plump, round, comfortable-looking bottle? Never mind the name of what is beside it; let us stick to the bottle, and distinguish it, if you like, by giving it a name of our own. Suppose we call it "our Stout Friend?" Very good. Our Stout Friend, by himself, is a most harmless and useful medicine. He is freely dispensed every day to tens of thousands of patients all over the civilized world. [...] *But* bring him into contact with something else [...] and let Samson himself be in that closed chamber, our Stout Friend will kill him in half-an-hour!'
> (pp. 776–7, italics in original)

This 'Stout Friend', a medicine that is usually used to cure and prevent illness, can very easily become a murder weapon. Applied to Ozias Midwinter's story, this notion suggests that the measures in place to anticipate or prevent obscure mental diseases ironically *create* the very shadows and phantoms they are most eager to overcome. In agreement with what the *Glasgow Medical Journal* said of Winslow, constant attempts to discover and control madness can, it seems, be maddening themselves. Collins's work suggests that the 'dangers' of womanhood, likewise, cannot only be the self-fulfilment of male fears, but fascinating indicators of the unhealthy elements residing in masculine minds as well.

Conclusion

> I married Helen. Villiers, that woman, if I can call her woman, corrupted my soul. [...] You, Villiers, you may think you know life, and London, and what goes on, day and night, in this dreadful city; for all I can say you have heard the talk of the vilest, but I tell you you can have no conception of what I know, no, not in your most fantastic, hideous dreams can you have imaged forth the faintest shadow of what I have heard – and seen. Yes, seen; I have seen the incredible, such horrors that even I myself sometimes stop in the middle of the street, and ask whether it is possible for a man to behold such things and live. In a year, Villiers, I was a ruined man, in body and soul, – in body and soul.[1]

In recent years, Arthur Machen's *The Great God Pan* (1894), from which the above extract is taken, has had a surge of interest from academics fascinated with late-nineteenth-century Gothicism and decadence. According to Roger Luckhurst, 'the text has become the quintessential text of late Victorian Gothic for many contemporary critics' because of its main female character, Helen Vaughan, and portrayals of London as a nightmarish 'city of resurrections'.[2] Helen, the illicit offspring of a working-class woman and a Pagan god (The Great God Pan), becomes a demonic and destructive harbinger of dissidence within London's fashionable circles. Like many female characters of the 1890s, she is represented as disturbingly over-sexualised and capable of leading unsuspecting men to destruction. She thus causes what the text calls a 'terrible epidemic of suicide' in the metropolis's well-to-do circles.[3] For some critics, the destructive *femme fatale* (as typified by Helen Vaughan) is an instantly recognisable product of the *fin-de-siècle*.[4] Although the increased number of such portrayals at the end of the nineteenth century cannot be denied, my study has aimed to show how the destructive female figure was very much a part of *mid*-Victorian culture.

Helen Vaughan and her sisters are not, therefore, unique to the *fin-de-siècle* but one outcome of the complex nexus of ideas and representations I have been discussing in the preceding chapters.

As Luckhurst observes, Machen only ever hints at the horrors posed by the existence of Helen Vaughan: 'Machen's Gothic tales of the 1890s', he notes, 'are full of doors shut firmly in our face'.[5] The exact nature of Helen's misdemeanours is thus never fully outlined. 'Such forces', Machen writes, 'cannot be named, cannot be spoken, cannot be imagined'.[6] Yet, despite such reserve, the text implies that Helen's sins are of a sexual nature. Moving from man to man in the capital, she operates like a venereal disease – infecting and destroying those she touches. As such, she is a physical, living signifier of sexual excess and danger. Although this links her to the inglorious portraits of womanhood explored by many late-nineteenth-century writers, it also suggests that Helen inherits much from characters like Lady Audley, Lydia Gwilt, and Charlotte St John. Helen Vaughan might not be as explosively violent as her sensational forebears, but, like them, she appears to confirm that 'human flesh may become the veil of a horror one dare not express'.[7] Like the passionate women portrayed in earlier popular fiction, legal history, and medical theory, Helen Vaughan, and, more broadly, the *fin-de-siècle femme fatale*, appeared to confirm presumptions that when women's sexuality became excessive, it became destructive. Late-Victorian texts also seemed to agree with earlier suggestions that such horrors often lurked beneath calm, deceptive, and beguiling feminine appearances.

This suggests, therefore, that there is an alternative way of thinking about representations of dangerous female characters. Rather than being the product of any given author's proto-feminist or misogynistic leanings, such depictions can be seen as a notion working its way through a large and complex web of ideas. It is with such intricate connections that this study has been primarily concerned. Helen Vaughan and her fatal sisters may have visible roots in the sensational villainesses of the 1860s, but future studies could well inquire how such portraits related to infamous criminal trials and medical theories of the late nineteenth century.[8] In terms of the mid-Victorian period, scholars could ask themselves what other images had a similar ability to move, with such telling results, between a range of the era's key disciplines.

I have suggested that the destructive woman figure had a specific poignancy, at mid century, because she spoke to a number of the era's ideologies. This book has not meant to argue that there was an increase in actual crimes committed by women at that time, but that allegedly violent women were given more attention in the period's media because they related to, supported, and allowed writers to explore a number of established beliefs. By the time it reached the times of Arthur Machen, the proliferation of dangerous female characters in fiction marked a hackneyed use of images that, in the 1860s, had been a fertile mode of expression. As we have seen, some thinkers at the latter time converted stories of female violence into narratives that sanctioned and strengthened controls enforced by a bourgeois- and male-driven culture. From stories like Madeline Smith's and Constance Kent's, for example, one discovers coded messages that aimed to regulate the behaviour of men and women (especially the latter) in such a way that retained traditional assignations of power.

Yet, according to Etienne Balibar and Pierre Macherey's important essay 'On Literature as an Ideological Form' (1981), literary texts reproduce ideologies in such a way that ideological 'contradictions' become 'unevenly resolved conflicts in the text'.[9] While one finds conservative notions writ large in fiction, one may also discover a map of their integral fault lines. This certainly appears to be the case with the sensation novels of the 1860s. Braddon, Wood, and Collins not only echoed some of their period's most conservative ideologies, but, in so doing, they also wrote narratives that provide modern scholars with indications of how those ideologies formed, operated, and failed.

Notes

Introduction

1. Jean Étienne Dominique Esquirol, *Des Maladies Mentales, Considérées sous les Rapports Médical, Hygiénique et Médico-légal* (1838); trans. E. K. Hunt as *Mental Maladies: A Treatise on Insanity* (Philadelphia: Lea and Blanchard, 1845), p. 362. Italics in original.
2. Ibid., p. 357.
3. Anon., 'The Lammonby Murder', *Times*, 13 February 1845, p. 5.
4. Ibid.
5. Mrs Henry Wood, *St. Martin's Eve* (1866; London: Richard Bentley and Son, 1895), p. 450.
6. See, for example, Andrew Scull, *Museums of Madness: The Social Organization of Insanity in Nineteenth-Century England* (London: Allen Lane, 1979); *Madhouses, Mad-doctors and Madmen: The Social History of Psychiatry in the Victorian Era*, ed. by Andrew Scull (Philadelphia: University of Pennsylvania Press, 1981); Elaine Showalter, *The Female Malady: Women, Madness and English Culture, 1830–1980* (1985; London: Virago Press, repr. 1987); Janet Oppenheim, *"Shattered Nerves": Doctors, Patients, and Depression in Victorian England* (Oxford: Oxford University Press, 1991).
7. See Mary S. Hartman, *Victorian Murderesses: A True History of Thirteen Respectable French and English Women Accused of Unspeakable Crimes* (1979; London: Robson Books, repr. 1985); Lucia Zedner, *Women, Crime, and Custody in Victorian England* (Oxford: Oxford University Press, 1991); and Judith Knelman, *Twisting in the Wind: The Murderess and the English Press* (Toronto: Toronto University Press, 1998).
8. See Winifred Hughes, *The Maniac in the Cellar: Sensation Novels of the 1860s* (Princeton: Princeton University Press, 1980); Patrick Brantlinger, 'What is "Sensational" about the "Sensation Novel"?' (1982) in *Wilkie Collins*, ed. by Lyn Pykett (London: Macmillan Press, 1998), pp. 30–57; Jenny Bourne Taylor, *In the Secret Theatre of Home: Wilkie Collins, Sensation Narrative, and Nineteenth-Century Psychology* (London: Routledge, 1988); Ann Cvetkovich, *Mixed Feelings: Feminism, Mass Culture, and Victorian Sensationalism* (New Brunswick: Rutgers University Press, 1992); Lyn Pykett, *The Improper Feminine: The Women's Sensation Novel and the New Woman Writing* (London: Routledge, 1992); Kate Flint, *The Woman Reader 1837–1914* (Oxford: Oxford University Press, 1993), pp. 274–93; and Lyn Pykett, *The Sensation Novel: from* The Woman in White *to* The Moonstone (Plymouth: Northcote House, 1994).
9. A recent collection of essays, edited by Andrew Maunder and Grace Moore, makes interesting connections between insanity, crime and popular culture; however, the terms 'madness', 'crime', and 'sensation' are linked in this work only as a means of grouping together fifteen essays of different scope and methodological approach. Unlike my study, Maunder and Moore's book does not offer a protracted analysis of the interdisciplinary connections between psychology, crime, and sensation fiction. See *Victorian Crime, Madness and Sensation*, ed. by Andrew Maunder and Grace Moore (Aldershot: Ashgate, 2004).

10. See, for example, Gillian Beer, *Darwin's Plots: Evolutionary Narrative in Darwin, George Eliot and Nineteenth-Century Fiction* (London: Routledge, 1983); Jenny Bourne Taylor, *Secret Theatre*; Sally Shuttleworth, *George Eliot and Nineteenth-Century Science: The Make-Believe of a Beginning* (Cambridge: Cambridge University Press, 1984) and *Charlotte Brontë and Victorian Psychology* (Cambridge: Cambridge University Press, 1996); Helen Small, *Love's Madness: Medicine, The Novel, and Female Insanity, 1800–1865* (Oxford: Oxford University Press, 1996); and Jane Wood, *Passion and Pathology in Victorian Fiction* (Oxford: Oxford University Press, 2001).
11. I have been inspired here by the work of Josephine McDonagh whose *Child Murder and British Culture 1720–1900* (Cambridge: Cambridge University Press, 2003) analyses the ubiquity of the image of infanticide by tracing its journey through a wealth of eighteenth and nineteenth-century materials.
12. See, for example, Beer's *Darwin's Plots* and Shuttleworth's *George Eliot and Nineteenth-Century Science* and *Charlotte Brontë and Victorian Psychology*. Two exceptions are provided by Taylor's *Secret Theatre* and Lawrence Jerome's *Victorian Detective Fiction and the Nature of Evidence: The Scientific Investigations of Poe, Dickens, and Doyle* (Hampshire: Palgrave Macmillan, 2003), both of which ask important questions about the interdisciplinary nature of popular fiction.
13. An exception is provided by Jill Newton Ainsley's article '"Some Mysterious Agency": Women, Violent Crime, and the Insanity Acquittal in the Victorian Courtroom', *Canadian Journal of History*, 35 (2000), pp. 37–55. In what is an essentially historical essay, Ainsley briefly implies that Braddon's *Lady Audley's Secret* is a novel that draws on the murder trial of Mary Ann Brough (discussed in chapter one) and contemporaneous theories on insanity and criminal responsibility.
14. Robert Lee Wolff, *Sensational Victorian: The Life and Fiction of Mary Elizabeth Braddon* (New York: Garland Publishing, 1979), p. 105. The exact details of Mary Maxwell's Irish exile have since been contested by Jennifer Carnell in *The Literary Lives of M. E. Braddon* (Hastings: The Sensation Press, 2000). Carnell claims that Mary Maxwell returned to her family in Dublin and was not committed to an asylum. See p. 115.
15. '"Devoted Disciple": The Letters of Mary Elizabeth Braddon to Sir Edward Bulwer Lytton, 1862–1873', ed. by Robert Lee Wolff, *Harvard Library Bulletin*, 12 (1974), pp. 5–35 and pp. 129–61 (p. 148).
16. Ibid., p. 149.
17. See J. S. Jacyna, 'Immanence or Transcendence: Theories of Life and Organization in Britain, 1790–1835' *Isis*, 74 (1983), pp. 310–29. On the Wood-Lawrence connection see Charles W. Wood, 'Mrs. Henry Wood. In Memoriam', *The Argosy*, 43 (1887), pp. 251–70, 334–53, 422–42 (pp. 251–70).
18. See chapter four for a more detailed discussion of Mrs Wood's use of medical books.
19. See William Baker, *Wilkie Collins's Library: A Reconstruction* (Connecticut and London: Greenwood Press, 2002) and Barbara Foss Leavy, 'Wilkie Collins's Cinderella: The History of Psychology and *The Woman in White*' *Dickens Studies Annual*, 10 (1982), pp. 91–141.
20. Quoted in Baker, *Wilkie Collins's Library*, p. 26.
21. Wolff, 'Devoted Disciple', p. 158.
22. Charles W. Wood, 'Mrs Henry Wood. In Memoriam', *The Argosy*, 43 (1887), pp. 251–70, 334–53, 422–42 (p. 436).
23. Deborah Wynne's *The Sensation Novel and the Victorian Family Magazine* (Hampshire: Palgrave Macmillan, 2001) has raised important issues relating to how we read sensation fiction in this original context.

24. On the presence of science in Victorian periodicals see Geoffrey Cantor and Sally Shuttleworth (eds) *Science Serialized: Representations of the Sciences in Nineteenth-Century Periodicals* (Cambridge, MA: The Massachusetts Institute of Technology Press, 2004) and Geoffrey Cantor, Gowan Dawson, Graeme Gooday, Richard Noakes, Sally Shuttleworth, and Jonathan Topham, *Science in the Nineteenth-Century Periodical* (Cambridge: Cambridge University Press, 2004).

1 Explosive materials: Legal, medical, and journalistic profiles of the violent woman

1. Anon., Untitled Report, *Times*, 25 October 1849, p. 4.
2. Anon., Untitled Report, *Times*, 25 August 1849, p. 5.
3. See Judith Knelman, *Twisting in the Wind: The Murderess and the English Press* (Toronto: University of Toronto Press, 1998), p. 31.
4. Anon., Untitled Report, *Times*, 25 August 1849, p. 5.
5. Anon., Untitled Report, *Times*, 14 November 1849, p. 4.
6. Charles Dickens attended the hangings and described the scene in a letter to *The Times*:

> Thieves, low prostitutes, ruffians, and vagabonds of every kind, flocked on to the ground, with every variety of offensive and foul behaviour. Fightings, faintings, whistlings, imitations of Punch, brutal jokes, tumultuous demonstrations of indecent delight when swooning women were dragged out of the crowd by the police with their dresses disordered, gave a new zest to the general entertainments. When the sun rose brightly – as it did – it gilded thousands upon thousands of upturned faces, so inexpressibly odious in their brutal mirth and callousness, that a man had cause to feel ashamed of the shape he wore, and to shrink from himself, as fashioned in the image of the Devil.
> Charles Dickens, 'To the Editor of the *Times*', *Times*, 14 November 1849, p. 4.

7. Anon., Untitled Report, *Times*, 27 October 1849, p. 5.
8. Ibid.
9. See Knelman, *Twisting*, p. 104.
10. Anon., Untitled Report, *Times*, 14 November 1849, p. 5.
11. Ibid. Italics in original.
12. Isabella Beeton, *Beeton's Book of Household Management* (London: S. O. Beeton, 1859), p. 908.
13. Ibid., p. 25.
14. Waif Wander [Mary Fortune], 'The White Maniac: A Doctor's Tale', http://gaslight.mtroyal.ab.ca/gaslight/whtmanic.htm [accessed 1 December 2006].
15. Ibid.
16. Anon., 'Woman in Her Psychological Relations', quoted in *Embodied Selves: An Anthology of Psychological Texts 1830–1890*, ed. by Jenny Bourne Taylor and Sally Shuttleworth (Oxford: Oxford University Press, 1998), pp. 170–6 (p. 172). These opinions are corroborated by Jane Austen's *Pride and Prejudice* (1813). Mrs Bennett, remarking on her daughters' lustful attractions to men in military uniform, says, 'I remember the time when I liked a red coat myself very well – and, indeed, I do still at my heart; [...] Colonel Forster looked very becoming the

other night at Sir William's in his regimentals'. Jane Austen, *Pride and Prejudice*, ed. by Robert P. Irvine (1813; Ontario, Canada: Broadview Press, 2002), p. 67.
17. Fortune, 'The White Maniac'.
18. Ibid.
19. Ibid. Italics in original.
20. Ibid.
21. Ibid.
22. Anon., 'Woman in Her Psychological Relations', p. 172.
23. Fortune, 'The White Maniac'.
24. Ibid.
25. Ibid.
26. Ibid.
27. Ibid.
28. Charlotte Brontë, *Jane Eyre*, ed. by Margaret Smith and Sally Shuttleworth (1847; Oxford: Oxford University Press, 2000), p. 213.
29. Anon., 'Double Murder by an Insane Sister', *Annual Register* (1860), p. 48.
30. Roger Smith, *Trial by Medicine: Insanity and Responsibility in Victorian Trials* (Edinburgh: Edinburgh University Press, 1981), p. 6.
31. J. G. Davey, 'Lectures on Insanity, Delivered at the Bristol Medical School During the Summer Session of 1855: Lecture II', *British Medical Journal* (1855), II, pp. 668–75 (671–2).
32. [Dinah Mulock Craik], 'In Her Teens', *Macmillan's Magazine*, 10 (1864), pp. 219–23 (p. 220).
33. Lawson Tait, *Diseases of Women* (1877; New York: William Wood and Company, 1879), p. 91.
34. Fortune, 'The White Maniac'.
35. Ibid.
36. Jean Étienne Dominique Esquirol, *Des Maladies Mentales, Considérées sous les Rapports Médical, Hygiénique et Médico-légal* (1838); trans. E. K. Hunt as *Mental Maladies: A Treatise on Insanity* (Philadelphia: Lea and Blanchard, 1845), p. 367.
37. Craik, 'In Her Teens', p. 219.
38. Alfred Swaine Taylor, *The Principles and Practice of Medical Jurisprudence*, 2 vols (1865; London: J. and A. Churchill, 1894), II, 486.
39. Anon., 'Central Criminal Court', *Times*, 17 June 1853, p. 7.
40. Ibid.
41. Taylor, *Principles and Practice*, II, 601.
42. Anon., 'Police', *Times*, 3 June 1853, p. 7.
43. Ibid.
44. Ibid.
45. Fortune, 'The White Maniac'.
46. Ibid.
47. Ibid.
48. Ibid.
49. Ibid.
50. Frederick C. Skey, 'Hysteria', *Lancet* (1864) I, pp. 31–2 (32).
51. T. W. Gairdner, 'Hysteria and Delirium Tremens', *Lancet* (1861), I, pp. 429–30 (429).
52. Janet Oppenheim, *"Shattered Nerves": Doctors, Patients, and Depression in Victorian England* (Oxford: Oxford University Press, 1991), p. 181.
53. Jane Wood, *Passion and Pathology in Victorian Fiction* (Oxford: Oxford University Press, 2001), p. 13 and p. 12.

54. Helen Small, *Love's Madness: Medicine, The Novel, and Female Insanity, 1800–1865* (Oxford: Oxford University Press, 1996), p. 16.
55. Julius Althaus, 'A Lecture on the Pathology and Treatment of Hysteria: Delivered at the Royal Infirmary for Diseases of the Chest', *British Medical Journal* (1866), I, pp. 245–8 (245).
56. D. De Berdt Hovell, Letter to the Editor, *Lancet* (1868), II, p. 219.
57. See, for example, Robert Brudenell Carter, *On the Pathology and Treatment of Hysteria* (London: John Churchill, 1853), p. 82; Frederick Skey, *Hysteria: Six Lectures* (1866; New York: Moorhead, Simpson, and Bond, 1868), pp. 48–9; Mark S. Micale, *Approaching Hysteria: Disease and its Interpretations* (New Jersey: Princeton University Press, 1995), pp. 161–8.
58. Althaus, 'A Lecture', p. 247 and p. 248.
59. Carter, *Pathology and Treatment*, p. 36.
60. James Cowles Prichard, *A Treatise on Insanity and Other Disorders Affecting the Mind* (1835; Philadelphia: Haswell, Barrington, and Haswell, 1837), p. 157.
61. Anon., 'Murder and Insanity', *Annual Register* (1863), pp. 157–61 (p. 158).
62. Ibid., p. 159.
63. Carter, *Pathology and Treatment*, p. 58.
64. Anon., 'Murder and Insanity', p. 159.
65. Ibid., p. 160.
66. Ibid.
67. Anon., 'Central Criminal Court', *Times*, 29 October 1863, p. 11. Italics in original.
68. Anon., 'Central Criminal Court', *Times*, 16 May 1845, p. 7.
69. Ibid.
70. Ibid.
71. Ibid.
72. Ibid.
73. Taylor, *Principles and Practice*, II, 565.
74. Ibid., II, 577.
75. Davey, 'Lectures on Insanity', p. 675. Esquirol, *Mental Maladies*, p. 407.
76. Davey, 'Lectures on Insanity', p. 675.
77. Mary S. Hartman, *Victorian Murderesses: A True History of Thirteen Respectable French and English Women Accused of Unspeakable Crimes* (1979; London: Robson Books, 1985), p. 72.
78. Anon., 'The Glasgow Poisoning', *Annual Register* (1857), p. 530.
79. Ibid., p. 590.
80. Ibid., p. 560.
81. Ibid., p. 574.
82. Madeline claimed that she had used the poison for cosmetic purposes: 'she says she had been told when at school in England, by a Miss Guibilei, that arsenic is good for the complexion. [...] She says that she poured it all into a basin and washed her face with it'. (ibid., p. 543.) The idea was later employed by Wilkie Collins in *The Law and the Lady* (1875). Sarah Macallan buys arsenic to improve her complexion but eventually uses it to commit suicide. Her husband Eustace is arraigned for her murder and, like Madeline Smith, given a 'not proven' verdict. For a discussion of Collins's appropriation of the Smith trial's details, see Jenny Bourne Taylor, 'Introduction', in Wilkie Collins, *The Law and the Lady*, ed. by Jenny Bourne Taylor (1875; Oxford: Oxford University Press, 1999), pp. vii–xxiv.
83. Anon., 'The Glasgow Poisoning', p. 533.
84. Ibid., pp. 534–5.
85. Ibid., p. 534.

86. Ibid., p. 587.
87. Ibid.
88. [Helen Taylor], 'Women and Criticism', *Macmillan's Magazine*, 14 (1866), pp. 335–40 (p. 340).
89. Anon. Review of C. H. F. Routh, *Infant Feeding and its Influence on Life; or, the Causes and Prevention of Infant Mortality*, British Medical Journal (1860), II, pp. 999–1000 (999).
90. C. H. F. Routh, *Infant Feeding and its Influence on Life; or, the Causes and Prevention of Infant Mortality* (1860; New York: William Wood and Company, 1879), p. 1.
91. Ibid.
92. In 1872, Routh claims, 123,596 infants died so that there was one death for every six births (see Routh, *Infant Feeding*, p. 1).
93. Esquirol, *Mental Maladies*, p. 392.
94. In 1865, John Tuke delivered a lecture at the Medico-Chirurgical Society in Edinburgh. He seemed to disagree with Esquirol by claiming that the insanity caused by pregnancy was not maniacal (explosive, violent) but melancholic (pensive, suicidal). See John Tuke, 'Special Correspondence: Edinburgh', *British Medical Journal* (1865), I, pp. 466–7.
95. Anon., 'Central Criminal Court', *Times*, 14 July 1863, p. 10.
96. Ibid.
97. Ibid.
98. Anon., 'Central Criminal Court', *Times*, 22 September 1865, p. 6.
99. Ibid.
100. Ibid.
101. Ibid.
102. Ibid.
103. Esquirol, *Mental Maladies*, pp. 269–70.
104. Although it is tempting to think otherwise, the synonyms 'mother' and 'smother' do not share a related derivation. Both are from the Old English, respectively, *mōdor* (mother) and *smorian* (to suffocate) (*Collins English Dictionary and Thesaurus*).
105. Esquirol, *Mental Maladies*, p. 89.
106. Ibid., p. 129.
107. See ibid., p. 130. Although he proposes that suppressed lochia causes insanity, Esquirol discredits the idea of 'milk on the brain'.
108. See Hilary Marland, *Dangerous Motherhood: Insanity and Childbirth in Victorian Britain* (Basingstoke: Palgrave Macmillan, 2004). See also Marland's 'Getting Away with Murder? Puerperal Insanity, Infanticide and the Defence Plea' in *Infanticide: Historical Perspectives on Child Murder and Concealment, 1550–2000*, ed. by Mark Jackson (Aldershot: Ashgate, 2002), pp. 168–92; and Cath Quinn, 'Images and Impulses: Representations of Puerperal Insanity and Infanticide in late Victorian England', in Jackson (ed.), *Infanticide*, pp. 193–215.
109. Robert Ferguson, 'Prefatory Essay', in Robert Gooch, *On Some of the Most Important Diseases Peculiar to Women* (1838; London: The New Sydenham Society, 1859), p. v.
110. Gooch, *Important Diseases*, p. 54 and p. 63.
111. Anon., 'Law and Insanity', *British Medical Journal* (1865), I, pp. 275–7 (275).
112. Prichard, *Treatise on Insanity*, p. 275.
113. Ibid., p. 276.
114. Anon., 'The Walworth Murders', *Annual Register* (1857), pp. 90–4 (p. 90).
115. Ibid.
116. Ibid., p. 91.

218 Notes

117. Ibid.
118. Ibid., p. 92.
119. Ibid.
120. Ibid., p. 94.
121. Routh, *Infant Feeding*, p. 58.
122. Ibid.
123. Ibid., pp. 103–8.
124. Ibid., p. 108.
125. Ibid.
126. Ibid., p. 111.
127. Ibid., p. 117.
128. Ibid., p. 120.
129. Ibid.
130. Ibid., p. 124.
131. Other writers were more explicit. See Sally Shuttleworth, 'Demonic Mothers: Ideologies of Bourgeois Motherhood in the Mid-Victorian Era', in *Rewriting the Victorians: Theory, History and the Politics of Gender*, ed. by L. M. Shires (London: Routledge, 1993), pp. 31–51, (p. 39).
132. Because of its location, Brough's crime was popularly known as 'The Esher Murders'. For historical studies of the Mary Ann Brough trial see Jill Newton Ainsley, '"Some Mysterious Agency": Women, Violent Crime, and the Insanity Acquittal in the Victorian Courtroom', *Canadian Journal of History*, 35 (2000), pp. 37–55; and Smith, *Trial by Medicine*, pp. 157–60.
133. After Brough's death, her body was given a post-mortem examination by Sir William Lawrence. He found extensive cerebral disease. Smith, *Trial by Medicine*, p. 160.
134. [Forbes Winslow], 'Recent Trials in Lunacy', *Journal of Psychological Medicine and Mental Pathology*, 7 (1854), pp. 609–25.
135. John Charles Bucknill, *Unsoundness of Mind in Relation to Criminal Acts* (1854; Philadelphia: Johnson and Company, 1856), p. 135.
136. Winslow, 'Recent Trials', p. 617. Italics in original.
137. Ibid., p. 615.
138. Ibid., p. 616.
139. Ibid., p. 617. Italics in original.
140. Anon., 'The Awful Tragedy at Esher', *Annual Register* (1854), pp. 93–7 (pp. 96–7).
141. Ibid., p. 97.
142. A. Meadows, 'Remarks on the Influence of Mental Impressions as a Cause of Bodily Deformity', *British Medical Journal* (1865), I, p. 626.
143. Robert J. Lee, *Maternal Impressions: A Consideration of the Effects of Mental Disturbance During Pregnancy Upon the Intellectual Development of the Child* (London: Smith, Elder and Company, 1875), p. 6.
144. Ibid., p. 15.
145. J. Waring-Curran, 'Case of Monstrosity Dependent on Mental Shock', *British Medical Journal* (1867), II, p. 468.
146. Ibid.
147. J. Hyde Houghton, 'Maternal Impressions', *British Medical Journal* (1867), II, pp. 468–9.
148. Francis Galton, *Hereditary Genius: An Inquiry into its Laws and Consequences* (London: Macmillan and Company, 1869), p. 1.
149. Ibid., p. 366.
150. Henry Maudsley, *The Physiology and Pathology of Mind* (London: Macmillan, 1867), p. 223.

151. W. Jung, 'Hereditary Tendency in Insanity', *Journal of Mental Science*, 25 (1867), pp. 106–7 (p. 106).
152. Esquirol, *Mental Maladies*, p. 49.
153. Frederick James Brown, 'Remarks on the Constitution of the Mind; and on Unsoundness of Mind', *British Medical Journal* (1866), II, p. 331.
154. See Daniel Pick, *Faces of Degeneration: A European Disorder, c. 1848–c. 1918* (Cambridge: Cambridge University Press, 1989; repr. 1993), pp. 109–52. On Lombroso's theories of criminal degeneracy see also William Greenslade, *Degeneration, Culture and the Novel 1880–1940* (Cambridge: Cambridge University Press, 1994), pp. 88–119.
155. Maudsley, *Physiology and Pathology*, p. 224.
156. Pick, *Faces of Degeneration*, p. 51.
157. Taylor, *Principles and Practice*, II, 506. Italics in original.
158. Ibid., p. 562.
159. Anon., 'The Brighton Poisonings', *Times*, 17 January 1872, p. 12.
160. Anon., 'The Brighton Poisoning Case', *Annual Register* (1872), pp. 189–201 (p. 198).
161. Ibid.
162. Ibid.
163. Ibid.
164. Quoted in Anon., 'Moral Insanity', *Journal of Mental Science*, 17 (1865), pp. 132–6 (p. 136).
165. Greenslade, *Degeneration*, p. 15.
166. Maudsley, *Physiology and Pathology*, p. 73.
167. Anon., 'The Old Maid's Petition', quoted in *Victorian Street Ballads*, ed. by W. Henderson (London: Country Life, 1937), p. 100.
168. [Anne Thackeray Ritchie], 'Toilers and Spinsters', *Cornhill Magazine*, 3 (1861), pp. 318–31 (p. 319).
169. Ibid., p. 320.
170. [R. Ashe King], 'A Tête-à-Tête Social Science Discussion', *Cornhill*, 10 (1864), pp. 569–82 (p. 572).
171. Ritchie, 'Toilers and Spinsters', pp. 321–2. This article is put to very good use by Nina Auerbach in *Woman and the Demon: The Life of a Victorian Myth* (Cambridge, MA: Harvard University Press, 1982), pp. 113–4.
172. King, 'Tête-à-Tête', pp. 570–1.
173. Forbes Winslow, *On the Obscure Diseases of the Brain and Disorders of the Mind* (1860; London: John Churchill and Sons, 1868), pp. 201–2.
174. Ibid., p. 202.
175. Anon., 'Woman In Her Psychological Relations', pp. 176–7. Italics in original.
176. See Mary Poovey, *Uneven Developments: The Ideological Work of Gender in Mid-Victorian England* (Chicago: University of Chicago Press, 1988), pp. 1–2.
177. Quoted in ibid., p. 1.
178. Ibid., p. 2.
179. Francis Skae, 'Climacteric Insanity in Women', *Journal of Mental Science*, 18 (1865), pp. 275–8 (pp. 275–6).
180. Edward John Tilt, *The Change of Life In Health and Disease: A Practical Treatise on the Nervous and Other Affections Incidental to Women at the Decline of Life* (London: John Churchill, 1857), p. 9.
181. [Catherine G. F. Gore], 'A Bewailment from Bath; or Poor Old Maids', *Blackwood's Edinburgh Magazine*, 55 (1844), pp. 199–201 (p. 201).
182. [Eliza Lynn Linton], 'Domestic Life' *Temple Bar*, 4 (1862), pp. 402–15 (p. 414).

183. Charles Dickens, *Great Expectations*, ed. by Robin Gilmore (1860–1; London: Everyman, 1994), p. 49.
184. See Greenslade, *Degeneration*, p. 2; and Wood, *Passion and Pathology*, p. 7, p. 163, and p. 176.
185. Skae, 'Climacteric Insanity', p. 275.
186. Ibid.
187. Ibid., p. 276.
188. Esquirol, *Mental Maladies*, p. 242.
189. Dickens, *Great Expectations*, p. 155.
190. Tilt, *The Change of Life*, p. 67 and pp. 269–70.
191. Ibid., p. 130.
192. See Knelman, *Twisting*, pp. 138–41.
193. Anon., 'Central Criminal Court', *Times*, 16 January 1872, p. 11.
194. Anon., 'The Alleged Poisoning at Brighton', *Times*, 8 September 1872, p. 9.
195. Ibid.
196. Anon., 'Central Criminal Court', *Times*, 16 January 1872, p. 11.
197. Anon., 'The Brighton Poisonings', *Times*, 17 January 1872, p. 12.
198. Ibid.
199. Anon., 'The Brighton Poisoning Case', *Annual Register* (1872), pp. 189–201 (p. 198).
200. Ibid., p. 195.
201. Ibid., p. 200.
202. [William Cyples], 'Granny Leatham's Revenge', *Cornhill*, 14 (1866), pp. 313–30 (p. 317).
203. Ibid.
204. Ibid., p. 322.

2 'The terrible chemistry of nature': The Road Murder and popular fiction

1. Anon., 'Barbarous Murder', *Times*, 3 July 1860, p. 12. Often called 'The Road Murder' because it occurred in a small village called Road, the crime has been researched most comprehensively by John Rhode, Yseult Bridges, and Mary Hartman. In *The Case of Constance Kent* (1928), Rhode accepts the version of the events that emerges from Victorian sources, while Bridges and Hartman aim to re-evaluate the crime's particulars in order to solve a mystery that, according to many, remains unsolved today. See John Rhode, *The Case of Constance Kent* (New York: Charles Scribner's Sons, 1928); Yseult Bridges, *The Tragedy at Road Hill House* (New York: Rhinehart and Company, 1954); and Mary S. Hartman, *Victorian Murderesses: A True History of Thirteen Respectable French and English Women Accused of Unspeakable Crimes* (1979; London: Robson Books, 1985), pp. 85–129.
2. Anon., 'The Recent Murder at Road', *Times*, 11 July 1860, p. 5.
3. A. D. Hutter, 'Dreams, Transformations and Literature: The Implications of Detective Fiction', in *Wilkie Collins*, ed. by Lyn Pykett (London: Macmillan, 1998), pp. 175–96. Hutter argues that it is the vocation of the police detective to purge the home of this foreign, criminal invasion.
4. Elizabeth Rose Gruner, 'Family Secrets and the Mysteries of *The Moonstone*', in Pykett, *Wilkie Collins*, pp. 221–43 (p. 222). See also Anthea Trodd, *Domestic Crime in the Victorian Novel* (London: Macmillan, 1989), pp. 19–25.
5. Anon., 'Barbarous Murder', *Times*, 3 July 1860, p. 12.

6. Gruner, 'Family Secrets', p. 222.
7. Anon., Untitled Report, *Times*, 20 April 1865, p. 8.
8. Bridges, *Tragedy at Road Hill House*, p. 158.
9. Charles Dickens, *Great Expectations*, ed. by Robin Gilmour (1860–1; London: Everyman, 1994), p. 11.
10. Joseph Stapleton, *The Great Crime of 1860: Being a Summary of the Facts Relating to the Murder Committed at Road; a Critical Review of its Social and Scientific Aspects, and an Authorised Account of the Family; with an Appendix Containing the Evidence Taken at the Various Inquiries* (London: E. Marlborough, 1861), p. 5.
11. 'S. P.'. 'The Road Murder', *Times*, 9 August 1860, p. 12. SP suggests that Francis saw a family member indulging in a scandalous act and that the boy was killed as a means of silencing him. This is the explanation favoured by many commentators, including Dickens, Bridges, and Hartman. All three suggest that Francis saw Samuel Kent fornicating with Elizabeth Gough and was consequently murdered by his father.
12. Ibid.
13. William A. Hammond, *Insanity in its Relations to Crime* (New York: D. Appleton and Company, 1873), pp. 74–5.
14. 'Medicus', 'The Road Mystery', *Times*, 30 October 1860, p. 6.
15. Jean Étienne Dominique Esquirol, *Des Maladies Mentales, Considérées sous les Rapports Médical, Hygiénique et Médico-légal* (1838); trans. E. K. Hunt as *Mental Maladies: A Treatise on Insanity* (Philadelphia: Lea and Blanchard, 1845), pp. 268–9.
16. Simon During, 'The Strange Case of Monomania: Patriarchy in Literature, Murder in *Middlemarch*, Drowning in *Daniel Deronda*', *Representations*, 0:23 (1988), pp. 86–104 (p. 86–7). Italics in original.
17. Esquirol, *Mental Maladies*, p. 22.
18. Anon., 'Apprehension of Miss Constance Kent', *Times*, 21 July 1860, p. 5.
19. Elaine and English Showalter, 'Victorian Women and Menstruation', in *Suffer and be Still: Women in the Victorian Age*, ed. by Martha Vicinus (London: Macmillan, 1972), pp. 38–44 (p. 43).
20. Anon., 'The Road Child Murder', *Times*, 10 November 1860, p. 11. Bridges and Hartman have argued that there were two, even three, nightshifts that the police confused and lost: one, caused by the menses of Mary Kent, Constance and Francis's older sister, the other probably worn by the murderer. The latter, they argue, was shown to Stapleton, the former was not. This evidence from Urch shows, however, that the nightshift seen by Stapleton, and the one found in the boiler-furnace were the same.
21. Elaine Showalter, *The Female Malady: Women, Madness and English Culture, 1830–1980* (London: Virago, 1987), p. 57.
22. Anon., 'The Road Child Murder', *Times*, 10 November 1860, p. 11. Interestingly, this piece of paper has been identified by Nick Rance as an article from the *Times* outlining Madeline Smith's alleged poisoning of L'Angelier. Constance Kent seems to have been fascinated with the Glasgow Poisoning. See Nick Rance, '"Victorian Values" and "Fast Young Ladies": from Madeline Smith to Ruth Rendell', in *Varieties of Victorianism: The Uses of a Past*, ed. by Gary Day (London: Macmillan, 1998), pp. 220–35 (pp. 228–9).
23. J. W. Stapleton, 'The Road Murder', *Times*, 13 November 1860, p. 10.
24. Anon., 'The Road Child Murder', *Times*, 15 November 1860, p. 10.
25. Anon., 'The Road Child Murder', *Times* (26 July 1860), p. 9.
26. S.P.,'The Road Murder', *Times* (9 August 1860), p. 12.

27. Henry Maudsley, *Body and Mind: An Inquiry into their Connection and Mutual Influence, Specially in Reference to Mental Disorders*, quoted in *Embodied Selves: An Anthology of Psychological Texts 1830–1890*, ed. by Jenny Bourne Taylor and Sally Shuttleworth (Oxford: Oxford University Press, 2000), pp. 204–6 (p. 206). Italics added.
28. Gillian Beer, 'Forging the Missing Link: Interdisciplinary Stories', in *Open Fields: Science in Cultural Encounter* (Oxford: Clarendon Press, 1996), pp. 115–45 (pp. 117–9).
29. Charles Locock, 'Menstruation, Pathology of', quoted in Taylor and Shuttleworth, *Embodied Selves*, pp. 201–3 (p. 201).
30. Anon., 'The Recent Murder at Road', *Times*, 11 July 1860, p. 5.
31. Anon., Untitled Report, *Times*, 20 April 1860, p. 8.
32. Anon., Untitled Report, *Times*, 27 April 1865, p. 10.
33. Anon., Untitled Report, *Lancet* (1865), II, pp. 70–1 (70). Italics added.
34. Anon., 'The Road Child Murder', *Times*, 23 July 1860, p. 12.
35. Anon., Untitled Report, *Lancet* (1862), II, pp. 70–1.
36. Forbes Winslow, *On the Obscure Diseases of the Brain and Disorders of the Mind* (1860; London: John Churchill, 1868), p. 78.
37. Stapleton, *The Great Crime*, p. 12.
38. Ibid., p. 21.
39. Anon., 'Barbarous Murder', *Times*, 3 July 1860, p. 12.
40. Anon., 'The Child Murder at Road', *Times*, 17 July 1860, p. 12.
41. Anon., Untitled Report, *Times*, 22 July 1865, p. 8.
42. Hartman, *Victorian Murderesses*, p. 109. In cutting off her hair, Constance also seems to have foreshadowed Jo's behaviour in *Little Women* (1868) who has a similar wish to be independent.
43. Anon., 'Justice to Criminal Lunatics', *British Medical Journal*, (1865), II, pp. 238–9 (239).
44. [Henry Mansel], 'Sensation Novels', *Quarterly Review*, 117 (1863), pp. 481–514 (p. 449 and p. 502).
45. [Margaret Oliphant], 'Novels', *Blackwood's Edinburgh Magazine*, 94 (1863), pp. 168–83 (p. 169).
46. Quoted in Bridges, *The Tragedy*, p. 187.
47. Quoted in Jennifer Carnell, *The Literary Lives of M. E. Braddon* (Hastings: The Sensation Press, 2000), p. 118.
48. Charles W. Wood, 'Mrs Henry Wood: In Memoriam', *The Argosy*, 43 (1887), pp. 251–70, 334–53, 422–42 (p. 436).
49. Mary Elizabeth Braddon, *Aurora Floyd*, 2 vols (Leipzig: Tauchnitz, 1863), II, 297.
50. Later (post-confession) editions of the novel (from which most modern editions are reprinted) do not feature this passage.
51. See Trodd, *Domestic Crime*, p. 23.
52. Mary Elizabeth Braddon, *Aurora Floyd*, ed. by P. D. Edwards (1863; Oxford: Oxford University Press, 1999), p. 5. Braddon's italics. Further references to this edition will be given in the text.
53. Jeni Curtis, 'The "Espaliered" Girl: Pruning the Docile Body in *Aurora Floyd*', in *Beyond Sensation: Mary Elizabeth Braddon in Context*, ed. by Marlene Tromp, Pamela K. Gilbert, and Aeron Haynie (New York: State University of New York Press, 2000), pp. 77–92.
54. Ibid., p. 90.
55. Anon., 'Woman in Her Psychological Relations', quoted in Taylor and Shuttleworth, *Embodied Selves*, pp. 170–6 (p. 171).

56. Of course, the broken riding-whip could be read as a symbol of emasculation. We could also surmise that the nickname 'Softy' carries connotations of impotence.
57. Mrs Henry Wood, *St. Martin's Eve* (1866; London: Bentley and Son, 1898), pp. 3–4. Italics in original. Further references to this edition will be given in the text.
58. Quoted in Bridges, *The Tragedy*, p. 108. Interestingly, Mrs Dallimore, wife to P.C. Dallimore, a local policeman, made some penetrative investigations of the Road Murder herself, having greater licence to discuss and explore more sensitive issues relating to the bloodstained nightdress(es). See Bridges, *The Tragedy*, pp. 106–9.
59. [Mrs Henry Wood], 'St. Martin's Eve', *New Monthly Magazine*, 99 (1853), pp. 327–42 (p. 337).
60. Ibid.
61. Stapleton, *The Great Crime*, p. 12.
62. Winslow, *Obscure Diseases*, p. 154.
63. John Charles Bucknill and Daniel Hack Tuke, *A Manual of Psychological Medicine* (London: Churchill, 1858), p. 273.
64. Andrew Wynter, *The Borderlands of Insanity and Other Allied Papers*, quoted in Taylor and Shuttleworth, *Embodied Selves*, pp. 280–1 (p. 281).
65. Anon., Untitled Report, *Lancet* (1865), II, p. 267.
66. Catherine Peters, *The King of Inventors: A Life of Wilkie Collins* (Reading: Minerva Press, 1992), p. 309. Some scholars are beginning to question whether Collins did create the sensation genre. In his M.Phil. thesis on the fiction of Mrs Henry Wood, for example, Michael Flowers has demonstrated how Wood was employing a style that might be called 'sensational' years before the publication of *The Woman in White* (1860) – the novel often credited as the first sensation novel. See Michael Flowers, 'Giving up her Ghosts: An Annotated Bibliography of the Short Supernatural Fiction of Ellen (Mrs Henry) Wood, 1814–1887' (unpublished M.Phil. thesis, University of Sheffield, 2003).
67. Wilkie Collins, *The Moonstone*, ed. by Sandra Kemp (1868; Harmondsworth: Penguin Books, 1998), p. 14. Further references to this edition will be given in the text.
68. Hutter has observed how 'the association to the moon further identifies the diamond with women' (see 'Dreams, Transformations', p. 184) but he does not discuss how this might refer to menstruation.
69. Ornella Moscucci, *The Science of Woman: Gynaecology and Gender in England 1800–1929* (Cambridge: Cambridge University Press, 1990; repr. 1993), p. 33.
70. Jenny Bourne Taylor, *In The Secret Theatre of Home: Wilkie Collins, Sensation Narrative, and Nineteenth-Century Psychology* (London: Routledge, 1988), pp. 197–8.
71. Francis C. Skey, *Hysteria: Six Lectures* (1866; New York: Moorhead, Simpson, and Bond, 1868), pp. 59–60. Winslow also writes, in the same year, that 'an hysterical patient [...] throws herself about in all directions; if in bed she rises and throws herself to the right and to the left [...] an hysterical woman keeps crying during the attack, and goes on moaning, or, towards the close, bursts into tears or into a laugh without any reason'. See Winslow, *Obscure Diseases*, p. 493.
72. In her discussion of Wilkie Collins as part-Female Gothic writer, Tamar Heller suggests that the Shivering Sands are a 'female sexual symbol' and that the shivering is a figuration of the female orgasm. See Tamar Heller, *Dead Secrets: Wilkie Collins and the Female Gothic* (New York: Yale University Press, 1992), p. 149.
73. See Moscucci, *The Science of Woman*, p. 33.
74. Peters, *King of Inventors*, p. 309.

3 'Frail erections': Exploiting violent women in the work of Mary Elizabeth Braddon

1. Quoted in Robert Lee Wolff, 'Devoted Disciple: The Letters of Mary Elizabeth Braddon to Sir Edward Bulwer Lytton, 1862–1873', *Harvard Library Bulletin*, 12 (1974), pp. 5–35 and pp. 129–61 (p. 158).
2. Ibid., p. 14.
3. Mary Elizabeth Braddon, *Lady Audley's Secret*, ed. by Jenny Bourne Taylor (1862; Harmondsworth: Penguin Classics, 1998) p. 252. Further references to this edition will be given in the text.
4. Jenny Bourne Taylor, 'Introduction', in *Lady Audley's Secret*, ed. by Taylor, p. xxxiii. See also Sally Shuttleworth, '"Preaching to the Nerves": Psychological Disorder in Sensation Fiction', in *A Question of Identity*, ed. by Marina Benjamin (NJ: Rutgers University Press, 1993), pp. 192–243 and Lynda Hart, *Fatal Women: Lesbian Sexuality and the Mark of Aggression* (London: Routledge, 1994), pp. 29–46.
5. Nina Auerbach, *Woman and the Demon: The Life of a Victorian Myth* (Cambridge, MA: Harvard University Press, 1983), pp. 93–6.
6. Anon., *My Secret Life*, ed. by James Kincaid (c. 1880; New York: Penguin Putnam, 1996), p. 74.
7. Wilkie Collins, 'A Passage in the Life of Perugino Potts', *Bentley's Miscellany*, 31 (1856), pp. 153–64, (p. 160).
8. T. Gaillard Thomas, *A Practical Treatise on the Diseases of Women* (1868; Philadelphia: Lea Brothers, 1891), p. 78.
9. Mary Elizabeth Braddon, *Garibaldi and Other Poems* (London: Bosworth and Harrison, 1861), pp. 195–6. Further references to this edition will be given in the text.
10. See Helen Small, *Love's Madness: Medicine, the Novel and Female Insanity, 1800–1865* (Oxford: Oxford University Press, 1996), pp. 1–32.
11. Braddon wrote about Charlotte Brontë that '*she* seems to me the only *genius* the weaker sex can point to in literature' (Wolff, 'Devoted Disciple', p. 150. Italics in original). Braddon's idea of a work of fictional genius was a form of realism coloured with occasional instances of spirituality and passion. In addition to Brontë, therefore, Braddon considered Dickens, Scott, and Bulwer as the nineteenth-century's true literary geniuses.
12. Mary Elizabeth Braddon, *The Trail of the Serpent*, ed. by Chris Willis (1861; New York: Random House, 2003), p. 121. Further references to this edition will be given in the text.
13. Anon., 'Catherine or Constance Wilson, The Poisoner', *Annual Register* (1862), pp. 453–62 (p. 459).
14. Ibid.
15. Anon., 'Central Criminal Court: Trial of Mrs Wilson for Murder', *Times*, 29 September 1862, p. 9.
16. The first publishers of *The Trail of the Serpent*, Empson of Beverly, asked Braddon to produce a 'compound of Dickens and G. W. M. Reynolds'. When Braddon first started working on *The Trail of the Serpent* in 1860, *A Tale of Two Cities* would have been Dickens's latest work. See Robert Lee Wolff, *Sensational Victorian: The Life and Fiction of Mary Elizabeth Braddon* (New York: Garland Publishing, 1979), pp. 113–5.
17. Quoted in Toru Sasaki and Norman Page 'Introduction', in Mary Elizabeth Braddon, *John Marchmont's Legacy*, ed. by Toru Sasaki and Norman Page (1863;

Oxford: Oxford University Press, 1999), p. xv. Further references to this edition will be given in the text.
18. Of course, we have another possible link to *Jane Eyre* in this scene featuring an interrupted marriage ceremony.
19. Shuttleworth, 'Preaching to the Nerves', p. 218.
20. As is shown by Taylor's persuasive introduction to the Penguin edition of the text.
21. Mary Elizabeth Braddon, *Aurora Floyd*, ed. by P. D. Edwards (1863; Oxford: Oxford University Press, 1996), p. 20. Further references to this edition will be given in the text. For a discussion of Aurora through the 'uncultivated plant' metaphor see Jenni Curtis, 'The "Espaliered" Girl: Pruning the Docile Body in *Aurora Floyd*', in *Beyond Sensation: Mary Elizabeth Braddon in Context*, ed. by Marlene Tromp, Pamela K. Gilbert, and Aeron Haynie (New York: State University of New York Press, 2000), pp. 77–92.
22. Josephine McDonagh, *Child Murder and British Culture, 1720–1900* (Cambridge: Cambridge University Press, 2003), p. 136.
23. Quoted in McDonagh, p. 106.
24. See Small, *Love's Madness*, p. 55.
25. Wolff, *Sensational Victorian*, p. 372.
26. Mary Elizabeth Braddon, *Lady Lisle* (1862; London: Simpkin, Marshall, Hamilton, Kent, 1891), p. 24. Further references to this edition will be given in the text.
27. Mary Elizabeth Braddon, *The Captain of the Vulture* (1862; London: Simpkin, Marshall, Hamilton, Kent, 1891), p. 89. Further references to this edition will be given in the text.
28. Mary Elizabeth Braddon, 'Lost and Found', in *Ralph the Bailiff and Other Stories* (1864; London: Simpkin, Marshall, Hamilton, Kent, 1891), pp. 171–307 (p. 257). Further references to this edition will be given in the text.
29. Charles Routh, *Infant Feeding and its Influence on Life; or, the Causes and Prevention of Infant Mortality* (1860; New York: William Wood and Company, 1879), p. 40.
30. Eliza Lynn Linton, 'Domestic Life', *Temple Bar*, 4 (1862), pp. 402–15 (p. 415).
31. [Catherine G. F. Gore], 'A Bewailment from Bath; or Poor Old Maids', *Blackwood's Edinburgh Magazine*, 55 (1844), pp. 199–201 (pp. 200–1). Italics in original.
32. Linton, 'Domestic Life', p. 414.
33. The name of the slums, 'Blind Peter', may also be significant here. Blindness, as we see in texts like *Jane Eyre* and Elizabeth Barrett Browning's *Aurora Leigh* (1856), was often used as a metaphor for emasculation. Physical emasculation, of course, is the fear at the heart of the 'vagina dentata' complex.
34. Mary Elizabeth Braddon, *Eleanor's Victory*, 2 vols (Leipzig: Bernhard Tauchnitz, 1863), I, 188.
35. Anon., 'A Word to Women by One of Themselves', *Temple Bar*, 2 (1861), pp. 54–61 (p. 58). In 1861 *Temple Bar* had two female correspondents, Mary Braddon and Eliza Lynn Linton. Although this article is unsigned, it is very likely to be written by Braddon. In her 'Domestic Life', for example, written for *Temple Bar* a year later, Linton's views on old maids differ widely to the ones expressed in 'A Word to Women'.
36. Linton, 'Domestic Life', p. 415.
37. Although I believe Braddon's use of the word was meant to remain ambiguous, it is perhaps significant that *Aurora Floyd* was printed side by side with a geological article discussing the reasons for collecting fossilised remains. See 'Clifton', 'The Recollections of a Geologist', *Temple Bar*, 4 (1862), pp. 473–80.
38. Anon., 'A Word to Women', p. 60.

39. Robert Buchanan, 'Society's Looking-Glass', *Temple Bar*, 6 (1862), pp. 129–37 (p. 132).
40. Wolff, 'Devoted Disciple', p. 130.
41. Buchanan, 'Looking Glass', p. 133.
42. Ibid, p. 132.

4 'Nest-building apes': Female follies and bourgeois culture in the novels of Mrs Henry Wood

1. Deborah Wynne, 'See What a Big Wide Bed it is!: Mrs Henry Wood and the Philistine Imagination', in *Feminist Readings of Victorian Popular Texts*, ed. by Emma Liggins and Daniel Duffy (Hampshire: Ashgate, 2001), pp. 89–107 (p. 95). In a recent article on *East Lynne*, Andrew Maunder seems inclined to agree. 'Mrs. Henry Wood', he concludes, 'must herself be re-evaluated as a guardian of bourgeois propriety and the moral health of the nation'. Andrew Maunder, '"Stepchildren of Nature": *East Lynne* and the Spectre of Female Degeneracy, 1860–1861', in *Victorian Crime, Madness and Sensation*, ed. by Andrew Maunder and Grace Moore (Hampshire: Ashgate, 2004), pp. 59–71 (p. 69).
2. Deborah Wynne, *The Sensation Novel and the Victorian Family Magazine* (Hampshire: Palgrave Macmillan, 2001), p. 70.
3. Samuel Smiles, *Self Help* (1859; London: Sphere Books, 1968), p. 138.
4. Henry Maudsley, *The Physiology and Pathology of Mind* (London: Macmillan, 1867), p. 205.
5. Henry Maudsley, 'On Some of the Causes of Insanity', *Journal of Mental Science*, 24 (1867), pp. 488–502.
6. Maudsley, *Physiology and Pathology*, p. 74.
7. John Hollingshead, 'Nest-Building Apes', *Once a Week* (19 July 1862), pp. 111–2 (p. 111).
8. Ibid., p. 112.
9. It should be recognised that, while Maudsley believed in this atavism as a degeneration into psychological aberration and infertility, he disagreed that it was a return to animalism. He writes, 'however much man may degenerate, he never really reverts to the type of any animal, though he may sometimes become very like his next of kind, the monkeys'. Maudsley, 'Causes of Insanity', p. 499.
10. Lyn Pykett, *The Improper Feminine: The Women's Sensation Novel and the New Woman Writing* (London: Routledge, 1992), p. 132.
11. Mrs Henry Wood, *East Lynne* (1862; London: Thomas Nelson and Sons, n.d.), pp. 213–4. Further references to this edition will be given in the text.
12. Smiles, *Self Help*, p. 232.
13. Isabella Beeton, *Beeton's Book of Household Management* (London: S. O. Beeton, 1859), p. 1034.
14. Sally Shuttleworth, 'Demonic Mothers: Ideologies of Bourgeois Motherhood in the Mid-Victorian Era', in *Rewriting the Victorians: Theory, History and the Politics of Gender*, ed. by Linda M Shires (London: Routledge, 1993), pp. 31–51 (p. 42).
15. Josephine McDonagh, *Child Murder and British Culture, 1720–1900* (Cambridge: Cambridge University Press, 2003), p. 130.
16. Wynne, *The Sensation Novel*, p. 70.
17. Pykett, *The Improper Feminine*, p. 50.
18. Charles Dickens, *Great Expectations*, ed. by Robin Gilmour (1860–1; London: J. M. Dent, 1994), p. 185.

19. 'A Proser', 'Domestic Hero Worship', *New Monthly Magazine*, 119 (1860), pp. 475–85 (p. 476).
20. Ibid., p. 478.
21. Ibid., p. 483.
22. Eliza Lynn Linton, 'Domestic Life', *Temple Bar*, 4 (1862), pp. 402–15 (p. 403).
23. Ibid.
24. Mrs Henry Wood, *Danesbury House* (1860; London: Ward, Lock and Company, n.d.), p. 15. Further references to this edition will be given in the text.
25. Mrs Henry Wood, *Mrs Halliburton's Troubles* (1862; London: Richard Bentley and Son, 1897), pp. 81–2. Further references to this edition will be given in the text.
26. Lord Thomson of Fleet, 'Introduction' in Smiles, *Self Help*, p. viii. Capitals in original.
27. Ibid., p. 177.
28. Ibid., p. 203.
29. Maudsley, *Physiology and Pathology*, p. 208.
30. See, for example, his later revision of *Physiology and Pathology of Mind*. In it he wrote:

> 'He is so spoiled', says the silly mother placidly of her child, as though she was saying something that was creditable to it, or at any rate that it was not very discreditable to her, little thinking of the terrible meaning of the words and the awful calamity which a spoiled life may be. It may justly be questioned whether the whole system of education at the present day does not err on the side of dangerous indulgence. [...] The aim of early education ought to be sound intellectual or moral discipline.
>
> Henry Maudsley, *The Physiology and Pathology of Mind*, reprinted and revised as *Pathology of Mind* (1867; New York: D. Appleton, 1894), pp. 162–3.

31. Smiles, *Self Help*, p. 233.
32. McDonagh, *Child Murder*, p. 88.
33. Ewing Whittle, 'On Infanticide and Abortion', *British Medical Journal* (1869), I, p. 262.
34. [Alfred Austin], 'Our Novels: The Sensational School', in *Temple Bar*, 29 (1870), pp. 410–24 (p. 415).
35. Mrs Henry Wood, *Lady Adelaide's Oath* (1867); reprinted as *Lady Adelaide* (London: Richard Bentley and Son, 1898), p. 426. Further references to this edition will be given in the text.
36. Maudsley, *Pathology of Mind*, p. 103.
37. Ibid.
38. [Lucy Coxon], 'A Few Tickets in the Matrimonial Lottery', *Temple Bar*, 19 (1867), pp. 138–43 (p. 138).
39. Ibid.
40. [William Black], 'Girl's Brothers', *Temple Bar*, 27 (1869), pp. 109–13 (p. 109 and p. 111).
41. Henry Maudsley, *Responsibility in Mental Disease* (1874; New York: D. Appleton, 1897), p. 25.
42. Maudsley, *Pathology of Mind*, p. 98.
43. Coxon, 'Matrimonial Lottery', p. 142.
44. Ibid.

45. Black, 'Girl's Brothers', p. 111.
46. Coxon, 'Matrimonial Lottery', p. 142.
47. Emma Liggins, 'Good Housekeeping? Domestic Economy and Suffering Wives in Mrs Henry Wood's Early Fiction', in *Feminist Readings*, ed. by Liggins and Duffy, pp. 53–68 (p. 62).
48. Mrs Henry Wood, *The Shadow of Ashlydyat* (1864; London: R. E. King, 1905), p. 17. Further references to this edition will be given in the text.
49. Charles W. Wood, *Memorials of Mrs Henry Wood* (London: Richard Bentley and Son, 1894), p. 262.
50. Smiles, *Self Help*, p. 138.
51. Maudsley, *Pathology of Mind*, p. 91.
52. Maudsley, *Pathology of Mind*, p. 139.
53. Smiles, *Self Help*, p. 234.
54. Maudsley, 'Causes of Insanity', p. 498.
55. Maudsley, 'Causes of Insanity', p. 493. Even Smiles suggested that there was a reciprocal connection between the mind and the lungs. In *Self Help* he wrote:

> A healthy breathing apparatus is as indispensable to the successful lawyer or politician as a well-cultured intellect. The thorough aëration of the blood, by free exposure to a large breathing surface in the lungs, is necessary to maintain that full vital power on which the vigorous working of the brain in so large a measure depends.

Smiles then lists some of the nineteenth century's most industrious men, calling them 'all full-chested men' *Self Help*, p. 207.
56. Mrs Henry Wood, *Verner's Pride* (1863; London: Richard Bentley and Son, 1896), p. 2. Further references to this edition will be given in the text.
57. Smiles, *Self Help*, p. 254.
58. Ibid., p. 256.
59. Mary Elizabeth Braddon, *Lady Audley's Secret*, ed. by Jenny Bourne Taylor (1862; Harmondsworth: Penguin Classics, 1998), p. 316.
60. The chapter in which Sibylla dies, for example, is called 'The Lamp Burnt Out At Last'. See pp. 451–6.
61. Mrs Henry Wood would often use the same characters and families in more than one novel. Lady Dane, mother to Harry Dane in *Lady Adelaide's Oath*, is related to the Verners of *Verner's Pride*.
62. Smiles, *Self Help*, p. 259. Italics in original.
63. 'K. T. L'., 'How to Deal with Our Rural Poor', *Once a Week* (12 July 1862), pp. 64–7 (p. 66). See also Anon., 'Help For The "Workies"', *Once a Week* (4 October 1862), pp. 399–402.
64. 'K. T. L'., 'How to Deal', p. 66.
65. Wood, *Verner's Pride*, p. 125.
66. Frederick Skey, *Hysteria: Sex Lectures* (1866; New York: Moorhead, Simpson and Bond, 1868), pp. 64–5.
67. Smiles, *Self Help*, pp. 150–1.
68. Wood, *Memorials*, p. 188.
69. Ibid., p. 50.
70. Ibid., pp. 188–9.

5 Hidden shadows: Dangerous women and obscure diseases in the novels of Wilkie Collins

1. In 1980, for example, Winifred Hughes argued that Collins 'aims directly at the foundation of Victorian social dogma [... because he] explores forbidden territories and releases hidden sources of energy'. Similarly, Philip O'Neill notes the way 'Collins is deliberately subverting the popular literary representation of women' by revealing how 'little can be taken at face value [and] appearance is not to be trusted'. More recently, Deborah Wynne has claimed that the author 'probed the underside of respectable domesticity, laying bare its corruptions and areas of vulnerability'. Winifred Hughes, *The Maniac in the Cellar: Sensation Novels of the 1860s* (Princeton, NJ: Princeton University Press, 1980), p. 144; Philip O'Neill, *Wilkie Collins: Women, Property and Propriety* (London: Macmillan, 1988), p. 5 and p. 172; Deborah Wynne, *The Sensation Novel and the Victorian Family Magazine* (Hampshire: Palgrave Macmillan, 2001), p. 149.
2. [William Black], 'Flirts and Flirtation', *Temple Bar*, 26 (1869), pp. 58–67 (pp. 64–5).
3. Jenny Bourne Taylor, *In The Secret Theatre of Home: Wilkie Collins, Sensation Narrative, and Nineteenth-Century Psychology* (London: Routledge, 1988), p. 7. Italics added.
4. [James Hinton], 'The Fairy Land of Science', *Cornhill Magazine*, 5 (1862), pp. 36–42 (pp. 37–8).
5. Collins's edition of *Obscure Diseases* was inscribed 'from the Author to Wilkie Collins'. See William Baker, *Wilkie Collins's Library: A Reconstruction* (London: Greenwood Press, 2002), p. 160.
6. Forbes Winslow, *On the Obscure Diseases of the Brain and Disorders of the Mind* (1860; London: John Churchill and Sons, 1868), p. xi.
7. Ibid., p. ix and pp. xi–xii.
8. Ibid., p. 142.
9. Ibid.
10. Ibid.
11. Ibid., pp. 576–7.
12. Wilkie Collins, 'A Shockingly Rude Article (Communicated by a Charming Woman)' (1858), in *My Miscellanies* (1863; London: Chatto and Windus, 1875), pp. 18–29 (p. 19 and p. 28).
13. Lillian Nayder, *Wilkie Collins* (New York: Twayne Publishers, 1997), p. 15.
14. Alexander Grinstein, *Wilkie Collins: Man of Mystery and Imagination* (Madison, CT: International Universities Press, 2003), p. 101 and p. 131.
15. Virginia Morris, *Double Jeopardy: Women Who Kill in Victorian Fiction* (Kentucky: The University Press of Kentucky, 1990), p. 105.
16. Ibid., p. 465.
17. Winslow, *Obscure Diseases*, p. 127 and p. 79.
18. Wilkie Collins, *The Woman in White*, ed. by John Sutherland (1860; Oxford: Oxford University Press, 1998), p. 569. Further references to this edition will be given in the text.
19. Anon., quoted in 'Dr. Forbes Winslow's Evidence in the Townley Case', *Journal of Mental Science*, 14 (1864), pp. 295–7 (pp. 296–7).
20. [J. W. Kaye], 'On Growing Old', *Cornhill*, 5 (1862), pp. 495–507 (p. 498).
21. Although the roles of Anne and Laura were played by the same actress in some dramatic reproductions of *The Woman in White*, there is no evidence of a production

wherein Glyde and Hartright were played by the same actor. I am indebted to Janice Norwood for this information.
22. For particularly insightful examples see chapter four of Ann Cvetkovich, *Mixed Feelings: Feminism, Mass Culture, and Victorian Sensationalism* (New Jersey: Rutgers University Press, 1992) and Walter M. Kendrick, 'The Sensationalism of *The Woman in White*', in *Wilkie Collins*, ed. by Lyn Pykett (London: Macmillan Press, 1998), pp. 70–87.
23. Wilkie Collins, *No Name*, ed. by Virginia Blain (1862; Oxford: Oxford University Press, 1998), p. 146. Italics in original. Further references to this edition will be given in the text.
24. Interestingly, Sheridan Le Fanu later adopted the biblical phrase for his volume of psychological short stories *In a Glass Darkly* (1872).
25. [Margarent Oliphant], Review of *No Name*, *Blackwood's Edinburgh Magazine*, 94 (1863), p. 170.
26. [Eneas Sweetland Dallas], 'On Physiognomy' and 'The First Principle of Physiognomy', *Cornhill*, 4 (1861), pp. 472–81 and pp. 569–81. Taylor also discusses Dallas's contribution to the *Cornhill* but only takes account of the first essay. See Taylor, *Secret Theatre*, p. 50, p. 51, and p. 258.
27. Dallas, 'On Physiognomy', p. 475.
28. Ibid., p. 472.
29. Dallas, 'The First Principle of Physiognomy', p. 579.
30. Ibid., p. 574.
31. Nayder, *Wilkie Collins*, p. 109.
32. Taylor, *Secret Theatre*, pp. 131–50.
33. Isaac Baker Brown, *On the Curability of Certain Forms of Insanity, Epilepsy, Catalepsy and Hysteria in Females* (London: Robert Hardwicke, 1866), p. 17. Italics in original.
34. Ornella Moscucci, *The Science of Woman: Gynaecology and Gender in England 1800–1929* (Cambridge: Cambridge University Press, 1990; repr. 1993), p. 115.
35. Mary Poovey, *Uneven Developments: The Ideological Work of Gender in Mid-Victorian England* (Chicago: The University of Chicago Press, 1988), pp. 24–50.
36. Forbes Winslow, *Lettsomian Lectures on Insanity* (London: John Churchill, 1854), p. 11.
37. Winslow, *Obscure Diseases*, pp. 101–2. Capitals in original. Winslow also aims to reinterpret the histories of tyrants in his *Lettsomian Lectures*. In that text, however, which predates Collins's short story, Winslow does not consider Queen Christina. The way in which he includes her story in the later *Obscure Diseases* suggests that he may have read and drawn on Collins's work.
38. Wilkie Collins, 'A Queen's Revenge' (1858), in *My Miscellanies*, pp. 159–70 (p. 160).
39. Ibid.
40. Ibid., p. 161.
41. Ibid., p. 164.
42. Winslow, *Obscure Diseases*, pp. 105–6.
43. Wilkie Collins, *Armadale*, ed. by Catherine Peters (1866; Oxford: Oxford University Press, 1999), pp. 54–5. Further references to this edition will be given in the text.
44. Winslow, *Lettsomian Lectures*, p. 156.
45. Henry Maudsley, *The Physiology and Pathology of Mind*, reprinted and revised as *Pathology of Mind* (1867; New York: D. Appleton, 1894), p. 88.
46. Wilkie Collins, *The Legacy of Cain* (1889; Gloucestershire: Sutton Publishing, 1995), p. 326.

47. Ibid., p. 221.
48. Maudsley, *Physiology and Pathology*, p. 103.
49. Winslow, *Obscure Diseases*, p. 526.
50. Ibid., p. 527.
51. Sir Benjamin Brodie, *Psychological Inquiries: Being a Series of Essays Intended to Illustrate the Mutual Relations of the Physical Organisation and the Mental Faculties* (1854), in *The Works of Sir Benjamin Collins Brodie*, ed. by Charles Hawkins, 3 vols (London: Longman, Green, Longman, Roberts, and Green, 1865), I, p. 161.
52. Jenny Bourne Taylor observes how Ozias's fatalism becomes a 'monomania [that] can work its own fulfilment' (*Secret Theatre*, p. 152) but, unlike the discussion I offer here, does not explore the role played by the dangerous woman in that process.
53. See Taylor, *Secret Theatre*, p. 159.
54. This episode has a lot in common with the passions of Eunice Gracedieu in *The Legacy of Cain*. Collins appears to recycle a lot of the same imagery when describing the return of Eunice's inherited emotions:

> I saw a fearful creature, with glittering eyes that threatened some unimaginable vengeance. Her lips were drawn back, they showed her clenched teeth. A burning red flush dyed her face. The hair of her head rose, little by little, slowly. And, most dreadful sight of all, she seemed, in the stillness of the house, to be *listening to something*.
>
> Collins, *The Legacy of Cain*, p. 296. Italics in original.

55. Jessica Maynard, 'Black Silk and Red Paisley: The Toxic Woman in Wilkie Collins's *Armadale*', in *Varieties of Victorianism: The Uses of a Past*, ed. by Gary Day (London: Macmillan, 1998), pp. 63–79 (p. 74).
56. [Mrs M. E. Owen], 'Criminal Women', *Cornhill*, 14 (1866), pp. 152–60 (p. 152).
57. Ibid., pp. 156–7.
58. Winslow, *Obscure Diseases*, p. 143.
59. Ibid., p. 144.
60. Maynard, 'Black Silk', p. 67.
61. Jenny Bourne Taylor has observed how the setting draws on mid-nineteenth-century medical ideas on the moral management of the insane but does not mention, as I do here, the concept of treating mental disorder with methods that the patient is incognisant of. See *Secret Theatre*, pp. 171–2.
62. Winslow, *Obscure Diseases*, p. 507.

Conclusion

1. Arthur Machen, 'The Great God Pan', in *Late Victorian Gothic Tales*, ed. by Roger Luckhurst (Oxford: Oxford University Press, 2005), pp. 183–233 (p. 232).
2. Ibid., p. 196.
3. Ibid., p. 218.
4. See, for example, Rebecca Stott, *The Fabrication of the late-Victorian Femme-Fatale: The Kiss of Death* (Basingstoke: Macmillan, 1992).
5. Luckhurst, Introduction, p. xxiv.
6. Machen, *The Great God Pan*, p. 225.
7. Ibid., p. 232.

8. Andrew Smith has looked at how the Whitechapel Murders and clinical ideas of syphilis relate to late-Victorian fictions in *Victorian Demons: Medicine, Masculinity and the Gothic at the Fin-de-Siècle* (Manchester: Manchester University Press, 2004), but he does not discuss representations of femininity, choosing to focus instead on questions of masculinity.
9. Etienne Balibar and Pierre Macherey, 'On Literature as an Ideological Form', quoted in Andrew Bennett and Nicholas Royle, *Introduction to Literature, Criticism and Theory* (Harlow: Pearson Routledge, 2004), p. 173.

Bibliography

Cases cited

BACON, MARTHA; 'The Walworth Murders', *Annual Register* (1857), pp. 90–4.
BRIXEY, MARTHA; 'Central Criminal Court', *Times*, 16 May 1845, p. 7; Eigen, *Unconscious Crime*, pp. 75–6; Smith, *Trial by Medicine*, pp. 155–7; Taylor, *Principles and Practice*, II, 565.
BROUGH, MARY ANN; 'The Awful Tragedy at Esher', *Annual Register* (1854), pp. 93–7; Ainsley, '"Some Mysterious Agency"', pp. 38–55; Bucknill, *Unsoundness of Mind*, p. 135; Knelman, *Twisting in the Wind*, pp. 69–71; Smith, *Trial by Medicine*, pp. 157–60; Winslow, 'Recent Trials in Lunacy', pp. 609–25.
CROSBY, JANE; 'The Lammonby Murder', *Times*, 13 February 1845, p. 5; Knelman, *Twisting in the Wind*, p. 134.
EDMUNDS, CHRISTIANA; 'The Brighton Poisoning Case', *Annual Register* 6 (1872), pp. 189–201; 'Central Criminal Court', *Times*, 16 January 1872, p. 11; 'The Brighton Poisonings', *Times*, pp. 17 January 1872, p. 12; 'The Alleged Poisoning at Brighton', *Times*, 8 September 1872, p. 9; Knelman, *Twisting in the Wind*, pp. 138–41.
KENT, CONSTANCE; 'Justice to Criminal Lunatics', *British Medical Journal* (1865), II, pp. 238–9; *Lancet* (1865), ii, pp. 70–1; *Times*, 20 April 1860, p. 8; 'Barbarous Murder', *Times*, 3 July 1860, p. 12; 'The Recent Murder at Road', *Times*, 11 July 1860, p. 5; 'The Child Murder at Road', *Times*, 17 July 1860, p. 12; 'Apprehension of Miss Constance Kent', *Times*, 21 July 1860, p. 5; 'The Road Child Murder', *Times*, 23 July 1860, p. 12; 'The Road Child Murder', *Times*, 26 July 1860, p. 9; 'S. P'. 'The Road Murder', letter to *Times*, 9 August 1860, p. 12; 'Medicus', 'The Road Mystery', letter to *Times*, 30 October 1860, p. 6; 'The Road Child Murder', *Times*, 10 November 1860, p. 11; J. W. Stapleton, 'The Road Murder', letter to *Times*, 13 November 1860, p. 10; 'The Road Child Murder', *Times*, 15 November 1860, p. 10; *Times*, 20 April 1865, p. 8; *Times*, 27 April 1865, p.10; *Times*, 22 July 1865, p. 8; Bridges, *The Tragedy at Road Hill House*; Hartman, *Victorian Murderesses*, pp. 85–129; Rance, 'Victorian Values', pp. 227–9; Rhode, *The Case of Constance Kent*; Stapleton, *The Great Crime of 1860*.
LACK, ESTHER; 'Central Criminal Court', *Times*, 22 September 1865, p. 6.
MANNING, MARIA; *Times*, 25 August 1849, p. 5; *Times*, 25 October 1849, p. 4; *Times*, 27 October 1849, p. 5; *Times*, 14 November 1849, p. 4; Knelman, *Twisting in the Wind*, pp. 101–5.
MINCHIN, SARAH; 'Police', *Times*, 3 June 1853, p. 7; 'Central Criminal Court', *Times*, 17 June 1853, p. 7; Taylor, *Principles and Practice*, II, 601.
MITCHELL, SARAH; 'Murder and Insanity', *Annual Register* (1863), pp. 157–61; 'Central Criminal Court', *Times*, 29 October 1863, p. 11.
PAYNE, MARY ANN; 'Central Criminal Court', *Times*, 14 July 1863, p. 10.
SCHOLES, MISS; 'Double Murder by an Insane Sister', *Annual Register* (1860), p. 48.
SMITH, MADELINE; 'The Glasgow Poisoning', *Annual Register* (1857), p. 530; Hartman, *Victorian Murderesses*, pp. 51–84; Rance, 'Victorian Values', pp. 220–34.
WILSON, CATHERINE; 'Catherine or Constance Wilson, The Poisoner', *Annual Register* (1862), pp. 453–62; 'Central Criminal Court: Trial of Mrs Wilson for Murder', *Times*, 29 September, 1862, p. 9.

Medical sources

Althaus, Julius, 'A Lecture on the Pathology and Treatment of Hysteria: Delivered at the Royal Infirmary for Diseases of the Chest', *British Medical Journal* (1866), I, pp. 245–8.
Anon., Review of Winslow, *Obscure Diseases*, *British Medical Journal* (1860), II, pp. 580–2, 581.
Anon., Review of C. H. F. Routh, *Infant Feeding and its Influence on Life; or, the Causes and Prevention of Infant Mortality*, *British Medical Journal* (1860), II, pp. 999–1000.
Anon., 'Dr. Forbes Winslow's Evidence in the Townley Case', *Journal of Mental Science*, 14 (1864), pp. 295–7.
Anon., 'Law and Insanity', *British Medical Journal* (1865) I, pp. 275–7.
Anon., 'Moral Insanity', *Journal of Mental Science*, 17 (1865), pp. 132–6.
Anon., 'Woman in Her Psychological Relations', in *Embodied Selves*, ed. by Taylor and Shuttleworth (Oxford: Oxford University Press, 1998), pp. 170–6.
Brodie, Sir Benjamin, *Psychological Inquiries: Being a Series of Essays Intended to Illustrate the Mutual Relations of the Physical Organisation and the Mental Faculties*, in *The Works of Sir Benjamin Collins Brodie*, ed. by Charles Hawkins, 3 vols (1854; London: Longman, Green, Longman, Roberts, and Green, 1865).
Brown, Frederick James, 'Remarks on the Constitution of the Mind; and on Unsoundness of Mind', *British Medical Journal* (1866), II, p. 331.
Brown, Isaac Baker, *On the Curability of Certain Forms of Insanity, Epilepsy, Catalepsy and Hysteria in Females* (London: Robert Hardwicke, 1866).
Bucknill, Charles, *Unsoundness of Mind in Relation to Criminal Acts* (1854; Philadelphia: Johnson & Co., 1856).
Bucknill, John Charles and Daniel Hack Tuke, *A Manual of Psychological Medicine* (London: Churchill, 1858).
Carter, Robert Brudenell, *On the Pathology and Treatment of Hysteria* (London: John Churchill, 1853).
Dallas, Eneas Sweetland, 'On Physiognomy', *Cornhill*, 4 (1861), pp. 472–81.
Dallas, Eneas Sweetland, 'The First Principle of Physiognomy', *Cornhill*, 4 (1861), pp. 569–81.
Davey, J. G., 'Lectures on Insanity, Delivered at the Bristol Medical School During the Summer Session of 1855: Lecture II', *British Medical Journal* (1855), II, pp. 668–75.
De Berdt Hovell, D., Letter to the Editor, *Lancet* (1868) II, p. 219.
Esquirol, Jean Étienne Dominique, *Des Maladies Mentales, Considérées sous les Rapports Médical, Hygiénique et Médico-légal* (1838); trans. E. K. Hunt as *Mental Maladies: A Treatise on Insanity* (Philadelphia: Lea and Blanchard, 1845).
Gairdner, T. W., 'Hysteria and Delirium Tremens', *Lancet* (1861) I, pp. 429–30.
Galton, Francis, *Hereditary Genius: An Inquiry into its Laws and Consequences* (London: Macmillan, 1869).
Gooch, Robert, *On Some of the Most Important Diseases Peculiar to Women* (1839; London, The New Sydenham Society, 1859).
Hammond, William, A., *Insanity in its Relations to Crime* (New York: D. Appleton and Company, 1873).
Houghton, J. Hyde, 'Maternal Impressions', *British Medical Journal* (1867), II, pp. 468–9.
Jung, W., 'Hereditary Tendency in Insanity', *Journal of Mental Science*, 25 (1867), pp. 106–7.
Lee, Robert J., *Maternal Impressions: A Consideration of the Effects of Mental Disturbance during Pregnancy upon the Intellectual Development of the Child* (London: Smith, Elder and Company, 1875).
Locock, Charles, 'Menstruation, Pathology of' in *Embodied Selves*, ed. by Taylor and Shuttleworth (Oxford: Oxford University Press, 1998), pp. 201–3.

Maudsley, Henry, 'On Some of the Causes of Insanity', *Journal of Mental Science*, 24 (1867), pp. 488–502.

Maudlsey, Henry, *The Physiology and Pathology of Mind* (London: Macmillan and Co., 1867).

Maudsley, Henry, *Body and Mind: An Inquiry into their Connection and Mutual Influence, Specially in Reference to Mental Disorders* (London: Macmillan, 1870).

Maudsley, Henry, *The Physiology and Pathology of Mind* (1867), revised as *Pathology of Mind* (New York: D. Appleton and Company, 1894).

Maudsley, Henry, *Responsibility in Mental Disease* (1874; New York: D. Appleton and Company, 1897).

Meadows, A., 'Remarks on the Influence of Mental Impressions as a Cause of Bodily Deformity', *British Medical Journal* (1865), I, p. 626.

Prichard, James Cowles, *A Treatise on Insanity and Other Disorders Affecting the Mind* (1835; Philadelphia: Haswell, Barrington, and Haswell, 1837).

Routh, C. H. F., *Infant Feeding and its Influence on Life; or, the Causes and Prevention of Infant Mortality* (1860; New York: William Wood and Company, 1879).

Skae, Francis, 'Climacteric Insanity in Women', *Journal of Mental Science*, 18 (1865), pp. 275–8.

Skey, Frederick C., 'Hysteria', *Lancet* (1864), I, pp. 31–2.

Skey, Frederick C., *Hysteria: Six Lectures* (1866; New York: Moorhead, Simpson, and Bond, 1868).

Tait, Lawson, *Diseases of Women* (1877; New York: William Wood and Company, 1879).

Taylor, Alfred Swaine, *The Principles and Practice of Medical Jurisprudence*, 2 vols (1865; London: J. and A. Churchill, 1894).

Thomas, T. Gaillard, *A Practical Treatise on the Diseases of Women* (1868; Philadelphia, Lea Brothers and Company, 1891).

Tilt, Edward John, *The Change of Life in Health and Disease: A Practical Treatise on the Nervous and Other Affections Incidental to Women at the Decline of Life* (London: John Churchill, 1857).

Tuke, John, 'Special Correspondence: Edinburgh', *British Medical Journal* (1865), I, pp. 466–7.

Waring-Curran, J., 'Case of Monstrosity Dependent on Mental Shock', *British Medical Journal* (1867), II, p. 468.

Whittle, Ewing, 'On Infanticide and Abortion', *British Medical Journal* (1869), I, p. 262.

Winslow, Forbes, *The Plea of Insanity in Criminal Cases* (London: H. Renshaw, 1843).

Winslow, Forbes, *On the Incubation of Insanity* (London: S. Highley, 1846).

Winslow, Forbes, 'Recent Trials in Lunacy', *Journal of Psychological Medicine and Mental Pathology*, 7 (1854), pp. 609–25.

Winslow, Forbes, *Lettsomian Lectures on Insanity* (London: John Churchill, 1854).

Winslow, Forbes, *On the Obscure Diseases of the Brain and Disorders of the Mind* (1860; London: John Churchill and Sons, 1868).

Wynter, Andrew, *The Borderlands of Insanity and Other Allied Papers*, in *Embodied Selves*, ed. by Taylor and Shuttleworth (Oxford: Oxford University Press, 1998), pp. 280–1.

Literary sources

Anon., 'The Old Maid's Petition', in *Victorian Street Ballads*, ed. by W. Henderson (London: Country Life, 1937), p. 100.

Austen, Jane, *Pride and Prejudice*, ed. by Robert P. Irvine (1813; Ontario, Canada: Broadview Press, 2002), p. 67.

Braddon, Mary Elizabeth, *Garibaldi and Other Poems* (London: Bosworth and Harrison, 1861).

Braddon, Mary Elizabeth, *Lady Lisle* (1861; London: Simpkin, Marshall, Hamilton, Kent, 1891).
Braddon, Mary Elizabeth, *The Trail of the Serpent*, ed. by Chris Willis (1861; New York: Random House, 2003).
Braddon, Mary Elizabeth, *Lady Audley's Secret*, ed. by Jenny Bourne Taylor (1862; Harmondsworth: Penguin Classics, 1998).
Braddon, Mary Elizabeth, *The Captain of the Vulture* (1862; London: Simpkin, Marshall, Hamilton, Kent, 1891).
Braddon, Mary Elizabeth, *Aurora Floyd*, ed. by P. D. Edwards (1863; Oxford: Oxford University Press, 1999).
Braddon, Mary Elizabeth, *Eleanor's Victory*, 2 vols (Leipzig: Bernhard Tauchnitz, 1863).
Braddon, Mary Elizabeth, *John Marchmont's Legacy*, ed. by Toru Sasaki and Norman Page (1863; Oxford: Oxford University Press, 1999).
Braddon, Mary Elizabeth. 'Lost and Found', in *Ralph the Bailiff and Other Stories* (1864; London: Simpkin, Marshall, Hamilton, Kent, 1891), pp. 171–307.
Brontë, Charlotte, *Jane Eyre*, ed. by Margaret Smith and Sally Shuttleworth (1847; Oxford: Oxford University Press, 2000).
Collins, Wilkie, 'A Passage in the Life of Perugino Potts', *Bentley's Miscellany*, 31 (1856), pp. 153–64.
Collins, Wilkie, 'A Queen's Revenge' (1858), in *My Miscellanies* (1863; London: Chatto and Windus, 1875), pp. 159–70.
Collins, Wilkie, *The Woman in White*, ed. by John Sutherland (1860; Oxford: Oxford University Press, 1998).
Collins, Wilkie, *No Name*, ed. by Virginia Blain (1862; Oxford: Oxford University Press, 1998).
Collins, Wilkie, *Armadale*, ed. by Catherine Peters (1866; Oxford: Oxford University Press, 1999).
Collins, Wilkie, *The Moonstone*, ed. by Sandra Kemp (1868; Harmondsworth: Penguin Books, 1998).
Collins, Wilkie, *The Law and the Lady*, ed. by Jenny Bourne Taylor (1875; Oxford: Oxford World's Classics, 1999).
Cyples, William, 'Granny Leatham's Revenge', *Cornhill*, 14 (1866), pp. 313–30.
Dickens, Charles, *Great Expectations*, ed. by Robin Gilmour (1860–1; London: Everyman, 1994).
Machen, Arthur, 'The Great God Pan', in *Late Victorian Gothic Tales*, ed. by Roger Luckhurst (Oxford: Oxford University Press, 2005), pp. 183–233.
Stoker, Bram, *Dracula*, ed. by Maurice Hindle, (1897; Harmondsworth: Penguin Classics, 1993).
Wander, Waif [Fortune, Mary], 'The White Maniac: A Doctor's Tale', http://gaslight.mtroyal.ab.ca/gaslight/whtmanic.htm [accessed 1 December 2006].
Wood, Mrs Henry, *Danesbury House* (1860; London: Ward, Lock and Company, n.d.).
Wood, Mrs Henry, *East Lynne* (1862; London: Thomas Nelson and Sons, n.d.).
Wood, Mrs Henry, *Mrs Halliburton's Troubles* (1862; London: Richard Bentley and Son, 1897).
Wood, Mrs Henry, *Verner's Pride* (1863; London: Richard Bentley and Son, 1896).
Wood, Mrs Henry, *The Shadow of Ashlydyat* (1864; London: R. E. King and Company, 1905).
Wood, Mrs Henry, 'St. Martin's Eve', *New Monthly Magazine*, 99 (1853), pp. 327–42.
Wood, Mrs Henry, *St. Martin's Eve* (1866; London: Richard Bentley and Son, 1895).
Wood, Mrs Henry, *Lady Adelaide's Oath* (1867), repr. as *Lady Adelaide* (London: Richard Bentley and Son, 1898).

General nineteenth-century sources

'A Proser', 'Domestic Hero Worship', *New Monthly Magazine*, 119 (1860), pp. 475–85.
Anon., 'A Word to Women by One of Themselves', *Temple Bar*, 2 (1861), pp. 54–61.
Anon., 'Help For The "Workies"', *Once a Week* (4 October 1862), pp. 399–402.
Anon., *My Secret Life*, ed. by James Kincaid (c. 1880; New York: Penguin Putnam, 1996).
Austin, Alfred, 'Our Novels: The Sensational School', *Temple Bar*, 29 (1870), pp. 410–24.
Beeton, Isabella, *Beeton's Book of Household Management* (London: S. O. Beeton, 1859).
Black, William, 'Flirts and Flirtation', *Temple Bar*, 26 (1869), pp. 58–67.
Black, William, 'Girls' Brothers', *Temple Bar*, 27 (1869), pp. 109–13.
Buchanan, Robert, 'Society's Looking-Glass', *Temple Bar*, 6 (1862), pp. 129–37.
'Clifton', 'The Recollections of a Geologist', *Temple Bar*, 4 (1862), pp. 473–80.
Collins, Wilkie, 'A Shockingly Rude Article (Communicated by a Charming Woman)' (1858), in *My Miscellanies* (1863; London: Chatto and Windus, 1875), pp. 18–29.
Coxon, Lucy, 'A Few Tickets in the Matrimonial Lottery', *Temple Bar*, 19 (March 1867), pp. 138–43.
Craik, Dinah Mulock, 'In Her Teens', *Macmillan's Magazine*, 10 (1864), pp. 219–23.
Gore, Catherine G. F., 'A Bewailment from Bath; or Poor Old Maids', *Blackwood's Edinburgh Magazine*, 55 (1844), pp. 199–201.
Hinton, James, 'The Fairy Land of Science', *Cornhill*, 5 (1862), pp. 36–42.
Hollingshead, John, 'Nest-Building Apes', *Once a Week* (19 July 1862), pp. 111–2.
Kaye, J. W., 'On Growing Old', *Cornhill*, 5 (1862), pp. 495–507.
King, R. Ashe, 'A Tête-à-Tête Social Science Discussion', *Cornhill*, 10 (1864), pp. 569–82.
'K. T. L.', 'How to Deal with Our Rural Poor', *Once a Week* (12 July 1862), pp. 64–7.
Linton, Eliza Lynn, 'Domestic Life', *Temple Bar*, 4 (March 1862), pp. 402–15.
Mansel, Henry, 'Sensation Novels', *Quarterly Review*, 117 (1863), pp. 481–514.
Oliphant, Margaret, Review of Wilkie Collins, *No Name*, *Blackwood's Edinburgh Magazine*, 94 (1863), p. 170.
Oliphant, Margaret, 'Novels', *Blackwood's Edinburgh Magazine*, 94 (1863), pp. 168–83.
Owen, Mrs M. E., 'Criminal Women', *Cornhill*, 14 (1866), pp. 152–60.
Ritchie, Anne Thackeray, 'Toilers and Spinsters', *Cornhill*, 3 (1861), pp. 318–31.
Smiles, Samuel, *Self Help* (1859; London: Sphere Books, 1968).
Stapleton, Joseph, *The Great Crime of 1860: Being a Summary of the Facts Relating to the Murder Committed at Road; a Critical Review of its Social and Scientific Aspects, and an Authorised Account of the Family; with an Appendix Containing the Evidence Taken at the Various Inquiries* (London: E. Marlborough, 1861).
Wood, Charles W., 'Mrs. Henry Wood. In Memoriam', *The Argosy*, 43 (1887), pp. 251–70, 334–53, 422–42.
Wood, Charles W., *Memorials of Mrs Henry Wood* (London: Richard Bentley and Son, 1894).

Secondary sources

Ainsley, Jill Newton, '"Some Mysterious Agency": Women, Violent Crime, and the Insanity Acquittal in the Victorian Courtroom', *Canadian Journal of History*, 35 (April 2000), pp. 37–55.
Auerbach, Nina, *Woman and the Demon: The Life of a Victorian Myth* (Cambridge, MA: Harvard University Press, 1982).
Bachman, Maria K. and Don Richard Cox (eds), *Reality's Dark Light: The Sensational Wilkie Collins* (Knoxville: The University of Tennessee Press, 2003).
Baker, William, *Wilkie Collin's Library: A Reconstruction* (London: Greenwood Press, 2002).

Baker, William, Andrew Gasson, Graham Law, and Paul Lewis (eds), *The Public Face of Wilkie Collins: The Collected Letters*, 4 vols (London: Pickering and Chatto, 2005).

Balibar, Etienne, and Pierre Macherey, 'On Literature as an Ideological Form', quoted in Andrew Bennett and Nicholas Royle, *Introduction to Literature, Criticism and Theory* (Harlow: Pearson Routledge, 2004).

Beer, Gillian, 'Forging the Missing Link: Interdisciplinary Stories', in *Open Fields: Science in Cultural Encounter* (Oxford: Clarendon Press, 1996), pp. 115–45.

Beer, Gillian, *Darwin's Plots: Evolutionary Narrative in Darwin, George Eliot and Nineteenth-Century Fiction* (London: Routledge, 1983).

Brantlinger, Patrick, 'What is "Sensational" about the "Sensation Novel"?' (1982) in *Wilkie Collins*, ed. by Lyn Pykett (London: Macmillan Press, 1998), pp. 30–57.

Bridges, Yseult, *The Tragedy at Road Hill House* (New York: Rhinehart and Company, 1954).

Cantor, Geoffrey and Sally Shuttleworth (eds), *Science Serialized: Representations of the Sciences in Nineteenth-Century Periodicals* (Cambridge, MA: The Massachusetts Institute of Technology Press, 2004).

Cantor, Geoffrey, Gowan Dawson, Graeme Gooday, Richard Noakes, Sally Shuttleworth, and Jonathan Topham, *Science in the Nineteenth-Century Periodical* (Cambridge: Cambridge University Press, 2004).

Carnell, Jennifer, *The Literary Lives of M. E. Braddon* (Hastings: The Sensation Press, 2000).

Curtis, Jeni, 'The "Espaliered" Girl: Pruning the Docile Body in *Aurora Floyd*', in Marlene Tromp, Pamela Gilbert, and Aeron Haynie (eds), *Beyond Sensation: Mary Elizabeth Braddon in Context* (New York: State University of New York Press), pp. 77–92.

Cvetkovich, Ann, *Mixed Feelings: Feminism, Mass Culture, and Victorian Sensationalism* (New Brunswick: Rutgers University Press, 1992).

During, Simon, 'The Strange Case of Monomania: Patriarchy in Literature, Murder in *Middlemarch*, Drowning in *Daniel Deronda*', *Representations*, 23 (Summer, 1988), pp. 86–104.

Eigen, Joel Peter, *Witnessing Insanity: Madness and Mad-Doctors in the English Court* (New Haven: Yale University Press, 1995).

Eigen, Joel Peter, *Unconscious Crime: Mental Absence and Criminal Responsibility in Victorian London* (Maryland: Johns Hopkins University Press, 2003).

Flint, Kate, *The Woman Reader 1837–1914* (Oxford: Oxford University Press, 1993).

Flowers, Michael, 'Giving up her Ghosts: An Annotated Bibliography of the Short Supernatural Fiction of Ellen (Mrs. Henry) Wood, 1814–1887' (unpublished M.Phil. thesis, University of Sheffield, 2003).

Gilbert, Pamela K., *Disease, Desire and the Body in Victorian Women's Popular Novels* (Cambridge: Cambridge University Press, 1997).

Greenslade, William, *Degeneration, Culture and the Novel 1880–1940* (Cambridge: Cambridge University Press, 1994).

Grinstein, Alexander, *Wilkie Collins: Man of Mystery and Imagination* (Madison and Connecticut: International Universities Press, 2003).

Gruner, Elizabeth Rose. 'Family Secrets and the Mysteries of *The Moonstone*' in *Wilkie Collins*, ed. by Lyn Pykett, pp. 221–43.

Harrison, Kimberly and Richard Fantina (eds), *Victorian Sensations: Essays on a Scandalous Genre* (Ohio: Ohio State University Press, 2006).

Hart, Lynda, *Fatal Women: Lesbian Sexuality and the Mark of Aggression* (London: Routledge, 1994).

Hartman, Mary S., *Victorian Murderesses: A True History of Thirteen Respectable French and English Women Accused of Unspeakable Crimes* (1979; London: Robson Books, 1985).
Heller, Tarmar, *Dead Secrets: Wilkie Collins and the Female Gothic* (New Haven: Yale University Press, 1992).
Hughes, Winifred, *The Maniac in the Cellar: Sensation Novels of the 1860s* (Princeton: Princeton University Press, 1980).
Hutter, A. D., 'Dreams, Transformations and Literature: The Implications of Detective Fiction', in *Wilkie Collins*, ed. by Lyn Pykett (London: Macmillan, 1998), pp. 175–96.
Jackson, Mark (ed.), *Infanticide: Historical Perspectives on Child Murder and Concealment, 1550–2000* (Aldershot: Ashgate, 2002).
Jacyna, J. S., 'Immanence or Transcendence: Theories of Life and Organization in Britain, 1790–1835', *Isis*, 74 (1983), pp. 310–29.
Kendrick, Walter M., 'The Sensationalism of *The Woman in White*', in *Wilkie Collins*, ed. by Lyn Pykett, pp. 70–87.
Knelman, Judith, *Twisting in the Wind: The Murderess and the English Press* (Toronto: Toronto University Press, 1998).
Leavy, Barbara Foss, 'Wilkie Collins's Cinderella: The History of Psychology and *The Woman in White*', *Dickens Studies Annual*, 10 (1982), pp. 91–141.
Liggins, Emma, 'The "Evil Days" of the Female Murderer: Subverted Marriage Plots and the Avoidance of Scandal in the Victorian Sensation Novel', *Journal of Victorian Culture*, 2:1 (Spring 1997), pp. 27–41.
Liggins, Emma, 'Good Housekeeping? Domestic Economy and Suffering Wives in Mrs Henry Wood's Early Fiction', in *Feminist Readings of Victorian Popular Texts*, ed. by Emma Liggins and Daniel Duffy (Hampshire: Ashgate, 2001), pp. 53–68.
Liggins, Emma and Daniel Duffy (eds), *Feminist Readings of Victorian Popular Texts* (Hampshire: Ashgate, 2001).
Mangham, Andrew, 'Hysterical Fictions: Mid-Nineteenth-Century Medical Constructions of Hysteria and the Fiction of Mary Elizabeth Braddon', *Wilkie Collins Society Journal*, 6 (November 2003), pp. 35–52.
Mangham, Andrew, '"Murdered at the Breast": Maternal Violence and the Self-Made Man in Popular Victorian Culture', *Critical Survey*, 16:1 (2004), pp. 20–34.
Mangham, Andrew (ed.), *Wilkie Collins: Interdisciplinary Essays* (Newcastle: Cambridge Scholars Publishing, 2007).
Marland, Hilary, 'Getting Away with Murder? Puerperal Insanity, Infanticide and the Defence Plea' in *Infanticide*, ed. by Mark Jackson, pp. 168–92.
Marland, Hilary, *Dangerous Motherhood: Insanity and Childbirth in Victorian Britain* (Basingstoke: Palgrave Macmillan, 2004).
Maunder, Andrew, '"Stepchildren of Nature": *East Lynne* and the Spectre of Female Degeneracy, 1860–1861', in *Victorian Crime, Madness and Sensation*, ed. by Andrew Maunder and Grace Moore (Hampshire: Ashgate, 2004), pp. 59–71.
Maunder, Andrew (ed.), *Varieties of Women's Sensation Fiction, 1855–1890*, 4 vols (London: Pickering and Chatto, 2004).
Maunder, Andrew and Grace Moore (eds), *Victorian Crime, Madness and Sensation* (Hampshire: Ashgate, 2004).
Maynard, Jessica, 'Black Silk and Red Paisley: The Toxic Woman in Wilkie Collins's *Armadale*', in *Varieties of Victorianism: The Uses of a Past*, ed. by Gary Day (London: Macmillan, 1998), pp. 63–79.
McDonagh, Josephine, *Child Murder and British Culture, 1720–1900* (Cambridge: Cambridge University Press, 2003).

Micale, Mark S., *Approaching Hysteria: Disease and its Interpretations* (Princeton: Princeton University Press, 1995).
Morris, Virginia, *Double Jeopardy: Women Who Kill in Victorian Fiction* (Kentucky: The University Press of Kentucky, 1990).
Moscucci, Ornella, *The Science of Woman: Gynaecology and Gender in England 1800–1929* (Cambridge: Cambridge University Press, 1993).
Nayder, Lillian, *Wilkie Collins* (New York: Twayne Publishers, 1997).
O'Neill, Philip, *Wilkie Collins: Women, Property and Propriety* (London: Macmillan, 1988).
Oppenheim, Janet, *'Shattered Nerves': Doctors, Patients, and Depression in Victorian England* (Oxford: Oxford University Press, 1991).
Peters, Catherine, *The King of Inventors: A Life of Wilkie Collins* (Reading: Minerva Press, 1992).
Pick, Daniel, *Faces of Degeneration: A European Disorder, c. 1848–c. 1918* (Cambridge: Cambridge University Press, 1993).
Pinto-Correia, Clara, *The Ovary of Eve: Eggs and Sperm and Preformation* (Chicago: University of Chicago Press, 1997).
Poovey, Mary, *Uneven Developments: The Ideological Work of Gender in Mid-Victorian England* (Chicago: The University of Chicago Press, 1988).
Pykett, Lyn, *The Improper Feminine: The Women's Sensation Novel and the New Woman Writing* (London: Routledge, 1992).
Pykett, Lyn, *The Sensation Novel: from* The Woman in White *to* The Moonstone (Plymouth: Northcote House, 1994).
Pykett, Lyn (ed.), *New Casebooks: Wilkie Collins* (London: Macmillan, 1998).
Rance, Nick, '"Victorian Values" and "Fast Young Ladies": from Madeline Smith to Ruth Rendell', in *Varieties of Victorianism: The Uses of a Past*, ed. by Gary Day (London: Macmillan, 1998), pp. 220–35.
Rhode, John, *The Case of Constance Kent* (New York: Charles Scribner's Sons, 1928).
Rylance, Rick, *Victorian Psychology and British Culture 1850–1880* (Oxford: Oxford University Press, 2000).
Scull, Andrew (ed.), *Madhouses, Mad-doctors and Madmen: The Social History of Psychiatry in the Victorian Era* (Philadelphia: University of Pennsylvania Press, 1981).
Scull, Andrew, *Museums of Madness: The Social Organization of Insanity in Nineteenth-Century England* (London: Allen Lane/New York: St. Martin's Press, 1979).
Showalter, Elaine and English Showalter, 'Victorian Women and Menstruation', in *Suffer and be Still: Women in the Victorian Age*, ed. by Martha Vicinus (London: Macmillan, 1972), pp. 38–44.
Showalter, Elaine, *The Female Malady: Women, Madness and English Culture, 1830–1980* (London: Virago, 1987).
Shuttleworth, Sally, *George Eliot and Nineteenth-Century Science: The Make-Believe of a Beginning* (Cambridge: Cambridge University Press, 1984).
Shuttleworth, Sally, 'Demonic Mothers: Ideologies of Bourgeois Motherhood in the Mid-Victorian Era' in *Rewriting the Victorians: Theory, History and the Politics of Gender*, ed. by Shires, Linda M. (London: Routledge, 1993), pp. 31–51.
Shuttleworth, Sally, '"Preaching to the Nerves": Psychological Disorder in Sensation Fiction', in *A Question of Identity*, ed. by Miranda Benjamin (New Brunswick, NJ: Rutgers University Press, 1993), pp. 192–243.
Shuttleworth, Sally, *Charlotte Brontë and Victorian Psychology* (Cambridge: Cambridge University Press, 1996).

Small, Helen, *Love's Madness: Medicine, The Novel, and Female Insanity, 1800–1865* (Oxford: Oxford University Press, 1996).

Smith, Andrew, *Victorian Demons: Medicine, Masculinity and the Gothic at the Fin-de-Siècle* (Manchester: Manchester University Press, 2004).

Stott, Rebecca, *The Fabrication of the late-Victorian Femme-Fatale: The Kiss of Death* (Basingstoke: Macmillan, 1992).

Taylor, Jenny Bourne (ed.), *The Cambridge Companion to Wilkie Collins* (Cambridge: Cambridge University Press, 2006).

Taylor, Jenny Bourne, *In the Secret Theatre of Home: Wilkie Collins, Sensation Narrative, and Nineteenth-Century Psychology* (London: Routledge, 1988).

Taylor, Jenny Bourne, 'Obscure Recesses: Locating the Victorian Unconscious' in *Writing and Victorianism*, ed. by Bullen, J. B. (New York: Longman, 1997), pp. 137–79.

Taylor, Jenny Bourne and Sally Shuttleworth (eds), *Embodied Selves: An Anthology of Psychological Texts 1830–1890* (Oxford: Oxford University Press, 2000).

Trodd, Anthea, *Domestic Crime in the Victorian Novel* (London: Macmillan, 1989).

Tromp, Marlene, Pamela K. Gilbert, and Aeron Haynie (eds), *Beyond Sensation: Mary Elizabeth Braddon in Context* (New York: State University of New York Press, 2000).

Wolff, Robert Lee (ed.), '"Devoted Disciple": The Letters of Mary Elizabeth Braddon to Sir Edward Bulwer Lytton, 1862–1873', *Harvard Library Bulletin*, 12 (1974), pp. 5–35 and pp. 129–61.

Wolff, Robert Lee, *Sensational Victorian: The Life and Fiction of Mary Elizabeth Braddon* (New York: Garland Publishing, 1979).

Wood, Jane, *Passion and Pathology in Victorian Fiction* (Oxford: Oxford University Press, 2001).

Wynne, Deborah, 'See What a Big Wide Bed it is!: Mrs Henry Wood and the Philistine Imagination', in *Feminist Readings*, ed. by Emma Liggins and Daniel Duffy (Hampshire: Ashgate, 2001), pp. 89–107.

Wynne, Deborah, *The Sensation Novel and the Victorian Family Magazine* (Hampshire: Palgrave, 2001).

Zedner, Lucia. *Women, Crime, and Custody in Victorian England* (Oxford: Oxford University Press, 1991).

Index

Abercrombie, John, 171
adaptation to modernity, 141–2, 151–4, 158
adolescence, 13–16, 18, 60, 184
adultery, 96, 99, 130–1, 161–2
alienation, 129, 154, 202
All the Year Round, 79, 172
Althaus, Julius, 18–19
ambition
 commercial, 90–6, 99–102, 106–7, 110–11, 118, 181
 social, 114, 119, 126–7, 129, 141–3
Annual Register, 12, 20, 22, 27–8, 32, 37
aristocracy, 108, 111–13, 132, 144
arson, 88–9, 95
Auerbach, Nina, 89
Austin, Alfred, 144

Bacon case, 27–8
Baker Brown, Isaac, 189
 On the Curability of Certain Forms of Insanity, 190
Balibar, Etienne
 'On Literature as an Ideological Form,' 211
Beer, Gillian, 58–9
Beeton, Isabella
 Household Management, 8–9, 132
Belgravia, 143
Bentley's Miscellany, 90
Bermondsey murder, 7–9
binary view of women, 66, 169, 185
births, monstrous, 33–4, 156
Black, William
 'Girl's Brothers,' 146–7, 169
Blackwood's Edinburgh Magazine, 43, 116
boundaries
 gender, 135–6, 156–7
 private and public, 134–5, 156–7
 transgression of, 42, 62–3, 109–10
Braddon, Mary Elizabeth, 4–5
 Aurora Floyd, 63–70, 103–4, 122–5
 The Captain of the Vulture, 109–10, 120–2

Eleanor's Victory, 119
Garibaldi and Other Poems, 64, 92–6
John Marchmont's Legacy, 100–3, 120
Lady Audley's Secret, 87–92, 94, 103, 107, 161, 165, 173
Lady Lisle, 108–13
'Lost and Found,' 113–16
Ralph the Bailif and Other Stories, 113
The Trail of the Serpent, 96–100, 104–7, 117–18
'Under the Sycamores,' 92–6
breast-feeding, 23–6, 29–32, 103, 113, 132
breeding, issues of, 47–8
 see also heredity; marriage
Brighton Poisoner, 44–8
British Medical Journal, 23, 27, 32, 35
Brixey case, 20–1, 70, 88, 97
Brodie, Sir Benjamin
 Psychological Inquiries, 199, 201
Brontë, Charlotte
 Jane Eyre, 12, 95, 165
 Shirley, 120, 157
Brough case, 30–2, 171
Brown, Frederick James, 35–6
Buchanan, Robert, 124–5
Bucknill, John Charles, 62–3, 75–6
 Unsoundness of Mind in Relation to Criminal Acts, 30–1
Bulwer-Lytton, Edward, 4, 87, 100
Burton, John Mould, 20–1, 70

Carter, Robert Brudenell, 19–20
Cathrow, William, 19–20
Chartists, 105
childbirth, 26–8, 31, 75–7, 103, 105
children
 corrupted, 45–7
 spoiled, 104, 108, 137–8
class difference, 105, 112, 166–8
 transgression of, 33–5, 39, 109–11, 113–16, 132
 see also aristocracy; middle classes; working classes

242

classification of women, 185
climacteric insanity (menopausal), 44, 46
clitoridectomy, 189–90
Collins, Wilkie, 4–5, 63, 169–72
  'A Passage in the Life of Perugino Potts,' 90
  'A Queen's Revenge,' 193–5
  Antonina, or the Fall of Rome, 172
  Armadale, 113–14, 196–208
  Basil, 170
  Heart and Science, 189
  The Legacy of Cain, 172, 198
  The Moonstone, 50, 79–86, 94, 192
  My Miscellanies, 172
  No Name, 182–93, 195–6
  The Woman in White, 12, 110, 170, 172–82, 196
commercial exploitation of women, 90–6, 99–102, 106–7, 110–11, 118, 181
contamination issues, 47–8, 201–2, 210
Cornhill magazine, 39–41, 47, 169, 176, 185, 201
Coxon, Lucy
  'A Few Tickets in the Matrimonial Lottery,' 146–7
Craik, Dinah Mulock
  'In Her Teens,' 13, 15
crime, motiveless, 54, 61
criminal cases
  Martha Bacon, 27–8
  Martha Brixey, 20–1, 70, 88, 97
  Mary Ann Brough, 30–2, 171
  Jane Crosby, 1–2, 73
  Christiana Edmunds, 36–8, 44–8, 119
  Constance Emily Kent *see* Road Murder
  Esther Lack, 25–6
  Maria Manning, 7–9, 55
  Sarah Minchin, 15–16
  Sarah Mitchell, 19–20
  Mary Ann Payne, 24–5
  Miss Scholes, 12
  Madeline Smith, 21–3, 58, 211
  Catherine Wilson, 98–9
criminality, physical signs of, 36
Crosby case, 1–2, 73
cunning, 19–20, 45–6
Curtis, Jeni, 66
Cyples, William
  'Granny Leatham's Revenge,' 47–8

Dallas, Eneas Sweetland, 185
Darwin, Charles
  Origin of Species, 34, 44, 126, 142
Davey, James, 13, 21
deceptive appearance of women, 15, 179–80, 185–8, 192, 210
  in Braddon, 67, 97–9, 161
  in Collins, 79–81, 169, 190–4
  in Wood, 74, 78–9, 136, 146–7, 160–1
deceptiveness
  of bourgeois respectability, 73, 131
  of surface appearance, 83, 99, 169–70, 172
deformity, 82–3
degeneration, 36, 38, 43–4, 123, 128–9, 144–5, 155
demonic 'other,' 170, 175, 196
desire and aggression, 18–19, 23, 176
desire and disgust, 184, 195
detection as obsession, 76–9, 82, 84–8, 172–4, 178, 180, 182–3, 192, 208
detectives, 55–8
  fictional, 70, 78–9, 82, 84–8, 94, 172–82
dialogism, 129
Dickens, Charles, 40, 63
  Great Expectations, 12, 16–17, 43–4, 47–8, 51, 119–20, 134, 154, 159
  A Tale of Two Cities, 51, 65
disappointment in love, 47, 93, 100–1, 106, 120, 122
disguises, 186–7, 190, 193
domestic authority, 149
'Domestic Hero Worship,' 134–5
domesticity of murder, 7–9, 50–2
Doubleday, Thomas, 164
  The True Theory of Population, 141–3
dreams, 200–2
During, Simon, 53–4

Edmunds case, 36–8, 44–8, 119
Eliot, George
  Middlemarch, 98
  The Mill on the Floss, 62
emasculation, 69, 95, 107, 121, 166
Esquirol, J. E. D., 15, 21, 24, 35, 44, 53–4
  Mental Maladies, 1, 14, 26
evolution, 34, 44, 126, 142, 151
  see also adaptation to modernity

excess
　maternal, 108–11, 132–3
　sexual, 21–3, 29–30, 33, 89, 130–1, 184, 202, 209–10

family life, sanctity of, 18, 29, 49–50, 59, 65
fatalism, 197–200
fears, 90, 98, 196
　self-reflective, 44, 197, 199, 205, 207
　of sexuality, 176–7, 182
　of women, 15, 41–2, 117, 121, 174–5, 192, 204
fecundity, 164, 167–8
femmes fatales, 165, 209–10
fin de siècle, 209–10
Fortune, Mary
　'White Maniac, The,' 9–12, 14–18, 53
foster siblings, 114–15
free will and determinism, 197–8

Galton, Francis
　Hereditary Genius, 34–5, 39
gender roles
　reversal of, 16–17, 63, 68, 92, 95, 193–6
　transgression of, 42, 62–3, 109–10
gentlemanly qualities, 159, 163, 168
Glasgow Medical Journal, 173–4
Gooch, Robert
　Diseases Peculiar to Women, 26–7
Greenslade, William, 38, 44
Greg, W. R.
　'Why Are Women Redundant?', 42
Grinstein, Alexander, 172
Gruner, Elizabeth Rose, 49–50, 54
gynaecology, 13–14, 21, 60, 80, 91, 189–90

Hammond, William A.
　Insanity in its Relations to Crime, 52, 55
Hardy, Thomas
　Jude the Obscure, 165
Hartman, Mary, 22
heredity
　biological, 35, 155, 158
　insanity, 30, 35–9, 60–2, 71–2, 77, 103, 112, 197
　psychological, 183, 197–9, 201–2, 204, 206–7
Hetley, Dr, 168

Hollingshead, John, 141
　'Nest-Building Apes,' 127–9, 141, 153–4, 163
Houghton, J. Hyde, 33
Household Words, 171–2
'How to Deal with Our Rural Poor,' 163–4
Hutter, A. D., 49
hybridity, 34–5, 59, 81
hysteria, 18–21, 68–9, 81–4, 89–90, 96, 100–3, 115, 147, 165–6

illegitimacy, 163–4
imagery and metaphor
　contamination and infection, 47–8, 201, 210
　explosive and volcanic, 26, 48, 51–3, 58, 73, 75, 100, 130, 161–2
　fertility, 155, 184
　fire and blood, 18, 93–4, 97–8, 161
　hysterical, 83, 107
　landscape as female, 94, 104–5, 117–18
　menstrual, 69, 80–1, 85, 88–9
　red and white, 9–12, 16–17, 65, 88, 175, 177, 179
　reptilian, 123–4, 187–8, 190
　sexual and phallic, 89–91, 94–5, 117, 192, 194
　shadows, 115, 148, 151–2, 196, 200–3
　smouldering fires, 44, 59, 67, 73–4, 89, 94, 98, 130, 186
independence of women, 39–40, 42, 62, 81, 102, 104, 119, 151–2
infant mortality, 24, 92, 105
infanticide, 24–8, 30, 49–50, 62, 71–2, 92, 104–6
insanity
　and alcoholism, 137
　climacteric (menopausal), 44, 46
　detection of, 19, 36, 39, 52–5, 76, 172–3
　hereditary, 30, 35–9, 60–2, 71–2, 77, 103, 112, 197
　as legal defence, 12, 19–20, 25–6, 28, 30, 35–8
　and menstruation, 58–9, 61
　monomania, 9–12, 14–18, 53–4, 87, 94, 102, 173–4, 180, 191, 199
　passed on in breast milk, 29–30
　puerperal mania, 26–8, 31, 75–7, 103, 105

pyromania, 1–2, 71–3
and unrequited love, 47, 93, 100–1, 106, 120, 122
intention and crimes, 203, 205, 207
irrational thoughts, 170–1

jealousy, 19, 71–2, 74–7, 101–2, 123, 130, 136, 161
Journal of Mental Science, 35–6, 44
Journal of Psychological Medicine, 10, 30
Jung, W., 35

Kaye, John, 176
Kent case *see* Road Murder
King, R. Ashe, 40–1
Knelman, Judith, 44

Lack case, 25–6
Lancet, The, 18–19, 60–1
Lavater, John Caspar, 185
Lee, Robert
  Maternal Impressions, 32–3
Liggins, Emma, 149
Linton, Eliza Lynn, 43, 116, 120, 135–6
Locock, Charles, 59
Lombroso, Cesare
  Criminal Man, 35–6
love-sickness, 47, 93, 100–1, 106, 120, 122
Luckhurst, Roger, 209–10

Machen, Arthur
  The Great God Pan, 209–10
Macherey, Pierre
  'On Literature as an Ideological Form,' 211
Macmillan's Magazine, 13
male dominance, 162–5, 179
male failure, 129, 136–40, 144, 146, 148–51, 153, 157
male gaze, 65–6, 68, 79, 83, 95–6, 99–100
male imagination, 69, 71, 86, 173, 177–8
male weakness, 108–10, 121, 145, 165–6
Manning case, 7–9, 55
Mansel, Henry, 63
Marland, Hilary, 26
marriage, 42, 134–6
  as a lottery, 146–9, 155, 160–1
masculinity in women, 184, 189, 195–6

Maudsley, Henry, 35–8, 46, 58–9, 129, 145, 151, 153, 198
  The Physiology and Pathology of Mind, 126–7, 138
  Responsibility in Mental Disease, 146–7
McDonagh, Josephine, 105, 132
McNaughten Rules, 12
medical witnesses, 13, 19–21, 30–1, 38, 46, 70
menopause, 39–48, 116–25
menstruation, 55–60
  dysfunction and aggression, 20–1, 88–9
  and hysteria, 19, 21
metaphor *see* imagery and metaphor
Micale, Mark, 19
middle classes, 111, 126–7, 129, 134, 136–7, 142–3
Minchin case, 15–16
missing link, search for, 58–9
Mitchell case, 19–20
modernity, adaptation to, 141–2, 151–4, 158
monomania, 9–12, 14–18, 53–4, 87, 94, 102, 173–4, 180, 191, 199
  see also obsession
Morel, Bénédict Augustin, 36
Morris, Virginia, 172
Moscucci, Ornella, 80
mothering
  excessive, 108–11, 132–3
  lack of, 104, 106
  and male success, 140–1
multiformity, 81–2
My Secret Life, 90
myth and tradition, 149, 151–2, 158

Nayder, Lillian, 172
nest-building apes, idea of, 127–9, 141, 153–4, 163
New Monthly Magazine, 72, 127, 134
Newgate Calendar, 5, 87
nightdress, search for, 55–7, 59

obsession, 122, 186, 191, 195, 199–201, 203
  detection as, 76–9, 82, 84–8, 172–4, 178, 180, 182–3, 192, 208
Obstetrical Society, 33
old maids, 39–42, 47, 120, 186
  realist writers as, 124–5
  see also surplus of women

Oliphant, Margaret, 63
Once a Week magazine, 127, 163–4
Oppenheim, Janet, 18
Owen, M. E.
  'Criminal Women,' 201–2

passion, 14, 19, 61, 111–12, 187–8
  in Braddon, 67–8, 70, 89, 93–7,
    99–102, 106–8, 116–20, 123,
    161, 165
  in Collins, 93–4, 194, 200–2, 204–6
  in Wood, 71–2, 74–7, 129–32, 136,
    161–2, 165, 168
  past, preoccupation with, 143, 149,
    151–3, 158
Payne case, 24–5
Peters, Catherine, 79–80, 85
physiognomy, 184–5
Pick, Daniel
  Faces of Degeneration, 36
Poovey, Mary
  Uneven Developments, 42
predestination, 199–200
pregnancy
  and psychological disorder, 24–5
  shock during, 32–3, 156
Prichard, James, 27
  Treatise on Insanity, 19
progress, notion of, 126–9, 131, 141,
  143, 152
projection, 177–80, 193, 196, 201, 203,
  205
promiscuity, 21–3, 29–30, 33, 89,
  130–1, 202
property ownership, 160
psychological inheritance, 197–9,
  201–2, 204, 206–7
psychopathology, 4, 38, 52–3, 83, 86,
  90, 174
psychosomatic illness, 115, 165–6,
  168, 181
puberty, 13–16, 58, 61
puerperal mania, 26–8, 31, 75–7,
  103, 105
Pykett, Lyn, 129, 134
pyromania, 1–2, 71–3

realism, 124–5
revenge, 44, 47–8, 72, 75, 96, 194
Ritchie, Anne Thackeray, 39–41

Road Murder, 49–63, 211
  and *Aurora Floyd*, 63–71
  and *The Moonstone*, 79–86
  and popular fiction, 63–4
  and *St Martin's Eve*, 71–9
Routh, Charles, 26–7
  Infant Feeding and its Influence on Life,
    23–5, 29–30, 113

Sala, George Augustus, 143
Saturday Review, 38
Scholes case, 12
science, 4, 169–70, 185, 188–91,
  195–6, 208
scientific materialism, 153
Scottish Temperance League, 137
scrutiny
  of potentially insane, 36, 39, 54,
    76–9, 171
  of women, 15, 18, 23, 36, 39, 52, 58,
    61, 68, 97, 104, 171, 185, 196
  see also self-scrutiny
self-control, 67, 73–4, 97, 111, 132–4,
  136, 138, 140
self-fulfilling prophecies, 200–1, 207–8
self-help ideology, 126–9, 136–8, 141,
  143, 149, 152–3, 159
self-made men, 111, 150
self-reflective suspicions, 196
self-scrutiny, 171, 181, 183, 198, 204
separate spheres ideology, 135–6,
  156–7
sexual awakening, 13–16, 18, 58, 60–1,
  184, 204
sexual connotations, 17, 63, 65, 84,
  89–91, 93–4, 117, 125
sexual desire and aggression, 18–19,
  23, 176
sexuality and creativity, 85–6
Shelley, Mary
  Frankenstein, 170
Showalter, Elaine
  The Female Malady, 55–6
Shuttleworth, Sally, 132
Skae, Dr Francis, 43–4
Skey, Frederick, 18, 82, 166–7
Small, Helen, 93
Smiles, Samuel, 129, 131, 141, 150,
  163, 167
  Self Help, 126, 137–8, 153, 159

Smith case, 21–3, 58, 211
Smith, Roger
  Trial by Medicine, 12
social climbing, 114, 119, 126–7, 129, 141–3
somnambulism, 15, 196
Standard, The, 8
Stapleton, Joseph, 51–2, 56–8, 75
  The Great Crime of 1860, 61
Stephens, Joseph Raynor, 105–6
sterility
  and failure to adapt, 152–5, 158
  and social climbing, 141–3
suicide, 30, 104, 106, 139, 209
superstition, 152–3, 158, 202
surplus of women, 40–4, 116, 120, 123

Tait, Lawson, 13–14, 60
Taylor, Alfred, 28, 36–7, 98, 107
  Principles and Practice of Medical Jurisprudence, 15, 21
Taylor, Helen, 23
Taylor, Jenny Bourne, 81, 88, 169, 200
telepathy, 114, 200
Temple Bar, 64, 116, 119–20, 135, 143–4, 146–7, 169
temptresses, women as, 175, 204
Thomas, Theodore Gaillard
  Practical Treatise on the Diseases of Women, 91
Tilt, Edward
  The Change of Life, 43–4
Times, The, 1–2, 7–8, 15–16, 20–1, 45, 64, 99
  Road Murder, 49–50, 52–3, 56–8, 60, 62–3
tradition and myth, 149, 151–2, 158
Trodd, Anthea, 49, 64–5
Tuke, Daniel, 75–6

unrequited love, 47, 93, 100–1, 106, 120, 122

'vagina dentata,' 84, 90, 117
vampirism, 12, 132, 148, 169
vulnerability, 176–7

Waring-Curran, J., 33
wet-nursing, 29–32, 113, 115–16
Whittle, Ewing
  'Infanticide and Abortion,' 142
Wilde, Oscar, 108
Wilson case, 98–9
Winslow, Forbes, 31–2, 61, 75, 171, 173–4
  Lettsomian Lectures on Insanity, 170
  On Obscure Diseases of the Brain, 30, 41, 170, 183, 198–9, 207
  The Plea of Insanity, 30
Wolff, Robert Lee, 4
  Sensational Victorian, 108
'Woman in Her Psychological Relations,' 10–11, 13, 42, 66
Wood, Charles, 150, 168
Wood, Jane, 18, 44
Wood, Mrs Henry, 4–5, 64, 126–9
  Danesbury House, 137–43
  East Lynne, 40, 129–36, 162
  Lady Adelaide's Oath, 143–9
  Mrs Haliburton's Troubles, 137–43
  The Shadow of Ashlydyat, 149–58
  St. Martin's Eve, 2, 71–9, 89, 161
  Verner's Pride, 158–68
Wordsworth, William
  'The Thorn,' 132
work ethic, 127, 137–8, 140, 142, 167–8
working classes, 105–6, 111, 113–14, 163–4, 167, 201
Wynne, Deborah, 126, 129, 134